BEYOND THE SEAS

PAT KELLY

Published by Silverbird Publishing
PO Box 72
Eltham Victoria 3095

First published in Australia 2020
This edition published 2020

Cover design, typesetting: WorkingType (www.workingtype.com.au)

Kelly, Pat
Beyond the Seas
ISBN: 978-0-6450020-0-3
pp382

ABOUT THE AUTHOR

The author was born in Scotland a year before World War II started, but swears she didn't cause it …

In January 1968 she arrived in Australia as a 'Ten Pound Tourist' with her, then, husband and four children.

After the breakup of her marriage after twenty-five years the author was contacted by a man named Mike Kelly, whom she had known in her teens and had had no contact with for nearly thirty years. Mike's marriage having broken up around the same time as the author's. On learning she was 'on the loose', he obtained her phone number by courtesy of his mother — International telephone enquiries — and the author's mother, so rang to see if she was okay.

One thing led to another, they were married in 1988 and returned to the Isle of Man to start a new life. On Mike's retirement, five years later, they followed the summers and spent half their lives in Australia and the other half in the Isle of Man.

In their months on the island each year, they ran a daffodil and plant nursery and were well known throughout the island for their roadside stall, where they sold their daffodils and plants.

As age caught up with them, they realised it was time to settle somewhere permanently. Being the warmer country, Australia won, and they moved there in 2014, to live in a retirement village in Lakes Entrance — one of the prettiest spots in Australia.

This, they both feel, will suit them until they climb in their boxes (but not for a long time yet) and move on to higher places.

BY THE SAME AUTHOR

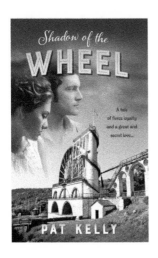 

Shadow of the Wheel

The mighty water-wheel at Laxey mines in the Isle of Man has been set in motion. In its great shadow, Sarah and Patrick have fallen in love. It is a love that must be kept secret, for Patrick is Irish. Sarah's mother — Judith — has lost her mind and blames an Irishman for her husband being imprisoned 'across the water' in Liverpool, where she can never visit him.

The two young lovers desperately desire to wed and be together, but Judith's increasing madness, which began when she lost some of her childher to a savage disease and deepened on her husband's incarceration, proved too strong a pull.

Sarah's deep loyalty to her mother also stands between the lovers, indeed life itself thwarts their every effort to find a way toward their happiness.

Patrick's friend — Robert — is going to Australia to make his fortune mining for gold and has asked Patrick to accompany him. With no other option and seemingly with the cards stacked against them, Patrick and Sarah are both heartbroken.

Knowing that her mother will never recover from her illness and will always need her support, Sarah tells Patrick he must go with Robert to make a life for himself without her, and to forget her, and the love they share.

Hedge of Thorns

The author, who hails from Scotland, spent many hours listening to her mother-in-law recount, in vivid detail, memories of her childhood days in the tiny village of Patrick, in the Isle of Man, during the First World War. As Lou talked, the author realised she was listening to history, a lot of which no one else could tell, and that if Lou were to die, all that history would be lost forever. So she wrote it all down and turned it into *Hedge of Thorns*.

In those days the village was dwarfed by the huge internment camp at Knockaloe, created for the accommodation of thousands of men classed as enemy aliens. Men whose only crimes were to have German, Austrian or Turkish origins.

Hedge of Thorns is a true account of the impact that the Great War and the monster of Knockaloe camp had on the lives of a Manx family which still followed the traditional crofting way of life. It is a most moving and memorable story of the stresses and strains which shattered the peaceful existence of a family whose loved ones were caught up in the emergencies of war.

Throughout Europe, during those dreadful war-torn years, millions of families were suffering similar deprivation, fear, loss and heartbreak.

Millions died in most dreadful ways and millions more eventually returned home crippled in either body or mind. Or both!

It was to be the war to end all wars, for no one could imagine such stupidity happening again but—!

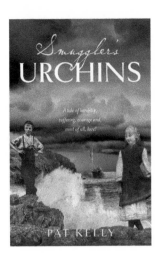

Smuggler's Urchins

It is the story of two young children, born into the poverty-stricken years of the Isle of Man, when drunkenness and smuggling were rife. Two children who were imprisoned for the heinous crime of stealing a scrap of food to keep themselves alive.

Daniel, worldly-wise, who has had to fend for himself for most of his ten years of life. Unwanted from birth, abandoned and unloved, he has had the strength to develop into a caring young man, old and mature for his age.

Eight-year-old Isabella, who had been forced to flee from home to escape being sold into prostitution by a depraved mother. Small for her age, she is frail and unable to look after herself.

Released from gaol in Castle Rushen in midwinter, with no home to go to, the children team up in a heartrending battle for survival. As they slither rapidly into further trouble and disaster looms, it is only their involvement with a smuggling family that saves them from deportation to the Americas ... or possibly even death!

To my best friend, my husband Mike Kelly
with thanks for many happy years together.

ACKNOWLEDGEMENTS

With thanks for their support and encouragement — to my children Dawn, Andrew, Alison and Kenneth.

Luke Harris at Working Type Studio for his guidance in the writing of my book.

Last but not least, my funny Irish/Manx friend, Keith Costain, who kept me laughing for a year through a bushfire, a pandemic, my husband's broken leg, then allowed me to 'borrow' him for my story.

THE ROUTE OF
'THE LADY JULIANA'

did, instead of stopping off for a jar of jough at the local, he went straight home to tell his wife about the poor little lass in the cell.

Mary, eyd and awed and said it was not right to lock a little child up like that. 'Only twelve years of age, you say, and you've locked her in a cell? How could you do that? If she's homeless and starving she needs to be helped, not locked up!' She stamped her foot angrily.

'I didn't want to, lass, believe me,' Michael said sadly, but I've let her *escape* so often before and people are beginning to look at me funny. It's my job, Mary, to catch criminals and take them off the streets and send them for justice. My job — an' I can't afford to lose it.'

Mary smiled sadly. 'I know love. You *have* to do it. But what sort of justice will she get? A young child like that. A criminal! The only proper justice would be for someone to start a foundling home or the likes to give a roof and food to these poor waifs.'

Michael nodded. 'Aye love. I agree. But it will never happen. There are so many. Douglas is alive with homeless children wandering the streets and stealing to survive. There would be too many to find room for. And who would pay for the food? Or for the roof they were sleeping under?'

'Aye, who?' Mary agreed. 'Anyway, at least we can give her something to get her through tonight. I'd made a pot of thick Manx broth for us for tonight, so I'll add a bit of water and there'll be enough for the lass to have some.'

Mary filled a large bowl and sent Michael to deliver it and a thick slice of warm, home-made bread, with the message that he was not getting his until Alice had hers.

Before he left, Michael begged, from Mary, a warm shawl that she rarely wore. 'The poor little lass has nowt to wear but a thin cotton dress,' he told her.

Mary found her largest, warmest shawl, and sent him on his

5

way with it. He was a good-hearted man she knew, and she also knew how much this must be hurting him.

When Michael returned to the watch house. Juan Killey was on duty. He was a man Michael did not like very much. A bit of a rough type and a bully.

'What you got there?' Juan asked, frowning.

'Just a shawl and a bowl of soup Mary has sent for the lass in the cell.'

Juan shook his head. 'You're soft in the head, you are. The girl's a thief. A common criminal. Why d'you want to go giving her food an' clothes?'

Michael clenched his teeth angrily. What business was it of Juan's who he gave food or clothes to? He was about to say so, then realised Juan was going to be in the station overnight, with poor Alice in the cell. If he was to make the other man angry now, the child might pay the price for it.

'She's nobut a child,' he said quietly. 'No child should have to go cold and hungry. It's only an old shawl Mary was going to throw out and a bit of the broth we're having for tea.'

Juan shrugged and shook his head. 'Please yourself. The most I would give her is a clip round the ear.'

Michael nodded but said nothing. If he gave Juan cause there was the risk that what he might give Alice was another black eye. Unlocking Alice's cell door, he found her huddled in the corner of the cot, almost blue with cold. Sitting beside her, he gently wrapped the warm shawl around her. It was a big one, almost like a blanket and she so small, it covered her well. Putting the spoon in her hand, he handed her the bread and the bowl of broth. 'Get this into you an' you'll feel a lot better, lass.'

Alice looked from bowl to spoon, as though she didn't know what they were. Then lifting the bowl to her mouth, she gulped the broth down in noisy slurps.

With a jerk of his head, he signalled them to come in. The four shackled prisoners shuffled up the slope, while Michael followed reluctantly behind, his hand on Alice's shoulder.

'I hope all goes well for you with the deemster,' he said quietly as John Cannon took her arm and led her toward the dungeon.

CHAPTER 2

It was with a heavy heart that Alice allowed herself to be led away. She twisted, once, to peep back past John, the prison warder, but Michael had gone from sight.

Until now, with Michael looking after her, she had not been scared. But now? Well, now was different. From now on she would have to fight her own battles. Nothing new there really, was there? For nearly three years now she had been doing just that. Ever since her mother had suddenly disappeared from her life.

Another guard appeared and he and John unshackled the prisoners. They were led between cold, grey stone walls. As they neared the end of the passage John took a bunch of large keys from his pocket and unlocked a heavy, well-worn door.

'In here,' he said, with a quick jerk of his head toward the door.

Maggie gently took Alice's hand. 'Come on, love. It's not all that bad. It's a roof over our heads for a few months and food in our bellies that we don't need to steal.'

Alice nodded. 'I've been here before. It's full of rats.'

Maggie scratched her head and nodded. 'Can't argue with you there, but nothing we can do about them. We'll just ha' to make the best of it. Let's find ourselves a corner as far to the back as we can.'

Alice sighed, followed Maggie into the cell, and shuddered as she heard the door clang shut behind her and the key grind in the lock. The sound had such a finality about it. As if telling her she would be there forever and never see daylight again.

There were at least a dozen other women in the dark, damp room, all looking with curiosity and some resentment at the new arrivals. To Alice, they all looked alike. The eyes that watched her all looked the same — empty and without hope.

The only light in the room came from a small opening set low at the front of the dungeon. It was only about two feet square, with two crossing bars. Alice started toward this source of light, but Maggie took her arm and led her away from it.

'We need to be as far away from there as we can get,' she told her quietly. 'That's where the rats come in. An' if there's a high tide or it's a bit stormy the sea comes in there too.'

Yes, Alice remembered now. Other times she had been here the other women would not let her have a space at the back and her tender young body had been a magnet to the vermin. She still bore some scars on her legs.

Maggie led her to the back. 'Come on Jenny, move yersel'.' She nudged a small hopeless looking woman with her toe. The woman glared resentfully at her, but shuffled along, pushing the woman on her other side.

'A bit further. There's two of us.'

Jenny grumbled but shoved a bit further along.

Maggie dumped herself on the floor and tugged at Alice's arm, nodding wordlessly toward the floor.

Alice slumped to the floor and Maggie put an arm around her shoulder. 'I'll look after you while I'm here, my love, but I might not always be, so just take care. They're a desperate lot in here, so keep an eye open always. An' keep that shawl wrapped tight around you or it'll be gone.'

13

Alice looked around. Shuddered. Memories flooded back of
previous stays in the prison. The times she had been bullied by
the older women who were bored and looking for a bit of amusement to help pass the time. They had not all been bad, though,
she remembered. Like Maggie, some had taken pity on her and
tried to protect her from the others. In times past, it had just been
bullying; she had nothing for them to steal. This time she had
her shawl, so knew she must stay alert and be ready to fight for it.

When night came Alice lay snuggled up to Maggie, her shawl
tucked well under her and wrapped partly around her friend. It
was the warmest and most secure she had felt since her mother
had vanished, and she slept soundly for a while.

Loud screams brought all the women suddenly wide awake.

'I've been bit!' a voice yelled in the dark.

Alice sat up quickly and tried to see who was making the commotion, but was blind in the darkness of the dungeon.

Maggie sat up and put a comforting arm around her. 'It was
bound to happen, love, they allus come in at night looking for a
piece of meat to chew on!'

Alice shuddered, remembering the times the piece of meat had
been her! She could hear people moving around in the darkness,
trying to beat off an unseen attacker. With a fearful sigh she lay
back down, making sure her shawl was well under her, but she
could not sleep soundly again. Her mind was too much on the
rats and the fear that they might come to her next.

For the rest of the night, Alice dozed fitfully, her ears on full
alert for any scuffling sounds. When, at long last, a glimmer of
light showed through the grill at the front of the cell she found
the communal bucket and thankfully relieved herself.

When the guard came later with a tray of bread and mugs of
water the women were instantly all around him snatching greedily at the bread. Try as he might to control them they were all

around him and too many for him to watch. Several were left without food, but the guard was used to this. They could sort themselves out, he wasn't going to risk being set upon. Leaving the tray of water mugs on the floor, he fled.

Maggie had managed to snatch the last piece of bread, but Alice had nothing. Without a word, she handed it to Alice.

Alice shook her head. 'Thank you, but it's yours. You need to eat too.'

'Don't you worry about me. I will eat!' So saying, she marched over to a woman who had two lumps of bread and snatched one out of her hand.

'Hey, you whore! That's mine!' The woman leaped to her feet and tried to grab the food back, but Maggie quickly whipped it out of her reach.

With a screech of fury the dirty, disheveled woman launched herself at Maggie, grabbed her hair, and brought her knee up quickly.

Quite used to street fighting, Maggie jerked her head aside so that the knee only caught her a glancing blow. With a quick flick of her wrist, she tossed the bread to Alice. 'Hold on to this, my lovely,' she called before returning her attention to her protagonist.

The vicious fight seemed, to Alice, to go on for hours, though it was probably more like fifteen minutes. There were no holds barred, no rules. Kicking, biting, hair pulling. She watched wide-eyed and trembling with fear for her friend.

The other women stood around cheering, shouting encouragement to one or the other of the fighters. All but Alice were thoroughly enjoying this bit of relief to their boredom.

At the end of it, Maggie returned to Alice, bruised and bleeding, but triumphant. She had won. This particular opponent would never pick on her again!

'Like I said, lovey, you must learn to look after yourself. I won't allus be here to fight your battles. You's only little, but you's fast. So, you'll have to learn to use your speed to win any fights.'

Alice looked at her friend. There was blood everywhere. From bites on her cheek and arms and from where a lump of hair had been torn from her head. There were many bruises coming, not least of all the embryo of a huge black eye. The eye itself was already closed.

If Maggie's the winner, then the other woman must be a mess, she thought. Glancing over, she saw the loser lying in the foetal position on the floor sobbing. During the fight, her other piece of bread had long since disappeared down someone else's gullet. Despite the woman's greed, Alice could not help feeling sorry for her.

The next few days dragged by painfully slowly, with no relief from the mind-crushing boredom. The only piece of hope that kept her going was that the deemster she would come before in court would not be a harsh one who would give her too long a sentence. Though maybe just until the end of winter might be good.

Deemster Quayle glared at the girl before him. He was thoroughly fed up with having these dirty, thieving, flea-ridden children paraded into his court. And he was sure he had seen this one before. Not certain though because he saw so many of them they all looked the same. Just dirty and scruffy. He screwed his face up in disgust.

'I've seen you before, haven't I, child?'

Alice quailed under his angry scrutiny and could only nod.

'Well, speak up girl. Yes or no?'

'Yes,' Alice nodded, then as an afterthought, added "sir."

The court reporter handed deemster Quayle a file, which he

opened and perused at length, his frown deepening with every minute that passed. Finally, he slammed the file shut and glared at Alice.

Shaking his head he said, 'This is your sixth time you have been brought before this court I see. Twice you were let off with a caution because of your young age. Three times you have been incarcerated. Yet still, you steal. Obviously you have learned nothing from your months in the dungeons, so it behoves me to take stronger action. I sentence you to seven years. To serve this punishment you will be transported to *parts beyond the seas.* Until you sail, you will be transferred to Newgate prison at the earliest opportunity.

Alice stared, wide-eyed at Deemster Quayle. What was he telling her? She didn't understand. Seven years! Seven years, for stealing a loaf of bread to stay alive. That was all she understood of it. Where did he say? Beyond the seas and Newgate prison. It all meant nothing to her.

'Where — sir?' she finally squeaked.

Deemster Quayle scowled at her. 'Newgate prison, in London, while you await transportation. Take her away guard, and bring in the next prisoner."

The guard grabbed Alice's arm in a grip that hurt. She could feel every finger biting into her skinny little arm and had no choice but to allow herself to be almost lifted off her feet and pushed ahead of him out of the courtroom.

In the doorway, she passed Maggie, who was being led into court. Alice gave her a teary, beseeching look, but there was no chance to speak. As the guard marched her back to the dungeon she questioned him about where she was to be sent, but he merely shrugged.

'Well, wherever it is,' she told herself, 'it can't be any worse than this place.' She had never heard of the places the deemster had mentioned. They must be at the other end of the island somewhere! Alice slumped to the floor, sitting on the tail of her shawl and wrapping the rest around herself.

It seemed like a lifetime but was probably only twenty minutes before Maggie was returned to the cell.

'How long's he given you?' she asked as she settled herself beside Alice.

'He said seven years.' Alice felt the tears prick the corner of her eyes but was determined not to let them fall.

'Seven bloody years?' Maggie almost screamed. 'Seven years! Just a child trying to stay alive. Has the man no heart? How does he think you will survive seven years in this hell hole?'

'I'm not to be here. The deemster said something about transport. He said I had to go to some place called Newgate, then another place beyond the seas. I don't know what he meant'

'Bloody hell!' Maggie shook her head in disbelief. 'The bastard's sending you to a foreign country. An' me too. They're fed up having us in their gaol here, so they're sending us away. I got seven years an all. He must be in a seven-year mood today. Probably his wife said 'no' to him last night! Don't you worry, my lass, wherever this new country is, we'll be goin' there together.'

Suddenly feeling a lot less frightened of what the future held, Alice threw her skinny arms around her new friend and gave her a huge hug. Her little chest fluttered as she tried to suppress her sobs.

Time passed painfully slowly while they awaited their fate. They learned that two of the other women in their cell were also to be transported, so they all waited in anticipation and fear of what the future would bring.

One night there was a terrible storm. A typical December

In all her waking hours Alice could feel Mavis' eyes on her. When she looked up the malevolence in those eyes made her shudder. Wordlessly, Mavis let Alice know that she was under threat. At night she curled in the safety of Maggie's arms, the two of them wrapped in the precious shawl. But the fear was always there.

'Just stay well clear of that one,' Maggie quietly advised. 'She's a bad un. I heard she's in here 'cos she organised a gang of prostitutes. All young girls, they was. Maybe not much older than you. Then she threatened and robbed the men the girls took up with. She's being sent away for seven years to this place beyond the seas.'

Alice nodded, wide eyed. 'I knew it must have been something bad, but I don't know how they work out the sentences. I was talking to Megan over there an' she says she just got caught drunk in the public lavatory. An' she's being transported for seven years too. An' all I did was pinch a loaf of bread to stay alive. It's not fair is it?'

Maggie gave a wan smile. 'Well, my love, life isn't fair. The older you get the more you realise it. It seems that no matter what a woman does wrong she gets the same sentence, unless she steals too much, or from the wrong person, then she gets burned at the stake.'

Alice gasped in horror. 'You mean set on fire?'

Lily, a gentle, quietly spoken girl whom Alice and Maggie had befriended joined in the conversation. 'I was in here the last time they did a burning.' Her eyes glistened with unshed tears and she shuddered at the memory.

'What had she done?' Alice asked nervously.

'From what I was told, her an' two men was caught makin' sixpence coins. An' it was a death sentence for that. Some said it wasn't right that she should be burned while the men was only hanged.'

'I don't think I fancy either.' Maggie shook her head sadly. 'But I suppose hanging would hurt less.'

'We could hear it all from in here. It was very early in the morning and first thing we heard was St. Sepulchre's bell ringing. Then we heard the crowd cheering an' knew the men was being taken out through the debtors' gate to the scaffold. For a long time — it must have been the best part of an hour we could hear the chaplain splatherin' on. We couldn't hear what he was saying, thank God! An' all this time the men were standin' on the scaffold, with hoods over their faces an' ropes around their necks, waiting to be hung up like hens in a butcher's window. As the platform dropped from beneath them, we heard the bang, then the cheer of the crowd.'

Maggie shook her head angrily. 'Dear God, is there no limit to the inhumanity of mankind?' she asked feelingly.

'Mary, who was waiting to be killed that day, was here and heard it all. Soon after, they came and dressed Mary in white an' took her out. By all accounts, she was made to stand on a stool and tied to a hefty stake that was set into the ground. Then they piled kindling an' wood all around her an' the sheriff's men put blazing torches to it. We could hear the crackling of the flames and Mary's screams for ever such a long time and we all just wished she would die quickly. Then she went quiet and all that was left was the terrible smell of burning meat.' Lily surreptitiously swiped a tear that escaped from the corner of her eye.

Maggie's face set in a mask of fury, while Alice was stunned to silence.

'I find it impossible to think that any man, who considers himself a man can set fire to a woman, for making false coins and listen to her scream until she is nothing more than a few cinders and ashes.' Maggie shook her head in disbelief.

Lily nodded her agreement. 'But they do! You see Sarah

over there?' she twitched her head toward a gaunt, dark-haired woman who had always seemed to keep much to herself. Almost as though she was in another world.

Alice and Maggie looked at the woman — well she was no more than a girl really — and nodded questioningly.

'Well,' Lily continued, 'She was a coiner too or so they said — and she has been sentenced to death, but it seems they are not quite sure what to do. The man she was caught with said he was the one and that she had nowt to do with the coining. He said she just happened to be in his room with him when the constables smashed their way in. But they wouldn't listen to him. They won't say when she has to die. They tell her when it's to be, then put it off a bit longer. Whenever she hears an execution happen she sinks more and more into herself. Wondering if the next to be screaming at the stake will be her.'

Alice sat in silence. Her mind could just not grasp the horror of such an act. Nor that anyone who called himself human could inflict such suffering on a fellow being. What hope was there for anyone in such a cruel world? How could any person stay in their right mind with something like that hanging over them? Her heart bled for poor Sarah.

Standing stiffly, Alice shuffled across the cell and sat beside Sarah. Without a word, she took the girl's hand in hers and squeezed it gently.

For a moment Sarah did not respond, then she returned the gesture, raised her eyes, and smiled sadly.

'Don't sit here by yourself,' Alice said quietly. 'Come an' sit with us. Maggie an' Lily are ever so kind. You'll feel better if you're not alone.'

For a moment Sarah didn't move, then she nodded, scrambled painfully to her feet, and let Alice lead her to where Maggie and Lily sat watching.

The worst of the plague passed, as did the winter. Though still bitterly cold in the cell, it became marginally less unbearable.

Alice and Maggie, who had spent most of the torturous months wrapped together in the shawl often wondered how they had survived. Even more did they wonder how the many women who had not even the comfort of a damp shawl had made it through to the spring alive. Sadly, many had not.

They were a foursome now, with the addition of Lily and Sarah, so felt just a little more secure. They huddled together in a corner keeping a wary eye on the other women.

In time, with friends to keep her mind off her fragile future, Sarah became less withdrawn, her eyes less vacant and sunken.

One day in mid-March the cell door was opened at a time that was not usual, and the head turnkey stood in the doorway looking around the cell, a scented kerchief held to his face.

He studied the paper in his hand. 'Right, when I call your name, I want you out in the corridor.'

The women eyed each other apprehensively.

The convicts shuffled nervously past him when their names were called and huddled together, under the watchful eye of another turnkey with a truncheon in his hand.

The list went on and on, until at least half the women had left the cell.

'Maggie Craster!'

Maggie stood, unmoving.

'Come on then woman!' the turnkey glared at her and put his hand on his cudgel.

'Where are you takin' us?' Maggie demanded.

'You'll find out when you get there!' the turnkey's face reddened.

'What about Alice?'

'Who?'

'Alice,' Maggie clutched at the girl's hand. 'My child!'

The man looked at his list and shook his head. 'Not on my list!'

'Well, if *she* doesn't go — I don't go!'

'You'll go where you're told! Now get yourself out here!'

Maggie clamped her lips, defiantly put her hands on her hips, glared at the turnkey, and stood her ground.

In a blaze of anger, he strode into the cell, his fury turning white-hot when he slipped on the slimy floor and almost fell. By the time he reached Maggie his cudgel was in his raised hand. He'd had his share of arguing with this unbearable lump of dirt, so without hesitation, he hit her a resounding crack across the side of her head.

As Maggie's knees folded Alice screamed and jumped to catch her.

The turnkey grabbed Maggie's shackles and dragged her, almost on her knees, from the cell. Like a sound from hell, the door clanged shut behind them, and the lock squealed!

'No!' Alice's agonised cry echoed around the cell. She threw herself against the door and crumpled to her knees on the steps, banging on it with her fist.

Lily rushed to kneel beside her.

'Where are they taking her? What are they going to do to her?' Alice sobbed.

Lily shrugged miserably.

The remaining women looked fearfully at each other. What was going on? Where were their cellmates being taken? No one was able to think of a reasonable explanation.

Mavis Crowe leered across the room, her malicious little dark eyes as bright and cold as diamonds. This was the moment she had been waiting for!

'Bet you're not so clever now you've lost your protector, are you girl?' she sneered. 'I'll have my shawl now!'

Alice tried to out-stare her but could not stop herself trembling.

Mavis heaved herself up off the putrid floor and started towards her.

Fearfully, Alice jumped to her feet, pulling the shawl tighter around herself.

With an evil laugh, Mavis grabbed the trailing end of the shawl and tried to jerk it out of her hand, but Alice hung on tight and was almost pulled off her feet.

'Little bitch!' Mavis hissed and aimed a kick at her legs.

Alice jumped back, dragging Mavis with her. Their feet went from under them and they landed in an untidy heap on the slimy floor, with Mavis on top and tiny Alice pinned helplessly beneath her.

Triumphantly, Mavis got a grip on the shawl. Alice, although winded, was aware enough to know she must hold on. Twisting it quickly around her arm, she clamped her teeth on Mavis' knuckle and bit as hard as she could.

When Mavis screamed and let go of the shawl, Alice improved her grip on it.

Mavis punched her hard in the face. Gripping the girl's hair, she pulled her head up and was about to smash it to the floor. A screech from behind made her turn her head and she only had time to glimpse Lily leaping at her before the younger girl seized her by the hair, pulled her head back, and bit her neck.

With a yell of fury, Mavis released Alice and leapt to her feet. Moving at surprising speed, she threw herself at Lily, who dodged quickly, and suddenly Mavis found a wall of women between herself and the two girls.

'Let me past!' she snarled.

The women stared at her, some fearfully, but no one moved.

'They're just a couple of bairns. Leave them alone,' said one brave woman, taking a half step forward.

With a look of pure hatred, Mavis leered at the women. 'You will regret this! You all will rue the day you turned against me! You will all pay!' Without another word, she went and sat on the floor in the far corner of the cell. For the remainder of the day, her venom-filled eyes roamed from one to the other of her fellow convicts. She would get even! One day, no matter how long it took, revenge would be hers!

Alice slept fitfully that night, with the shawl wrapped tightly around herself and Lily. It was hers! No one would have it from her!

A tugging at the shawl during the night brought her half-awake, but before she could gather her wits, she felt it being pulled from over her. Opening her eyes, she saw a figure bending over her in the darkness and realised immediately that this could only be Mavis. Instinctively she tightened her grip on the precious blanket, but before she could do more Mavis punched her hard in the face and yanked it from her grasp.

Scuttling to the far corner of the cell, Mavis dropped her winnings to the floor and sat on it. Alice moved to follow her, but Lucy and Sarah, awakened by the fight, held her back.

'Tomorrow,' Lily whispered. 'We'll sort her out tomorrow, when there is light to see by. There's nowhere she can hide it.'

Alice, seeing the sense in it, nodded. 'Yes — tomorrow!' She tried to sleep but lay awake with pain in her face and head. Both felt as though they were about to burst right open.

When tomorrow came, Lily saw to her horror, the damage Mavis had done to Alice. Her friend's left eye was black and so swollen she could not open it. The back of her head bled, where it had hit the floor when her face was punched.

'Oh, dear God! What did the bitch do to you?'

'I think she punched me, but I was not properly awake. I must get my shawl back from her.'

Lily nodded. 'We'll think of a way, but we'll have to take care. Catch her unawares.'

Sarah glared across the cell to where Mavis sat, her face an ugly mask.

'We will make her suffer!' she said with feeling.

Alice nodded, then winced as the movement hurt her head.

Mavis squatted at the far side of the cell, wrapped in the shawl. Her nasty little eyes never leaving Alice, she wore a malevolent look of triumph.

Before the two girls could hatch any sort of a plot to recover Alice's property, the turnkey arrived with his kerchief over his face and his list in his hand.

'Right, I gotta take some more of you out. Same as last time. When I call your name I want you in the corridor pretty sharp-ish.' He studied his list and called out several names, including Alice Moore and Lily Jenkins.

The two girls looked at each other and clung together.

'Where are we to go? Where are you taking us?' Alice asked.

'You'll find out when you get there, won't you,' the man replied unhelpfully. 'Now just get yourselves out in the passage.'

'What about Sarah?'

The turnkey snorted. 'She stays!'

'No. You *must* let her come with us!'

'Wrong missy. She *must* stay here. There's a stake an' a pile of kindling waiting for her!'

'No!'

'Yes!' the man grabbed the back of Alice's dress and started to drag her to the door.

Alice took a deep breath and pointed to Mavis. 'That woman stole my shawl.'

The turnkey glanced over at Mavis, who leered challengingly back at him. Deciding it wasn't worth stepping inside that hell hole to recover a shawl, he shrugged. 'Well, it looks like it's hers now, doesn't it?'

'But — -!'

Before she could say another word, the gaoler jerked her by the shoulder and almost threw her into the passage. Alice could only manage one last glimpse of her shawl before he shut the door.

CHAPTER 5

———

Protesting loudly, the women were herded along the passage and out into a dark, sunless yard that held several tubs of water. They were each handed a rough towel, a hard brush and a bar of carbolic soap.

'Get your clothes off an' get in a tub. You's have all got to scrub yersel's clean. And I mean clean. Once we think you've done it right you'll be given two new dresses each.'

Some of the women, many of whose crimes had been prostitution, wasted no time in throwing off their filthy clothes and stepping into the tubs. When they found the water was as icy cold as the day itself, they all protested loudly.

Their shouts and profanities, however, fell on deaf ear.

Alice, Lucy, and one of the other girls hung back. Much as they wanted to be clean, they were hesitant about undressing in front of the turnkeys. They stood, huddled together, waiting for the men to leave.

'Well, get on with it,' the turnkey ordered. When they still hesitated, he told them, 'if you don't get a move on, I'll come an' scrub you myself!' He leered at them for a moment then smiled. 'Maybe you would like that. Is that what you're waiting for?' Smiling nastily, he took a step toward them.

Shaking with fear and embarrassment the girls attempted to keep their backs turned while they quickly disposed of their filthy clothes and scrambled into the tubs.

Alice gasped with shock when the coldness of the water hit her. Recovering quickly, she thought how wonderful it was to be able to wash. She couldn't remember how long it was since she had been clean. Not since long before she was captured! Perhaps if she scrubbed hard enough and washed her hair thoroughly the carbolic soap would kill all the fleas, lice, and any of the other blood-sucking creatures that had inhabited her hair and body. To this end, she scrubbed every inch of her body until it was almost raw. She washed her hair over and over until finally, she stank of carbolic, but she felt clean.

Cold it may have been but she felt she happily could stay in that tub forever — until the turnkey came over and leered at her.

'Are you goin' to get out o' there some time, or would you like me to come in and join you?' he asked' smirking nastily.

Grabbing the towel she had dropped on the ground beside the tub, she held it in front of herself as she climbed out. The turnkey handed her a dress made from some rough material that made her itch a bit. She didn't mind that. It was not as bad as the assortment of wildlife she had just scrubbed from her body. She would get used to it. What mattered was that it was clean! She was clean! When she had finished dressing, the turnkey shoved another dress into her hands.

'You gotta have this to wear when that one needs washing, so they says.'

Surprised, but grateful, Alice accepted it and thanked the man. Her happier mood soon left her when she, once again, had shackles fastened around her ankles.

Surgeon Simpson arrived looking quite angry and gave all the convicts a cursory examination. After a quick nod to the head turnkey, he stomped out of the yard.

He well knew that many of these women had a venereal disease. Some were over sixty! What use were they going to be in the forming and growth of a new colony? No use! Governor Phillip wanted women who could work hard and who would breed and increase the population. Not women too old to reproduce and women suffering the clap who would take their diseases into the new colony. Women who would never be in really good health again. What he couldn't know, of course, was that the new colony was already rife with a variety of venereal diseases! However, he had been ordered to pass as many women as possible so, reluctantly, that was what he was doing.

The surgeon knew, as did many in the Home Office and the Admiralty, that the *first fleet* had been poorly prepared for the voyage. That so far there was no evidence that the fleet had even arrived safely in this new country. Yet they had been gathering ships for a second fleet! How could any government be so stupidly inhuman, he wondered? So irresponsible? It seemed to him that the only interest the Home Office had in these poor people was how to rid the country of them. It was clear to him that their lives meant nothing!

When the *Prince of Wales*, the first ship to return from Botany Bay, appeared in the Thames early in March, Surgeon Simpson felt some relief. He knew the destination of thousands of convicts had been sealed. but at least now it seemed possible that there would be some sort of civilisation for them to arrive in. Now that the government knew the first fleet had arrived and had set up a colony there, this was how they would clear much of the overcrowding in English gaols.

He had read all the reports. It was the headlines in all the newspapers. Port Jackson, it had been named, and prison clerks throughout the country were being swamped with paperwork authorising the movement of convicts.

In less than a week after the arrival of the *Prince of Wales*, many of the female convicts who had been sentenced to transportation to Parts Beyond the Seas were being hustled out of prisons and sent speeding toward London.

Surgeon Simpson shook his head sadly. What, he wondered, would become of these poor wretches he had just examined? Would they make it to this Port Jackson to be used as breeding sows, or would they perish on the way?

Without too much protest, the little group of women was led out through the gates of Newgate prison, to where stood a rickety cart with two thin, sad-looking horses in the traces. The women, shackles cutting their ankles, struggled into the cart and the turnkey sat up in the front with the driver.

'Same place as yesterday,' the turnkey ordered. The driver clicked his tongue and the horses wearily started to plod.

'Where are you taking us?' one of the women asked tentatively.

The turnkey looked round briefly. 'A place called Galleons Reach.'

'Well what's there? Why are you taking us there?' the woman persisted.

'Cos that's where your ship is!'

'Ship?'

'Yeah. To take you wherever it is you're being sent.'

More questions were thrown at the man, but he was bored with the women. He just wanted to get rid of them and get back to Newgate. Perhaps, he thought, if he was quick enough, he might snatch time for a jug of ale on his way back. He ran his tongue over his lips at the thought.

The cart bumped and swayed on a rough road which eventually

brought them to the river. On reaching Blackfriars Bridge, the carter pulled on the reins, shouting, 'whoa, you buggers' and with a weary sigh the horses dragged to a standstill.

'Come on you lot!' the turnkey barked. 'Get yersels down to that boat — an' be quick about it!'

The women were hustled out of the cart and down some worn stone steps to where they were loaded into a waiting lighter. As soon as they were aboard the oarsmen bent to their task and the lighter pulled away from the dock.

As early in the morning as it was, the waters of the Port of London were crowded with craft of all descriptions.

Alice was amazed at the number of tall-masted ships that were littered around the waters and moored at the docksides. More than she could imagine even existed, and so big! Huge! Much larger than any she had ever seen before.

A blackish haze hung over the river and, when asked, one of the oarsmen told them it was caused by dust from the colliers.

The lightermen had to run the gauntlet of all this shipping, constantly dodging and maneuvering to avoid collisions.

Past the north bank of the Thames, the convicts were rowed, the poor souls shivering in the cold of an early March dawn. Southwards down Limehouse reach, where Alice could see the skeletons of partly constructed ships. Beyond those was an area crowded with what one of the lightermen said were military and merchant ships.

They came to an area that looked like a huge building site and the lighterman told them it was to be a military barracks. In this same stretch of the river, an odour came to Alice that she remembered from her coach journey into London. Looking around she could see, scattered on the river, the broken and dismasted ghost ships in which prisoners were being held. Each of these ships, she remembered, were known as *the hulks* and were home to hundreds of poor, suffering men. Men who were kept in chains, given almost no food, and expected to slave on the docks every moment there was daylight to see by.

Alice remembered hearing on the very healthy prison grapevine, that some of these poor souls had been held on *the hulks* for years. How, she wondered, could any of them survive so long.

As the lighter carefully picked its way between these hulks the women could see men, chained together, being loaded onto other boats to be taken ashore and start their labours.

Some of the men waved and called out. Though Alice could not make out their words, she felt a certain empathy for the poor, miserable fellow human beings.

As they rounded a bend in the river the convicts caught sight of another large ship, anchored on the water.

The turnkey pointed to it. 'That there is where you're going,' he told them. 'Just a short boat ride now an' I'll be rid of the lot of you!'

As they neared the ship, It had three masts and, as far as she could see, two decks. Even the largest ship she had seen in Douglas harbour was small in comparison She could see a name in large letters on the bow, but could not tell what it said.

The lighter came up against the side of the ship and the bowman grabbed a huge net that hung down the length of it. Another crewman in the stern caught hold of the net and held it tightly.

'Get yourselves up there,' the turnkey ordered.

Bewildered, and not knowing what was expected of them, the women looked, first at each other, then at the turnkey.

With an angry sigh, the exasperated man shouted, 'My God! Are you all really as stupid as you look?' He grabbed a handful of the net and shook it towards them. 'Get hold of this and climb!'

When the women still sat looking puzzled the turnkey drew

his baton. 'You've got until I count to five, then I'm going to crack the skull of any of yous whats left in this boat.'

As one, the women struggled to their feet and grabbed for the net.

Being young and agile, Alice managed it quite well and as she neared the top she was grabbed by strong hands and hauled unceremoniously over the side and onto the deck. Landing in a heap, she hurriedly scrambled to her feet and adjusted her skirts.

Lily was close behind her and glancing over the side, they saw that some of their companions, partly because of their chains, were struggling badly. A few had lost their footing and were hanging on for dear life with at least one leg caught through the net.

A few of the crew went over the side to disentangle them and help them to the top.

At last, everyone was aboard and struggling to their feet.

The carter was paid his half-a-crown a per head delivery fee and he and the turnkey were rowed back to shore.

The man who had hauled Alice onto the ship collected the women and lined them up.

'Now, this here ship is named the *Lady Juliana*, and it's what is called a three-masted barque. In command of it is Captain Aitken. You'll find if you behave yourselves proper he'll be a fair man. Cap'n won't have women in chains on his ship. I'm James Reed an' first thing he says I've got to do is get them irons off you. So just line up by this anvil an' I'll have 'em off you in just a tick.'

The women obediently lined up and, true to his word, James very quickly knocked off the rivets and their chains fell away.

This was the first time, Alice realised, she had been free of chains for seven or eight months. No words she knew could describe the feeling it stirred in her. Her heart flew with joy and she felt tears in her eyes.

Alice had noticed a stocky, round-faced man and a taller, well-dressed man who had been watching the procedure from a distance. As the last manacle and shackle dropped to the deck they approached the women.

'Can I have your attention for a moment, ladies?' the stocky man asked. 'I'm Lieutenant Thomas Edgar, master of this ship and government agent. I have been appointed to look after your welfare for the duration of the voyage. This gentleman with me is Surgeon Richard Alley, who will assist me in making sure you are all well cared for and kept in as good health as possible.'

The women stood quietly, listening and covertly studying the two men. There was a bit of quiet murmuring, but no one spoke aloud.

'Before I ask James to take you to your accommodation, I need to ask you all a few questions. I'm afraid His Majesty's servants just dump you on us without telling us anything about you. So that we know exactly who we have aboard, I just need to ask your names, ages, and the crimes you were convicted of.'

This last comment brought a few snorts and grumbles.

One by one the women were interviewed. Alice noticed the odd raised eyebrow and a glance exchanged between Lieutenant Edgar and the surgeon when one of their charges admitted to prostitution.

When Alice's turn came and she confessed she had stolen a loaf of bread to be able to stay alive, both men looked truly shocked and saddened.

'What of your parents? Surely they fed you?' Richard Alley asked.

'My Daa died when I was a baby and my Mam just disappeared about three years ago.'

'Disappeared? What do you mean? People don't just disappear.'

Alice shrugged. 'Well, my Mam did! She went out one day to get some food for us and never came back!'

'Have you been alone ever since? Caring for yourself?' Thomas Edgar questioned.

Alice nodded.

'For three years?'

She twitched a shoulder. 'I had to. There was no one else.'

'And what age are you, child?'

'Fourteen. I'll be fifteen in the summer.'

The two men looked startled.

'Fourteen? I thought you much younger,' Robert frowned and shook his head. *Maybe she was from small parents*, he thought. *Or perhaps her size was due to years of deprivation*. Whichever, it saddened him to see a girl so young and vulnerable looking, on a ship of this sort. He would have to keep a wary eye on this child.

Turning away from the women, Thomas directed a quick nod at James, who quickly took charge of them.

'Now, if you'll follow me, ladies,' he said cheerfully, 'I'll take you to your cabin.'

Alice felt her heart give a little jump of joy. This was the first time since her arrest that she had been spoken to as though she was a person, rather than a lump of filth.

James led them to a hatch and directed them down a ladder. Awaiting her turn, Alice noticed, attached to the hatch, a heavy iron grating with bolts.

With a sigh, she reasoned they were to be put below decks and imprisoned by these iron grills.

So, this was to be her home. For how long, she wondered? She had no idea. Still, it could not be worse than Newgate. Nothing could be worse than Newgate! Nor even anywhere near as bad.

And at least she was rid of her chains! Her wrists and ankles, now ulcerated, would have the chance to heal.

Alice's first sensation, on descending the ladder, was of a pleasant scent of new wood. Her second was of darkness, claustrophobia, and human sweat.

Lily, who was as scared as *she*, clung to her hand.

'Alice! Alice Moore!' a voice called from the darkness. Frowning, her eyes not yet adjusted, she peered around.

Suddenly arms were around her and she was engulfed in a crushing hug.

'Don't say you've forgotten your old friend already?'

'Maggie? Oh, Maggie, I thought I would never see you again,' she cried joyfully. Swiping a tear from her cheek, she returned the hug. 'And Lily is with me.'

Maggie quickly included Lily in the hug. 'It's a real pleasure to have my hands free an' be able to give you both a proper cuddle.'

Maggie led them over to the side, where a lantern was hanging and Alice saw that there were many shelves fastened there. 'These are our beds,' Maggie told them, nodding towards the shelves. 'That steward fellow, James, said five or six of us had to share each shelf for sleeping. They're a bit hard but better than the stinking floor at Newgate!'

'Oh Maggie, I don't care about a hard bed. What matters is that we are out of that terrible gaol and are all together. We are all going to this new country, which *must* be better than the one we are leaving!' A shadow crossed her face and a tear came to her eye. 'All except Sarah!'

'What's with Sarah?' Maggie asked anxiously.

'The turnkey said,' she stopped and fought for a breath before she could continue. 'He said she has to stay and burn at the stake!' she gulped.

'Oh, dear God!' was all Maggie could think of to say. 'When

you hear of things like this it makes you wonder if there really is a God in Heaven, doesn't it?'

Alice nodded and looked up at her, sobbing, and as she did so her hair fell away from her face.

Maggie stared at her, in horror, for a moment then she gently gripped her chin and turned her face to the light. 'Who did this to you, lass?' she asked tightly.

'Mavis Crowe. She stole my shawl and hit me when I tried to stop her.'

Maggie looked around furiously. 'Did she come with you today?'

Alice shook her head. 'No, thank God!'

Maggie pursed her lips. 'Well, she'd just better pray they keep her in Newgate, for if I see her again, she will be dead!'

Grasping her friend's arm, Alice shook it slightly. 'You will do no such thing, Maggie Craster. Evil as she is, she is not worth you being burned to a cinder! Tell me, have you heard anything about where we are being sent?'

'Aye. A bit. James Reed — he seems to be a good man. Easy to talk to. Doesn't look down his nose at us. He says we are to go to a new country that belongs to England. Somewhere called Port Jackson, he said. A fleet was sent out there a couple of years or so ago with some marines and about eight hundred convicts. The idea was for them to start a new colony.'

'And have they?' Alice was not altogether sure she understood too much of this.

'It seems a ship arrived back a week or so ago that went with that fleet and the news is that they arrived safely, though quite a few of the convicts died on the way. This fellow, James, says he hasn't been there but has heard it is a very hot country.'

'Good! I could do with some heat!' Alice said with feeling.

'Well, lass, this ship isn't what you would call hot, but it's a hell of a sight warmer than Newgate!'

Alice nodded her appreciation.

'Anyway,' Maggie continued, 'James told me that at first, the plans were to send both male and female convicts on this ship. Either that or women and a battalion of marines to relieve the ones who went out with the first fleet. Then they changed their minds and decided they would only send women. It seems not enough went with Governor Phillip's fleet, so they need a lot more of us out there.'

Alice sat quietly for a few minutes, trying to digest all this news.

'There was something else he told me.' Maggie studied Alice thoughtfully for a few moments. 'How old are you Alice?'

Alice was startled for a moment. Why was Maggie suddenly interested in her age? 'I'm fourteen. Why?'

'Fourteen! I thought you much younger. James says there are to be no convict men on this ship. The only men on board will be the crew. It seems, if James is to be believed, that the captain had given each crewman permission, for the voyage, to take himself a *wife* from amongst the women!'

Alice's eyes widened. 'A wife? But surely many of the crew will be married already?'

Maggie laughed and shook her head. 'Probably *most* of them are, but it will be wife in name only. And only until we reach this place we are being sent to.'

'Then what?' asked Lily.

'Then we're just convict women again. Nothing else. The sailors will go sailing off around the world again and if any of us should bear infants as a result, we will be left to cope with them on our own!'

Alice shuddered at the thought. 'Thank the good Lord I'm too young to marry,' she said with feeling.

'Well, just don't tell anyone what age you really are,' Maggie reminded her firmly.

Alice shook her head. 'They already know.'

Maggie clamped her top lip between her teeth and sighed. 'Who did you tell?'

'That man. I think he said he was the master of the ship. Or something. And the surgeon.'

Maggie nodded and sighed again. 'Then we must just hope they keep it to themselves. If anyone else asks, tell them you're twelve. You're small enough. You'll be believed.'

'Do we have to stay down here in this box?' Alice decided it was time for a change of subject. 'Or will we be permitted to go on deck sometimes. After all those months in that stinking hell hole, I crave fresh air. It was worth the cold on the cart and the lighter coming here to have a fresh wind in my face.' Alice looked longingly towards the ladder.

Maggie smiled and nodded. 'I know just what you mean. All that time in Newgate I thought I would never be clean again. Yes, we are allowed on deck, for we can not escape. Unless you want to jump in the Thames and try to swim for shore.'

Lily snorted and said, 'no fear!'

The three women made their way on deck and stood for a moment breathing the cold air. It bore the stink of the sewage in the river, but to those who had spent months in Newgate prison, it smelled fresh and clean.

A few of the crew, busy about their shipboard duties, paused and appraised the two women and the young girl.

Seeing their looks, Maggie put her face next to Alice's and whispered, 'Don't forget what I told you about your age, else one of them will have you laid before you know it!'

They stood for quite some time watching the hustle and bustle across the water on the dockside and listening to the resulting clamour. They could see chain gangs of prisoners on the quayside, wearily passing heavy burdens from one to the other. Freed temporarily from the hulks, they were treated as slaves. Now and again one would slip and fall and the men either side of him would drag him to his feet. If they weren't quick enough a guard would come with his truncheon and whack his head.

Though she knew none of them, Alice found she had a tear on her cheek for their suffering.

Occasionally, as they stood there, a crewman would stop for a word or two or to make a ribald comment.

James joined them to chat for a few minutes.

'They're sizing us up and trying to decide which of us they want to take as a *wife*,' Maggie said drily.

Startled, Alice studied her friend, not sure whether she was being serious.

'Settling in alright are you ladies?'

Three heads nodded. 'How long are we going to be here?' Alice asked. 'Do you know when we sail?'

James shook his head. 'It won't be for a while yet. The ship is nowhere near ready, but they've already sent over one hundred of you ladies from Newgate in the last two days. And a couple of young babies! Don't know how they'll go on the long voyage! I heard they had just sent you lot here now to get rid of some of the overcrowding in Newgate. An' there's a lot more to come from other prisons. There are to be two hundred or more of you by the time we sail. I reckon all the fellows who went out with the first fleet will be glad to see you lot when you arrive. One of the men from the *Prince of Wales* said they're a bit short of females in this new colony.'

Alice was amused to see the gleam in James' eye whenever he looked at Maggie. After he had left them she giggled and whispered, 'He's taken a fancy to you!'.

Maggie gave her a good-natured slap on the arm. 'Don't be silly, girl!'

The following day was sunny and warm for the time of year. Many of the women were sitting around the deck, enjoying the unaccustomed warmth of sunshine on their faces.

Alice, Maggie, and Lily were again standing at the rail, watching the activity on the docks, when suddenly an order came for them to go below to their quarters.

'I wonder what's happening,' Alice hated having to be shut in the specially constructed cabin in the orlop deck.

Maggie shrugged. 'They're probably just bringing more convicts on board. I think I saw a lighter coming this way with quite a few aboard. The captain must think that while they're busy doing other things we'll pinch the ship from under them.'

They went below and sat on the bed watching the ladder to see who would come down. While they waited, they could hear female voices and the sound of metal hitting metal.

'Aye, it's more of us,' Maggie confirmed. 'That's the rivets being knocked out of the chains.'

Before long, their new neighbours started scrambling down the ladder.

'By God, it's herself,' Maggie hissed.

'Who?' Alice peered into the semi-gloom, and her heart sank. Mavis Crowe! Of all the people it might have been, she was the last one Alice could have wished to see.

Maggie said no more. She just sat watching Mavis, her eyes unblinking, much as a lion would watch its prey. When Mavis was settled, with her back turned, Maggie strode across the cabin. She thrust her knee into the other woman's back, simultaneously grabbing a handful of hair and jerking her head. Mavis' head snapped back dangerously.

'I'll have my girl's shawl that you stole from her,' Maggie snarled.

Mavis tried to struggle but was helpless. Her head was so far back that she could not get breath down her throat.

'The shawl, I said!' Maggie glared down into the other woman's eyes. 'You give me it or I'll break your bloody neck. I'm only a smidgeon away from doing it right now!' she warned. Suddenly releasing her prisoner, she reached down and yanked the shawl from Mavis' grasp. 'You touch Alice again and you are dead!' she warned.

Hatred burned from Mavis' eyes, but Alice noticed she was trembling. She hoped against all hope that this would be the end of the matter and there would be no more trouble.

The days passed pleasantly. As Maggie had said, the ship was quite a bit warmer than Newgate, but most important of all was that their wooden bed, hard though it was, was dry and did not smell unpleasant. After Newgate, their accommodation was luxurious. Although, if James was correct, and there were another hundred or more women to come, it would be very crowded.

Time will tell, Alice thought. *Time will tell!*

CHAPTER 6

———•••———

A lice stood idly watching the flurry of activity across the water. A few feet away Maggie and James leaned on the rail, their foreheads almost touching as they talked quietly and laughed together. She smiled to herself and shook her head. *And she tries to tell me,* she thought, *that James is not interested in her!*

Lily had drifted away; Alice knew not where; with a sailor who had been showing a keen interest in her. While she was pleased to see her friends making friends and perhaps finding romance, she couldn't help feeling a little lonely and abandoned.

Suddenly she became aware there was someone leaning on the rail a few feet away. Turning, she found a tall, skinny young lad studying her through the darkest eyes she had ever seen. He was a stranger, not someone she had seen on board before.

Realising he had been caught out staring at Alice, the boy reddened, averted his gaze and turned quickly to look down into the grubby water.

Flustered by his scrutiny, Alice half turned her back and continued to look out over the water. To her eyes it looked greasy and turgid, the ripples rounded by the scum that floated on the river's surface. *Not surprising,* she thought, *considering the amount of human waste that was dumped into it.* Every day, with a knot of disgust in her stomach, she had watched as the buckets of human waste and kitchen refuse were tossed over the rail.

James had told them once that all the ships on the river did the same. 'Well, what else is there to do with it all?' he asked, shrugging and laughing at the horror on their faces.

Thinking about this, and all the *Hulks* with their vast number of convicts, Alice shuddered. It surprised her that the river wasn't solid.

'Are you all alone?' A quiet voice suddenly sounded in her ear.

Alice spun around, to find the boy had moved nearer to her.

Taking a quick backward step, she frowned at him. 'What does it look like?' She was aware she was being rude, but apart from the rough ragamuffins she had come across thieving in Douglas, she was unused to boys.

'I'm sorry,' the boy dropped his eyes and shuffled the feet he was now studying. 'I wasn't being nosy. I just thought you looked lonely.' He shifted his gaze upward to look at her again.

'S'all right,' Alice shrugged and half turned away. 'I am a bit lonely sometimes,' she added as an afterthought.

'Me too.' He nibbled his lip and sighed.

Alice turned to look at the lad. *He does look a bit sad and lonely,* she thought. 'You have all your friends on the ship for company,' she told him quietly.

The boy grimaced. 'I don't really know any of them. This is my first time on a ship. I don't even know whether I'll like it.'

'Why come then?'

He shrugged. 'My dad said I had to!'

'Why, what did you do?' Alice was starting to feel a stirring of interest in this sad-looking boy.

He shook his head. Didn' do nuthin'. It's just there's six

younger than me at home an' my Dad said it was time I left an' made my own way in the world. A mate of his got me this job.'

'That's sad,' Alice said quietly. 'You must miss them.'

The boy nodded. "Specially my Mum and my little brother what's a year younger than me. We was great mates. They was both crying when my Dad took me away.'

Alice nodded. 'My Mam would have cried too.'

'Can we be friends? My name is Danny Williams.'

Alice studied him for a moment. *It would be nice to have a friend near my own age*, she thought. Nodding, she said, 'Yes I would like that. I'm Alice Moore.'

Danny moved a bit closer and they both turned to look out across the river.

'Why are you here?' he asked quietly.

Alice gave an unladylike snort. 'Because the deemster said I must!'

Danny looked a bit disconcerted for a moment. 'No, I meant what did you do wrong to deserve to be sent away?'

'I was hungry, so I stole a loaf of bread!'

Not knowing how to respond, Danny sighed and looked sadly out across the water. He absently scuffed his toe into the deck. 'What about your parents? Did they not feed you?' he eventually asked.

Alice felt her eyes fill with tears and clamped her top lip between her teeth. 'I didn't have a Dad. Or at least I never knew him, and my Mam just disappeared a few years ago. She just went out one day an' never came back. After that, the only way to get food was to steal it! I used to pull potatoes and turnips from the fields and pinch bread an' bits of fruit from the market. A fish sometimes if I could.'

Danny shook his head in sorrow. 'That's sad. Really sad!' he said quietly. 'An they're sending you to this new country far away, all for a loaf of bread?'

Alice shrugged. 'Well, it wasn't the first time I'd been caught, so I guess the deemster thought it best to just get rid of me for once and for all! This way I won't bother him again.'

Danny angrily shook his head. 'That's wrong though. You're nobbut a child!'

'I'm fourteen, soon be fifteen,' Alice said indignantly.

Danny looked startled. 'You ain't? Are you? I thought you was about twelve'.

Alice shook her head. 'I'll be fifteen in August.'

'You're not much younger'n me then. I turned fifteen at Christmas.'

A shout from the poop deck made them both turn around.

'Get yourself up here, Williams, there's work to be done. You're not here to chase women!'

Alice saw one of the crew-men beckoning angrily.

'Sorry. Got to go. I'll see you later, I hope.' Danny turned and ran to get on with his work.

Watching him go, Alice smiled to herself. *Yes, it would be nice to have a young friend during the voyage!*

In the weeks that followed Maggie covertly watched the developing friendship between Alice and the young deck-hand with a degree of satisfaction. She no longer felt quite the same responsibility towards the girl and felt freer to pursue her own developing romance with James.

Lily, also, had quite a strong friendship underway with another of the sailors, Duncan Greig. 'I've some news for you,' she announced one day when she, Alice and Lily were together at the rail.

Both her friends turned their eyes to her. 'Which is?' Maggie asked.

'Well, you know the Captain said all the crew could take a wife for the voyage?' she asked hesitantly.

Alice nodded and Maggie said, 'Yes.'

'Well Duncan, that's the sailor I've been spending time with, has asked me to be his *wife*. If I do, I can go and stay in his quarters with him. It will be more comfortable, he says, and not as crowded as in our cabin.'

Maggie gave her a long, penetrating look before asking, 'and what did you tell him?'

'I said I would,' Lily dropped her gaze to study the deck.

'I don't blame you.' Maggie squeezed her shoulder. 'James asked me the same thing an' I told him I would think about it.'

Alice's head shot up and she stared at her friend. 'What about me? I'll be alone!' she said miserably.

Maggie put a comforting arm around her. 'No, you won't, love. You have your little friend, Danny, and we will still be here during the day for you to talk to when the men are working. It is only at night we won't be here.'

Slightly mollified, Alice nodded. *They were right, of course,* she thought, *but she would still miss them in the* evenings. Her mind turned to Mavis, and the possible danger of being unprotected in the nights.

Plucking up her courage, she said, 'I suppose you would be more comfortable if you did go with James. He's nice and he treats us with respect. I like him, so I think you should say *'yes'* to him.' Half of her wanted Maggie to refuse, but the other half wanted happiness for her friend.

Maggie stood, gazing thoughtfully out across the river for some minutes. Finally, she turned to Alice, studying her face as she asked, 'Are you sure you wouldn't mind? You would be alright, wouldn't you? Tell me if you won't.'

Alice thought about it for a moment. She knew she would feel bereft. Would miss her terribly at night. Of course, she would. But she found her strongest feeling was that she was pleased.

Maggie deserved only the best, and in Alice's mind, James was the best.

Smiling, she nodded. 'You needn't worry about me. I will be fine.'

Maggie gave her a quick hug. This child and her happiness meant the world to her.

Maggie and Lily wasted no time. Having made their decision, they moved to the men's quarters that night.

After they had gone, Alice lingered on the deck for as long as possible, until the cold of the evening finally drove her below decks. She looked around for friendly faces. There were some she knew, who smiled at her, but they had settled into their own group of friends and did not invite her to join.

Dragging her feet, she wandered sadly to her bed-space. All the weeks she had been on board the *Lady Juliana* she had lain snugly between Maggie and Lily. Now there would be only space where they had lain. Or more likely their spaces would be filled to ease the overcrowding.

With a weary sigh, she sat on the bed with her back against the ship's side. Pulling her feet up, wrapping her arms around her shins she rested her forehead on her knees. Smiling to herself she drifted off into a daydream about Danny and how much she was enjoying their blossoming friendship.

Suddenly she became aware that someone had sat beside her and she opened her eyes, finding, to her horror, that it was Mavis Crowe.

'What do you want?' she asked, with as much aggression as she could muster. Realising her lips were trembling, she drew them in and clamped her teeth on them.

'Just a friendly visit,' Mavis replied, with an evil glitter in her eyes that was anything *but* friendly.

73

'Well, I can do without your friendship!' Alice snapped.

'No, now that's where you're wrong. Now your protector has gone, you see, you'll need a new one. That will be me!'

Alice hitched along the bed away from Mavis. 'I don't need protection. Not from you or anyone else.'

'Oh, I think you do. There's some rough bitches on this boat an' they'll come after a soft little lass like you.' Mavis slid along to close the gap between herself and Alice.

'I can look after myself.' Alice moved a bit further and found herself right at the edge of the bed.

Mavis threw her head back and gave a harsh, barking laugh that made Alice shudder.

'You couldn't look after a bowl of buttermilk, let alone yourself. No, you need protection. An' the price of that protection will be that shawl you're so fond of.'

Alice jumped to her feet, hugging the shawl tightly around herself. 'No! You won't have it! Never!' Her eyes blazed as she faced up to the older woman.

With startling speed, Mavis leapt forward, grabbed the shawl, and gave it a swift jerk.

Hanging on tightly, Alice was jerked off her feet, rocketed towards her protagonist, bounced off her, and went sprawling full length on the deck. Still, she clung to her precious wrap. 'It was a present from a friend and you're not having it!' she shouted from the floor.

Standing above the prone girl, Mavis sneered down at her. 'Well, that's what you think,' she snarled as she dropped to land her full weight, knees first, on Alice's midriff.

With all the breath driven out of her and gasping for air, Alice curled her knees up and tried to turn on her side.

'I'll have *my* shawl now!' Mavis tried again to yank it away and when Alice hung on, she punched repeatedly at the side of her face.

Alice lay, desperately trying to defend her face without releasing the precious shawl, but just as she thought she was about to be beaten unconscious, Mavis suddenly fell away from her.

'Leave the child alone, you evil bitch! You'll have *me* to deal with if you hurt her again.'

Fearing another beating, at first, Alice did not dare to raise her head. When she did, she saw a woman whom she knew had come from Lincoln gaol, standing nearby with Mavis spreadeagled at her feet. Alice painfully dragged herself to a sitting position and nervously watched Mavis.

Mavis half rose from the floor and cast her a venomous glance, but when the other woman took a step towards her, she scrambled rapidly to her feet. When the woman raised a beefy fist, she scuttled off to her own bed.

'Have a mind,' the woman shouted after her. 'Stay away from the child or you'll be dead!'

'An' you'll need to keep an eye behind you always, or you'll be the first one to die!' Mavis shouted back; brave again from a distance.

Alice's saviour squatted beside her. Brushing the blood-soaked hair away from her face, she inspected the damage Mavis had wrought. 'You all right? You need to see the surgeon?' Taking her arm, she helped Alice up onto her bed.

Alice shook her head and wiggled her jaw a bit. 'No. I think it's just cuts and bruises. I'd rather not go to the surgeon.'

The woman nodded thoughtfully. 'Well, my name's Gracie West. You'd best come over and join me and my friends in our bed. You won't be safe to stay here now your friends are gone.'

Alice gratefully followed her new friend across the cabin, aware every moment of Mavis' eyes burning into her back.

Gracie introduced her three friends as Jean, Winnie, and Megan, then found a clean rag from somewhere and gently cleaned the blood from Alice's face. It was not as bad as she had first feared, just a couple of good-sized cuts and a few bruises.

Utterly exhausted, Alice lay down between Gracie and Megan and quickly fell into a deep sleep. She felt safe with her new friends. Mavis could not hurt her while they were there.

At some time during the night, she awoke to find herself wrapped tightly in Gracie's arms. It was too tight for comfort, so she wriggled away a bit, then drifted back to sleep, feeling content and secure with the warmth from the bodies on either side of her and the protection they gave her.

'Who did this?' Maggie asked angrily when she saw Alice's face the following morning.

'Mavis. She said that now you were gone I would need protection. She told me she would give me that, but the price I would have to pay would be my shawl.'

'Still after that, is she?' Maggie asked grimly.

Alice nodded. 'Aye, but I told her I didn't need protection and she couldn't have the shawl.

Tight-lipped, Maggie nodded but said nothing.

'Well, we had a fight an' she was winning,' Alice continued, 'then just as I thought I could hang on no longer and I was about to pass out another lady dragged her off me an' gave her a thumping. She told her if she hurt me again, she would kill her!'

'Good of her,' Maggie said thoughtfully. 'Who was this woman an' what did she want from you in return?'

'She just didn't like to see me being hurt. An' to make sure I was safe from Mavis, she took me over to her bed-space to share it with her and her three friends. I had to sleep between her and one of her friends to make sure Mavis couldn't creep up on me in the night.'

'These women? Where are they from? Do I know them?' Maggie frowned.

Alice shrugged. 'I dunno. You might. They're from Lincoln gaol and slept over the other end of the cabin from us.'

Maggie nodded. 'I think I know who you mean. A big woman about my age and three younger ones?'

'Aye.'

'Well, they might be all right. Or they might not. Just watch yourself around them. Be very careful.'

Alice studied her friend thoughtfully. When she glanced at Lily the other girl nodded and said quietly, 'I agree with Maggie. Just stay alert around them.'

'OK.' Alice agreed. Her new friends seemed very nice, but she knew Maggie was usually a good judge. Though she had no idea what it was Maggie feared from them, she would do as she asked and be wary when with them. She just hoped she hadn't stepped from Mavis' fire into their frying pan.

At that moment Danny appeared beside her and laid a gentle hand on her shoulder. Studying her anxiously, he asked, 'what happened to your face?'

Alice gave a weary smile. 'Just one of the women. She wanted my shawl.'

Danny scowled and put an arm around her shoulder. 'Well, if she hurts you again you tell me an' I'll sort her out!'

Alice looked at skinny little Danny and giggled. 'You haven't seen her. She would fell a stevedore with one punch!'

Danny laughed. 'Well, she'd have to catch me first. I can dodge pretty quick an' my Dad taught me how to look after myself. I'll look after you too,' he finished bravely.

Alice shrugged. 'Thank you. I like having you for a friend,' she smiled up at him, 'but you needn't worry about me. I have found four nice new friends who are more than a match for Mavis Crowe. They will keep me safe at night when you can't be there to watch over me.'

Turning to speak to Maggie, Alice found that she and Lily had discreetly drifted away and were leaning on the rail several yards away.

In the days that followed Alice found herself looking for Danny whenever she was on deck. Maggie and Lily spent quite a bit of time with her, but she found that even when she was with them, her eyes were roaming the deck looking for the thin little figure.

Maggie noticed her distraction and smiled to herself. *Maybe not so much of a child as she looked, after all*, she thought with a knowing nod to herself

While they were in dock there was not a great deal for the crew to do, so to Alice's joy Danny had quite a bit of time to spare, most of which he spent with her.

At nights, Alice slept uneasily. Often she awoke to find herself locked tightly in Gracie's arms. In the first days, Gracie would allow her a bit of space when she wriggled away from her, but as the days passed, she resisted and continued with her tight hug. Behind her, Alice heard strange sounds from her other three new friends and felt a lot of movement against her back. Aware, always of Maggie and Lily's warning, she became more uncomfortable with every night that passed.

'I just don't like being so close to someone,' Alice confided in her two friends one day. 'She holds me so tight at night I can hardly breathe. An' if she comes near me during the day she's always touching me. Stroking my face or my arms or trying to put her arms around me. I don't like it.'

Maggie pursed her lips. 'I thought there was something odd about that one. An' her three friends. There's some women what like other women instead of men. I think those four must be that type. You stay away from them. Find yourself some new friends.'

Alice sighed. 'That's not so easy. If I won't sleep alongside them Mavis will get to me. At least Gracie an' the other three don't knock me about — or steal my shawl.'

Maggie scratched her forehead thoughtfully. 'Well, you tell that Gracie you don't like being held at night, 'cos it keeps you awake. An' if any of them try any funny business wi' you, you let me know an' I'll think of some way out of it.'

'I'm real grateful to you for keeping me safe from Mavis,' Alice said quietly when they were preparing for bed that night, 'but I don't want you to hug me no more. It makes me uncomfortable an' I can't sleep proper.'

Gracie frowned and studied her for a moment. 'Don't you, now? Well, that's the price you pay for having me an' my friends protecting you. I like a nice cuddle at night.'

'Well I don't like it. An' I don't want you to do it.'

Gracie shrugged. 'Well, that's your bad luck then isn't it? Unless you want Mavis turned loose on you again, you'll just have to put up with it!'

At that, she turned and walked away, shaking her head and laughing as she went.

That night, to Alice's relief, Gracie only held her quite loosely and she fell asleep quite quickly. Only to awaken suddenly with the feel of Gracie's hand trying to push its way between her legs. Horrified, she put her hands against Gracie's chest and tried to push herself away.

Gracie held tightly to her. 'Come on girlie, just let me in there and I promise you'll enjoy it. Much more pleasure than any man can give you!'

'No! I don't want it! Let me go!' Alice screamed, and in a

strange corner of her mind, she registered the other women in the cabin starting to stir.

Gracie gave an evil-sounding laugh and managed to force her hand home. 'Now, just relax and enjoy it.'

In a last desperate effort, Alice dug her finger nails into Gracie's neck and twisted with all her strength.

Gracie screamed and clutched at her neck.

Grabbing the chance, Alice leapt from the bed and fled to the far side of the cabin.

'You bitch!' Gracie yelled. 'I'll make you regret that. You will have no one to protect you now, an' there will be four of us you will have to fear as well! So be warned!'

Alice was aware of the other women in the cabin peering through the darkness, but not a word was said. No one offered to help her, and the bed-space she had shared with Maggie and Lily had long ago been filled. Fighting tears, she stumbled over to the companionway and curled into a ball of misery on the floor.

'Who was it this time?' Maggie asked angrily. She had only had to take one look at Alice in the morning to see that something dire had happened.

Alice glanced nervously over her shoulder. 'Gracie. She tried to … to do things I didn't want her to do. An' when I said I didn't want it, she tried to force me. I dug my fingernails into her neck an' that made her let go of me, but she says they're all going to come after me. They were all giving me looks this morning so hot they would have fried an egg. Mavis too!'

Maggie ran her fingers through her hair. 'Well, they'll ha' to get past me first!' she said grimly.

Alice gave a weary smile and shook her head. 'You're not there at night an' that's when they'll come after me.'

'I'll come back to the orlop. James will have to do without me. I can't leave you to the mercy of them witches.'

Alice choked down a sob. 'You can't do that for me. It's not fair on you or James. I'll manage to stay away from them.'

'Going to stay awake twenty-four hours a day from now till *whenever* are you? I *will* do it. It's my decision. I'll tell James when I see him.'

Alice shook her head again but was lost for words. A large part of her wanted to have Maggie there to protect her. Another part of her did not want to get in the way of her friend's happiness.

Lily joined them soon afterward and was quickly told of Alice's unhappy tale. After that nothing more was said for quite some time as the three of them sat by the rail, watching the workers grafting on the dock across the river and trying to think of a solution.

'You like Danny, don't you?' Lily suddenly broke the silence.

Startled out of her reverie, Alice looked at her friend and nodded her head.

Maggie frowned questioningly.

'Well, you could ask him if he would take you as his wife.'

'She's nobbut a child!' Maggie said angrily.

'She's only a short kick away from bein' fifteen,' Lily shot back. 'Just because she only looks ten or eleven doesn't mean nothin'. She's nearly a woman. So why shouldn't she be a wife?'

Maggie nodded thoughtfully and looked questioningly at Alice. 'How do you feel about the idea?'

Alice scratched the side of her face. 'I don't know. I hadn't even thought about that sort of thing.

'You would be safe from them women at night,' Lily encouraged.

'Yes ...but,' Alice sighed and twitched her shoulders. 'Anyway, he hasn't asked me and he might not want me.'

Maggie studied her for a moment. 'It's my bet he wouldn't say no. You've got to remember, he may look like only a skinny little boy, but it's my bet he would want to do what men like to do if he had you in his bed.'

Alice looked quickly at Maggie, her eyes wide with alarm. 'You mean …?'

Maggie nodded. 'I have no doubt, living in the street for years, you will have seen the sort of thing men and women get up to.'

Alice nodded. She had often seen prostitutes plying their trade in the back alleys of Douglas. Had watched in some fascination at times. They had looked, most of the time, as if they were enjoying the activity. She had seen money change hands, so knew the women were paid for it. At times, recently, she had even wondered if that might be a better way to survive than to steal food. The trouble was that she didn't quite know what it entailed. Prostitution, she knew, was the reason Maggie was imprisoned. The reason, in fact, she was being sent *beyond the seas*.

'Think carefully before you decide,' Maggie said quietly. 'It's a big step for such a little girl.'

Alice smiled and shook her head. 'I really don't know why we're discussing it. Danny has never mentioned any such thing. He probably wouldn't want a wife.'

'It wouldn't be forever though. It would only be until we reach this new land. Then Danny, I should think, will have to go with the ship when it leaves.'

'Think about it. Then if you decide it is what you want, then ask him.' Lily suggested.

Alice shook her head. 'I couldn't do that. It's just too forward! And I wouldn't know what to do!'

Maggie gave a loud guffaw. 'Oh, you would soon learn. Nature would guide you!'

Lily smiled and nodded. Until she had become Duncan's *wife* she'd had no experience with men, but she *had* learned — and quickly!

'I don't think I can bear another night down there.' Alice nodded toward the hatch to the convict's quarters. 'To stay safe, I had stay awake all last night, but I can't go without sleep forever!'

Maggie nodded. 'Right. Well, tell Danny. Ask Danny.'

'Tell me what? What's happened?'

The three women turned from the rail at the sound of his voice behind them.

Alice gasped and felt the heat rise to her face. How long had he been standing there, she wondered.

'Some of the women gave her a beating last night and it's not safe for her to be down there wi' them any more,' Maggie answered before Alice could say a word.

Danny immediately looked concerned. 'Why? Why did they beat her?'

'Because she wouldn't do something they wanted her to do. Now it's too dangerous for her to stay among them. They're bad women.'

'Well, I'll tell the captain and the surgeon. They'll tell the women to stop,' Danny said earnestly. 'I'll go now.' He turned to hurry away, but Maggie grabbed his arm.

'That won't do no good. It won't stop them and will probably make them worse.'

'What can we do then?' Danny asked in consternation. 'We can't leave her to be beaten.'

Maggie nodded her agreement. 'You really do like Alice don't you?'

'Oh yes! We's real good friends,' he replied enthusiastically.

'Well, how would you feel about making her your *wife*?'

Startled, Danny's head shot round to anchor his gaze on Maggie. 'Wife? I'm too young to have a wife.'

Mortified, Alice wanted to curl up in a ball and die of embarrassment.

'Just for the voyage. To keep her safe,' Maggie encouraged. 'Captain Aitken said all the members of the crew can take a *wife* for the voyage. You're on the crew are you not?'

Danny nodded dumbly. 'Yes ... but. Well, I'm only fifteen. I don't know as he'd have meant one so young,' he mumbled in confusion.

Maggie laughed quietly. 'Maybe. But he did say *every* crew member. Think about it for a while, but don't take too long. Alice won't be safe down there tonight.'

Danny shook his head, as though to clear his thoughts. Finally, he turned and took hold of Alice's hand. What do you think of it? Would you want to be my *wife?*'

Embarrassed, but at the same time excited, Alice nodded. 'Well, I do like you a lot. An' I'm scared to go back to the orlop.'

Danny nodded thoughtfully and one of the crew-men chose that moment to shout at him. 'Hey, Williams, get yourself up here. There's work to be done.'

'I'll think on it an' talk to you later,' he said quietly, before hurrying away.

'He'll say *yes*,' Maggie said with confidence when he had left..

CHAPTER 7

Maggie was right! An hour or so later Danny drifted back to where Alice, Maggie, and Lily sat on the deck with their backs to the rail.

Looking a bit uncomfortable, he stumbled over words as he said, 'I — um — I asked my mate about it — um — you know — um — if,' he stopped, red-faced. Scuffing the toe of his boot into the deck he continued, 'if the captain would let me have a *wife*.'

'And the answer was?' Maggie prompted.

Danny shuffled uncomfortably, 'he said I was on the crew and the captain said *all* the crew, so that would mean me too. Then he told me to go grab my little wench!' he ended in a rush.

Maggie gave a barking laugh and thumped him on the back so hard that he nearly went flying. 'Congratulations,' she said heartily.

Danny turned to Alice. It seemed to him she hadn't said very much about it. Her friend had done all the talking and he had no idea of how Alice felt. 'How about you, Alice,' he asked quietly. 'Is it really what you want to do? Just say if it isn't. I don't want to put pressure on you.'

Alice smiled and shook her head slightly. 'The only people putting any pressure on me are them there.' She nodded toward the hatch. 'I like you a lot and I know I'll be safe wi' you. You won't give me a beating.'

Danny's face lit up in a wide grin and he shook his head vehemently. 'No, 'course I won't. I ain't never hit no one in my life. I'm real pleased! When I get a break from work, I'll come an' take you to my berth.'

He wanted to give her a great big hug and a kiss but decided he'd better not. Too many eyes watching.

True to his word, Danny came and collected Alice an hour or so later. Taking her hand, he led her to the forecastle, which was where the ordinary seamen were housed. Shyly, he pointed to a bunk, which was one amongst many. 'This is mine,' he said quietly.

Alice looked in wonder at Danny's bed. It had a mattress. Albeit a thin one, it was a mattress! Her heart leapt with excitement. She hadn't slept on a mattress since her mother had vanished and the landlord had kicked her out of the house.

Thinking back sadly, she remembered the months after her mother disappeared, when she had hung around near the house. It hadn't been much of a house, but all that her mother could afford. It was always cold and damp — even in the summer. When it rained they had to put pots under where the roof leaked, but at least it was a roof over their heads. Poor though it was, her mother had made it a home. It was full of love, and that was what mattered.

Then one night her mother had gone out — and just disappeared. When the rent had gone unpaid for several weeks the landlord had come, grabbed her by the scruff of her neck and thrown her out into the street.

Many a night she had slept on the doorstep, hoping against hope that her mother would magically reappear. When winter came, she'd had to abandon her vigil and had crept in to sleep on the floor of a nearby church. Her mother, it would appear, had simply vanished from God's earth, so it seemed fair that she should make her bed in His house.

Shaking herself back to the present, Alice looked up at Danny with a tear pricking her eye.

Danny saw the tear and took her hand. 'If it's no good. If you won't like it here, just tell me. I don't want you to be here if you won't be happy.'

'Oh, I will! I will be happy here. It's just that seeing the mattress made me think of things I'd rather forget.'

Danny looked shocked but said nothing for a moment. He wanted to ask what upset her so much about a mattress but thought better of it. 'Do you have any stuff to bring here?' he asked finally.

Alice shrugged and gave a sad smile. 'I only have this shawl and another dress they gave me at the prison before they brought me here.'

'Best go an' get it an' bring it here. Get Maggie to go down wi' you so's that woman don't get yer.'

Alice nodded and left him there.

Maggie was more than happy to lend her protection, then went back with her to Danny's little corner.

'You'll be cosy here, girl. And safe and comfortable.' Taking Alice's hand, she turned her to face her. Gripping her shoulders, she looked intensely into the girl's face. Maggie knew that many a girl Alice's age had had experience with men; in fact, she knew quite a few who had taken to the streets as a way of making a living. She, herself had not been much older than Alice was now when she had entered into a life of prostitution. However, she was fairly sure Alice was still an innocent.

'Now, I want you to listen to me, girl. And pay attention and answer me honestly.'

Alice met her eye with a steady gaze and nodded.

'Have you ever done anything with a man — or a boy? You know what I mean don't you?'

Alice thought for a moment. 'You mean what the street women do with men in the alleys?' she asked finally.

Maggie nodded.

'I've seen them do strange things and get money for it, but I'm not very sure what it is they do,' Alice twitched her nose and shrugged.

Maggie sighed and pursed her lips. It was as she had thought. She sat down on the bunk, pulled Alice down beside her, and explained the facts of man-woman relationships.

Alice sat quietly, wide-eyed as she listened. 'I see,' she said finally. 'Well, most of them look as if they enjoy it. And this is what Danny will expect me to do then?'

Maggie nodded. 'That's what wives do. It's good for some, not for others. Depends on how much the man cares.'

Alice smiled, 'Well, it sounds a bit strange but better than having to stay in the orlop cabin with them women!'

'Well, just a word of warning; doing that is what makes a baby. You don't want one o' them, not at your age. So be careful. Make sure an' tell Danny that if he wants to do it, he has to pull out of you before he comes.'

Alice frowned, perplexed. 'Comes where?'

Maggie sighed and shook her head. She had forgotten how innocent a girl could be. 'Comes inside you! Just tell him, he'll know what you mean. An' always remember, when we get to this new country *we* will be staying there, but Danny will be leaving again when the ship sails. So don't you go getting too fond of him, an' don't go getting with child either.'

Alice shrugged. 'I'll tell him,' she promised.

It was a beautiful, balmy early summer's day. Alice, Maggie, and Lily spent most of it sitting on the deck, backs against the rail enjoying the sunshine while they chatted and dozed. Now and again one of their beaus would stop for a word or two as they passed. Danny always had a huge grin on his face and was clearly looking forward to the night to come.

Alice turned her face to the sun, enjoying its warmth. Puffy white clouds drifted lazily across a perfect cerulean sky. Gulls swirled across her vision, mewing as they constantly searched for food. Though what they might find fit to eat in this putrid, stinking river, she was not sure.

This must be what real happiness is, she thought. Good friends. Nice food and as much of it as she needed. This had never happened to her before. As long as she could remember, she had always been hungry. And now, a comfortable bed and a nice protector to share it with. *Could anyone ask for more?* she wondered. This experience of being comfortable on the ship made her wonder if she had ever been truly happy before. Even with her mother there, life had been a struggle and there had never been much food. Warmth was a stranger to her. There had been love, though. In abundance. Alice had never doubted her mother's love. Nor had she resented the fact that she was often left alone in the cottage at night. Her mother had worked mostly at night, cleaning business houses, she had said, to earn the money to keep them housed and fed.

For the first time, Alice suddenly felt glad she had been arrested and sentenced to go beyond the seas. If not for that, she would not be here now and about to start living as a wife to Danny. Second, only to Maggie, she thought Danny was her best friend. She knew instinctively that he would be kind. *This would be luxury*, she thought. *To be snuggled up in bed with Danny — and on a mattress! Luxury!*

When the day had grown old and the crew finished their shift, the men who had taken *wives* collected them and took them back to their quarters. They sat around in several groups, drinking rum and telling bawdy stories.

Alice, while enjoying the camaraderie, didn't understand a lot of the stories. The men might as well have been speaking a different language. However, she reckoned she would learn it in time.

Eventually, as evening turned to night, the couples started drifting off to their bunks. Danny shyly took Alice's hand. 'Do you want to come to bed yet?' he asked nervously.

Alice gazed back at him, lost for words for a moment. Did she? All day, she had thought about it. Wondered about it. Part of her was happy about it. She had been looking forward to being Danny's wife, but apprehensive about the things Maggie had told her she would have to do. Apprehensive, but at the same time looking forward to it. To the adventure of something new. A feral part of her, the woman, knew instinctively that she wanted to be a physical wife to Danny. The little girl still in her feared the act, and the pain she thought it might bring.

In the end, it did not happen that night. Danny wordlessly led her to his bunk. 'You'd better go against the wall in case I get called during the night, or you're still asleep in the morning when I have to go on duty.'

Alice obediently climbed into the bunk and felt a sudden wave of joy at the comfort the thin mattress brought. She tried not to think of the rank stone floor in Newgate Gaol, but the memory did, for a moment, hit her with some force and her stomach heaved. Pushing the unpleasant thought aside, she averted her eyes shyly as Danny divested himself of his outer clothes. He climbed nervously in beside her and they lay stiffly on their backs, neither of them quite sure what they should do.

Eventually, Danny said, 'Well, I guess we better go to sleep.'

Alice nodded. 'Goodnight then.' With mixed feelings, she turned to face the wall. For some inexplicable reason, she felt a tear prick her eye. She had expected more. What had she expected? She didn't know, but was irrationally disappointed when it did not happen.

'G'night,' Danny replied quietly. A moment later Alice felt him turn in the bed and his arm gently creep around her. Smiling to herself, she snuggled back against him and felt his arm tighten.

Feeling happier and more secure than she ever had, Alice fell into a deep sleep. When she awoke in the morning Danny had gone, and she had not felt him leave.

'Well, how did it go?' Maggie asked when they met for breakfast. 'Was he gentle with you?'

Alice twitched a shoulder and grimaced, the feeling of disappointment returning. 'He didn't do anything. He said we should go to sleep. So, we did.'

'Is that all?' Maggie asked in disbelief. 'Nothing? He did nothing?'

'He put his arm across me, is all.'

'He must be pretty special then. Or a bit funny, is all I can say.' Maggie shook her head.

That evening followed the same pattern, but during the night it changed. Alice was wakened by the feel of his hand on her newly budding breast and had a surge of a feeling that was completely new to her. What was this feeling? She didn't know, but she liked it. It was warm and exciting. Without any real thought, she pressed herself back against him, heard him gasp and was rewarded by the feel of him harden against her.

This must be the thing Maggie had told her about, the thing he would put inside her. Suddenly the woman in her wanted that. She couldn't have explained why, nor did she know it was just the way of nature; the natural urge to reproduce. All she knew was that she wanted the feel of that special part of Danny inside her.

Around her, she heard the murmurs, giggles and grunts she had heard when she had spied on the prostitutes in the alleys. They all sounded to be enjoying whatever they were doing and she longed to try it.

Nothing more happened, though Alice waited with bated breath for Danny to make his next move. After a while, she realised that he had slept through his bodily reaction and had known nothing about it. Almost weeping tears of frustration and an unreasonable feeling of rejection, Alice finally fell back to sleep.

Danny lay, motionless and uncomfortable, with Alice's buttocks pressed against him. He, also, was experiencing feelings he had never felt before. He had masturbated in the past. Of course, he had! What fifteen-year-old boy had not? But this was different.

When Danny felt his penis swell at the touch of Alice's bottom he thought he must die of embarrassment. Afraid he might lose control of himself, he did not dare let her know he was awake in case she moved and his resolve crumbled. He struggled to keep his breath steady so that she would think he was asleep.

His older cousin, George, had often boasted, proudly, of the things he did with a multitude of girls, though Danny was sure he exaggerated. So Danny knew what males and females did, but had never felt any real interest — until now. He had always thought girls a bit silly and giggly — until now.

He remembered that on one occasion his father had overheard George's boasts and had taken him aside afterward. 'Don't pay any attention to George,' he had said quietly. 'He's a bad boy and a bad influence. Most of the things he says he does are just lies to make himself look and feel important.'

Danny had nodded. That was just about what he had been thinking.

'Always remember,' his father had continued, 'That women and girls have to be respected. You do know what it is that George claims he does with girls, do you not?'

'More or less. I have a pretty good idea anyway.'

'Yes, well,' his father had added, 'You've been brought up as a good Christian boy and when you are with a girl, no matter how strongly you may feel, you must behave as a good Christian man. You must never, *never* do that sort of thing with any woman until she is your wife. Do you understand?'

Danny had nodded enthusiastically and said 'yes' he did understand and 'no' he would never do *it* until he was wed. The promise didn't seem like any great sacrifice.

And he had meant it. It was something he had never put much thought into. Girls were pretty boring and uninteresting, weren't they? He had preferred knocking about with his friends, getting into petty, harmless mischief.

Then he had met Alice. The small, lost-looking, childlike waif, for whom he had felt instant sympathy. Her sadness echoed his feelings at being parted from his family and he felt the need to be a friend to her. And he had needed a friend too if he was to be honest. That had been all he was looking for when he first spoke to her. Friendship; which had quickly become more than that. Danny was a bit confused about just what it *had* become. He had quickly realised she needed protection, but it was more than that too!

Then her friend had suggested that to keep her safe he should make her his wife. A wife, for goodness sake, at fifteen. While it had seemed a ridiculous suggestion, he had to admit he had felt a frisson of excitement ripple through him at the thought. It would be good to not have to watch her being battoned below decks every night. Nice to have her in his cabin and so near to him, he thought. But only for her protection, of course!

Now, here he was, sharing a bed with her and his treacherous body desiring to do the things his father had told him he must never do until he was wed. But then, again, he *was* wed, wasn't he? Well, in a sort of way. The captain said it was alright for him to take a wife. So it *was* alright wasn't it? Or was it. It might not be so hard for him if she didn't look so young. If she wasn't so small and child-like! In his heart, if he was honest with himself, he knew they could not sleep together for months on end without taking the ultimate step.

Without thinking, Danny heaved a mighty sigh, then mentally kicked himself for possibly letting Alice know he was awake. When she didn't stir, he almost sighed with relief, but instead eased himself gently away, to put a bit of space between them. He desperately needed to masturbate, to relieve this awful pressure, but was aware that would almost certainly awaken her. Instead, he clasped the delicate little breast a little more firmly and eventually drifted off to sleep.

Alice was alone in the bunk when she awakened. She lay for a while, thinking about the night before. Had it happened? Or had she dreamed it? Nodding to herself, she decided she really had gone to sleep with Danny's gentle, warm hand on her. It had been nice. She had felt secure, but she knew instinctively it had not been enough. Well, maybe tonight! She nodded again. Yes. Tonight!

'I know he wanted it,' she told Maggie when they met on the deck later. 'At least a part of him did. But he was asleep, and it went no further. Then when I awakened, he was gone.'

Maggie laughed. 'And what about you? Did you want it?' She raised a quizzical eyebrow.

Alice was thoughtful for a moment, but before she could answer she was interrupted by the arrival of Lily.

'Any news this morning?' Lily asked cheerily when she joined them. It was pretty obvious *she* had enjoyed her night.

Maggie rolled her eyes heavenward and shook her head. 'Not a lot, but we're gettin' there.'

Alice had to repeat her tale of woe.

'Do you want him to do it?' she echoed Maggie's question.

Alice sighed and nodded. 'I think so. I don't know why, but I nearly cried when he slept on. I could hear everyone around doing it, and it made me want to.'

'Mayhaps he wasn't asleep,' Maggie suggested. 'Perhaps he was embarrassed his body had let him down an' he doesn't want to push you into anything you don't want to do!'

'I can't see what your problem is,' Lily said, with a shrug. 'Don't sleep with your back to him. Face him, cuddle him and when *it* swells up just get hold of it!'

Alice gasped and gaped at her friend. What a suggestion! Did she really mean it? With a shake of her head, she said, 'I can't do that!'

'Why not?'

'It's too ... well, too forward. I wouldn't have the nerve.'

Lily shook her head and sighed.

'No need to be so forward,' Maggie interceded. 'Like Lily

said, don't put your back to him when you go to bed. Face him and when his penis swells, just press against him an' move a bit. Should get him started!'

'Do you think so? But what if it doesn't?'

'I don't think so — I know so! For sure. He won't be able to stop himself then!'

Maggie saw Danny approaching and quickly changed the subject.

'I wonder how poor Sarah is,' she said, gazing sadly over the river.

'I hope they haven't burned her,' Alice said quietly. She remembered how badly Sarah had been coping with her dreadful situation before she had drawn her into her little group of friends.

'Who's Sarah? What do you mean — burned?'

A tear escaped and Alice impatiently swiped it away. 'Sarah was a friend in the gaol who was to be burned at the stake. She was left behind when we were sent here.' Alice sighed and shook her head. 'She was so frightened. I don't know how she will be getting on wi' us gone.'

Danny blanched and shivered. 'Burned? Not while she's alive, surely? How can they do that to anyone? What had she done that was so bad?'

'She'd done nothing,' Maggie said quietly. 'Except be in the wrong place when the constables did a raid.'

'How sad. How can people be so cruel? It shouldn't be allowed.' Shaking his head he wandered off to get on with his work.

Alice went to bed that night with her heart beating a healthy tattoo against her ribs. Did she have the courage to follow her friends' advice? She didn't know. Climbing into the bunk, she lay with her back to the wall, waiting nervously for Danny to join her.

Seeing her facing him, Danny hesitated. Should he face her, or face away from her? It would be pretty dangerous to face her, wouldn't it? But just looking at her, so small yet appealing, he had no doubt of what he wanted. Or what his body wanted! He felt an erection starting and slipped quickly into bed before, (he hoped), she could see it. Lying stiffly on his back, he stared into the space above him and hoped his swelling would subside.

Alice lay beside him, waiting for him to turn and face her, and wondering what her next move should be if he didn't. After a few minutes, she put a tentative hand on his chest and felt him stiffen and draw a quick breath.

With a groan, Danny put from his mind, his promise to his father. Well, she *was* his wife, wasn't she? The captain said she was. So it was alright wasn't it, for him to do *it*? Turning on his side, he gently put his arms around her and drew her to him. Not wishing to frighten her, he tried to keep his back bent so that his penis wouldn't press against her, but Alice had her own ideas.

As soon as Danny's arms went around her, Alice slipped closer, pressing herself to him, snuggling her face against his neck.

Placing his fingers under her chin he raised her face and attempted his first-ever kiss. A first also for Alice, she pressed closed lips against his. Danny instinctively moved his head and their lips parted, turning it into a close and intimate and enjoyable moment.

In an agony of desire, Danny tightened the hug and let nature take over. Moving his hand to her breast he said quietly, 'I've never done this before. 'Do you know what to do?'

Alice shook her head slightly. 'No. I've never done it either. But Maggie said to tell you you have to pull out before you come. She said you would know what she meant.'

Danny felt momentarily shocked and embarrassed to know she had discussed this with her friends. It seemed so cold-blooded and intrusive. However, this longed-for union with Alice quickly swept that from his mind. 'Yes,' he agreed quietly, 'I know what she meant.'

After a fair bit of fumbling and repositioning, Alice felt a quick stab of pain, tensed, and gasped.

Quick to sense her feelings, Danny paused. 'Did I hurt you? Do you want me to take it out?' he asked, praying her answer would be '*no*'.

Enjoying the feeling of warmth and love and belonging it gave her to have him inside her, Alice shook her head. 'It was only for a moment. I like it,' she reassured him.

Disappointingly, the pleasure was only brief. Before either of them had time to enjoy it it was all over. Danny felt himself coming and tried to pull out. Alice's legs, wrapped around his, slowed him down and he could only pray he had been in time.

'I'm sorry,' he whispered, feeling wretched. 'I didn't think it would happen so fast.'

Alice lay silent, her mind spinning. Was that it then? Surely there was more. When she had watched the women in the alleys, the rutting had usually gone on for quite a while. And the sounds of lovemaking she heard around her now seemed endless. She felt bereft and couldn't think what to say. Still enjoying the closeness and warmth of his body, she snuggled so close to Danny they became as one.

'I'm sorry,' he repeated.

'It's alright,' Alice told him quietly and kissed his cheek. 'Maybe it's because it's the first time.'

'Aye,' Danny nodded enthusiastically. 'Next time it will be better,' he finished on a happier note.

She put her hand down to caress this very special part of her lover. It responded instantly, so *next time* didn't take long to arrive — and it *was* better.

CHAPTER 8

With her friends and her support now gone, Sarah retreated into herself and was soon huddled down in a corner, expecting at every moment that the priest would come and the white dress would be brought to her. Every time she heard the gaoler's key turn in the lock, she stared blindly at the door, wondering if this was to be *it*. The day for the prayer and the walk to the stake!

Conditions in the gaol, though still unbearably squalid, had improved. With only a few women left in the cells, the air was not so foul. For a short while, those who were left behind could sleep on the platforms that passed for beds, without having to pay for them. So at least they were off the urine-soaked and bug-infested floor and could sleep dry. However, as more women arrived from around the country, the cells began to fill again, and the *beds* were again only for those with money.

The food had improved too, but not in taste or quality. It was just that there was more of it!

In her state of misery, Sarah hardly appreciated this improvement, so occupied was her mind with what lay before her; so overwhelming the terror that stalked her.

It was several weeks after her friends had been taken to

— heaven alone knew where — that the turnkey arrived at an unusual hour. With a sneer on his ugly face, he stood looking around at the women in the cell.

'I expect some of you will already have heard,' he began pompously, 'that our beloved King George has been suffering an illness of the mind.' Pausing to look around, he was met by a cell full of blank faces.

'It is with great joy that I am able to tell you he has now recovered his health.' He stopped again, looking at the women and awaiting a response.

Few came. There was only an odd, murmured ribald comment. One, from the back of the cell, shouted, 'It brings me no joy! What the hell difference does it make to us whether he's sane or totally gone in the head?'

The man in the doorway frowned and tutted. Really, these women had no hearts! 'It is wonderful news,' he told them sternly. 'The whole country is rejoicing. There are parties in the streets, with free food and drinks.'

'Where's our share of it then? What do we care about what the rest of the country is doing while we starve?'

The turnkey snorted and glared at the dirty, smelly creatures before him and said, 'Well, if you hadn't done crimes an' got yersels locked up in here you would be out in the streets where the free food is, would you not?'

The women shook their heads and, losing what little interest they'd had, turned away. Clearly, the turnkey had only come to gloat!

One day, late in April, the cell door flew open with a crash. The turnkey stood, looked around the cell and consulted a sheet of paper he held in his hand. 'Right. Same as last time,' he started, 'when I call your name, I want you out in the passage. He read out six names and the frightened women shuffled past him. All of those called knew well that they had a death sentence hanging over their heads! So, what was going on? Was this to be *the* day? Their last day!

'Sarah Jenkins,' the gaoler called, finally.

Sarah stood rooted to the spot, frozen with fear and unable to put one foot in front of the other.

The turnkey glared at her. 'Get yersel out here quick or I'll take my truncheon to you,' he growled as he started to pull the weapon from his belt.

Sarah shuffled nervously towards him and sidled past, never taking her frightened eyes from him for a moment.

When they reached the yard there were many other women there. They were all as confused and scared as Sarah. Terror showed in every pair of eyes as the women looked fearfully at each other. With hearts of lead, they whispered amongst themselves. They soon realised that every one of the twenty-three gathered there were under sentence of death. They all knew that, although the female cells were no longer crowded, the gaol, in general, was still grossly overcrowded, with more prisoners arriving every day. They feared they were all going to be quickly put to the stake to make space in the cells.

Once they were all present, the women were herded, trembling with fear, along *Dead Man's Walk* to the courtroom.

The recorder looked at the convicts over his spectacles and his face distorted with disgust. The smell assaulted his nostrils from across the courtroom and he held a perfumed kerchief to his face.

'I have no doubt you have all heard the wonderful news, that our beloved King George has recovered from the illness he suffered,' he looked up, his eyes travelling along the mob of frightened, stony-faced women. After a moment's hesitation, he gave a slight shake of his head and continued, 'as part of our thanksgiving, it has been decided to grant a pardon to you all, on certain conditions,' he began.

Bewildered, the women all looked blankly at each other. What *was* the man talking about?

With the failure to get any reaction, the recorder ploughed on with his speech. 'The conditions are that instead of burning at the stake, you will be sentenced to transportation to Port Jackson — a new English colony beyond the seas.'

The women continued to look confused, so he then read out fourteen names and told them they were to be transported *for the term of their natural lives!* To the remaining women, he said 'And the rest of you are sentenced to spend seven years in this new colony. After that, you will be free to return if you so wish.'

The recorder asked if they accepted the terms of the pardon.

Once it had sunk in what he was telling them, Sarah and fifteen of the others agreed to the conditions. Seven did not!

'I will die by the laws of my own country before I will be sent to another for the rest of my life!' said one.

Another spoke up. 'I agree! I would sooner die than be shipped to this unknown place for the rest of my natural life. I did not commit the crime for which I have been condemned and I will not accept transportation.'

In disbelief, the recorder glared at this unbelievable rejection of this generous, and in his view, undeserved, offer of reprieve made by His gracious Majesty. Angrily, he warned them that if they did not accept the king's pardon now, they would not have another chance.

'Every woman who refuses to accept the pardon now will be ordered for immediate execution!' he shouted.

The women well knew that *immediate execution* meant it would be carried out within days. They had all heard, only a month or so earlier, the priest's long incantation in the street outside their cell. They had heard the bang of the trapdoors open and the crack of the necks as eleven or twelve men were hanged.

Even this memory did not move them from their determination not to be transported. They vowed they would fight for a reprieve that allowed them to stay in England.

The recorder shrugged. He did not really care if they threw their lives away. 'If that's the way you want it, then that's the way it will be.' He stood to leave the court.

'Return the prisoners to their cells,' he ordered, and the turnkeys ushered the women from the court to hustle them back along *Dead Man's Walk*.

Sarah, and the other six women from her cell who had been waiting to burn at the stake, stared at the turnkey, hardly daring to believe they had heard the judge correctly.

While their gaoler fumbled with the keys to their cell, Sarah managed to rasp, past a huge lump in her throat, 'Is it true what he said? We're not to die? We're really not to die?'

The man looked at her and his face twisted in disgust. 'No. More's the pity! It is not my decision, and if you ask me it's better than you deserve. You are to live. I'll be glad to get rid of you, so the sooner they transport you the better!' On that note, he managed to get the door open and he jerked his head towards the cell.

The women stumbled down the steps and looked at each other in disbelief as the cell door slammed shut behind them.

A babble of noise broke out as the other women who had been left in the cell demanded to know what was going on.

'We are to live!' Sarah said quietly. 'The judge told us we were to be transported to some place called Port Jackson.'

For a few moments, there was a stunned silence, then the cell erupted into a cacophony of shouts and cheers.

Alice, Maggie, and Lily stood on the deck of the *Lady Juliana*, watching as yet another lighter appeared from behind a ship near the bend in the river.

Maggie cupped a hand over her eyes and peered at the distant craft. 'Looks like it might be more women,' she murmured. During the last few weeks, they had seen several boat-loads of female convicts arrive. They had watched one coach arrive on the quay across the river, with fourteen frozen, half-starved women chained to its outside. They, poor souls had come from Lincoln prison and had been shackled in those seats for over thirty-six hours.

Their plight brought back to Alice and Maggie, memories of their journey from Liverpool to Newgate.

When the new arrivals' manacles had been removed and they were brought down to the cabin some of the kinder women wrapped their own blankets around them to get some heat back into their bones. Alice had been only too happy to lend her shawl.

Now it looked as if there was yet another boatload on its way.

Maggie shook her head. 'If they send any more, they'll sink the ship. The orlop cabin is too crowded already! Thank God we're out of it an' living in comfort wi' our men!'

As was usual, when a lighter full of new convicts arrived, the women, *the wives* included, were all ordered to go below, so had no chance to see who was in the approaching lighter. They sat on the edge of the beds, listening to the sounds from the deck.

Alice and her friends found themselves to be the recipients of hateful glares from Mavis and Gracie and their cronies but met the looks with no sign of fear. They knew that as soon as the new arrivals had been unfettered, they would be allowed back on deck.

When the metallic clink of the hammer on rivets ceased, they heard the now familiar voice of Thomas Edgar, the agent, talking to the women; welcoming them aboard, and asking his usual questions.

With interest, they watched the ladder to see who the newest arrivals would be. Most of the women they had known in Newgate were on the *Lady Juliana* already, so they thought it unlikely they would know any of these newcomers, but still, they watched. Until they were permitted to return to the deck it was something to help pass the time, wasn't it?

Suddenly Alice squealed, 'Sarah!' Leaping from the bed, she ran across the cabin, throwing herself at the girl who had only just got her feet to the deck.

Maggie and Lily were close behind. All eager to give their friend a huge, welcoming hug.

Almost dancing with joy, Alice clung to Sarah's hands. 'I can't believe you're here! When they took me away, I didn't believe I would see you again? What happened? Are you here to stay? Are you coming with us?' Alice's questions tripped over themselves.

Maggie gave her a little shake. 'Come on, child. Give the girl a chance to answer.'

'I know. I'm sorry. I'm just so happy,' Alice gushed.

'Well, we were all taken to the courtroom,' Sarah began. 'All the women who were condemned to die. The Judge told us that we were *all* to be reprieved, so long as we agreed to be transported. I and six of the others had to go for seven years, the rest for the whole of their lives!'

'What brought that about?' Puzzled, Maggie shook her head.

'Well, they told us King George has been sick in the head but has recovered. So, to celebrate they have decided to spare us the stake!'

'By all that's wonderful,' Maggie enthused. 'It's the first sensible thing the law has done. I bet everyone fell over themselves to agree.'

A shadow crossed Sarah's face and she shook her head. 'Not everyone. Sixteen of us agreed, but seven said they would rather die than be sent across the seas to live the rest of their lives in a foreign country.'

Alice shook her head in disbelief. 'Surely being alive is more important than where you live.'

Lily nodded. 'Of course, it is. You can surely make a life for yourself wherever you are.'

Maggie nodded. 'I'm leaving three little childher behind, to go to this Port Jackson and it's most likely I'll never see them again. But if I'm alive there is always some chance, is there not? Perhaps one day they will come an' find me.'

There was such a sad longing in her voice that Alice felt the tears prick her eyes. Instinctively, she moved closer to Maggie and put an arm around her.

'I am to *live!*' Sarah said tremulously. 'I am to live, and I still can't really believe it!' Suddenly she folded into a heap on the deck, where she sat racked with sobs, her whole body shaking.

Alice sat down and hugged her friend. 'Hey, you should be happy, not weeping,' she said quietly.

Sarah nodded and wiped a hand across her cheek. 'You don't know what it feels like. You *can't* know how it feels. To live for all those months knowing that one day you are going to be tied to a stake and set on fire. I was there the last time they did a burning! I can still hear Mary's screams. I can still smell her burning flesh. And all this time I have known that in the end, that was going to happen to me! I waken at night hearing and smelling it over and over again. And I have lived with the knowledge that one day that would be my fate!'

'Now it's *not* going to happen!' Alice wrapped her arms around Sarah and gave her a tight cuddle.

'Every time that cell door opened,' Sarah continued, as though she had not heard, 'I feared they were bringing the white dress, and this was my day to burn!' She sobbed in great gulps of air.

Alice tightened her hug but held her silence. She could tell her friend needed to unburden.

'I can't even begin to tell you how that felt,' Sarah continued. 'It wasn't the dying that frightened me. It was the burning! The pain! Hearing myself screaming for help that I knew would not, could not come. Feeling and smelling my own flesh burning!' Her head fell forwards and her sobbing continued. 'When they came to take us before the recorder that last time I was shaking so much, with fear, that I could hardly walk!' A huge sob shook her. 'I was so scared in *Dead Man's Walk*, I peed in my bloomers!'

Alice vaguely heard the other reprieved women sobbing and, for the first time fully realised how the wait must have felt for them.

'What if they change their minds again?' Sarah wailed. 'What if this is some cruel joke and they come and take us back to Newgate again?'

Maggie suddenly grabbed her and bundled her into her arms. Holding the girl tightly to her, she had her hand at the back of Sarah's head, pressing her face against her neck. Biting her lip she struggled to hold back her own tears.

'I can understand your fears, my lovely, but that is not going to happen. You are going to live! Like us, you are going to be transported to this *part beyond the seas*; wherever that might be! James Reed says it's a good warm place. It looks certain we are going there together, on this ship.'

'Wherever it is it *must* be better than Newgate gaol!' Alice said with certainty. 'We'll be together, and we'll look after each other!'

Maggie nodded enthusiastically. 'If I had a gin, I'd drink to that. Thank heaven the king recovered his wits in time!'

After a while, Sarah's sobs ended and she even managed a

watery smile. 'When they put us in the cart this morning none of us knew where we were going. We were all terrified. I never imagined you would all be waiting here to greet me. This is a most wonderful day!'

'It is indeed,' Alice agreed with feeling.

The four friends went on deck and watched all the activity across the water until the light faded from the day and the chill of evening moved in.

Sadly, as evening turned to night, Sarah had to leave her friends and go below decks alone.

'It's not too nice down there, but it won't be for long. We'll find you a husband soon,' Maggie told her as they were parting.

Sarah gave a sad smile. 'I think I've probably used up all my luck just by getting here. From what you tell me all the crew have already found themselves wives. Whatever it is like down there, it will be heaven to me. I am to live. That is all that matters.'

With those words, she lowered herself into the hatch to join her fellow reprieved.

During the next few weeks, life on the *Lady Juliana* settled into a comfortable routine. The cabin, measuring no more than two-thousand square feet, gradually became overcrowded as ever more women arrived to find a space in it.

Sarah found it uncomfortable but made no complaint. Whenever she felt like grumbling, she reminded herself it was better than the stake.

'How many more are they going to send?' Maggie asked James, one day.

He pulled a face and shrugged. 'Dunno, but there's not much room for many more. They reckon there's more'n two hundred of you already! They'll be whooping with excitement when we land you lot at Port Jackson, I reckon!'

Maggie rolled her eyes skywards and shook her head. *What else would be a man's first thought?* She wondered.

'There'll be a few more crew arriving tomorrow,' he continued, 'So mayhap we'll be able to find a *husband* an' get Sarah away from the mob down there.'

Maggie nodded enthusiastically. It sat hard with her that Sarah was trapped in the orlop while she, Lily and Alice, slept in luxury. She had watched Alice grow in confidence and happiness since she had joined Danny and felt sure she had been right to encourage them, young though they were. If Danny had not taken the lass under his protection there was no saying what some of the older, rougher men might have done to her. There were men, she knew, who preferred children for their pleasures. She nodded her head in satisfaction and decided she must vet the new crew members when they arrived, and pick the best for Sarah.

As the time neared for their departure from London, Alice and her friends were unceasingly amazed at the number of convicts who had visitors. The activity on board was beyond belief to them.

Many of the visitors were parents, who had attended court and watched in horror and disbelief as their daughters were convicted of crimes that they swore they did not commit. Many of them had made long coach journeys from the furthest ends of the country to reach the *Lady Juliana*. Even at this late date, they were desperately begging the authorities to pardon their daughters. Almost on bended knees, they offered themselves as surety to guarantee their child's future good behaviour, if the authorities would only reconsider and order a release!

Their pleas fell on deaf ears. The law had made its decision and would stand by it. Besides, the new colony at Port Jackson was desperately in need of more women, wasn't it?

The parents knew in their hearts they would not succeed, but they would go on pleading for their daughters' release until the moment the ship set sail. They knew that once the huge hawsers fell away, they would almost certainly never see their girls again.

A constant stream of people came on board with letters they wanted delivering to sons or husbands or brothers who were currently with the marine corps that had accompanied the first fleet to Sydney Cove.

Some parents had taken loans and impoverished themselves to enable them to give their daughter a little money. They hoped this might buy their child a more comfortable life in the new colony.

Danny told Alice of one of the women on board, Jane Gordon, whose husband had pleaded with the courts, on her behalf to try to win her a pardon and avoid her deportation. Her crime, he claimed, had been committed under the influence of her mother, an evil woman who was now dead. After she had been incarcerated for six months his plea finally fell on ears that were not deaf. Her husband happily offered securities for her and she was granted her freedom. As Jane's husband led her, hand in hand down the gangplank, a huge cheer went up from the women who had gathered on the deck to watch her leave.

Newspapermen and illustrators came on board, each one looking for a story. A special story of hardship and heartbreak that would sell papers and make money for him, or at least favourably impress his editor.

The *Lady Juliana* was different! It was newsworthy! The likes of what was taking place on this ship had never happened before and every journalist worth his salt wanted a piece of it.

Alice, who looked nothing like her fourteen years, watched it all in awe. A few of the newspapermen thought it might make good press that such a young child was being transported. Some questioned her briefly but on learning her true age, decided the theft of a loaf of bread was not newsworthy, and quickly moved on to find someone more interesting.

'We're sailin' day after tomorrow,' Danny told Alice one night as they lay entwined in each other's arms. 'It will be nice to be on our way, but I hope I don't get sea-sick. I've never been on a ship at sea.'

'I was once. When they brought me over from the Isle of Man, but I was half unconscious.'

'There's goin' to be a big party tomorrow night, so it could get a bit noisy. I'll look after you though.'

Alice nodded and cuddled closer. She always felt safe when she was with Danny.'

The following day many of the women watched from the deck as rowing boats arrived laden with barrels of gin.

'It's going to be one hell of a party tonight with all that gin,' Maggie observed.

'I've never tasted gin,' Alice frowned. 'Is it nice?'

'It is when you're drinking it. Not so nice after, when your head feels fit to burst!' Maggie laughed. 'I wouldn't advise you to try it. You stick with lime juice or summat.'

Danny sat close beside Alice during the party. At first, she found it fun. There was singing, dancing, and laughter, but as the evening wore on and the excess of gin made its mark, both crew and convicts became more and more raucous, she started to feel frightened and clung tightly to Danny's hand.

When things started to get out of hand and fights were threatening, Danny quietly led Alice away to their bunk and they made love.

They were awakened in the morning by the captain's bullhorn blaring, calling all crew members on deck.

Danny leapt from the bunk, hurriedly pulled his clothes on, and raced away.

Feeling bereft and a little frightened, Alice pulled the covers up to her chin and lay listening to feet banging around on the deck above her and angry voices shouting.

What on earth is happening, she wondered. Was the ship about to sail? Was it about to sink?

Hurrying into her clothes, she made her way on deck, pushed and pulled around by other *wives* trying to do the same. Once there, she found herself embroiled amid utter chaos.

The women from the orlop deck were being dragged up through the hatch and roughly lined up.

Alice found her friends and they huddled nervously together watching the goings-on.

The crew scrambled around, looking in every nook and possible hiding place. Even the lifeboats were searched. In the end, there was a count of heads.

The captain, the surgeon, and the agent stood by the bridge in earnest and sometimes heated conversation.

Captain Aitken threw his hand in the air and shook his head. 'Well, no matter. We sail this morning and if they haven't been found and returned by then we shall have to leave without them. They will have to be sent with one of the other ships when they're captured.' Turning abruptly, he stormed away.

Maggie saw James approaching and grabbed his arm. 'What's happened?'

James tried to keep the grin from his face but did not quite succeed. 'We've lost four of our girls.'

'Lost? How can you lose them on a ship in the middle of the river?'

James gave a loud guffaw. 'It's quite easy if the guard is peeved about being put on guard when the rest of the ship is partying. You let him have a taste of what's up your skirt an' ply him wi' gin until he passes out. Then you just climb over the side and get into the boat some of your friends have obligingly rowed across for you. Vanished in the night an' the captain says we must go without them. We'll be leaving very soon.'

Alice felt a ripple of excitement, tinged with fear, run through her belly. A small part of her looked forward to leaving this stinking river, while another part was apprehensive about the long journey ahead across the mighty ocean to this *place beyond the seas.*

CHAPTER 9

—⋅⋅—

Alice and many of the other women leaned over the rail, excitedly watching the activity on the water.

It was a beautiful July day. The sky a vivid blue; made brighter by Alice's excitement; with only an occasional puff of white cloud to break the colour. She turned her face skyward and closed her eyes, enjoying the warmth of this beautiful summer day. Opening her eyes again, she looked along the deck and notice an unusual amount of activity.

Thomas Edgar, the master and government agent came down from the bridge and demanded silence. When he finally had the women's attention, he ordered them to the orlop deck, amidst a volley of loud protests, he ushered them down the hatch. Those who tried to refuse were roughly manhandled and pushed down the ladder by crew members.

'Why've we gotta go down there?' Mavis Crowe asked, belligerent as ever.

'Because the captain says so and because I'm carrying out his orders,' Thomas replied patiently.

'Why though? 'Tis a nice day to be on deck an' we wants to say *goodbye* to England.'

'There'll be plenty of time for that. We won't be clear of these shores for some weeks yet. And you *have* to stay below because it's not safe on deck. This is the busiest time on a ship. There's going to be men running all over and we can't have you lot getting in their way — for your sakes as well as theirs. We don't want anyone getting knocked over and their bones broken. We'll let you out again as soon as things quieten down again an' you'll be safe.'

The grumbling continued, but despite that, every convict was secured and the hatch was shut and tightly screwed down.

Alice had almost forgotten what it was like in the dark, crowded conditions of the orlop cabin. It smelled of stale sweat, and the odour from the river seemed to lie like a stinking blanket just about nose high.

Alice and her three friends huddled together close to one of the open glasses, but that was a futile effort, for the air that came in was almost as bad as the air that ws already there.

'It's starting to make me feel sick. I'd forgot how bad it was down here,' Alice whispered after only a few minutes.

Maggie put an arm around her. 'It won't be for long. Then they'll let us out into the fresh air again. Well, if you could call it fresh. Just try to think of something good until then. Think how nice it is to be spending your nights with Danny instead of down here in this stinking hell-hole with scum like Mavis.'

Not daring to open her mouth, Alice merely nodded

They sat clutching each other in terrified silence for what seemed like an eternity.

From above, there was a cacophony of unfamiliar noises; snapping banging and cracking that made them fear the ship was splitting apart. James later told them those were the sounds of the wind filling the sails and making the ropes snap tight. The worst of the screeching and clattering, he told them, had been the ropes as the sails were hoisted into position, and the raising of the giant anchor.

There was endless shouting and cursing and the convicts could hear the captain bellowing on his bullhorn. Feet stamped and banged on the deck above their heads as the crew obeyed their orders.

Eventually, the women felt a change in the attitude of the ship. It seemed to them that it was moving. At last, after a whole lifetime in their dark dungeon, they heard the bolts being undrawn on the hatch and a welcome beam of daylight shone down on them.

James stuck his head down the opening. 'You can come out now, ladies,' he told them cheerfully.

'Thank God for that,' Maggie said with feeling. 'I'd have been ill too if I'd had to stay down here much longer. Come on girl, let's get out of this hell-hole.' Grabbing Alice's arm she dragged her toward the hatch and they scuttled quickly up on deck.

The day was still glorious. Even more so. The sky was bluer, the air fresher, but Alice saw none of it as she ran to the rail and emptied her breakfast into the water.

With her heart leaping and turning somersaults, Alice was spellbound as she stood looking skyward. The *Lady Juliana* now appeared completely different; larger somehow. The three masts, which until now had stood empty, appeared to be a tangle of tightly stretched ropes. these were alive with crewmen who ceaselessly scrambled around trimming the sails. She surveyed the huge sails, now taking the wind that drove the mighty ship before it.

In no time, it seemed, the dockland buildings and moored ships slipped past and were left behind.

In all the docks, as they passed, there was constant activity as ships were loaded and unloaded.

So, this was it! The start of her journey. Until now it had been like a very enjoyable holiday to Alice. After all the years of living on the streets and having to steal to stay clothed and fed, her weeks on the anchored ship had probably been the happiest and most comfortable of her life. But now. Well, what now? What lay ahead? She didn't know, and she feared the unknown. If it was left to her she would have been happy to spend the rest of her life on this beautiful ship with Danny. Her friends were there for her though. If she became too scared, she would always have them to lean on. And they on her, if need be!

In the last couple of weeks Alice, Maggie, and Lily had watched, with interest, a growing friendship for Sarah with one of the newest crew members. Just a few nights ago she had moved out of the orlop cabin and into his quarters.

He seemed a nice young man and Maggie had nodded her head in approval. 'Better than being stuck in that overcrowded hell-hole for months,' she muttered to Alice and Lily. 'We'll all be more comfortable for our voyage to wherever we're going.'

As the day wore on the river gradually widened, the water became less oily and foul-smelling. There was a fresh, sweetness in the breeze that Alice reveled in. She could see through the surface of the water now and the odd shoal of fish that flitted and swirled beneath it.

Alice gazed over the rail, thinking that the water now looked much more like the clean water that ran out into Douglas Bay. For a moment she thought sadly about the island she had left behind and would never see again, but she shrugged her shoulders and shook the thought away. What she must remember, she told herself, was how bad her life had been on the island. This was her life now; this ship, and somewhere in the future, these *parts beyond the seas.*

The *Lady Juliana* was on her own now, her sails filled and surging over the water.

The women on board felt a mixture of emotions.

To Alice and many of the others, although they were apprehensive, they also had a feeling of joy and freedom. Behind them was a lifetime of hardship and suffering, from which they were happy to escape. There was a great adventure ahead for these women. But to Maggie and, indeed, most of the other women, it was a heart-wrenching moment. A large percentage of the convicts were leaving family behind. Children, like Maggie's three, parents, siblings, husbands. And to all of them, the only country they had ever known. They all knew they would almost certainly never see their families or their country again.

A wind picked up early in the afternoon and filled the sails. The ship responded joyfully, dancing her way easily through the white-capped waves, making good speed as she scudded past the English coast.

There was land to both sides of the ship at first and the convicts watched it with interest and delight.

James stopped beside them briefly to point at a town on the larboard side. That there's Southend-on-Sea, where all the hoity-toities go for their holidays,' he informed them before he went rushing off again.

The sudden activity on board left the women breathless. Until then there had not been much for the crew to do apart from keep the ship clean. They'd had quite an easy time of it until now, with women pleased to help them, wash and repair their clothes and keep them warm and satisfied at night.

And the women *had* been keen. Alice had watched and giggled at the antics of some of them as they had tried to attract a man. Even fat, ugly old Mavis Crowe had been sidling up to some, squeezing their buttocks — among other things. Offering them a fumble under her bodice. To Alice's amusement Mavis had met with no luck and was clearly becoming more frustrated and angry at every rejection.

It was not surprising, Alice thought. With over two hundred women on the ship and no more than three dozen men, they could take their pick. There were plenty of females, far younger and more succulent looking than Mavis Crowe.

Every time that woman looked at Alice the girl almost shrivelled at the hatred she saw in those evil eyes.

Watching through the eyes of near innocence, Alice was amazed and confused by the number of partners some of the men seemed to take on. A few of them she noticed seemed to take a different woman to their bed every night.

One evening, as they stood hand in hand on the deck, Alice asked Danny about this strange behaviour.

Danny shook his head, laughed, put an arm around her, and told her that by the time they reached the open sea almost all the men would have taken a wife. 'Even the captain and surgeon Alley,' he said quietly. 'An' they's married men. Mind, most of the crew's married I suppose, but some men's like that. One woman ain't enough for a lot of men and James says it's every sailor's right to take a female. An' if the woman he chooses don't want him, then it's just her bad luck her, cos' she's got to let him have her. Surgeon Alley has been checking a lot of the women to make sure they ain't got the clap, what a lot of them has 'cos they was in prison for prostitution.'

Alice smiled sadly. 'I don't think women have got many rights when it comes to men, have they? And what about their *wives* too? Don't they have any rights?'

Danny gave her a long, worried look. 'You don't think I've taken you just because it's my *right*, do you? I certainly don't think I have a right to you. I want you here with me, so you'll be safe an' not be bullied.'

Alice took his hand and smiled. 'No, I know. And you *do* look after me. I've never felt so safe, or so happy, in my life as I do with you. I like being with you and I'm happy you want me as your wife. I know full well it was kindness made you ask me.'

Danny's face lit up in a beaming smile. 'But I like the things we do in bed too!' He gave her a mischievous look as he slipped his hand inside her bodice and gave her a quick squeeze.

Alice playfully slapped his hand away and he looked around quickly hoping no one had been watching.

Maggie had seen, and as a flush spread up from his neck, she shook her head slightly, wagged a finger at him, then winked.

Alice stood on the deck with her back to the rail. She had wakened early, when Danny had slipped out of the bunk to start his watch and, feeling a bit queasy, she had left the forecastle cabin to find some fresh air.

There was a fresh wind blowing, making the ship roll more than usual, which accounted for her fragile stomach. The sails were full, and the *Lady Juliana* picked up her skirts and flew across the sea. Alice guessed that if they kept up this pace they would be in this new land before they knew it.

The sky was still the bright orange of early morning, just before the sun would creep over the horizon. There were a few large ugly patches of roiling purple cloud and Alice prayed it did not mean there was a storm coming. Never would she forget the storm they survived on the little fishing boat when they were being taken from the island to Newgate gaol. She shuddered at the memory of *that* place. But this was a bigger ship, wasn't it? The *Lady Juliana* would not toss around like that little fishing boat, would it? It was like a nightmare now and she wondered how she had survived it. But for Maggie, she would surely have perished.

Far above her head, she saw a cloud of birds. There must have been thousands of them. She remembered such birds on the island and being told they were starlings. By some strange instinct, the whole flock constantly changed direction and shape and swooped and swirled as if in some previously agreed pattern. Fascinated, she watched, wide-eyed, and wondered why with such sudden changes of direction the birds did not collide and fall from the sky. After a few minutes the flock drifted off out of sight in the distance, and all that was left was a handful of noisy gulls gliding and mewing above her head as they followed the ship.

Her eyes finished their scan of the sky and wandered to where a figure stood on a timber spar far above her head. The sailor fiddled with a canvas then glanced down. On seeing Alice he waved, and her heart stopped for a moment when she realised it was Danny. Of course, she had seen him up there many a time since they had sailed, but it never ceased to frighten her. He climbed the ropes like a monkey. Swung across the rigging from sail to sail and she knew that one slip, one missed catch on a rope and he would plunge forty or fifty feet to almost certain death.

Irritated by her cowardice she muttered, 'Mustn't think of that. He won't fall. What would I do? He wouldn't leave me like that.' Alice forced her eyes away from him to where she could see the other hands moving around, constantly changing the set of the canvasses. Danny had told her once that there were about twenty separate sails which were set and then adjusted as needed, depending on the strength and direction of the wind. Watching the men move endlessly about the rigging high above her head, Alice had a fleeting thought that they looked as if they were performing some strange dance. She knew, because Danny had told her, that all this activity with the sails was essential to the ship's movement and direction through the water and to keep her speed to a maximum.

121

Sighing, Alice turned her attention to the activity at a lower level. Wherever she looked there was the appearance of frantic activity. A constant tide of men moved backward and forward on the deck and up and down ropes like monkeys. No one stayed still for more than a few moments, except for the man high up at the very top of the mast. The *lookout* Danny had called him.

The *Lady Juliana* sailed along smoothly for several days, driven by a light wind that kept the sails filled. Even so, the women found it difficult to walk. Until they became accustomed to the rolling of the ship, they had to be very careful how they put their feet down, particularly when using the ladders. It was all too easy to find the rung you were about to put your foot on swing away from you, and either leave you hanging by your hands or dumped unceremoniously on the deck below. Many a bruise and several broken bones were won this way!

England was always in sight, but after a few days, Alice realised that she could also see land far away on the larboard side of the ship.

The women puzzled over this land for quite some time, wondering whether they were sailing up some wide channel. Eventually, with a shake her head Maggie caught James' arm as he passed. 'What's that land over there she asked, is it still part of England?'

James shook his head. 'No that's another country. it's called France. I must go now, or the captain will put me in irons.' With that, he twitched his arm free and hurried across the deck.'

'Another country?' Alice asked. 'I wonder if that is the country we are going to.'

Maggie shook her head. I shouldn't think so. 'They told us it would take months to get there and we have only been sailing for a few days.'

Alice wasn't sure whether to be pleased or sorry. Though she was not greatly enjoying this voyage and the sickness it caused, part of her dreaded reaching this *place beyond the seas* for fear that she might lose Danny. It would be worth tolerating her illness to put off a possible parting for as long as possible. He was so kind and loving, but she could not imagine him not being with her. Such an idea did not bear thinking about.

Standing at the starboard rail, the women were awed by the site of towering sheer white cliffs.

'I remember there were cliffs at Onchan head and Douglas head,' Alice said breathlessly, 'but they were grey; dark grey and not anywhere near as high as these white cliffs.'

Maggie nodded her agreement as she studied the huge white formations.

James stopped in passing, following their gaze to the cliffs. 'Them there is the White Cliffs of Dover. And those houses you can see in the distance is the town of Dover. Another few days and we will be in Portsmouth. We have to stop there to take on more water and provisions. Once we have all we need we'll be sailing off to start the rest of our voyage.'

'What's this Portsmouth like then,' Maggie asked. 'Is it a big town?'

'Yes. It's a big, busy port. The captain says we're to meet up with a ship called the Guardian. It is to be fully laden with provisions, mostly food, for this new colony you are being sent to.'

'Is that the one that passed us a few days before we left Galleons Reach?' Lily asked.

James nodded. 'Aye. There were supposed to be five ships sailing with the second fleet, but the captain has heard the other three ships will not be ready to leave for some months. There's been some sort of a mix-up and delays. I heard they have only recently commissioned the other three ships. So there will only be us and the *Guardian* sailing.'

'There should be plenty for us to watch while we are in Portsmouth then,' Alice said hopefully.

'Aye,' James agreed, 'An' plenty you'd rather not see as well, I think.'

Maggie give him a questioning look. 'What would that be then?'

James gave a shrug and a sad sigh. 'More of those hulks like there was on the Thames.'

'What? And are there convicts in them too?' she asked in horror.

James nodded. 'It's a sad thing. People shouldn't be kept like that. Like animals. No — *worse* than animals. Some of them have been there for three years and more I was told.'

Alice looks sadly towards Dover with a tear in her eye. 'We shall have to hope then that all the convicts from the hulks are sent to this new land with this fleet. This second fleet, as they call it.' She shook her head and heaved a great sigh.

Portsmouth, when they reached it, did indeed come as an eye-opener. The port was crammed with boats and ships of all sizes.

Alice watched, wide-eyed, the massive amount of shipping movement on the water. To her unknowing eyes, it looked like completely disorganised chaos as the craft jostled for position. There hardly seemed to be an unoccupied spot of water.

Quite soon Alice could smell a familiar odour — the stink of the hulks. Only now, after the days of beautiful fresh sea air, it seemed more sour and unbearable than ever.

Peering into the distance, her eyes located the dismasted, crumbling wrecks of ships. Far away but, unfortunately, near enough for the smell to carry to her on the prevailing wind. Screwing her nose up, she turned her back to them.

Moored not far away, Alice could see the *Guardian*. She

remembered it passing a few days before they had left Galleons Reach, and James had told her it was a supply ship, and would be sailing alongside them as part of the second fleet. There was a lot of activity around the *Guardian*, with boats being rowed out, piled high with wooden crates and large barrels. These were put into large strong nets and manhandled to the deck off the ship. From there they quickly disappeared below deck.

To most of the women on board the *Lady Juliana*, it seemed a strange few days they spent in Portsmouth. They watched with interest as men were rowed out from the shore, and a few even from the hulks. When asked, James explained that Thomas Edgar, agent, having a kind heart, had agreed to allow visits from husbands. The ones who came from shore we're almost certainly saying goodbye to their wives for the last time. For those who came from the hulks, it might be a temporary farewell as they hoped to be reunited *beyond the seas* in the months to come.

It's just as well, Alice thought with a wry smile, '*that these visiting men are not aware that some of their wives have already been taken as wives for the crew.*'

One sad visitation that brought tears to Alice's eyes was that of a mother being reunited briefly with her four young children. The children were brought aboard one afternoon, and Alice watched sadly as they squealed with delight and ran into their mother's arms. A tear ran down her face when their visiting time was over and they were dragged away screaming, for she knew they would almost certainly never see their mother again. Nor she, them.

The poor mother tried to run after them but was restrained by crew members. Arms outstretched she screamed their names. The children tried to pull away and run back to her but were quickly bundled over the rail and lowered into the waiting boat. The woman pulled herself free and ran to the rail, sobbing as she watched the boat being rowed toward the shore.

Watching her, Thomas Edgar shook his head, sighed then, fearful she might jump over the rail and try to swim after them, he moved to her side and gently took her arm.

'Come, my girl,' he said quietly. 'It's best if you don't watch.'

'I have to,' she replied with a catch in her voice, ''tis probably the last time I will ever set eyes on them.'

Thomas let go of her arm, but stood close at hand watching as she stood sobbing at the rail.

The mother's eyes stayed glued to the little boat until it disappeared amongst the crowd of ships, then she crumpled, sobbing to the deck.

The *Lady Juliana's* stay in Portsmouth was a short one. Captain Aitken had a meeting with the captain of the *Guardian*, who told him his ship would not be ready to sail for many weeks, as many of the provisions he was to take to the new colony had not yet arrived. On hearing this captain Aitken decided he could wait no longer and would set sail alone.

Within days the frantic activity onboard resumed. The anchor was wound up and she set sail for their next port of call which was to be a place called Plymouth. There, James told them, the ship was to be fully provisioned for the next part of their voyage.

The following morning captain Aitken told his officers that he was not going to wait in Plymouth for the *Guardian*. It was taking too long altogether. There had already been too many delays, so once the *Lady Juliana* had all the supplies she needed he wanted to be underway.

There was a scurry of activity on deck, with all hands busy with their allotted tasks.

Alice watched, with her heart heavy in her chest, as Danny climbed the ropes to the highest level and swung out onto the furthest reaches of the spars.

A small boat arrived, and the women watched with interest and curiosity as it took up position toward the front of the *Lady Juliana*.

With a lot of squealing and clanking the anchor was winched up.

A ripple of excitement ran through the women on the deck as the *Lady Juliana* caught the wind and started to surge forward. She followed the small ship, a pilot to guide them safely past the shoals; so Danny told Alice; that surrounded the Isle of Wight. Once safely at sea again, *Lady Juliana* turned westward and headed to Plymouth under full sail.

If Alice had thought Portsmouth to be crowded with ships, she saw now, that was as nothing compared with Plymouth. This was, so James informed them, One of the busiest ports in England. Every kind of shipping imaginable was crammed into the Sound.

As far as the eye could see, the shore was occupied by shipyards and repair yards. There were also vast stretches of market gardens who's fruit and vegetables supplied the ships that came from and sailed to every corner of the world.

The women lined the rails and watched as empty water casks were taken ashore in lighters. Some time later they were returned, filled, to the *Lady Juliana* and the stronger men of the crew heaved them on board. This took a full day but was an essential task and the barrels of sweet water, which came from Dartmoor, would be enjoyed by all on board until they reached their next port, at Santa Cruz.

In the days that followed, a steady stream of lighters moved backward and forward between ship and shore, carrying provisions to the *Lady Juliana*. Hauled on board, these were carried away and quickly stored below deck.

Alice watched all this activity with avid interest. Leaning far over the rail at times, She saw the huge crates being lifted on deck, until she was sure there could be room for no more in the hold.

'I gotta help the carpenters tomorrow,' Danny told her one night as they snuggled together.

'The carpenters?' Alice Asked, puzzled. 'I didn't know you worked with wood.'

'I don't, but Mr. Edgar said I have to help to build pens for some live animals and cages for hens.'

'Live animals? Where will they put those then?'

'On the deck, he says.'

Alice shrugged. It seemed a strange thing to do, and where would the women spend their days? *It will make it terrible hard to sit on the decks if they are full of animals,* she thought.

The following morning the women watched, intrigued as the carpenters measured and sawed and hammered. Whenever they got in the way, they were roughly shoved aside, until eventually they were all huddled at one end of the deck, becoming more annoyed by the minute.

'Just look at the mess they are making of the deck,' Maggie grumbled. 'I suppose the Captain will expect us to clean up after all this lot!'

There was great excitement the next morning when lighters, filled with an assortment of animals was hitched up tight to the side of the *Lady Juliana*.

The convicts crowded into a small amount of deck that was not taken up by pens and cages.

Alice edged herself to the front of the crowd and found herself a small space against the rail. The entertainment she enjoyed for the next few hours made her forget her fragile stomach for a while.

The smaller animals, sheep and goats and hens were passed

up by hand from the lighter, but when it came to the larger creatures it was, to Alice, a good comedy show and she found herself giggling as she watched.

Cattle and large pigs were brought, one at a time, from their pens in the lighter and forced into strong canvas slings. Once these were secured around them the men on the *Lady Juliana* heaved on the ropes and, sweating profusely, dragged them on board the ship and securely fastened them into pens.

Throughout the day the air was filled with the sounds of cattle bellowing, pigs squealing, and men cursing. And by the end of it all, the deck was awash with steaming excrement.

'More bloody cleaning,' Lily grumbled to Duncan when he stopped for a moment to chat to her. 'How do they expect us to keep the deck clean with all these animals shitting on it?'

'Well,' he laughed. 'Captain and Mr. Edgar say you convict women have to be kept busy to stop you getting into any mischief.'

That night Alice was disappointed, but understanding, when Danny wanted nothing more than to sleep. She had come to look forward to their nocturnal activities, but could see how very tired he was. With a sigh, she cuddled up to him and fell asleep.

In the morning the few women who were brave enough to share the deck with the animals we're interested to see yet another lighter approaching, this time filled was women.

They watched as a man scrambled aboard and the captain went to meet him, his expression puzzled.

'I've brought you another eighteen convicts you are to take to the new colony with you,' he said, handing Captain Aitken a piece of paper.

Frowning, the captain shoved The paper back into the man's hand. 'I haven't been notified about this,' he said angrily.

The man shrugged and held the paper out to him. 'Well, that's the orders. You gotta take them. Them's from prisons in this area and it wasn't worth sending them to London just to bring them back here again. So the orders is that you has to take them.'

'Who's orders?' Thomas Edgar, the agent, asked as he joined them.

'Admiralty,' the man replied with a shrug of his shoulders. 'They make the decisions, and what they say goes.'

With an angry snort, captain Aitken snatched the paper from the man's hand. 'How the hell am I expected to keep any kind of control When I don't know how many passengers I am going to have on this ship? Well, I suppose we had better get them aboard, then we'll be sailing straight away. We'll just have to make our provisions stretch a bit further.'

The poor, grubby looking women were manhandled onto the *Lady Juliana*, and once they were all aboard, James knocked off their shackles, Once free, they were taken below to the orlop cabin.

Earlier residents, who had been unable to find a sailor to move in with, eyed the new arrivals suspiciously. When told by Thomas Edgar that they must squeeze together more tightly to make room, there was endless grumbling. Mavis Crowe was the loudest protester.

After a lot of shouting, and arm waving, Thomas reached the end of his patience. 'Well, the choice is yours. either you move along and make room for these new ladies, or you can spend a few days in the brig on bread and water.'

In a show of bravado, Mavis, hands on hips, glared at him and spat on the deck at his feet, but when he took a step toward her, she backed away, collected her belongings, and shuffled along the shelf bed.

Thomas pursed his lips, nodded, then told her angrily to clean up the mess she had just made.

Listening to the altercation from the deck above, Alice and her friends had a fit of the giggles.

'Serves the evil bitch right,' Maggie said, with no small amount of satisfaction. 'I'd have liked to see him put her in the brig for the whole of the voyage. Let's hope there is someone tougher than her amongst the newcomers.'

Once again Thomas Edgar permitted the relatives of these women to come aboard to say a final farewell to daughters, wives, sisters, and sweethearts before they sailed out of their lives forever.

Alice wept again as one young mother was visited by three young children, whom she hadn't seen since she had been incarcerated in Exeter jail three years previously.

The eldest child. A boy of about six, recognised her immediately and with the squeal of delight ran into her open arms. The two younger children eyed her suspiciously at first, then, more slowly, followed their brother into her arms.

Watching, Maggie sat with tears streaming down her face. It brought back too many raw memories of when her children were taken away from her. Their screams and pleas to her not to leave them, cut cruelly through her mind.

When time ran out and the visit had to end the woman clung, sobbing, to the children and they to her. The husband, with agony in his eyes, picked up the two younger children and, as he walked away, told the older child to come with him. When the child continued to cling to his mother, Thomas Edgar gently unlocked his arms from around her neck and followed the father to the gangplank.

The mother tried to run after him but surgeon Alley took hold of her arms and gently, but firmly held her back.

As Thomas carried the child to the ladder, he screamed and struggled to escape, with his arms outstretched towards his mother.

When they were out of sight the mother crumpled to the deck and lay curled in ball sobbing, knowing that was the last sight she would ever have of her children.

Shortly after the last relative left the ship, the women were all ordered below decks, and the hatch screwed down behind them. They all sat in glum misery listening to the mixture of now familiars sounds, as the ship prepared to leave Plymouth and England forever.

CHAPTER 10

O n the morning of the 29th of July, the women were once again ordered down the hatch, into the orlop hold, where they listened resignedly as they heard the screws turn to lock them in. A few grumbled, but most had come to accept that this temporary imprisonment was all part and parcel of setting sail.

Within minutes the butterflies which seemed to live constantly in Alice's stomach these days went into hysterics. She felt as if the whole of her insides were tying in knots, her heart fluttered, her head spun and she felt faint.

'I do hope they're not going to keep us down here too long,' she said miserably.

Maggie put a motherly arm around her shoulder and gave her a gentle squeeze. 'I know just how you feel,' she said quietly, 'but you know James said we have to be down here for our own safety.'

Alice nodded. Yes, she *did* remember, but remembering did not make the smell any less foul, or her stomach less queasy.

Once again the women listened to the racket of preparing the ship to sail. The snapping and cracking of the sails and ropes, running feet thumping on the deck, the captain's bullhorn, and the shouting and cursing of the men. But having grown used to it by now, they no longer found it so frightening.

At last, when she was sure could not survive much longer, Alice heard the hatch being opened. Heaving a hearty sigh of relief, she rushed to climb out onto the deck to gulp down great lungs full of fresh air.

Most of the other women thankfully scrambled out behind her, pulling, shouting and swearing at each other as they went. Several were knocked over in the rush, or pulled from the ladder and thrown on the ground, but few stopped to help them.

Alice rushed straight to the rail, and holding on to it, sucked hungrily at the sweet fresh air.

With topsails set and taking the wind, the *Lady Juliana* moved swiftly out of Cawsand Bay on the outgoing tide.

With a heavy feeling in her heart, Alice watched Plymouth shrinking into the distance. So this was it! The leaving of England, never to return! No chance now of ever being able to trace her mother. Now she would have to face the rest of her life not knowing why she had disappeared. It had been a struggle for her Mam, she knew, to keep her fed and clothed but she also knew her mother had loved her and had done the best she could for her. Though there had never been enough food, she had seen her mother go without, herself, to give her daughter what small amounts she had managed to scavenge or steal. There had never been a shortage of love. Hugs and kisses had always been plentiful. So why, she wondered, why had this woman she loved abandoned her? She would never believe her mother had left willingly. So, what *had* happened to her? Had she been set upon and robbed? Murdered perhaps? Alice sighed sadly. Well, now she would never know, would she?

'What's on your mind?'

Turning her head, Alice found Maggie leaning on the rail beside her. So lost, had she been in her thoughts, that she had neither seen nor heard her friend coming.

Alice drew in her breath on a shuddering sigh. 'I was just thinking about my Mam,' she said sadly. 'Wondering whatever happened to her. It saddens me to know I will never see the Isle of Man or my mother again. I can only hope that wherever she is she is well and happy.'

Maggie put an arm around her shoulder and gave her a gentle squeeze. 'It's best not to think of it, love,' she said quietly. 'You can drive yourself mad that way. Have you ever thought that perhaps she might be imprisoned somewhere?' She bit her lip and studied the girl thoughtfully. 'Or it is possible, you know, that she might no longer be alive.'

Alice nodded and bit back tears. 'Aye, I have thought of it, but I don't want to. I don't want to believe she is dead. But nor do I want to believe she just walked away and forgot about me. I just don't know *what* to believe.'

Maggie shook her head. 'I know how you must feel,' she said quietly. 'I just hope that my children never come to believe I abandoned them. If your Mam loves you as much as I care for my children, and she is still alive somewhere, I know how much she must be suffering. You don't know what real suffering is until you lose a child.'

Alice choked back a sob And leaned over the rail, gazing into the dark blue water of the Sound.

Throwing her head up boldly she fixed Maggie with a penetrating look. 'I *will* find her someday. That is a promise I make to my Mam and to myself. One day I will find a way to return to the island and somehow I will find out what happened to her. I won't stop looking until I know. Of this, I vow.'

Maggie thought she had never seen such determination on

such a young face. Was it possible, she wondered, whether, in years to come, her children would care so much about her fate. At least, unlike Alice, they knew that she had not willingly left them. Could it be possible that some time in the future they would come looking for her? How wonderful that would be!

Deciding it was time they moved on to a more cheerful subject, Maggie pointed up to a headland they were passing. 'See them big black things up there,' she said. 'James says they are huge guns that were put there to defend this corner of England from invaders.'

'Invaders from where?' Alice thought she should at least try to show some interest, and looked, briefly, up at the guns.

Maggie shrugged. 'I don't know, wherever invaders come from I suppose. James didn't say.'

As Plymouth and England became nothing more than a grey haze on the horizon, Alice heaved a heavy sigh and turned to look toward the bow of the ship. That must be the only way to look now, she told herself. Forward — to the future was her only direction. Until the day came when she could find her way back to the Isle of Man!

The ship looked very different now. Where before there had been a lot of empty deck space, there were now penned animals, cages of hens, and an assortment of temporary huts that had been erected to store provisions that could not be found space for below decks.

What little deck space was left, was crowded, with the convicts vying for every little inch of room.

The women had formed into gangs. Most of them were hard, made tough by a lifetime of struggling to survive. Now, the most violent had appointed themselves leaders and formed gangs, stealing anything they took a fancy to from the other women. Any who tried to resist them were harshly dealt with. They enjoyed beating and kicking anyone they took a dislike to, just for the fun of it.

Others, the non-vicious amongst them, had also formed into groups, like Alice and her three friends, as an act of self-defense. No lone woman was safe from the packs.

One of the worst of these gang leaders was Mavis Crowe, Who continually tried to pick fights with the other women and very often members of the crew. To keep herself out of trouble as much as possible Alice always tried to be aware of where Mavis was, and steer well clear. At least her shawl was safe now, as the weather was warmer and she left it folded on Danny's bunk. She, Maggie, Lily, and Sarah tried always to be together when they were not with their chosen menfolk.

Hearing raised voices, Alice swiftly turned her back to the rail and faced the direction of the altercation. With a sigh and a shake of her head, she noted that it was Mavis once again causing the trouble. Her group of gangster mates stood behind her, looking threatening, as she tried to bully one of the younger women. She was pulling at the bodice of the girl's dress and trying to push her hand inside it.

The woman; not much more than a girl really; faced Mavis, Tried to push her hand away, and shook her head angrily. 'No! it's mine. My father gave it to me, and you're not having it. I shall need it when I get to the end of this voyage to give me a good start in this new colony.'

Mavis sniggered. 'Think you're something special, do you, because you have a father who gives you money? Well, you are right, it does make you special to *me* because you are going to make me richer. You can give me it now and then tell your lovely father I said thank you. I'll have it from you now or, believe me, you won't reach the new colony.' Her face, ugly to start with, became suddenly the personification of evil in Alice's eyes.

The girl, Jenny, shook her head, clutched a hand to her breast and took a backward step. 'You're not having it! My father had to take out a loan against his house to get this.'

With startling speed for a woman of her bulk, Mavis leaped forward, grabbed Jenny by the hair and in one movement brought her knee up into the girl's stomach.

Jenny screamed and fell to the deck, clutching her bodice with one hand and her stomach with the other.

Alice gasped in horror and took a step forward but Maggie's hand on her arm stopped her.

'Stay out of it,' Maggie advised quietly. 'The bitch has it in for you already. Don't throw fuel on the fire or you will live — or die — to regret it.'

'Someone has to help her,' Alice said angrily. 'Mavis will kill her if she isn't stopped.'

'Yes, but not you. Mavis' thugs would crush you long before you could reach her. She's already after your blood without you inviting more trouble. Anyway, help is coming now.' She nodded toward Alice's right.

Following the direction of Maggie's gaze, Alice saw Thomas Edgar, surgeon Richard Alley and several of the crew rushing to the scene.

Without wasting a moment, Thomas grabbed Mavis by the back of her clothes and threw her away from the helpless girl on the deck. He gave a nod of satisfaction when she landed flat on her back, cracking her head on the boards.

Her face a mask of hatred and holding the back of her head, Mavis leaped to her feet and stumbled toward Thomas.

Before she had taken more than two steps surgeon Alley caught her arm and one of the men took hold of her dress. In a flash, Mavis swung around and brought her knee with great force into the poor man's groin.

With an agonized scream, the man clutched the injured area and dropped, writhing, to the deck.

In an instant, two more of the crew grabbed her and threw her unceremoniously to the ground.

'Take her below and lock her up,' Thomas said angrily when they had dragged her to her feet.

The grim-faced crewman who had suffered her knee struggled painfully to his feet, twisted her arm up her back, grabbed a handful of her hair, and with the help of another man all but threw her down the hatch. With relish, he screwed it shut.

Turning to Richard Alley, Thomas shook his head. 'Why does the stupid woman keep doing this?' he asked. 'She causes trouble and gets herself locked down in the hold every single day. Surely she can't enjoy being in that stinking hell hole?'

Stuck for an answer, Richard shrugged his shoulders and threw his hands up in a gesture of helplessness. 'Something is going on with that woman that I just can't fathom. She seems to deliberately make trouble where there is no trouble to be found.'

Thomas nodded. 'There's a reason for it and by hook or by crook I am going to find it.'

Richard frowned. 'Have you notice that she slurs her words? If I didn't know she had no access to alcohol, I would think she was drunk.'

Thomas chewed thoughtfully on the inside of his lip. 'Aye, I'd had that same thought, but I can't think where she could be getting any. There's something going on though. I'll look into it and I *will* find the answer.'

The *Lady Juliana* slipped steadfastly through the waves on the wings of a firm, but gentle breeze.

Captain Aitken had always been a stickler for cleanliness. It was his conviction that a clean ship was a healthy ship. It was also his opinion that the convicts had to be kept busy to prevent them from becoming bored and creating mischief. To this end, he determined that it would be the women's job to keep the *Lady Juliana* as clean and as disease-free as possible. So within days of the first convicts coming on board in the Thames, he had set them to work as cleaners.

Water was bucketed up from the sea. The women lined up and knelt shoulder to shoulder, scrubbing the decks with holystones. The walls were scrubbed with vinegar, and whitewashed.

Very aware of the risk of typhus having been brought aboard the ship from infested gaols, captain Aitken ordered that, whenever possible, pots of pitch should be boiled below decks, in the hope that this would keep the disease at bay.

Whether it was this precaution or sheer coincidence, no one would know but, with help from surgeon Alley, the few women who did come on board with typhus recovered and the disease did not spread.

The convicts were also set a task of making and repairing shirts for the crew.

Alice happily applied herself to the work the captain had allotted to the women. She was happy to work at any task she was set. She found the scrubbing of the decks hard work, for she did not really have the strength this required. However, she persevered, built up strength, and made a good and thorough job of it. This, though, had become a lot more difficult with the arrival of all the livestock. Before scrubbing, the decks now had to be swabbed and all the urine and faeces washed overboard. Her favourite job was sewing, especially when the shirt she was stitching was Danny's, and her greatest fear was of being ordered to scrub the orlop deck, but thankfully surgeon Alley had foreseen the danger she would be in there and had demanded that she must never be sent down there to work.

Finishing her scrubbing, Alice straightened up and tipped her pail of dirty water over the rail. Putting her arms above her head she happily stretched the kinks out of her back. For a while, she lingered at the rail, sadly watching the coast of Cornwall as it slipped past in the distance.

It looked such a peaceful, yet rugged stretch of land, with its jagged grey cliffs and blanket of green fields stretching away as far as the eye could see.

James had pointed out a picturesque town and told the four women it was called Falmouth.

It was two days now since they had sailed from Plymouth and as she enjoyed the view, Alice realised the ship appeared to have turned shortly after they had passed a rugged headland that one of the crew told them was called Lizard Point. England was now definitely not to starboard.

Danny had told her that they would soon be turning South, leaving England behind and sailing down off the coast of France.

The sun appeared at a different angle also, and Alice fancied the sea seemed a bit rougher. She sensed the *Lady Juliana's* head adopted a different attitude in these new waters.

A sudden feeling of melancholy made her heart feel heavy and she hurried to the stern.

Watching Alice go, Maggie sensed the sadness in her. It was in her too, for she was leaving behind the three people she loved most in the world. What Alice was leaving, she thought sadly, was a lifetime of hunger, degradation, misery, and a mother who may or may not have abandoned her. Sighing, and noticing Mavis Crowe sidling toward Alice, she hoisted herself to her feet, emptied her pail, and went to join her friend.

'No way back now,' she said quietly.

Alice nodded wordlessly, then shook her head. 'No,' she agreed. 'No way back. Not for now, but however long it may take, one day I *will* be back to find my Mam.'

Maggie gave her a sideways look and shook her head slightly, but said nothing. *Aye, and one-day pigs might fly*, she thought.

'I think today is the day I would have turned fifteen if my Mam was still here,' Alice said quietly. 'The last day of July.'

'Would have?' Maggie questioned. 'Well, whether she's here or not it still must be your birth anniversary, must it not?'

Alice shook her head. 'It doesn't feel like a birthday without her. She always made a fuss and gave me a cake. I know she probably stole it, But she loved me enough to take that risk.'

Maggie nodded, put her arms around Alice, and gave her a tight hug. 'Just for today let's pretend I'm your Mam, an' we'll go to the galley an' see if we can talk the cook into giving us a bit of cake.'

Alice buried her face in Maggie's shoulder, threw her arms tight around her, and burst into tears.

Maggie held her tightly and just let her cry. She could think of nothing to say that would bring the child any comfort.

Lily and Sarah joined them soon afterward, and the four of them stood hand in hand, leaning on the rail, as they watched England fade slowly into the distance. The fields above the cliffs gradually faded from a verdant green until they became just a part of the misty grey of the cliffs and finally disappeared beyond the horizon.

Alice heaved a tremulous sigh, straightened up, and stepped quickly back from the rail. Her heart felt as if it was tearing apart inside her and just for a moment, she'd had a frightening desire to jump over the rail and swim back to England.

As though reading her mind, Maggie took hold of her arm and squeezed it gently. 'No way back,' she said quietly, 'and remember you can't swim.'

Alice nodded and gave a tired smile. 'So now we sail into whatever the future has in store for us. At least we're warm and comfortable and well-fed.'

Maggie laughed. 'And talking about food, let's go and get you that birthday cake.'

With the tension of the moment broken, Alice and her three friends chattered happily as they went to find the cook. Luckily the cook, Jessie, who was on duty when they arrived, was a friendly, gentle woman whom Thomas Edgar had assigned to the galley. Jessie had been given the position because she claimed to have been a chef, at one time, in a top London restaurant. No one was sure whether this claim was fact or fiction, but she cooked well so crew and convicts alike were happy to let her stay in the galley.

On hearing Alice's story, Jessie was delighted to oblige. As luck would have it she had just taken a batch of cakes from the oven A few minutes earlier. After rummaging in some drawers for a few minutes she produced a rather sad looking candle and jammed it into the middle of the cake. Wrapping it in a clean cloth She handed it to Maggie.

'Don't let any of them other women see it.' Jessie warned. 'Them's a greedy lot and some of them would cut your throat as soon as look at you if they saw you with it.'

Sniffing back a tear, Alice gave Jessie a tight hug. 'Thank you,' she said with a tremor in her voice, 'thank you so much. You don't know how much this means to me.'

Jessie ruffled her hair. 'Get away with you girl,' she said fondly. 'It's only a bit of cake, an' you're one of the nice ones. You deserve something nice on your special day.'

Taking care to keep their prize well hidden, Alice and her friends hid behind one of the makeshift huts that now littered the deck. Whispering and giggling amongst themselves they enjoyed every crumb of the beautiful warm fruitcake.

CHAPTER 11

———

It was a perfect summer's day. The *Lady Juliana* scudded briskly along under a perfect blue sky, with only an occasional little powdery puff of white cloud to break it.

Most of the convicts had finished their chores and were lounging around the deck. As usual, the bullies and the roughest of the women were making their presence known, hassling and sneering at the ones who wanted only to be left in peace. If they did not get the desired reaction they progressed to pinching, hair pulling, kicking and punching. There were constant shouts, squeals and often the sounds of sobbing.

After a while Thomas Edgar or the surgeon would come down from the forecastle and put a stop to it. This usually meant banishing the trouble makers to the orlop hold, surprising everyone with their willingness to accept this punishment.

Alice leaned against the rail, her friends around her, and was thankful she had their protection. Danny's too. How wonderful it was to have him to care for her. She was sure he must be the nicest person she had ever known. Well, second maybe to Maggie, that was. If only she did not feel so wretched all the time, she thought, life would be perfect, she was warmer and better fed now then she could ever remember being in her whole life.

There was no land in sight. Not a bird to be seen anywhere. Not even the greedy, noisy gulls that had been ever-present in the Thames and the two harbour towns they had stopped in. Nothing to see now, but the white-capped, ever-shifting sea.

Watching the moving peaks and hollows of the water, Alice felt dizzy and her head spun. As a wave of faintness swept over her, she turned her back to the rail and slumped to the deck.

Maggie immediately dropped to her knees beside her, her face a picture of concern. In the previous few weeks, she had watched the girl becoming steadily more listless.

Putting a comforting arm around her friend's shoulder, she asked, 'What ails you, love?'

Alice shrugged and shook her head miserably. 'I just feel so sick all the time and now I have moments of feeling faint as well. I thought it would get better once I was used to the movement of the ship, but if anything it has got worse.'

Maggie eyed her speculatively, put a hand to her mouth, and chewed on the inside of her cheek for a moment. 'I think perhaps it might be a good idea if you went and had a check-up with the surgeon.'

Alice surveyed her friend with a puzzled frown, Then she smiled and shook her head. 'Wouldn't do any good, I don't think. He's very kind and no doubt a good surgeon, but he wouldn't be able to stop ship rocking would he?'

Maggie sighed and wondered just what was the best way to tell Alice what it was she suspected. 'Well,' she started hesitantly, 'I think it is possible you might be with child and the best way to find out for certain is to ask surgeon Alley to check.'

Alice stared uncomprehendingly at her for a few moments, not being able to make any sense of what her friend was saying. What was this about a child? 'I don't know what you mean,' she said with a frown and an abrupt shake of her head.

Maggie drew in a deep breath. This was going to be difficult. 'I mean just what I said. With all this sickness, and now feeling dizzy and faint. It seems possible to me that you might be with child.'

Shaking her head, Alice turned away from her. 'No,' she said emphatically, 'it's only the movement of the ship,'

Maggie pursed her lips. 'The sickness perhaps, but not the dizziness and faintness as well.'

Alice felt her heart thundering against her ribs. A child? It couldn't be, could it? A baby? 'It can't be,' she said finally. 'I'm only fifteen.'

Maggie sighed. How naive could this girl be, she wondered. 'Girls much younger than you have had babies, you know. I did warn you, before you became Danny's wife, to take care and make sure he pulled out before he came. Did he always do that?'

Alice dropped her gaze, scuffed her toe against the deck and shrugged one shoulder. Shaking her head, she said quietly, 'most times he did, but sometimes he was too slow.'

Maggie snorted and rolled her eyes to heaven. 'Then we had best go and see surgeon Alley,' she said decisively.

The following morning saw Alice and Maggie in line for the surgeon's sick roll. Maggie held firmly to Alice's hand And chattered cheerfully to her in an attempt to keep her calm, while the poor child struggled to stop herself trembling.

Alice hadn't dared voice Maggie's suspicions to Danny last night. She had considered it but was feeling totally confused and frightened. Finally, she decided it was best to wait until she was sure; one way or the other; so she had kept quiet and lain awake all night worrying. If Maggie was right, how would he feel about it? How would he react? Would he be angry, she wondered, or would he be pleased? How *could* he be pleased to face fatherhood at only sixteen years of age? With absolute dread, she feared he would no longer want her as his *wife* and she would have to return to the danger and horror of sharing the orlop hold with Mavis, Gracie, and the myriad of other evil bullies.

When she told Maggie of her fears, her friend just shook her head. Taking Alice's trembling hands in hers, she said, 'Now listen here girl, Danny's a nice boy an' he cares about you. Baby or not, he would never send you back into that hell hole. He knows full well how dangerous it would be for you down there.'

Despite Maggie's confidence, Alice still could not help but be afraid, She was not sure which she feared most; the fact of being told she was to become a mother or Danny's possible reaction to the news.

After what felt like hours in the line, Alice's turn came and she found herself standing, speechless, before the surgeon. By this time she was shaking uncontrollably and it was left to Maggie to tell surgeon Alley why they were there.

The man put his fingers to his lips, rubbed his chin and muttered, 'Oh dear God,' then gave a slight shake of his head. This was something he had feared, but had hoped would not happen, when Alice became Danny's *wife*. Then he reminded himself of why it had been so important to get the girl out of the orlop. He'd had very mixed feelings about the arrangement at the time but had known that most certainly her life would have been in danger had she been left amongst those other dreadful women. She would certainly have come to a great deal of harm. There was no doubt in his mind that she would have been severely beaten — or worse — throughout the voyage. So provided her small body could survive the rigours of childbirth, this would almost certainly be the lesser of the two evils.

It saddened him that he had not had the means to prevent this from happening. Alice was just one of many women; mainly young girls below their twenties; who had become pregnant. And the voyage was still young. How many babies, he wondered, would he be called upon to deliver? How many would survive? And how many of these young mothers would live to reach this new colony? A ship tossing around on the ocean, possibly a stormy one, was far from the ideal place to bring a child into the world. A dangerous place for both mother and infant.

The Admiralty had obviously planned for this, of course, for he had been provided with facilities and supplies for a multitude of births. He could see now that the powers that ruled the country had been more than willing to put these women's lives at risk. It had become obvious that their only interest was in colonizing this new country — and as quickly as possible, by whatever means available. That was what had spurred their decision to send a ship filled with over two hundred female convicts. Prostitutes and innocent young girls alike, it was clear that they were being sent to Port Jackson to be used as breeding sows!

Several of the sailors had brought the woman of their choice to him to be examined to make sure and did not have the clap, before taking her as a *wife*. If the poor soul was found to be infected, she would be immediately discarded and the man would seek another mate. Most of the men though preferred the younger girls, who had a far better chance of being clean.

Surgeon Alley was also aware that quite a few of the men who had taken a *wife* were unfaithful and frequently visited the orlop deck at night. As half the women on board the *Lady Juliana* were being transported because they had been convicted of prostitution, he feared these men would be bringing venereal diseases back to their innocent young *wives*. Several of these girls were now pregnant and he worried about how it might affect their babies.

Rubbing a weary hand across his brow, he thought sadly of his own situation. In all honesty, how could he condemn the behaviour of the crew when every man on board the ship; himself included; from captain down to deck hand had found himself a woman?

In his early years at sea, he had felt guilty about betraying his wife every time he took a woman in a foreign port. Now he realised suddenly that the guilt was all but gone. Like any other sea-going man he had the same needs. Months, and sometimes years without returning home, were too long to expect any red-blooded man to remain celibate. So through time he had ceased to regard himself as an unfaithful husband and had accepted his philandering as the right of a sailor.

A wife in every port, the saying was, but with this voyage there had been no need to wait to reach a port. The Admiralty had very kindly provided them with over two hundred captive women to choose from. Most of them too unsavory for him to have considered, but also many comely maidens amongst them. It had not taken him too long to find himself a mate, a clean and pretty eighteen-year-old, and he had made as sure as it was possible to be, that he would not burden her with child. He knew that when the ship sailed from Port Jackson he would almost certainly have to leave with it, abandoning the poor mother to fend for herself and a very young baby in what was almost certain to be appalling living conditions. Arriving in this new world would be frightening enough for her without having the worry of a baby added to it.

To ensure her safety, he had brought a good supply of *English overcoats* to protect against causing an unwanted pregnancy and also to alleviate the danger to himself of contracting any disease.

Also, he could not accept the idea of any child of his being left to face, heaven alone knew what kind of a future. Like everyone else, he had read the stories in the newspapers claiming that in this new land there were black savages who killed and ate the white settlers.

Suddenly waking from his reverie, he became aware of the woman and girl standing before him regarding him in some puzzlement.

With a quick shake of his head to clear his thoughts, he sadly studied the child before him; for that's all she was; a mere child, as was the boy who had taken her as a wife. He could only be, what, sixteen? Certainly no more.

With an unhappy sigh, he instructed Alice to climb on the bed and bend her legs at the knees so that he could examine her.

Alice obeyed and lay fighting tears caused more by embarrassment than the discomfort of the examination itself.

'All right Alice, you can sit up now,' he told her solemnly, as he took a backward step.

Alice did so, dangling her legs over the side of the bed and watching the surgeon intently. *He looks sad*, she thought, *but does that mean he has good news or bad news for me?*

Drawing in a heavy breath he said, 'Well Alice, I regret to have to tell you that you are, indeed, to have a child.'

Alice stared at him in numb shock. *So Maggie was right*, she thought. A baby! Danny's baby! Her hand moved instinctively her belly. Her head spun and her thoughts turned somersaults. She was really going to have Danny's baby!

Worried by her lack of response, Maggie sat up beside her and put an arm around her. 'Are you all right, love,' she asked anxiously.

Alice turned to look at her and nodded absently. 'I think so,' she said quietly. Was she all right, she wondered. She didn't know how she felt. Dazed, would probably be the best description. Pressing gently on her stomach, she tried to digest what she had just been told. Looking down at her hand, her eyes misted. *Underneath my hand, Danny's baby is growing. I hope he'll be pleased.*

Surgeon Richard Alley studied her anxiously. He could only hope she would survive this. It worried him that the child was so small. However, what was done could not be undone, so all that remained was for him to do the best he could for her.

'I'm sorry, Alice,' he said quietly, 'but I have a lot of people waiting to consult with me, so I'm going to have to ask you to leave. I do promise you, though, that I will take the best care of you that I possibly can. You must come to see me regularly so that I can check that things are going alright with you.'

Alice nodded And slipped down from the bed. She felt dazed, and wondered if she was going to wake up any minute. Could it be true? What there really a baby; Danny's baby; growing inside her, or was it only a dream?

Watching the woman and the child leave his infirmary, Richard Alley shook his head sadly and muttered, 'babies having babies!'

'Well, I was right, wasn't I? So what now? How do you feel about it?' Maggie fired the questions at Alice as they stepped out onto the deck.

Alice drew a deep breath, looked up to where a golden ray of sunshine stabbed through black clouds, and ran both hands through her hair.

With a quick shrug and head-shake, she said, 'I really don't know. I don't know what to think or how I feel. I'm scared that I will have a lot of pain, and I'm frightened that I won't know how to look after it. I've never thought about having a baby, but know I will love it. I will love it with every part of my body and my soul, just as my mother loved me.

Maggie smiled sadly and nodded her head. Just as she had, and still did, love the three children she had been taken away from. It had always saddened her that she did not know, so could not tell her children who their father was, but she loved them no less for that. She loved Alice too, but not with quite the same kind of love. She just felt so heart-wrenchingly sorry for the child.

'I'll be here for you my lovely', she said quietly, rubbing her hand gently across Alice's shoulder. 'Don't ever doubt that. You will always be able to rely on me.' Her heart was filled with sadness and fear, for she knew only too well what Alice would have to face in the months to come. It was hard enough to go through the rigours of carrying and birthing a child when you were a grown-up and you had both feet on solid ground. What must it be like, she wondered, to have to go through childbirth in the confines of a constantly tossing ship? If she had been a religious person she would have said a prayer — but she wasn't, so she didn't.

'I'll have to tell Danny soon,' Alice said fearfully. 'What do you think he will say? will he be annoyed, do you think?'

Maggie worried a fingernail for a few moments before replying. 'Well, I would think his first reaction will be shock. Then if he knows anything about how babies are made, he should not be altogether surprised. After that, well I just don't know. It's not the same for him as it is for you, remember. This child is always going to be *your* responsibility.'

Alice gazed up at her, her face puckered in a puzzled frown. 'I know he cares about me so maybe when we get to this new country he will marry me properly and we will be a family.'

Maggie sighed sadly and fiddled with a loose end of the rigging that was flapping in the wind. How, she wondered could she bring home to Alice, the full truth of the situation without being too brutal. There was no way. However, she said it, the child was going to be upset.

'It can't be like that, my lovely,' she said quietly. 'Even if Danny is pleased and cares about the child, you will only be able to play at being a family until we reach Port Jackson. He is signed on as crew, so when the ship leaves he will have to go with it.'

Alice stamped her foot and glared at Maggie, her lips set stubbornly. 'If he cares he will sign off and stay with us.'

Maggie sighed and shook her head. 'I'm afraid that's not the way it works. Once you sign on you must stay with the ship until the voyage is completed. To keep the costs as low as possible a ship sails with the smallest number of crew possible. If only one man is missing it makes things very difficult for the remainder of the crew. The captain would never allow Danny to stay behind. When the ship leaves, Danny *will* go with it!'

Alice glared angrily at her for a moment, then turning quickly she ran up to the forecastle. Scrambling into Danny's bunk and feeling, somehow, betrayed she burst into tears. 'I thought Maggie was my friend,' she mumbled, 'I don't like her now.' She sobbed into the mattress until she fell into a troubled sleep.

That was where Danny found her several hours later when his watch finished. He had been concerned when he had not seen her for a while. He had found Maggie, but all she would tell him was that Alice was upset and that he should talk to her about it. He had not been able to go looking for her until now and had worried about her all afternoon.

Looking down at her now, curled in his bunk, her face stained with tears and the canvas below it wet, she just looked like a very young and vulnerable child. He was reminded, suddenly, of his much younger, sister, and his heart bled.

Kneeling, he gripped Alice's shoulder and shook her gently.

Alice's red-rimmed eyes flew open, and for a moment she looked like a startled rabbit, On recognising Danny, she sat up, threw her arms around his neck, and again burst into tears.

Embracing her firmly, Danny stood up, carrying her with him And gently stood her on her feet.

Crushing herself against him, Alice buried her face in his chest and wept against it. Huge hiccuping sobs rumbled up from the pit of her stomach.

Confused and worried Danny held her tightly and just let her cry for a few minutes. 'Hush now,' he said eventually, 'Whatever's upsetting you, it can't be as bad as all that surely?'

Alice fell into another bout of sobbing. 'Oh, but it is. It is! It's worse than you could ever imagine.'

Danny felt sick. A lump of lead sank heavily in his stomach. 'I saw you and Maggie in the line for the surgeon this morning,' he said quietly. 'Is this upset anything to do with that?'

Alice nodded, gave another hiccoughing sob and clung so tightly to Danny that they became almost one.

Danny felt his heart sinking and he gently tried to push her away so that he could see into her eyes, but she clung too tightly.

'Tell me then,' he requested, as a feeling of doom settled over him. 'What did surgeon Alley say that has upset you so badly?'

'H — h — h — he said,' Alice started, but she was shaking so badly that she could hardly speak. Pressing her face to Danny's chest, she struggled to control her tremors and get her thoughts into order. What should she say? How would he react? Would he be angry? She couldn't tell him. Wouldn't tell him. Despairingly, she shook her head at herself. She *had* to tell him, didn't she? Of course, she did. He was going to find out anyway. Drawing a deep, tremulous breath she loosened her grip on him.

Unable to look him in the eyes, for fear of what she might see there, she studied a button on his shirt. 'Surgeon Alley says I am with child,' she said quickly — heard his indrawn breath and felt him stiffen.

CHAPTER 12

———

Danny felt as though he had been kicked in the stomach. With child? Surely that was not what Alice had said. It couldn't be. She was too young. *He* was too young!

Gently disentangling her arms from around him, he gripped her shoulders held her at arm's length, and looked searchingly into her face.

Alice stood with her head hanging, looking dejectedly at the deck and trembling.

Danny put two fingers under her chin and gently raised her head, but still, she kept her eyes downcast.

'Look at me, Alice,' he said quietly.

Alice raised teary red eyes and drew in a shuddering breath.

'Did you say you are with child?' Danny asked, noticing as he did so that she was shaking uncontrollably.

Alice bit on her lip and nodded fearfully.

Danny studied her in silence. His heart thundered in his chest and he didn't know what to say. Completely lost for words. What did one say in this sort of situation? Eventually, he said, 'I'm sorry,' in a faltering voice.

Alice nodded and a tear escaped, to trickle down her cheek and drip from her chin.

'Don't cry. Please don't cry. I'm so sorry,' Danny wiped away her tears with the back of his fingers. 'I didn't mean this to happen.' He felt tears pricking at his own eyes and he couldn't get his mind around the enormity of little Alice bearing a child. His child!

Alice dropped her head again and on seeing yet more tears flow, Danny drew her back into his arms.

'What do we do now?' he asked.

Alice gave a shaky jerk of her head. 'I don't know,' she mumbled, 'but it's there now and will stay there until it is born. What is there that can be done?'

Danny folded himself down onto the deck beside his bunk and drew Alice down with him, holding her in a gentle embrace.

It crossed his mind briefly to wonder what his father would have to say to him when he was told. The pleasures he had enjoyed with Alice were exactly what his father had told him he must never do until he was wed. Well, he had failed to obey his father, hadn't he and now look where it had led. Alice was to become the mother of his child!

Danny struggled to justify himself, in his own mind, by telling himself that Alice was his wife. For this voyage at least. His mind would not accept it. He knew that in reality, Alice was *not* his wife, but now she was to pay the price for what his father would tell him was *his* sin. His chest heaved in a guilty sigh. As Alice had said, what was there that could be done? He must think — but what to think? There must be something. His mind was just a mass of jumbled panic. Right at that moment, he felt like some sort of evil monster. To have inflicted such horror on this little girl he loved so much was unforgivable.

Loved? Now that was a new thought. Was this feeling he had for her the great love that people talked about? Until now, he had thought it just a deep friendship — with the added bonus of the pleasures he had at night. Now, he suddenly realised that it was more than mere friendship he felt.

Alice sat snuggled up tightly, her arms locked around him, face pressed against his damp shirt. 'Do you still want me to be your wife, or will you send me back to the orlop?' she asked fearfully.

Danny drew a quick breath. 'Why would I do that?' he questioned. 'What makes you think I would send you back there ?'

Alice shrugged miserably and bit back a sob. 'I thought maybe you would be angry with me and also that you wouldn't want me if I am going to get fat. There are plenty of other girls who would be happy to be your wife.'

Danny drew a sharp breath. Holding her at arm's length, he raised her face to force her to look into his eyes. 'Please don't ever think that of me. Don't ever believe I would treat you so badly. I think I love you! No — I *know* I love you and I want you to be with me. I don't care if you get fat — it will be my fault if you do. I mean *when* you do. If I am angry with anyone, I'm angry with myself for causing this. There is no other girl on this ship that I would want.'

Eyes swimming with tears, Alice moved her head and pressed her cheek against the fingers that had been holding her chin. 'Did you mean that?' she asked.

'Mean what? I meant it all. Every word I said.'

'That you love me. Did you mean that?'

Danny hesitated for the briefest moment. Did he mean it? Yes, He *had* meant it. Did he love her, really? Well, he had never enjoyed a girl's company so much. Nor had he ever felt so protective toward anyone other than his little sister. So he must love her, mustn't he?

'Yes,' he said quietly, drawing her to him again. 'I meant it.'

'Even when I'm fat? You promise you won't send me back to the orlop, do you? Please,' she pleaded nervously.

'I could never do that to you,' Danny said quickly. 'It would be too dangerous. I care too much and I want you with me, where you are safe. And our baby,' he added as an afterthought. 'And if you get too fat to fit in the bunk with me, you will just have to sleep on the deck,' He said cheekily.

Alice drew her head back, gazed up at him. 'I wouldn't mind the deck,' she said quietly, 'just as long as I don't have to go back to the orlop.'

Danny laughed and shook her gently. 'That was meant as a joke. If anyone sleeps on the deck it will be me. 'You and our baby must be comfortable.'

'Our baby,' Alice whispered quietly.

Danny smiled down at her and nodded thoughtfully. 'Yes. *Our* baby.' His mind wandered back to when his younger siblings were born. He remembered clearly the days when the midwife had come bustling in and chased him and his brothers and sister out into the street, with Danny tasked to look after the young ones. They had sat on the step, at times half-heartedly kicking a ball around, frequently glancing at the door until they were told they could come back inside.

Each time, there had been a new baby. To young Danny, they had seemed magical creatures. He could never have imagined such a tiny person, so perfect in every way. In wonder, he had touched the tiny starfish fingers, thrilling when they had gripped his larger one and gazing in awe at the minute, perfect fingernails. And he had loved each baby on sight.

He had been a good brother he hoped, playing with them, taking them for walks, caring for them when his mother was tired, and often protecting them from bullies. In a way, he realised now, he missed them more than he did his parents, And he hoped that they were not missing him as badly and sadly as he missed them. He supposed that was probably what had brought Alice to his attention the first time he had seen her. She had looked to him to be not much older than his ten-year-old sister, Jennifer, and she had looked so lost and lonely. The big brother in him had reached out to her.

How he missed his little sister, he thought sadly. Maybe it *would* be nice to have a baby of his own.

'It will be alright,' he said thoughtfully, 'I'll look after you both.'

Alice worried her lower lip with her teeth. 'But what will happen after we get to Port Jackson? Maggie says you will have to leave when the ship sails again.'

Danny frowned and shrugged one shoulder dismissively. 'I'll tell the captain I need to stay with you and I'm sure he will release me. He is a fair man.'

Alice still looked worried and tearful. 'But Maggie said ...'

Danny put a finger over her lips. 'What does Maggie know,' he asked crossly. 'I know she's a good friend, but maybe you shouldn't pay too much attention to everything she says. I'm sure the captain will allow me to stay behind with you. But if he does not, I shall just have to hide until the ship has sailed.

Alice nodded, wanting to believe him but not wholly convinced. If he did try to hide, would not the captain send out a search party to find him? Then he would probably be given the cat! However, she did have to admit that she felt much happier now. She trusted Danny and convinced herself that he would work something out with the captain. The world didn't seem quite such a black place now she had broken her news to Danny and he had taken it so well.

'Oh Maggie,' Alice said excitedly. 'Danny was really happy about the baby. He says he loves babies and misses all his little brothers and sisters, so he will be very happy to have one of his own.'

Maggie sighed and pursed her lips. Shaking her head slightly she muttered, 'Oh dear.'

Puzzled, Alice frowned at her. 'Why do you say that?' she asked. 'I thought you would be pleased.'

'It pleases me that he is not unhappy about the babe. But it worries me, for both your sakes that he will not be here to be a father to it after we reach Port Jackson. How badly is it going to break his heart when he has to sail away and leave you both, I wonder.'

Alice laughed and nodded her head enthusiastically. 'But Danny *will* be here to be a father. He will be with us. He says Captain Aitken is a fair man and he is sure he will allow him to remain behind when the ship sails. And he says that if the captain says *no*, then he will just hide until the ship has sailed.'

Maggie looked around quickly and put a finger to her lips. 'Don't say things like that,' she hissed. 'Sound carries at sea and you never know who might be listening.'

Alice glanced around and was relieved to see there was no one close by apart from Lily and Sarah, whom she knew she could trust.

Maggie turned to lean on the rail, looking first at the sea, then raising her eyes to watch a fluffy white cloud, like a playful lamb, that broke the otherwise unblemished blue sky, as it scudded toward the horizon. Dropping her eyes to the deck, she worried it with her toe.

What to do now, she wondered? James had told her that to keep down costs, ships sailed with the absolute minimum of crew required. the illness or death of even one man could cause extreme hardship for the rest of the crew. Knowing that, it seemed very unlikely to her that Captain Aitken would allow Danny to stay with Alice. Should she tell the child this? And would it do any good if she did? Might it cause ill-feeling between Alice and Maggie, just when the girl would most need her support?

Maggie had never seen Alice so happy. For goodness sake, the child was even excited by the prospect of having a baby! Would it be fair of her to destroy that happiness by laying down the frightening bare facts? Deciding it would be best to leave Alice with her dreams, she hugged her and told her how lovely it was that Danny, even at his young age, was keen to take on the responsibility of fatherhood.

Let the girl be happy throughout the voyage, she thought. It would be time enough when they reached Port Jackson and the axe fell. She could see no point in Alice having to live in fear throughout her pregnancy and the long sea journey. Leave her to her happiness, she decided, and Maggie would be there to pick up the pieces when the time came.

This decided, she drew Alice to her and folded her in a hug. 'If you're happy then so am I,' she reassured her. Luckily the girl could not see the worried expression on her face. They would work it out if and when Danny was forced to leave.

Lily opened her mouth and was about to speak, but Maggie widened her eyes and gave a tiny shake of her head, so she said nothing. Raising her eyebrows and shaking her head sadly she leaned on the rail and gazed at the water. What, she wondered, would become of that poor little girl? Well, they must all be sure to give her all the help she needed when things went wrong — as they almost certainly would.

Was the sea getting rougher, she wondered. Until now, to her relief, they had sailed on calm seas. Now, she fancied the waves seemed higher and the troughs deeper. 'I do hope there is not a storm coming,' she said quietly. 'Duncan said we might be running into a storm. He said there are often storms along this area of the coast.'

Maggie nodded. 'Aye, James said the same. 'We must just hope it doesn't happen, but if it does we have no choice but to put up with it.'

Alice clung to Danny in terror. One hand desperately gripped the bunk and the other clutched at Danny, her fingernails digging into his flesh.

Danny winced, grumbled gently, and moved to loosen her grip.

The *Lady Juliana* tossed around like a twig in a whirlpool. One moment the bow was high in the air, fighting valiantly to scramble out of a trough. In the next, it was slanted downward as the ship fell into the next black hole in the churning water. At the same time, it rolled violently from side to side, roiling and heaving in an angry sea.

The crew had rushed to reef the sails when the storm had struck. Alice had sat, terrified, lest Danny should lose his grip and be swept overboard. She could hear Captain Aitken's bullhorn, but could not make out what he was saying.

The klaxon sounded, calling all hands on deck and Danny moved quickly to respond. as he struggled to disentangle himself from both Alice and the bunk. She clung to him ever more tightly.

'Don't leave me,' she pleaded fearfully.

'I have to,' he said quietly. 'The captain needs us all on deck. I'll be back as soon as I can.' Giving her a quick kiss on the cheek, he gently pulled himself free and hurried away.

'Be careful. Don't get swept overboard,' she called after him.

All around her in the forecastle, Alice could hear the sounds of men grumbling as they stumbled from their bunks, and women screaming and pleading with them not to leave. But leave they did — as they must.

To Alice's ears, it sounded as if the ship was grumbling and screaming also. She had never heard such a frightening noise. There was such a squealing and creaking all around that she was sure the *Lady Juliana* was being torn apart by the merciless sea.

The bunk, it seemed to Alice, would be sloping towards one

side of the ship, then with one sharp movement it's would be to the other side. As the bow of the ship topped a wave and plunged down into the trough the fixture holding the bunk snapped like a whip crack. Alice would momentarily hang in mid-air, then would crash down onto the bunk. Hanging on in fear, she felt certain the bunk would break free and she'd be thrown to the deck at any moment.

Above her head, the lantern swung and leapt around wildly, like some mad Dervishes' dance.

As the night wore on, the fury of the storm increased. More and more frequently massive volumes of water crashed against walls of the forecastle. Each time the *Lady Juliana* seemed to falter and shudder as though she had been hit some terrible blow.

Alice clung in terror to her pitching, jerking bunk and felt more ill than she ever had her life.

This was the night her life was going to end. She knew it without a doubt. Tonight she was going to die! Her bladder desperately needed to be emptied, but she knew it was impossible to go to the heads, which was no more than an open platform with holes cut in it and lashed to the aftermost section of the bowsprit. This was the means by which the sailors and women relieved themselves directly into the sea below, rinsing themselves off afterwards from a bucket of seawater. Alice shuddered at the mere thought of it. She had never felt comfortable going there at the best of times, but in this terrible storm, it was not safe even to leave the bunk and squat on the deck. Her only consolation, lying on the bunk as her emptying bladder brought relief from her pain, was that all the other women would be in the same miserable condition.

When it had become clear that a storm was imminent, the hens and animals had been brought from the deck for safety. Some were in the forecastle, tethered to the bunk posts. Unable

163

to keep their feet on the relentlessly tossing deck they slithered backwards and forwards on their sides squealing and bleating in pain and terror.

Cages of poultry slipped and tumbled ceaselessly with every lurch and leap of the ship. The noise of the animals, added to the relentless din of the wind and the seas, made Alice feel as if her head was going to burst right open.

Well, Alice thought, *the mess the poor animals will be making makes my few cups full of pee seem like nothing!*

The Storm continued through the night And Alice lay in fear and misery, wondering whether she would ever see Danny again and worrying in case he might have been swept overboard.

She found herself thinking about the women in the orlop and was concerned about how they were faring. Most of the goats and sheep and a lot of the cages of poultry had been taken down there.

It must surely he very wet down there too? With the weight of water that had been landing on the deck for hours, almost certainly much of it must have found its way to the lower deck. Would all the women and animals down there drown? Had they already?

How wonderful it was that Danny had taken her as his wife. But for that, she would almost certainly be down in that hell hole with its the hatch screwed down above her. The thought of it made her shudder.

It felt like a whole lifetime of terror that Alice lay clinging to the bunk, but it was probably closer to twenty hours. The wild tossing and heaving gradually decreased until the *Lady Juliana* was merely riding atop a restless swell.

When the ship was behaving less boisterously, Alice dared to climb down to the deck. The boards were slick and treacherous underfoot with all the animal and human excrescences.

Clinging tightly to both wall and bunk, she surveyed the cabin through frightened eyes.

Many of the animals lay writhing on the floor, many squealing in pain with obviously broken limbs. Some, Alice was certain, were dead.

Quite a few of the other women had also dared to leave their bunks and, like Alice, now stood clinging to anything they could reach to keep their footing on the slippery rolling deck.

Alice could feel her wet skirt sticking coldly to her legs and felt a wave of embarrassment sweep over her. Looking around she felt a little better when she could see the other woman were in the same sorry state.

Maggie headed towards her holding grimly to anything she could manage to get a grip on. Reaching Alice, she put her arms around her. 'Are you alright my lovely,' She asked quietly.

Alice nodded and whispered, 'Aye.' Dropping her eyes she added quietly, 'But I couldn't go to the heads when that storm was on an' now I'm in the most awful mess.'

Maggie gave a great shout of laughter. 'Do you think any of us did? Anyone fool enough to go and sit over that hole, with nothing below them but the raging sea, would surely have been swept away. Even the men would not have gone to the heads in that storm. If a bit of a mess is all you have suffered, you don't have a worry. When the sea has calmed a bit more we can change our clothes and wash the soiled ones.'

When calm at last descended and the orlop hatch opened, the women who stumbled gratefully out onto the deck were a sorry looking sight. None had been able to stay on the shelves that passed as beds, so had endured the storm sliding Around the deck in an ever-increasing slimy mess deposited by both terrified women and animals.

Captain Aitken immediately ordered that the ship be thoroughly scrubbed from stem to stern. The women were quickly supplied with mops and holystones and put to work.

Thankful to be clean and dry again Alice had even been happy to scrub herself with the terrible, stinking carbolic soap that she usually hated.

Now she happily settled to the task of scrubbing and holystoning the deck. Busy in the forecastle she became aware of a commotion out on the main deck. She and a few of the other women gathered by the door to watch the goings-on.

Mavis Crow, the most troublesome and abusive of the women was sneering and trying to provoke one of the sailors. Alice was not surprised, she had so often watched and listened as Mavis infuriated the men with her foul language and insinuations.

'I bet Your mother can't tell you who your father is,' She taunted.

The sailor ignored her, turned his back, and carried on with his work.

Mavis scowled and walked round in front of him. Planting a heavy foot on the rope he was trying to coil she continued, 'Well, whoever he was he must have been a better man than you.' Her lip curled as she looked him up and down.

The man jerked the rope out from under her foot, stood up, and turned to walk away.

Mavis glared after him, her face a mask of fury. 'Skinny little weasel like you Wouldn't be able to get it up enough to put any woman with child,' she shouted after him.

One of her gang members sniggered and Mavis gave her a look that would have shrivelled a less hardened woman in an instant. 'He's gonna regret that! No one walks away from me,' she snarled.

Moving to the next nearest sailor Mavis hurled off a long string of curses and abusive language then waited for the man's reaction.

This man also behaved as if he had not heard her.

This happened several times more, and Mavis became more furious every time. She tried it on one of the officers, her language more foul than ever, But he merely nodded to her, smiled and kept on walking.

Alice watched all this with great curiosity. Usually, when Mavis started her ranting, the men would react angrily. It was only her gang of rough, vicious women who stood behind her, that stopped the sailors punishing her nastiness.

Maggie stood beside Alice, as curious as she. 'What do you suppose is happening there? There's something strange going on.'

Alice nodded her head in agreement, then shook it and shrugged. 'I dunno,' was all she could think of to say.

Not prepared to be ignored any longer and burning with fury, Mavis stormed up onto the quarter deck, still shouting obscenities.

The watching women gasped. This was an act that any of the sailors would be flogged for. So what, they wondered, would be Mavis' punishment. As one, they all prayed that the evil woman would be given twice as many lashes of the cat's tail.

Maggie grabbed James' arm as he hurried past. 'What's happening wi' Mavis? The sailors are just acting as if they don't hear her.'

James smiled and tapped a forefinger to the side of his nose. 'You'll find out in a minute. I'll tell you later what's been going on, but I've a job to do right now.' He hurried away to where Thomas Edgar, the master and government agent had been standing, grimly watching Mavis' antics.

After a moment's conversation, the two men approached Mavis and each grabbed an arm. Half marching half dragging, they hauled her to where a barrel stood on the deck.

As a seaman lifted the barrel, Alice noticed it had a hole cut in the top and another at either side.

All the women stood on the deck, and with the exception of Mavis' gang, they all smiled as they waited expectantly.

James and Thomas Edgar lifted the barrel over Mavis and lowered it, forcing her arms out through the holes in the sides and dropping it until her head appeared through the top.

Thomas surveyed her and nodded and rubbed his hands with satisfaction. 'There, that should keep you out of mischief for a while,' he said finally.

Not wanting to lose face in front of her gang, Mavis cavorted and danced around the quarterdeck. She strutted cockily while the women watched from the main deck below.

The men roared with laughter and jeered, delighted to see her being made such a fool of. The women, on the other hand, were afraid to show their amusement, for fear that if they did Mavis would get her revenge in the not too distant future.

It did not take long before the heavy wooden barrel, resting on her shoulders became severely painful. Mavis tried to figure out a way of sitting, but could not. Instead, she tried squatting, so that the bottom of the barrel was resting on the deck. This didn't last long because her fat legs were squeezed so tightly that her knees and ankles quickly cramped.

Standing again, with the help of some of her gang members, she pleaded with Thomas and James to release her. This they agreed to do if she promised to stop her bullying; stop swearing at and tormenting the men and, also, to stop being the last one up on deck to start work in the morning and first to go down the ladder into the orlop at night.

This she eagerly agreed to, and the promise having been made, the barrel was lifted off her.

The watching women quickly departed to resume their work, not wanting to be Mavis' first encounter.

When James' watch ended Maggie collared him before he went

to his bunk.

'Me and the girls,' She glanced quickly at her three friends, 'was wondering why the men all acted as if they didn't hear the dreadful things Mavis was saying to them.'

James gave a loud gust of laughter. 'Well, it's like this you see. 'I was doing a stock check in the forward hold, which is right next to where the women are bedded in the orlop. I found that one hawkshead of port held nothing but empty bottles. Another hawkshead proved to be half empty, with the empty bottles pushed to the back and full ones placed in front of them. When I pulled it out I found a hole in the bulkhead dividing the hold from the women's quarters. I realised straight away then why Mavis and her cronies were all was so keen to be locked in the orlop as punishment. While there they had been having drinking parties, which explains their strange behaviour once they were released.'

'Well, I never!' was all Maggie could think of to say before all four women dissolved into a fit of the giggles.

'Anyway,' James continued, 'I put everything back where it was, so they wouldn't know I had found it, then I went and told Thomas Edgar.

'What did Mr Edgar say?' Alice asked, a bit bemused.

'He came up with this idea of the barrel. He reckoned that would be a better punishment than putting her where she could fill herself up with port. Told me to tell the sailors not to react when she started her nastiness and instructed me to be ready with the barrel. Do you think that will have taught her a good enough lesson?'

Maggie pursed her lips. 'Maybe for a little while, but my guess is that she is just so truly nasty that the lesson will not last very long.'

It took less than a week for Mavis to prove Maggie correct. Determined that anyone who had taken pleasure from her barreling would pay a high price, her bullying became more brutal than ever before.

Alice sat In a patch of shade on the deck when she had finished her work and gazed happily up at the beautiful cerulean sky. To her, it was the perfect day. There was not a single cloud to blemish the heavens. The heat had been a bit uncomfortable while she had been working, but she was not about to complain. For so much of her life, she had been cold it was unbelievably pleasant to be warm all the time.

Slowly her eyes started to close. Leaning back against the wall, she allowed her head to droop and within moments she was quite soundly asleep.

Suddenly she was grabbed by the hair, hauled to her feet, then thrown across the deck. Unable to save herself she slid across the deck, landing hard up against the rail. Before she had time to gather her senses her assailant was upon her. Held down by her hair and unable to defend herself, she felt blows raining on her face and a foot kicking at her lower body. Instinctively she curled into a tight ball to protect her baby. Still, the blows to her head continued, but the kicking foot contacted only her back and buttocks.

Just as she felt consciousness slipping away, she heard shouting and the blows suddenly ceased.

Arms were around her, trying to hug her, but instinctively she stayed curled up, with one arm up to protect her head the other clutched to her belly.

'It's me, love,' she heard and with relief recognised Maggie's voice.

Slowly she relaxed and allowed Maggie to pull her from the

deck and into her arms. Somewhere, but at a distance, she could hear a woman screeching obscenities as she was dragged away.

A man's voice now — and she realised Surgeon Alley was with her. Very gently he took her from Maggie's arms and carefully laid her on the deck.

'I need you to tell me if you have pain anywhere, Alice.'

Alice nodded. 'Everywhere hurts,' she sobbed.

Surgeon Alley smiled sadly. 'Everywhere is bruised, but I mean any more severe pain than just bruising.'

'Just bruising?' Maggie growled. 'Isn't that bad enough?'

The surgeon scowled at her. 'Please, will you just keep quiet. I need to examine her. I know you're a good friend to her, but she has more need of me at this moment.'

Maggie lowered her head and looked sheepish. 'Sorry.'

Finishing his examination, Richard Alley was fairly sure there were no bones broken. However, he was concerned that there may have been damage done by the blow to her head. His main worry though was for the unborn baby Alice carried. Picking her up very gently he carried her in his arms to the hospital.

Once there, he gave her a good dose of laudanum in the hope that it would lessen her shock and reduce the risk of her miscarrying. He allowed her no visitors for the rest of the day as he wished her to sleep for as long as possible.

In the morning she seemed well rested and recovered from her ordeal so Richard allowed Danny to visit before his watch started.

'Why did she do it?' he asked, concern etched in every line of his face.

Alice shook her head and shrugged. 'I don't know,' she sobbed. 'I had fallen asleep on the deck and was awakened when she's lifted me up by my hair, threw me down, and started hitting me. I couldn't get up and I thought I was going to die. I thought she was going to kill my — our baby.'

Danny put his arms around her and she clung to him weeping uncontrollably.

'Hush now,' he said quietly. 'It's over now and the surgeon says you are alright and our baby is still safely inside you. Don't cry.'

Richard Alley poked his head around the door, smiling to himself. 'Let her cry,' he told Danny. 'That will probably be the best medicine for her.'

Danny nodded, tightened his arms around her and kissed the top of her head. 'She won't do it again,' He told her grimly. 'The evil bitch won't ever hurt you again.'

Alice lifted her head to look questioningly up at him. 'Who was it? Who attacked me? I didn't see who was doing it!'

'Mavis Crow, it was. But she paid the price. I don't think she will ever dare to do anything like that to anyone again.'

'Why, what happened to her?'

The captain and Mr Edgar said that as she refused to take a warning then she was to be punished like any of the sailors who disobeyed. So she was bound with her arms and legs splayed and given twelve lashes with the cat o' nine tails. She will neither sit down nor lie on her back for quite some time an' the captain told her that if she's goin' to swear like a man, and continue her bullying ways, she will receive the same punishment as a man every time she causes trouble or uses foul language. Only, Captain says, the number of lashes will increase every time.'

Despite what she had been through Alice started to giggle, so Danny was able to start his watch knowing she was well on the road to recovery.

CHAPTER 13

The *Lady Juliana* sailed on Southward and as she did the weather grew warmer.

Just over two weeks out from Plymouth, and with Alice quickly recovering from her beating, islands started appearing to starboard. When asked, James explained that these were known as The Canary Archipelago. The winds started to increase and became quite fierce at times, which made the women fearful of another storm like the one they had already experienced.

'Won't come to nothing much,' James assured Maggie and her three friends. 'It always gets a bit gusty around these parts. We'll be stopping soon to replenish our stores.'

Under full sail, the *Lady Juliana* cut speedily through the waves. A ripple of excitement ran through convicts when they saw they were coming closer to a large island. Peering into the distance they could see a harbour with a large assortment of vessels.

'James told me this place was called Santa Cruz de Tenerife.' Maggie enjoyed airing her newly found knowledge to anyone who would listen. 'We're going to dock here for a while 'cos they have to get more food an' water an' animals to keep us going on the next part of our voyage.'

'Oh thank goodness,' Alice said feelingly. 'It will be so nice to walk on ground that doesn't move under your feet all the time.'

Maggie laughed. 'Oh, I don't know about that,' she said,

shaking her head. 'I don't suppose they're likely to let us off the ship in case we run off.'

'What would be the point in running off?' Sarah asked. 'Where could you run to on an island?'

Maggie shrugged. How would she know? 'I suppose you could hide until the ship had sailed,' she suggested. 'There's a lot of us who could easily earn a living here.'

Alice frowned questioningly and Maggie laughed. 'If you don't know, I won't explain it.'

Captain Aitken stood on the forecastle with his speaking trumpet, briefly surveying the women on the deck below him. Then raising the horn to his face he bellowed, 'I want all you women in your quarters right away'.

A murmur of grumbling rippled through the women on the deck.

'It's too bleeding hot down there,' one of the women shouted, and many of the others nodded their heads and mumbled in agreement.

Mavis stared defiantly up at him. Hands on hips, she shouted, 'What have we got to go down there for? Us likes being on deck in this nice warm weather.'

Captain Aitken glared down at her. 'You will go below because I said you have to! I have to have the decks cleared of prisoners. There will be no more argument.'

Mavis stood her ground, her head poked forward aggressively and her lips clamped tightly together.

Captain Aitken stared her down for a long moment, then he smiled. 'Do you really wish to meet the cat again?' he asked.

For a brief moment Mavis maintained her stance, then she dropped her eyes and turned away.

The captain nodded to a group of crewmen who were standing

at the ready. Without hesitation, the men moved in on the women herding them, in some cases dragging them, and pushing them down the ladder. The hatch was battened down behind them

Alice felt her stomach turn at the mere thought of being locked down below on a day as hot as this. She knew that both the heat and the stench would be unbearable and thanked God yet again for allowing Danny to take her as his wife.

James tipped Maggie a nod and she led the *wives*, without argument, to their berths in the forecastle.

Alice and her three friends settled themselves on the floor, prepared to chat quietly until they were allowed out on deck again.

Listening to the noises from the deck that had now become quite familiar to them, they could tell that the sails were being reduced. They heard the terrific sharp crack of the canvassing; the scream of the rigging as the mainsails came down. The *Lady Juliana* responded quickly and straight away the women could feel the difference in her behaviour.

Suddenly the air resounded with an enormous boom, which seemed to echo around the forecastle.

The few babies who had accompanied their mothers on the voyage started screaming. Women jumped to their feet in terror as a third boom rent the air, and many of them rushed to the door of the forecastle.

James and another crewman stood outside the door and prevented the women leaving.

'What's happening?' Maggie asked fearfully. 'Are those cannons? Why are they firing at us?'

James shook his head and laughed. 'Don't be frightened,' he said. 'They always fire an eleven gun salute when a ship comes into the bay.'

'Well, you might have warned us,' Maggie grumbled. 'It near scared the living daylights out of us. Half of us have peed our pants.'

175

James laughed again. 'Sorry. I didn't think of it. You'd best all go and sit down again until we've docked and the captain says you can come out.'

The sounds of the waves against the hull quietened as the ship moved into the protection of the headland, and calmer waters.

The listening women in the forecastle heard the rattle and screech of the anchor cable. The ship drifted for a few moments then came to a gentle halt, held securely by the massive forward anchor. There was a sudden total silence while the woman looked at each other, each waiting expectantly for the next sounds to come.

Eventually, they heard Captain Aitken bellow through his horn to the crew to release the prisoners from the hold. As one, the women in the forecastle stood and headed for the door.

Spilling out onto the deck they rushed to the rail, eager for the first glimpse of a foreign shore.

'I don't know what I was expecting,' Maggie said, shaking her head. 'But it wasn't this.'

'The Isle of man is better than this,' Alice said quietly. 'Look how dirty that beach is.'

'Look at that castle,' Sarah added, frowning toward the distant structure. 'It's nowhere near as grand as Castle Rushen.'

Alice looked in wonder at this strange place they had arrived in. Beyond the castle, she could see mountains that were hazy in the August heat. There was a stone harbour which was full of ships which James informed them were slave ships, that had come from Africa and were bound for the Americas.

On the hill, there were fortifications and a row of huge guns. 'I suppose them guns is what gave us such a fright,' Lily said, pointing up at them.'

'I don't like the smell here,' Alice said as she looked down into the murky water. 'It's as bad as London and Plymouth.'

'That will be coming from the slave ships,' James said sadly.

'You wouldn't believe how badly those poor people are treated. And I wouldn't want to try to tell you.'

'What? Worse than we was treated in gaol?' Maggie asked, shaking her head in disbelief.

James nodded his head. 'Much worse,' he said grimly. 'Much, much worse.'

The four friends watched curiously as the captain's barque was lowered into the water.

'What's happening now,' Alice asked Danny.

'I heard tell the captain, as her majesty's representative on the ship, has to go and ask the Spanish governor for permission to land.'

Alice frowned thoughtfully. 'What will happen to us then if this governor fellow won't give his permission?'

Danny looked startled for a moment, then he gave a helpless shrug. 'I don't know. I suppose we wouldn't be able to land then.'

'Would we have to go back to England then?' Alice asked hopefully.

Before Danny could answer, James, who was just passing at that moment and heard the question, stopped beside them. He told them laughingly, 'That won't happen. It is just a formality, that he must ask. A courtesy, really, that has to be observed. Our ship docking here is worth too much revenue for them to refuse us entry.'

Captain Aitken, dressed in his best breeches, gave last-minute instructions to the mate. 'The first thing that must be done is to get all the water barrels refilled. The water we brought on board in Plymouth is pretty rancid by now, so any of them that still contain any water must be emptied.'

The mate gave a bit of a sloppy salute and nodded cheerfully. 'I'll be on to it Sir, as soon as the deck is clear.'

'Good.' Captain Aitken nodded his approval. 'Ready when you are, Master.' Turning, he raised questioning eyebrows at Thomas Edgar, who had been standing patiently behind him.

The two men crammed their tricorn hats on their heads and climbed down into the barque.

'Well, that will be them away for a feast like none of us has never known and a belly full of best brandy to go with it, no doubt. While we stay here and do all the work,' James muttered.

Many of the women and some of the crewmen lined the rails to watch the departing boat. Most of them were unaware of the curious looks they were receiving from both the shore and the other boats.

As soon as the captain's barque had pulled away, James gave an order, and the seamen set to work heaving the empty water casks up from the bowels of the ship. They rolled the empty barrels along the deck to be lowered into the waiting long boats. As usual, any woman who got in their way was unceremoniously pushed aside. This often lead to a stream of foul language and insinuations directed at their mothers, but the men studiously ignored most of it.

The water they had brought on board in Plymouth some three weeks earlier had become brackish and was unpleasant to drink. The sailors emptied each cask that still contained water and the women watched with interest as it ran along the deck, to find the scuppers and gurgle off into the sea.

The barrows were rowed to the pier to be filled with beautiful clean, clear water from the mountains beyond the town.

While keeping a watchful eye on the sailors to make sure they were not slacking, James stood talking to Alice and her three friends.

'The water here is good,' he told them, 'it comes down from a River in the mountains. Then it is carried by way of an aqueduct into the bay. It supplies Santa Cruz and also much of it is run into the storage tanks you see at the end of the pier. This they sell it to ships that dock here.'

Alice watched as another empty cask was lowered into the longboat. 'It will be lovely to have fresh water,' she said feelingly. 'The stuff we had didn't just taste foul it stank as well.'

James frowned at her. 'Well you just be careful with this new water, girl,' he warned. 'Just because it tastes good and fresh, don't any of you drink too much of it too quickly.'

Maggie snorted. 'What harm can a drop of fresh water do?' she asked derisively.

'It can give you are terrible bellyache,' James warned. 'I've seen it many a time, and believe me, you would not enjoy it. You would likely get diarrhea and would spend days fighting the other women for a place at the heads.'

'With drinking water? Clean water?' Alice questioned.

James nodded. 'Yes — water. If you drink too much too quickly it can be bad. Especially for you Alice, being with child an' all.'

The whole of that day seemed to be taken up with the water collection. Most of the women sat in whatever shade they could find, enjoying the spectacle of the sailors struggling to hoist the heavy barrels back on deck.

When Captain Aitken returned from visiting governor Branquefort, he stood for a few moments, studying the mass of water barrels. Nodding his head as if coming to a decision he headed for the bridge.

A few moments later, he reappeared on deck with his speaking trumpet in his hand. 'We're going to be in Santa Cruz for quite some time. It is my decision, that as fresh water is plentiful here we should take advantage of it to get the salt washed out of our clothes. Once we leave here it will be quite some time before we are able to do this again. After we leave Santa Cruz the washing will all have to be done in salt water again. First thing in the morning I want all you women out here with soap and buckets of water. The crew and officers will give you all the clothes they can spare, and they must be washed as well as all your own clothes.'

'I'm not washing clothes for any sailor,' Mavis spoke from just behind Alice.

Realising suddenly just how close Mavis was, Alice moved rapidly out of reach.

Thomas Edgar, who had been standing just behind Mavis, shot out a beefy hand and grabbed the back of her dress, and a good lump of her hair to go with it. 'You'll bloody do what the captain tells you,' he snarled. 'I'll bring you my shirts and trousers first thing in the morning — and just be sure you do no damage to them or you will go before the cat again.'

As he stormed away, Mavis glared at his retreating back with a venomous look of sheer hatred.

Maggie, who had been watching this exchange with sheer glee up to now, shuddered when she saw the look. 'God,' she whispered, 'I wouldn't like to be in his shoes if he ever bumps into her on a dark night!'

The following morning the convicts were given orders to forgo all their normal cleaning work and to spend the day, instead, scrubbing every piece of clothing that could be found.

It was with great relief that the sailors brought out all their clothing and piled it on the deck.

While they were at sea there was not a drop of fresh water to be spared, so all dirty clothing had, through necessity, to be washed in salt water. Though this made the women's skirts stiff and itchy, this was little compared with the discomfort the officers suffered. Their britches fitted tightly around the crotch, their shirts snug around the collar and underarms, which caused them rashes and boils. The ordinary seamen fared better, for their trousers and shirts were much looser to allow for their constant activity.

Carefully supervised fires were lit on the deck and huge caldrons of water brought to the boil.

The only way to get the mountains of clothes clean was by boiling and beating. The women stood around the caldrons in groups, taking turns at stirring the clothes with a stout piece of wood. Then they would be fished out and when cool enough one of the group would get hold of the item and spend several minutes beating it against the deck.

The deck ran like a river of mucky water as it was thrashed out of the clothes. When the water in a cauldron became too dirty, a shout went up and women scattered as one of the sailors tipped the huge vessel on its side. Like a steaming tidal wave, the water would gush across the deck to gurgle out through the scuppers and add yet more pollution to the water of the harbour.

When the men's clothes were done and spread over every available space around the ship, the women started on their own washing. Stripping off as many layers of clothing as possible, but retaining the minimum amount for decency, they then set about cleaning their clothes. When all was done and everything spread to dry, they looked around at the strangely adorned ship, nodding with satisfaction.

Once the men's clothes were washed and drying, the women were able to relax a bit. They found it wonderful to have their hands and arms in water that was not full of salt and irritating to their skins. The ship came alive to the sound of their squeals and giggles as they splashed water and chased each other around the deck swinging dripping wet clothes at each other.

On the shore and the many ships in the harbour, men stopped work, to watch in puzzled amazement, the frivolity on the ship. While most of them enjoyed the sight of a shipload of women, some of them quite shapely, prancing around the deck semi-naked, they scratched their heads in bewilderment.

Who are these women, they asked each other? *Where have they come from? And to where are they going?* No one in the harbour of Santa Cruz had seen the likes before, and probably never would again.

It did not take long for word to spread that it was a shipload of whores bound for some new country around the other side of the world.

Everything the women could find had been boiled and beaten until it was spotless. Even the mattresses, to the relief of the *wives* who had been sharing them, not only with their *husbands* but also with quite a wide variety of livestock.

While all this was going on sailors rowed backward and forward to the pier, refilling the water casks the women had emptied.

Alice was thankful that James had warned them against drinking too much of the fresh water too quickly, for many of the women, suffering bouts of diarrhoea, had to repeatedly rush to the heads for relief. As the day wore on their deposits into the calm bay, combined with those from the slave ship quickly polluted the water around the *Lady Juliana*.

During the three weeks at sea, the convict women had become used to the fresh air and Alice now frequently found her stomach heaving with the now unaccustomed stench.

'I thought we had left all this behind us when we sailed from Plymouth,' she grumbled. 'I do hope we won't be here too long.'

Maggie nodded her agreement. 'Maybe James would have a word with surgeon Alley. 'If *he* will speak to the captain perhaps he will allow us to leave the ship and go inland a ways to get away from the smell.'

Alice perked up immediately. 'Oh do you think he will?' she asked eagerly.

Maggie shrugged. 'I dunno, but it's worth asking. If we don't, we have no chance. I'll ask James what he thinks.'

When asked, James drew his fingers across his mouth. he shook his head doubtfully. 'I shouldn't think so love,' he said. 'Half the women would never come back if they were allowed off the ship.'

Maggie nodded understandingly. 'I thought maybe you could ask — for Alice. I think surgeon Alley is a bit concerned about her. Maybe if you explain to him that the smell is making her sick, he might put a word in the captain's ear.'

James shrugged and dragged in a deep breath, 'I'll certainly ask, but don't you be getting too hopeful, because I'm fairly sure the answer will be *no*.

Surgeon Alley shook his head decisively. 'No I'm sorry James, but there is no chance at all of the captain agreeing to that. He has given permission for the officers to spend nights ashore when it is their spell off duty. It is also possible he might allow their *wives* to spend nights with them there.'

James shuffled his feet and studied the deck for a few moments. He sighed. It was the answer he had expected, but he didn't like letting Maggie down. Or Alice, for that matter. He had become rather fond of the child.

'Well Sir, it's just that Maggie is worried about her. The smell from the heads and the convict ships is making her ill. She really needs to be off the ship and inland from the Harbour if possible. Even if it is only for a few hours during the day.'

Surgeon Richard Alley shook his head again and pursed his

lips. 'I understand, James. Really I do, but she is not the only pregnant woman on the ship. If we were to let the women go ashore there would have to be a crewman to keep an eye on each one. And we just do not have enough men to do that.'

James scratched his head and look thoughtfully into the distance. 'Could Danny maybe take Alice ashore? He could do it during a time he is not on watch. He would make sure she didn't flee.'

The surgeon shook his head again. 'I know Alice would not run away, but we cannot make exceptions for one of the women.'

James opened his mouth to speak again, but surgeon Alley held up a hand to silence him. 'Can't you see that if Alice was allowed the privilege then the other women would demand that they be given the same rights. Then if we did not give in to them we could well have a mutiny on our hands.'

James sighed and nodded. 'Aye Sir. I do understand, but I just feel so sorry for the little girl. I have a daughter about the same age as Alice and it would pain me to think that she could ever be in the same situation. I just wanted to try an' make things easier for the lass.'

Richard Alley smiled sadly, laid his hands on James' shoulder, and gave it a friendly squeeze. 'I know, James. I would love to help her too, but it just is not possible. Even the sailors who go ashore will have to have an officer with them to prevent them from getting into fights. If it's any consolation, a man named Watkin Tench, a lieutenant who sailed with the first fleet, said that there is *little to please a traveler in Tenerife,* So she won't be missing much by staying on board. I will have a word with Thomas Edgar, the government agent, and ask him to speak to the captain. Don't get your hopes up though, because I'm pretty sure the captain will not agree.'

'Well thank you anyway, Sir,' James said sadly as he turned away, 'but I don't really think that will be any consolation at all,'

Now he would have to go and break the news to Maggie! He just hoped he would not be refused his husband's rights tonight because of his failure with the surgeon.

Alice tried not to breathe too deeply as she stood on the deck gazing over to the rather strange and exotic looking township that was Santa Cruz. How she would have loved to get off this stinking ship, if only for one hour. So much looked to be happening in the town. People hustled and bustled around, sometimes giving a shove if someone did not get out of their way quickly enough. Men carried wooden crates that Alice presumed must hold fish or perhaps fruit.

In the distance, she could hear bells — church bells — and more than one set by the sound of things. They seemed to ring constantly throughout all the hours of daylight.

The waters of the harbour were a constant hive of activity. Alice enjoyed passing the hours watching a myriad of small boats shuffling backward and forwards between all the ships.

She watched enviously whenever the officer's *wives* climbed down into the longboat and were rowed ashore.

'I'd give anything to be going with them,' she told her friends, sighing heartily.

Maggie put a comforting arm around her shoulder. 'I know, love. James did his best, I'm sure, to persuade the officers, but they would not be swayed.'

Alice nodded mutely and turned her attention once more to the view across the bay. Away in the distance, a long way away she thought, she could see a mountain. She puzzled over it for a while because it appeared to be capped with snow. How could that be, she wondered, for on the ship it was almost unbearably hot. In the Isle of Man, there was only snow in very cold weather. She did not have the knowledge to realise that this mountain, Pico de Teide, on Tenerife was far higher than any she had ever seen before and had a cap of snow on it for most of the year.

In the forecastle at night, the women who had been allowed ashore were full of excitement at the wonders they had seen in this strange foreign town.

'They all talk in a funny language and I couldn't understand a single thing they were saying', one woman complained.

'Nor could I,' another agreed. 'And they flap their hands around and shout all the time. The buildings are so strange too, not at all like the ones in London.

'There are beggars everywhere too,' another of the women joined in. 'They sit on the ground. holding their grubby hands out and pester you for money. As if I have any money to give them. And I wouldn't if I had!' she finished with a snort.

'The people are all brown, and there are bright-coloured flowering trees in the street. the women are all dressed in black, with scarves around their heads so that you wouldn't know whether they have any hair,' the first woman continued with her story. 'Everywhere you go there are holes in the walls of buildings with little statues in them. An' there was a huge brightly coloured statue of a woman, what my *husband* told me was a statue of the Virgin Mary.'

'Who?'

The first speaker shrugged. 'Buggered if I know, but it must be something to do with the church because there were a lot of priests and nuns wandering around, and every time they passed this statue they crossed themselves.'

'Well, I saw this fancy looking building. George told me it was the Governor's palace, but I think he was wrong. I've seen Buckingham Palace, you know, where the King lives, an' this place what they said the governor calls a palace is only like a big fancy house. It's not a *real* Palace like our King's.'

Within days of the *Lady Juliana* arriving at Santa Cruz word had got around, both in the town and on the other ships, that there was, in the harbour, a ship full of prostitutes from London. Soon, every able-bodied man in Santa Cruz, it seemed, was set on finding his way out to the ship for his share of the goods.

In the most part, the word was being spread by the sailors from the *Lady Juliana*, who were not averse to lining their pockets by doing a bit of pimping.

Bemused by it all, Alice watched boats roll out from the shore carrying townsmen. Added to this there was a constant stream of small boats arriving from the other ships.

Women crowded around, waiting to grab a man as soon as he climbed over the rail. Then as soon as she had ensured he had sufficient money the pair would quickly disappear to either the orlop or the forecastle.

Shortly afterward the couple would reappear. The customer would pay the sailor who had pimped, climb over the rail, and be gone.

The woman would rejoin the crowd at the rail awaiting her next chance at some income.

'Are they really selling themselves? Being bedded by these men? Alice asked in wonder.

Maggie laughed and nodded. 'Of course, they are. They want to have some money before they get to this new country and selling their bodies is an easy way to do it.'

'Easy?' Sarah questioned. 'To lie under some sweaty, smelly stranger while he does *that* to you. Do you *really* call that easy?'

'It's easier than an awful lot of the work I've had to put my back into,' Maggie said with a grimace. 'It only takes a few minutes, and on this ship, it will be safer than in a city.'

'I don't see how,' Lily joined in. 'Once they've got you on your back, they can do anything they want, I reckon.'

Maggie shook her head. 'They can when they have you in a back alley. Some of them have ropes and belts and whips and can't get the pleasure from fornication unless they are causing you pain.'

'They can just as easily do that here, can they not?' Alice asked doubtfully.

Maggie shook her head. 'No, because if they tried to do anything evil to you here, you would only have to scream and the sailors would save you. In the city, you can scream as loud as you like and no one will help you.'

'I still wouldn't want to,' Alice said adamantly. 'I don't ever want to do that with anyone else but Danny.'

Maggie gave her a sideways glance and rolled her eyes. 'Well, let's just hope you never need to,' she said quietly.

Sarah shook her head as she watched an officer from one of the other ships lay his arm across the shoulders of one of the younger, prettier girls and slip his hand inside her bodice.

The girl giggled and the pair quickly disappeared into the forecastle.

'I'm surprised the captain allows it,' Sarah said angrily. 'They are so blatant about it that he can't help but see what is going on on his ship.'

Maggie smiled. 'Well, of course, he sees it, but part of his job is to make sure the crew stay happy, an' they won't be happy If the captain won't allow them a bit of slap and tickle and the chance to earn an extra few pounds. James says it's always the same in every port they go into, the crew always go onshore and find themselves a prostitute. It's what happens at sea. They are away from home so much of the time they need their comforts. That's the way men are. No doubt Captain Aitken will always have his share too.'

'But he's got a *wife* on the ship,' Alice said, puzzled.

'Aye. An' a proper one at home,' Maggie agreed. 'But you can bet on it that many of the men on board who have taken *wives* on board are sneaking down to the orlop for a bit extra some nights!'

Alice and her two young friends looked at each other in dismay. 'Well Danny wouldn't,' she said adamantly.

'Probably not, because he's too young an' innocent,' Maggie agreed. 'But you put most men on a ship half-filled with over two hundred women an' most of them will make the most of it.'

'Do you think James does?' Lily asked.

Maggie shrugged. 'Probably. I don't ask. Anyhow, while we're here and all these men coming on board with bulging pockets, I might make some money myself.'

'You don't mean — ?' Alice started.

Maggie nodded. 'I do mean.'

Alice looked aghast and threw a startled look at her other two friends. ?'

Shaking her head, Maggie laughed. 'If you could just see the looks on all your faces. How do you all think I have got the money to feed my three children all these years? How do you think I even came to have the children. And why do you think I was convicted and put on this ship?'

Alice shook her head in disbelief. 'But I always thought you were so — -,' she halted, trying to think of the right word.

'Nice?' Maggie finished for her. 'I'm still the same person, who would die to protect you, you know. All I do is sell the use of my body. It's *my* body, so I do no one any harm. It doesn't make me a bad person.'

'Does James know?' Sarah asked, wide-eyed.

Maggie laughed. 'Of course, he does. He's not a young innocent and to him, I'm just a comfortable bedmate until the end of the voyage. We've talked about it and he's going to find some clean-looking men for me while we're here. That way he'll make a bit of extra money too.'

Alice shook her head sadly. It was beyond her to imagine a woman doing, for money, the things she and Danny did in his bunk at night. It upset her, also, to know that James was pimping for Maggie.

In the days that followed she watched sadly as Maggie took James's choice of men to the forecastle and saw them hand over their payment to James.

So it went on during all their time in San Cruz.

Many of the men arriving to board the *Lady Juliana* were officers, rowed across from other ships in the harbour. These fellows, always arrived carrying cigars, port, or whisky for Captain Aitken and we're always warmly welcomed aboard.

Alice noticed that that several of the younger girls, who had been examined by the surgeon and declared to be free of the clap, were kept for use by only the visiting officers. Having had their share of pleasure from the chosen girl, they would then spend a pleasant while smoking and drinking with Captain Aitken. Then they would go on their merry way, to return and repeat this all a few days later.

Even while all this depravity, to Alice's eyes, was going on, she noticed there was always an officer keeping a careful eye on the comings and goings of both the convict women and the men who visited them.

There was always the danger that one of the women might sell her favours, not for money, but for a sailor on a ship returning to England, to smuggle her away from the *Lady Juliana* and hide her on his ship. It was only a small risk but had to be watched out for just the same.

CHAPTER 14

——◆——

A round the middle of September, the *Lady Juliana* finally
weighed anchor and sailed out of Santa Cruz harbour.
The women, many of them considerably richer, one
or two of them possibly with child, several with newly acquired
diseases, lined the rails and waved to the other ships and the men
who watched from the shore.

All the casks were now filled with fresh, clean water. The
animals' pens were filled again with noisy, mess-making livestock,
and the ship was fully provisioned. She had been re-christened
The Floating Brothel by the residents of Santa Cruz and the seamen and officers of all the other ships in the harbour. Her cargo
of convicts would no doubt be sadly missed in Santa Cruz.

Two ships, currently carrying baubles to exchange for slaves
when they reached African shores, followed the *Lady Juliana*
out. Since they were all heading in the same direction and ready
to sail, the captains had decided it would be sensible to sail in
convoy. A decision that pleased some of the women who had
not become *wives*, for they were still able, on many occasions, to
have visits from the crewmen on the slavers, with whom they
had formed relationships.

Maggie smiled as she watched the sailors from the slave ships rowing across on their daily vigil. They eagerly scrambled up the nets to the deck of the *Lady Juliana* and hustled the woman of their choice down to the orlop. The women, every bit as eager, squealed and giggled and pretended to swat away the men's wandering hands as they hurried down the steps.

'Well, I can't say I expected all this activity and excitement when we sailed from London. Nor would the sailors on the slavers. If the ships stay together until we reach the next port it will keep a lot of the women happier than they have been since they failed to become a *wife*,' Maggie commented laughingly.

Lily pursed her lips. 'Aye,' she muttered, 'What about the ones who haven't snared a man this time either?'

'It will probably make them even more unpleasant than they were before — if that possible. So we will all have to be a lot more careful from now on,' Maggie said grimly. Turning to Alice she added, 'just you make sure you are never alone from now on. Make sure you keep your eyes open for Mavis.'

Alice nodded and looked around fearfully. 'I will be very careful and try hard not to let her catch me alone.'

'Don't you be worrying,' Sarah told her earnestly, 'we'll all be watching out for you.'

'Anyway, she knows now that if she harms you she will be meeting with the *cat*,' Lily added. 'I don't think she will dare to hurt you again.'

Maggie looked doubtful but said nothing. The last thing she wanted was to frighten the child too much. She just wished to make her wary.

For several days the three ships sailed in close convoy down the coast of Tenerife.

When she had finished her chores Alice spent many hours each day watching the island slip past. It's verdant hills and the snow-capped Pico del Teide in the distance reminded her slightly of the Isle of man. Only slightly though, for it was a much larger island and the mountain much higher. So high, in fact, that it took several days to disappear behind the horizon.

Once it had gone there was nothing to look at except the empty ocean and the two accompanying slave ships which trailed closely behind.

Alice felt a strange sense of loneliness then. Although she had not been allowed to go ashore in Santa Cruz, there had been hustle and bustle everywhere. There had been an activity of some sort all the time; on the pier; on the dirty looking beach; on the water and the surrounding ships and most especially on the *Lady Juliana*. Now there was nothing but the restless ocean lapping and sucking at the hull of the ship. And the poor animals and hens in their cages on the deck awaiting their turn to go in the stew pot.

Well, there was one thing to be grateful for, Alice thought, they had left behind them in Santa Cruz, the stink of the effluent that flowed constantly from the Lady Juliana and the flotilla of slave ships. Anything that now went overboard from the heads was swiftly dispersed and left behind.

Alice had not missed seeing the venomous looks Mavis directed at her, so she ensured that whenever possible she was surrounded by friends. On the odd occasion she did find herself alone she made sure she had something solid at her back, a clear vision all around her and a quick escape route planned.

To all on board the *Lady Juliana*, the week that followed seemed long and slow. The ship was headed into the wind and seemed to the women not to be moving at all. she just seemed to be lifeless, wallowing gently on an oily sea. A tired old lady.

'This voyage is going to take forever,' Alice grumbled.

Lily nodded her agreement. 'We're going backwards. That's what I think.'

Maggie laughed. 'I think you'll find we are still making progress. But if we are going backwards, perhaps we will end up back in Plymouth and they won't bother trying again to send us to wherever it is.'

Sarah merely smiled and shook her head at all this nonsense.

There were a few women on board who were unperturbed by the slow progress, for the lack of movement and the calm seas made it easy for their beaus to row over more often from the slave ships. Because of this, there were fewer fights on board amongst the women and for a while, a reasonable calm reigned on the *Lady Juliana*.

A shout of 'land ahoy' from the lookout at the masthead brought a flurry of activity from everyone on deck. All eyes peered ahead into the distance. Following the direction of his pointing arm, they strained to see land — and saw nothing.

In the hours that followed, Alice kept an anxious watch. She didn't like the sea. Oh, it was alright to look at, but not to be floating around in the middle of it. It made her feel vulnerable — and now she had two lives to worry about.

At last! At last, she saw a little dark roughness on the horizon and realised she was seeing land.

Grabbing Maggie's arm, and almost hopping with excitement, she pointed. 'It's there! Look, over there. Land, at last.'

Maggie looked, smiled, and nodded her head. 'I see it, but it's still a long way off so just calm yourself.'

To Alice's dismay, the *Lady Juliana* stayed well clear of the land. She stood at the rail and watch sadly as it passed to starboard. Was that it, she wondered? Was that the closest they were going to come to land? Were they going to be bobbing around on this blessed lump of wood forever?

That night, she asked Danny the same questions and he laughed, then hugged her tightly just to show her he had meant no offense.

'That first land we passed today Mr. Edgar told me, is called Sao Nicolau and the second was Boa Vista. They are two of the Cabo Verde Islands. We will be stopping in at the largest island, further south. We should get there tomorrow unless the wind fails, and he said we will be buying some animals there to keep us fed for the next part of our voyage.'

Alice smiled and snuggled suggestively against him. 'Good, it will be nice to be near land again.' Her hand slipped down between them and Danny responded eagerly.

As promised, The following day canvas flapped and banged loudly as the sails were lowered. Chains rattled and squealed as the *Lady Juliana* dropped anchor in a small grubby looking harbour.

Alice studied it doubtfully. 'I don't think I much like the look of this place,' she told James as she studied the poor looking hovels on the shore. 'It doesn't look as fancy as the last harbour we were in.'

'Nor is it,' James agreed. 'You see, Santa Cruz is owned by the Spanish. This place here belongs to Portugal, which is a much poorer nation. Most of the people in the Cabo Verde islands only scrape in enough money, either by hard work or theft, to keep them alive. They are very poor people, and a lot are not too honest either. This is one port where you should be very glad that you will not be allowed ashore.'

'I hope we don't stay here too long then,' Sarah joined in.

'We won't,' James promised. 'The boss man in this place, a

Portuguese fellow by the name of Captain Moor, lives a good distance out of town because he doesn't like the smell here. He charges a mooring fee and it takes his guard a good day to get here from his palace. If we can leave before the guard gets here Captain Aitken will be able to avoid paying the fee. Captain just needs to buy some more animals and fill up the water casks, then we'll be on our way as quickly as he can manage. we won't stay more than one day here if he can help it.

'More animals?' Alice queried.

James nodded. 'Aye, more animals. We'll need as many as we can fit on-board, for the next stretch of our voyage is a very long one.'

Alice didn't like the sound of that at all and her dismay showed in her face.

Seeing it James smiled and give her shoulder a gentle punch. 'At least in this port, my lady,' he said laughingly, 'you won't have to worry about the morals of your friend Maggie. There's not a man in Santiago who could afford her services.'

Alice felt the flush run up from her chest to the top of her head and James laughed again.

'Did I tell you,' he asked, 'that the Portuguese named this town after me?'

'What nonsense,' Maggie scoffed. 'I bet they have never even heard of you.'

'They did,' James insisted. 'Santiago means Saint James In Portuguese.'

'Well, they got that wrong then didn't they?' Maggie quipped. 'If there is one thing you are *not* it is a Saint!'

James laughed and give a dismissive flap of his hand, before moving away from them to continue his work.

Alice and her friends stayed where they were and chatted happily as they watched the activity on the water.

Hens. goats and sheep were rowed across from the pier and hauled, complaining noisily onto the ship. Once they had them on board, the sailors grabbed handfuls of their fleece, dragged them, across the deck and fastened them into their cages and pens. By the time this was done the deck was again a slippery mess of urine and faeces.

Maggie pursed her lips and shook her head. 'I suppose when they've finished playing with the animals they will expect us to scrub the decks again,' she grumbled.

'Why did they make us do it this morning?' Alice asked, 'when they knew they were going to make this mess.'

James, who overheard this question as he was passing, stopped to explain. 'Well you see it's like this,' he started, 'the captain likes to keep all you women busy because it's when you have no work to do that you start causing trouble.'

'I don't cause any trouble,' Alice said, rounding on him indignantly.

'Oh, well no, I didn't mean you, Alice,' James defended himself. 'I was talking about the women what does make trouble.'

Maggie laughed and punched his arm. 'I think you had better go and get on with your work before you get yourself into any more trouble,' she suggested.

James nodded and smiled. 'Maybe you're right,' he agreed. 'Anyway, they'll be bringing the bullocks across soon and I guarantee that you will find that a sight worth watching.' On that note, he took his leave.

'Did he say bullocks?' Sarah asked.

Frowning, Alice agreed that was what it sounded like.

'Well they'll have to take the ship over to the pier,' Maggie said thoughtfully. 'They'll never be able to get animals that size into the rowing boats.'

She was right about that but wrong about the ship being

197

docked. It remained firmly at anchor.

Watching in wonder from the rail, the women saw several bullocks being herded onto the shore. One was roped to the rowing boat and as the sailors pulled on the oars The poor creature dug its hooves in, bellowed angrily, and tried to back up onto the beach. After a few moments of confusion, men ran forward brandishing stout sticks and started whacking the bullock's rear end. The animal leapt around bucking, kicking, and bellowing. Its tormentors ran around shouting, swearing, and swinging their sticks. Others made their way cautiously to the bullock's head, caught hold of the rope, and started dragging it into the sea. Eventually, the poor creature was overpowered and dragged into deep water. Once it was out of its depth, it was left with no choice but to start swimming as the rowing boat towed it towards the *Lady Juliana*.

The women lining the decks watched this battle with growing amusement.

'How on earth are they going to lift a huge creature like that out of the sea and get it onto the ship?' Alice asked, thinking it would take stronger men than any they had on the ship to lift such a heavy burden.

Maggie shook her head and snorted in amusement. 'Your guess is as good as mine, Alice, but I suppose they will have done it before, so they must know a way.'

Alice nodded and returned her attention to the strange activity on the water.

The rowing boat bumped against the side of the ship and one of the men held fast to the boarding net while others shortened the rope and pulled the frightened bullock alongside.

Sailors scrambled down with ropes and boarding nets and in a surprisingly short time the bullock was secured and hauled, manfully aboard the Lady Juliana.

Several more of the poor creatures were swum out to the ship and heaved on board, while the convicts watched with avid interest. This was the most entertaining spectacle they had seen for many a long day.

Once this chore was completed, the sailors began the arduous task of replenishing the water supplies.

Unlike Santa Cruz, where the water was piped to tanks on the pier, here, in Porto Praya it had to be brought from a well, which was well over half a mile away from the beach. A pathway had been constructed, along which the barrels had to be rolled to the well and back. Once back on the beach, the casks had to be firmly tied together and floated out to the ship.

The sailors grunted and swore as they heaved the heavy, slippery casks across the deck to lower them and store them in the hold. Any woman who got in their way was more often than not, treated to a long spiel of foul language.

Several of the women were sent flying, to land in an undignified heap on the slippery, dung covered deck. One had a heavy cask roll over her ankles and was carried off to the surgeon with some suspected broken bones.

Alice apprehensively watched all this dangerous activity and made sure she kept well out of the way.

Maggie, protective as ever, kept a firm hold on Alice's arm to make sure she was not knocked or pushed into the path of the busy sailors. At the same time, she kept a wary eye on Mavis Crowe, who was lingering nearby with a dangerous gleam in her eye.

As the last barrel was being rolled across the deck, Alice stepped away from the rail and Maggie loosened her grip on her arm.

Without a second wasted, Mavis leaped forward, grabbed Alice's arm, swung her around, and at the same time gave her a mighty shove.

Too late, Maggie tried to tighten her grip, but Alice was snatched away from her and went flying, face down across the slippery deck, and into the path of the heavy water cask.

The sailor who was rolling it made a grab to try to stop it but could not get a grip. It rolled on, hitting Alice's lower half with a resounding crunch.

Maggie threw herself on the deck beside Alice. Cradling her head in her lap she screamed, 'Fetch the surgeon! For God's sake, someone fetch Surgeon Alley. Quickly!'

Alice lay curled on her side on the deck, her face pressed against Maggie's lap and her right clutching the rough cloth of her friend's skirt. Clenching her teeth against a fierce pain in her side, she struggled not to scream.

Somewhere in an only half-conscious part of her mind, she could hear shouting and swearing and sounds of a struggle.

Maggie gently stroked the child's hair, at the same time watching the drama developing on the deck.

Immediately Alice had been thrown to the ground sailors and women alike lunged at Mavis, dragged her to the deck, and fought each other to get close enough land a blow on her.

Within a minute or two Thomas Edgar, and Richard Alley appeared on the outskirts of the melee.

Thomas quickly took control of the ruckus on the deck, shouting angrily until the mob stepped back to reveal a battered and bloody Mavis Crowe lying prone on the deck. Thomas prodded her with the toe of his boot and as soon as she sat up, ordered her to be put in chains and taken to the brig.

A couple of the sailors gleefully heaved her to her feet, shackled her wrists and ankles and without mercy dragged her down the companionway to the brig.

While all this was going on Richard Alley rushed straight to Alice and dropped on his knees beside her.

'Don't try to move, lass,' he told her quietly. 'Tell me, do you have any pain anywhere.'

Alice nodded, then winced. 'My head hurts,' she sobbed. Letting go of her grip on Maggie's skirt, she moved her hand to her lower ribs. 'And down here.'

Richard gently checked her head. There was a graze, which he touched carefully, and decided it was probably not too dangerous. Removing Alice's hand He pressed lightly on her ribs and was concerned to see her flinch.

'That hurt did it?' he asked needlessly.

Alice bit on her lips and nodded. 'Yes,' she whispered.

'I think you might have some broken ribs, so I'll get you to the infirmary and check you well.'

Picking her up easily, he once more carried her to the hospital and laid her gently on the bed.

Danny, having heard the commotion and seen her carried away came scurrying into the infirmary behind them. 'Is Alice alright,' he asked anxiously. 'What's that evil whore done to her this time?'

'That's what I'm about to find out,' Surgeon Alley replied. 'I think she might not be too bad,' he reassured.

'But the baby?' Danny wailed, almost in tears, 'what about our baby? Will he be alright?'

Richard Alley frowned at him. 'I think it might be a good idea if you just wait outside until I have examined Alice,' he instructed quietly.

Danny hesitated, but Maggie took his arm firmly and led him away. At the door, he turned around, gave Alice a last concerned look then reluctantly followed Maggie.

After a thorough but gentle examination, the surgeon was somewhat relieved to be able to advise Alice that although she had two or three broken ribs, there was no further damage, apart from several large bruises.

Smiling, he told her, 'Well you're going to be rather sore for a few days and you will have to be very careful how you move. You might find breathing a little painful, but you're young, so your ribs should heal quickly and it shouldn't take you too long to recover.'

'My baby — ?' Alice began,

'Should be alright,' Richard Alley reassured her. 'The barrel hit against your side, as far as I can see, so the baby will probably not have been harmed. I would like to keep you in the infirmary for a day or two just in case the shock causes any problems, but I don't want this to worry you.'

Alice frowned and pursed her lips. 'Do I *have* to stay?'

The surgeon studied her speculatively for a moment then nodded. 'I would just like to keep an eye on you. It is merely a precaution.'

Alice sighed and nodded. It was only for a few days, after all, and it was to ensure the safety of her baby. So she would stay.

Mavis was kept securely locked in the windowless, stinking brig for two days while Captain Aitken tried to decide her punishment. It went against the grain with him to have a woman flogged, but past experience had taught him that a visit from the cat was the only way to control that wretched woman. With a sigh, he decided that this time she would have twelve lashes instead of the six he had ordered for her in the past. Perhaps that would make her think twice before she caused trouble again, but he did not hold out much hope. Or maybe this time he would give her the full cat, which had nine knotted thongs, instead of the 'boy's pussy' he had ordered for her last time. It was a much gentler instrument, having only five thongs, that had been invented for the punishment of young boy's In the crew. The pussy had not acted as any kind of deterrent previously with Mavis Crowe so, yes, this time she would have to feel the weight of the full cat.

Having made this decision, Captain Aitken sighed and nodded to himself.

Alice Found that for some reason she could not keep her mind off the fate that Mavis Crowe had brought down upon her own head. Though she had not, thankfully, been in the brig herself, Danny had told her about it

It was a dreadful place to be, he had told her and most people — at least those with any sense — would make sure they never made a second visit to it. It was a tiny room — if indeed it could be called a room — deep in the bowels of the ship. It had no windows and when the door was locked there was no way for fresh air to enter. What air there was, was further polluted by the stench creeping up between the boards, which came from the sand which was used as ballast and contaminated by human waste of all sorts. Probably there were also the decomposing corpses of rats and mice and insects that had been trapped and died down there during the years the *Lady Juliana* had sailed the seas.

After a short while Alice became uncomfortable lying on the bunk and bored with her own company. Carefully easing herself upright, she hobbled painfully to the door and was about to step outside when surgeon Alley appeared around the corner.

Stopping abruptly, he frowned at Alice and shook his head. 'You should not be out here girl,' he told her. 'You need to rest.'

Alice put on her most appealing look. 'Oh please just let me go out and sit by the rail. I am so lonely in here And I'm sure it would do me good to sit in the sun, by the rail.'

Richard Alley chewed the inside of his lip thoughtfully. 'If

I allow it, do you promise you will stay seated and not try to wander around?'

'Oh yes, I promise,' Alice said eagerly. She would happily have agreed to stand on her head if need be, to get out of that depressing infirmary.

Richard took her arm and walked her slowly to the rail. Sitting her gently on a crate, he wagged a finger under her nose. 'Now don't you dare move from there, or I will have you straight back inside. Do you understand?'

Alice nodded enthusiastically.

After giving her a last ferocious look, Richard Alley turned away and went on about his business.

Alice watched as small boats rowed out to the Lady Juliana, but she knew James had said that in this port there were no men with money in their pockets to buy the services of the ladies on the ship. Instead, these shabby boats brought islanders keen to exchange their boatloads of food for any clothing or jewellery the convicts might be willing to part with.

Though most of the women had little or nothing to spare for these offerings, There were a few fairly affluent convicts who had managed somehow to bring trunks on board, in addition to considerable sums of money, with which they had bought themselves more comfortable accommodation and many special little perks during their voyage.

Alice watched with interest as these women of means cheerfully traded clothing and other knick-knacks for Portuguese wines and a tasty looking variety of native fruits. *How nice it would be*, she thought, *to have some money or trinkets to swap with the boatmen for some fresh fruit.* However, she had nothing to trade, except for her spare dress, which she *could* not part with and her shawl which she *would* not part with. So no matter how her mouth watered, she would have to make do with whatever food the ship's cook provided.

Her friends sat close by, ready to protect her from any possible threat or to help her back to the infirmary if she should feel ill.

They all watched with amusement, the antics of the local peasants in their leaky boats as they bartered with the sailors and the better-off convicts.

Alice smiled to herself. She had no doubt there would be trouble later when the women had downed a good share of the wine and port they were buying.

Suddenly the air was rent with shouts and screams. Alice turned quickly towards the sound and winced as her cracked ribs stabbed her in protest.

Sailors backed up the steps from the brig dragging someone behind them. Amidst a volley of screeching and swearing, Mavis Crowe was heaved on deck. It took four strong men to hold her, while she fought, kicking, swearing and trying to bite as they dragged her along.

When they finally had her where they wanted her they tied her arms and legs securely to the shrouds, spread to form the shape of a cross.

A burly sailor, who had repulsed Mavis's advances early in the voyage and had his mother's name loudly denigrated ever since, stood nearby fondling the red handle of the cat of nine tails.

Alice looked at it and shuddered, her eyes wide in horror. It was a dreadful-looking contraption. It was about two and a half feet long and from the red handle hung nine narrow thongs, which were knotted every few inches. The ends of the thongs had metal tips.

Surely, Alice thought, they were not going to use this to whip Mavis. She had thought the boy's pussy they had used last time what bad enough, but this *cat* looked truly vicious.

The sailor wielding the *cat* kept his eye on Thomas Edgar and at his nod delivered the first blow with all his strength. There was a gleam of pleasure in his eye, for, at last, he was getting what he felt to be a fitting revenge on this evil monster of a woman.

At the first blow, Mavis gave an unearthly screech and Alice flinched. Part of her wanted Mavis to be punished and she knew it must be a severe punishment for there to be any chance that she would behave better in the future. Still, this whipping seemed to Alice to be almost inhuman. But then she asked herself had the beating Mavis had given her been the act of a human?

She didn't want to watch but found she could not tear her eyes away from the woman bound to the shrouds. If she was honest with herself, somewhere deep in her chest she did feel a little excitement and pleasure. This creature had tried to kill her baby, so surely she deserved any punishment she was given.

Most of the other women stood around waving their arms, some with clenched fists as they cheered and shouted encouragement to the sailor who wielded the cat.

Twelve lashes in all, Mavis was given and by the end, she just lay still in the shrouds.

Surgeon Alley gave her a quick examination Then ordered that she be taken back to the brig.

'Not the infirmary?' Thomas Edgar questioned.

The surgeon shook his head. 'No. I don't want her there because Alice will be sleeping there for a couple of nights. Mavis will live and she'll be in no more pain in the brig than in the infirmary. I'll keep an eye on her there.'

Thomas Edgar nodded his agreement and gave the order to the sailors, who cut her free, and two of them carried her back to the brig, leaving a trail of blood across the deck.

Alice looked at Mavis as she was carried past, saw that her back just looked like raw meat, and felt her stomach heave. All of a sudden she didn't feel too well so asked Maggie to help her back to the infirmary. Her one hope now was that this would send a strong enough message to Mavis.

Shortly after the flogging and with all the water safely stored in the hold, and all the animals on board and in their pens, Captain Aitken gave the order to sail.

'No sign yet of the governor's lackey,' He told Thomas Edgar. 'So let's set sail and get out of this miserable port before he arrives looking for payment.'

The women, now accustomed to being cleared from the deck at such times, allowed themselves to be herded to the orlop and the forecastle, without too much complaint. Besides, having watched Mavis' downfall, none was too keen to risk the captain's wrath.

Maggie, concerned as ever for Alice's safety, took her arm to steady her as she returned to the infirmary. From there they listened to the din as the ship was readied to sail.

As always feet thudded backward and forwards across the deck. The anchor chain squealed and clanked; men uttered loud obscenities; rigging screeched and sails flapped and cracked noisily. Finally, it all quietened and the *Lady Juliana* moved gracefully Towards the Harbour mouth.

Captain Aitken gave a satisfied smile. His ship was fully stocked with both water and food And into the bargain he had managed to dodge paying the port fees.

At some time in the early hours of morning Alice awakened In her lonely bed with a strange feeling in her abdomen. Fearing for her baby she screamed For surgeon Alley, who quickly arrived in his nightgown and cap.

'What is it? What's happened?' he asked anxiously.

Alice looked up at him with wide, frightened eyes. 'I feel funny,' she sobbed. 'Something is happening with the baby and it doesn't feel right.'

'Well let's not panic yet. It is probably nothing for you to worry about, so just let me check you over and I'll see what I can find. First of all, tell me what has happened to frighten you so much?'

After careful examination, Richard Alley smiled at his young patient. 'Well, I'm very happy to tell you, my child that you're strange feeling is just your baby giving you a bit of a kick to let you know that he is there, and he is well.'

Alice looked at him in wonder and slipped her hand onto her belly. 'My baby,' she whispered, 'it's really real and it moved.'

Richard Alley smiled and nodded. 'Now I suggest we all get some sleep,' he said cheerfully.

CHAPTER 15

—•••—

The slave ships that had run from Porta Praya with them followed closely in their wake as the *Lady Juliana* scudded happily along ahead of constant north-easterly trade winds.

The ladies of the *Lady Juliana* who had found soul mates on the slavers continued to enjoy both the financial rewards and the physical pleasures of their unions.

Captain Aitken, who was well aware that some of the women might try to escape with their lovers, gave Thomas Edgar the task of carefully checking every male visitor before he left the ship to ensure it was not one of the convicts dressed in her lover's clothes.

On an odd occasion, one would be caught and would be dragged, screaming profanities, before the captain. Alice smiled to herself as she watched the shenanigans. She just wished one of the slavers' crew would successfully smuggle Mavis Crowe and spirit her away. She thought it likely that Thomas Edgar would turn a blind eye if he saw that particular troublemaker going over the rail. Not much chance of *that* though was there? Pity!

Now and again her hand crept to her belly to feel the ever-increasing movement of the child inside her. Every little twitch of life gave her a feeling of excitement she could not put into words. And such an overpowering sense of love.

The small amount of work that was needed for trimming the sails in these steady conditions left the crew with plenty of time to attend to routine, but necessary maintenance and repairs.

Some of the crewmen laid out sailcloth on the deck and after cutting out a complete new set of sails, set about stitching them with huge needles and very thick twine.

'What's all that about? What are they making?' Maggie asked James. She, Alice and several of the other women had been requested to help with the stitching. While Alice had not had the strength to push the needle through, Maggie had managed for a while until her fingers became too sore to carry on.

'A new set of sails,' James replied.

'Why?' Alice asked. I can't see nothing wrong with the sails we've got.'

James smiled and nodded. 'You're quite right,' he agreed. 'There is nothing wrong with them but after we leave Cape Town there is a chance that we might need some more sails.'

'Why?

James thought for a moment. How much should tell the girl? He didn't want to alarm her too much. In the end, he settled for, 'Well, you see it can get a bit windy in the Southern Ocean so if a sail tears we must have another to immediately replace it.'

'I see,' was all Alice said, but she didn't really see at all and she did not like the sound of winds strong enough to tear such strong canvas.

Under Maggie's watchful eye, Alice spent much of her time sitting in the shade picking oakum. It was a dreary task, she thought, but at least it did not take too much effort and gave her plenty of time to daydream. It did make her fingers sore though and after a few hours of picking, they became quite raw and bled a bit.

'Why do we have to do this?' she had asked James early on. 'Why don't they just throw these frayed old ropes into the sea?'

James had laughed and told her, 'Our *Lady Juliana* needs all the hemp fluff you are producing.'

'Why?' What, she wondered, would a ship do with all this grubby fluff.

''Tis needed to push between the boards of the ship to seal any spaces,' James replied before walking away.

Alice was left none the wiser, but day after day she carried on with her boring task without complaint.

Danny, on the other hand, complained bitterly about one of the tasks he had been given. 'I don't know what the captain thinks I've done wrong,' he grumbled. He says I've to slush down the masts and that's a job that's usually given when you've done summat wrong.'

James laughed. I think you just happened to be in the wrong place at the right moment. You were probably just in his line of sight when he thought of the idea. It's a task that has to be done to keep the wood of the masts from drying out an' keep the tackle running smooth.'

'Well, I still don't think it's fair. I work hard an' do everything he tells me. I never make no trouble.'

'Yes, well I think maybe it would be a good idea if you just went an' got the grease from the galley an' got started before he *does* get annoyed with you,' James said quietly as he saw the captain eyeing them from the bridge.

Still grumbling to himself, Danny went down to the galley and collected a huge bucket of grease. With a sigh, he started the long climb to the masthead, from where he started the downward journey, rubbing the grease into the mast by hand as he went and making sure he did not miss a patch. He painstakingly forced the thick muck into even the smallest of cracks. All the time, he was terrified his greasy hands would lose their tenuous grip and he would plummet to the boards below. Looking down, the deck looked a frightening distance away. He could see the other crewmen looking up at him and laughing. Feeling resentful, he was sure that slushing was probably by far the most unpleasant task he had been given since starting the voyage.

This quiet spell on the water allowed Captain Aitken to set in motion a little money-making venture he had in mind.

When first charged with taking his shipload of female convicts to this new world, he had realised that with so few women sailing with the first fleet, there would be likely to be few, or possibly no, seamstresses nor weaving facilities in the new colony. Almost certainly by now, there would be no soap for washing either, and most of the clothing that had gone out with the first fleet would be well worn by now. With this in mind, he had purchased bolts of linen which he had stored very carefully where it could not possibly be damaged.

Thomas Edgar had it in his records what employment if any, the women had in past lives. From this list, Captain Aitken was able to choose twenty whom he thought, and they agreed, would be the best needlewomen on the ship. The bolts of cloth were brought out and the twenty chosen women were set the task of cutting out and stitching shirts, trousers and cloaks. Once these were made, they were carefully stored away, to be sold on arrival in Port Jackson.

Alice watched all this with interest and envy. How she would love to be able to sew and to stitch clothes for her baby, but she had never been taught. If her mother had known any needlework, she had not passed the skill on to her daughter. Perhaps, she wondered, if she asked one of the kinder women, she might teach her some of her crafting skills. The knowledge might serve her well in this new world she was heading for. Sidling up beside the group of women, she settled herself beside one who had always seemed friendly and watched with avid interest every move the woman made. Happily, the lady, whose name, Alice learned, was Mary, enjoyed her company and was willing to teach her.

Once she felt she had a reasonable idea of how it was done, she begged Thomas Edgar to ask the captain to allow her some of the scraps to try to fashion some baby clothes.

Thomas Edgar nodded. 'I'll ask him. I can't see any objections because the larger scraps are just used as cleaning rags and the smaller ones are thrown out,' he replied. It impressed him that a girl so young was so keen to learn and to do these things for herself, He could see her being a useful asset to the new colony.

When faced with the question Captain Aitken was quick to agree. Like most of the other officers, he liked Alice and respected her keenness to make things better for herself.

'I have good news for you, Alice,' Thomas told her an hour or so later. 'Captain says you can have as many of the scraps as you need. An' he says once you have enough for your own baby you can make some more and sell them when you get to Port Jackson. There's bound to be some babies there by now and possibly not many good clothes for them.'

Alice, almost dancing with joy, threw her arms around Thomas and hugged him. Realising what she had done, she backed away, red-faced and apologetic.

'I'm s-s-s-sorry,' she stammered. 'I didn't mean to do that.'

Thomas tried to look severe but seeing how distressed the child was, he quickly changed his scowl to a smile. 'No harm done girlie, but best if you don't get in the habit of it,' he told her quietly.

Still a bit pink and shaky, Alice gave him a watery smile and turned away to start picking up all the offcuts from the needle-womens' labours. Taking them into a shaded corner of the deck, she sat cross-legged and started to try to work out a pattern in her mind.

Mary joined her and cheerfully gave her lessons in design.

'This could stand you in good stead when we reach Port Jackson,' she said. 'If you can sell the clothes you make on the ship it will give you a bit of money to start you off there. If there is no one there already making children's' clothes — and almost certainly there won't be — you could maybe set up a little business there,' she suggested.

Alice's eyes lit up. 'Maybe we could do it together,' she said hopefully.

Mary smiled and shook her head. 'Bless you, child, I'll make a lot more money plying my trade when we get there. Very few women came with the first fleet, so there will be a lot of men who will be pretty desperate to pay well for the services of a lively woman by now. And I'll be more than happy to meet their need!'

Alice nodded sadly. Even though she enjoyed her lovemaking with Danny, she couldn't imagine lying with another man. Would it be as good with another man? Might it be better? Could she bring herself to be so intimate with a man she did not know or care about? Then she thought of some of the grubby, rough men she had seen the women of the *Lady Juliana* taking to their beds and decided *she* couldn't do it. Not for *any* amount of money, she could not. She had learned enough during her time on the ship, to know of the dangers of catching diseases from lying with men. And she knew that her first experience with Danny had been his first too, so neither of them was in any danger of contracting the dreaded pox.

While she stitched, Alice enjoyed watching the activities of the other women. Once the day's main chores were done, the goats were milked and all the animals were fed. The number of pigs cows goats and hens contained in such a small area still amazed her.

Keeping the deck clean of their waste was a never-ending task and Alice was relieved that Surgeon Alley had ordered that she must do no more of this arduous, smelly work.

There was a lot of horseplay amongst the women that usually started off light-hearted but very often became aggressive. Thomas Edgar, ever watchful was very quick to break up any fights that began. Also, with so much time on their hands, he had to keep an eagle eye on the sailors if the banter between them and the convict women became too heated.

Alice was interested to notice an increase in shipping soon after the left Porto Praya. There was not a day that passed when they did not see at least one other ship and often there were quite a few. Ships of all shapes and sizes.

In one restful moment Alice and her three friends, along with the four *husbands* sat around the deck watching yet another ship pass.

'Why are there suddenly so many,' she asked, as yet another one slipped past, heading north.

'Because this is the main sea route between Europe, Africa, and the Americas. At least that's what James told me.'

'What are they carrying then? And where are they going?' Knowing James had sailed these seas for many years, Alice looked, this time to him for an answer.

'Different things and different places. 'Some will go east with cargoes from different parts of Europe to the Cape — in Africa, and some further on to the Spice Islands. They bring arms too, you know.'

'Arms?' Alice questioned.

James gave a thoughtful nod. 'Guns and ammunition — for our soldiers who are fighting in Africa. They return with their holds full of exotic spices and silks and teas. Some are coming from the west, from the Americas and the Caribbean an' they bring coffee and tobacco and sugar for the rich folk in England and Europe. Probably other things too, but I don't know what.'

'Those slave ships that have been with us since we left Santa Cruz will go east to Africa. There they will unload whatever cargo they are carrying, probably cloth materials and all sorts of fancy beads and trinkets they can use to buy slaves. This done they will fill their holds with black slaves to take to the Americas and the Caribbean, to the cotton, coffee and sugar plantations.' He stopped for a moment, thinking sadly about those poor slaves. He had seen, so often at the slave markets how cruelly the miserable black people were treated by the rich white men who bought them.

His mind went back to the first time he had seen these poor creatures being bartered in the market in the Caribbean.

'Years ago when I was in the Caribbean and I went with my captain — Captain Larkan, he was — and we watched all these black people being herded into the town square all shackled together. Most of the poor devils looked more dead than alive, after weeks of being chained down in the holds of the slave ships with little to eat or drink. They were hardly able to stay on their feet but were yelled at to stand straight and keep their heads up because the traders wanted them to look as strong as possible. Most of them had few if any clothes, but if they could not manage to stay upright they were lashed around their heads and bodies with stout canes or leather tipped whips.' James sighed and shook his head before continuing.

Alice and her three friends listened in wide-eyed horror.

'When I ask Captain Larkan where these poor black people came from and why they were treated so badly,' James went on with his story. 'He told me that about 300 years ago, Pope Nicholas V granted the kings of Spain and Portugal *full and free permission to invade search out, capture and subjugate all the*

Saracens and pagans and any other unbelievers and to reduce their persons into perpetual slavery. This is the excuse they use for hunting down these poor people and stealing them away from their homes and families. If truth be known, the real reason is money. Slaves are needed to grow the precious crops of cotton, tobacco, and sugar in the Caribbean islands and the Americas.'

'And for this, they are taken by force and mistreated? Are they ever returned to their homes?' Maggie asked sadly.

James shook his head and took a deep breath. 'No never. Captain Larkan told me That they were so badly treated and starved of food during the voyage to America that at least one in every ten of them perished at sea.'

'Oh, those poor people,' Alice said, in horror.

James nodded his agreement. 'There was lots of overfed white men at the slave markets, who turned up in fancy carriages,' James continued. 'The cruel buggers poked and prodded these poor people. Pulled the men around, checked their — um — bits and pieces, often giving an extra tight squeeze and a twist to cause as much pain as possible. Then their teeth were checked and if they tried to resist they whacked them with their riding crops.'

'How terrible,' Alice gasped. 'Did they not fight?'

James shook his head sadly and drew in a tremulous breath. 'A few tried, but they were cruelly beaten to near death in front of all the other slaves. Very quickly no one else tried to resist. The way they treated the women was even worse. If they were young and attractive the boss men would check if they were virgins an' if they were they would pay more for them. They would be taken home to keep the boss man pleasured. If the poor girl was unfortunate enough to have a baby, more often than not the child was eventually taken from its mother and sold into slavery elsewhere. It didn't matter to the master that the child was half his.'

James shook his head, took a deep breath, and continued, 'Once they get the slaves to their farms they treat them far worse than they do their animals, for of course, they are cheaper to replace. They are given paltry rations and often are worked until they just drop on the ground with exhaustion and die. Or are beaten to death! Much of the sugar grown in the Caribbean islands is taken to New England where it is made into rum. This is then shipped to Africa and used to barter for more slaves to grow more sugar to buy more slaves — and so the evil circle continues.'

'Why do they need more slaves, when they have so many already?' Sarah asked.

'For two reasons. Their farms are growing quickly and many of the slaves they already have die of either disease, starvation, overwork, or a beating, and need to be replaced.'

They all sat in horrified silence for a few moments until Alice decided it was time for a change of subject.

'And what of the others?' she prompted.

'Other what?'

'Ships. All the other ships we are seeing.'

'All following what is called triangle trade. Because of the way the trade winds blow it is faster to sail south before turning west to the Caribbean. Until we reached the Cape Verde islands we were following the eastern leg of the Golden Triangle And since leaving Porto Praya we have cut across the southern corner of it to Rio de Janeiro in Brazil. The ships you see going north are taking things like sugar, molasses, manufactured goods and all sorts of cash crops to Europe.'

'Did you see that ship that passed ahead of us a few minutes ago?' Danny was speaking again.

Alice brought her mind back to him and nodded. 'That strange looking one? Yes.'

'That was what they call a whaler. They go to the southern

oceans to catch whales. Those are huge fish, the biggest creatures on God's earth James says. They use their meat to eat, their fat to make tallow for candles and something called ambergris, what comes from their stomachs, they use to make perfume.'

Alice wrinkled her nose. 'Well, I won't wear perfume then. I don't want to smell like a fish!'

James laughed. 'Well I don't know what they do with it, but I promise you it does not make the perfume smell fishy.'

Alice shook her head in confusion. All these ships carrying things from one part of the world to the other and back again. Why, she wondered, did they not just grow or make everything they needed in their own countries? Would that not be simpler and less costly?

'This place We are going to — what did you call it Cape something?'

'Cape Town,' James agreed.

'Is that where we are going? Is that where Port Jackson is?'

James laughed and shook his head. 'Bless you, no love. There is a long way to go after the Cape.'

Alice hung her head in dismay. 'I wish this voyage could be over,' she said quietly. I don't like being on the sea. It frightens me — 'specially with the baby coming. I want to be on firm land not at sea when our baby is born.'

'Don't get too frightened lassie,' James comforted, 'Captain Aitken says he may linger in Cape Town for a while. As you know, there are 6 or 7 babies due to be born soon, and the captain would prefer that to happen in a port rather than when we are at sea.'

Alice brightened immediately. 'Oh I do hope he does,' she said with feeling.

Not long after this, the slave ships turned east towards the collection of European settlements around the mouth of the River Gambia to pick up their cargo of slaves.

James remembered stories he had heard while in Gambia, of a shipment of two hundred British convicts who had been landed on the Gambian shores many years before. They had been a first fleet intended to colonise that area of Africa. Sadly, all bar fifty of them perished. Whether through starvation, disease, or murder by the natives he did not know, but it did cross his mind to wonder whether the same fate might have occurred to the first fleet to Botany Bay. Before leaving London he had heard that the *Prince of Wales*, one of the ships from the first fleet, had arrived with the news that the colonists were alive and well. He also knew that had been over a year before the *Prince of Wales* reached London, so what might have become of the settlers since then?

Watching the slave ships go, James sadly shook his head. He knew only too well what lay in store for the poor miserable creatures those ships would be transporting. On occasion while in the Caribbean he had seen young girls, fighting to stay alive, selling their bodies for just a handful of food.

He was not the only one sorry to see the ships go. The women who had been enjoying the company of their crews for many weeks also sadly watched their departure.

CHAPTER 16

———

The *Lady Juliana* changed course, to head speedily in a south-westerly direction ahead of steady winds. There was not a lot of work needed in trimming the sails so the crew had quite a bit of time on their hands. To fill this time many of them took to dangling fishing lines over the side. The wives of the successful fisherman benefitted from their men's catches And were probably better fed than they had ever been before. In these warmer waters, the fish they found themselves eating were varieties they had neither heard of nor tasted before, but it mattered not. It was fresh, nutritious, tasty, it filled their bellies and their health improved.

To Alice's joy, Danny was one of the lucky ones who very regularly made a good catch, which he usually shared not only with her but with her three friends. One day he hooked a huge bonito that leapt and thrashed around the deck until one of the sailors grabbed it by the tail, swung it with all his strength and smashed its head against the cleansing block.

Although cringing at each blow, Alice was stunned by a range of bright colours that lit its body as the life left it.

The women soon came to realise that the custom at sea was that any fish caught belonged to the person who hooked it. Very quickly many of the women who did not have a man to provide for her availed themselves of string and hooks. When the lookout at the masthead shouted and pointed to where he had seen a school of fish, these women were quick to pull in their lines and join the rush to drop them in the water on the side of the ship where the school had been spotted.

One day an unusually excited shout from the masthead had everyone on deck gazing out over the starboard side of the ship. Less than a hundred yards away a dozen or more large fish were leaping high out of the water, pirouetting in the air and slicing cleanly back through the waves, to disappear for a few moments beneath the water, before jumping again.

'Oh how beautiful,' Alice murmured. 'Did you see them, Maggie?'

'See what?' Maggie turned to look over the ocean just us several of the huge fish leapt from the water again, much closer to the *Lady Juliana* than before. Startled, she took an involuntary backward step. 'Oh, how huge! What are they?'

'Them's dolphins,' A passing sailor told her, leaving none of them much the wiser.

Alice's heart skipped a few beats with the excitement of seeing these beautiful big creatures playing so close to the ship.

'Oh look,' she cried, pointing, as several of the dolphins again broke the water. 'There are some babies too!' At that moment her own baby reacted to her excitement and gave her a hefty kick. Unconsciously she laid her hand her belly, waiting to enjoy the next movement.

The dolphins looked, to her, to be such beautiful, graceful creatures as they swam and dived and leapt. In her eyes they were the most beautiful fish she had ever seen and she could have happily watched them all day.

Spellbound by the beautiful scene, she did not at first notice the bosun hurrying to the rail with his harpoon in his hand.

Alice had seen him catch sharks several times with this dreadful looking weapon and had been horrified to see the barbaric way in which the fish was caught. And a little frightened when she saw its teeth. However, if she was to be honest with herself, she did enjoy eating the share she was given of this tasty fish.

Catching a movement from the corner of her eye, she now saw the bosun at the rail with his feet spread wide, bracing himself, against the gentle movement of the ship. His arm was raised ready to give a mighty heave and send his evil missile speeding towards its target.

Realising his intention, Alice screamed 'no' and took an involuntary step towards him.

Maggie grabbed her arm. 'Let it be,' she said quietly. 'It has to be. It's only a fish and we have to eat.'

'But they're so beautiful,' Alice replied with a tear in her eye. 'And so trusting to swim this close to the ship.'

Maggie nodded. 'Aye, but still only a fish.'

Alice watched sadly as the bosun drew back his arm and with a mighty heave sent the dreadful barbed missile speeding towards its prey. She willed it to miss its target, but the bosun was expert and she winced when she heard the crunch of the harpoon penetrating the dolphin's leathery skin.

Looking over the side of the *Lady Juliana*, Alice watched miserably as the ill-fated creature fought for its life. It leapt high out of the water, the harpoon firmly embedded in its flesh and the rope trailing behind it. She prayed for its success as it dived below the water in a desperate bid for freedom.

However, it was a fight doomed for failure.

Three sailors leapt forward and grabbed the rope to avoid the bosun being pulled overboard and their meal being lost.

Alice crossed her fingers and wished the dolphin luck, at the same time knowing the vicious barbs on the harpoon would prevent it being pulled out.

To make sure of his catch, the bosun's arm swung again. A second harpoon flew through the air and found its mark as unerringly as the first. The battle lasted quite a long time, but eventually, the dolphin gave a last tired flip of its tail, turned on its side, and lay still.

The lighter was launched and swiftly recovered the animal. A rope was attached to its tail and it was unceremoniously hauled on board by block and tackle.

Alice took one look at the poor animal lying bleeding on the deck and ran in tears to her bunk in the forecastle.

A creature that size provided a good meal for all on board, so that night everyone ate well — except Alice, who felt sick even at the thought of eating it.

Danny was catching plenty of fish and Alice was certain her baby was benefiting from this nutrition as it seemed to get livelier every day. She herself was better fed than she had been at any time in her life. Her health improved and despite her rapidly growing belly, she became ever more energetic.

Whatever time she had free from her chores Alice spent cutting and stitching baby clothes. These, she gave to Thomas Edgar when they were finished and he stowed them away carefully in his locker to ensure they would suffer no water damage and could not be stolen. She smiled to herself when she imagined running her own little business in this new colony she was going to. In her daydreams Danny was always at her side, helping her in her shop. Perhaps he would be running the shop, collecting supplies and making deliveries while she sat in a corner behind the counter doing her cutting and stitching. It was a happy dream that helped to keep her contented throughout the dreary voyage and the discomforts of pregnancy.

As they neared the equator and the doldrums the air became more humid and moist by the day until it was almost unbearable. What little breeze there was, was so hot that it did not give much relief.

Alice took to carrying a towel, but no matter how often she wiped her face neck and arms she could not dry the perspiration. she developed rashes under her arms and around the neckline of her dress. If only she still had her own ragged summer dress, but that had been taken from her when she was leaving Newgate and she had been given these dreadful rough, grey itchy things. How she would have loved to just throw them off and run around the deck naked. Instead, she had to make do with dowsing herself frequently from the water keg. This brought a little relief, but not much, as the water was quite warm.

Many of the women took to pulling their skirts well up whenever they were sitting. This wanton display of their feminine assets drew many leering looks and lewd comments from the sailors.

Alice spent most of her time, once her light duties were completed, sitting in the shade, always with her back against something solid trying to stitch clothes. Time and time again, she threw them on the deck with a grunt of exasperation. The cloth was damp, the sewing cotton was damp *everything* was damp. her sweating fingers could not grip the needle properly which made it almost impossible to draw the cotton through the cloth. Most of the surfaces on the ship, it seemed to Alice seemed to be developing a coating of mould. She had heard the sailors complaining that their pocket knives had become so rusty as to be almost useless.

Surgeon Alley repeatedly told the women and crewmen they must make sure they drank a good quantity of water in the dreadful tropical heat. He was very conscious of the danger of dehydration, which could be fatal. In particular, he was concerned about the well being of the pregnant women.

Following his instructions Alice kept a cup of water beside her whenever possible, refilling it frequently from the cask. It was too warm to refresh her, but did make her feel a little less queasy.

Alice sensed an uneasiness in the ship throughout the day and she knew Danny was frightened of what might be done to him. The younger members of the crew, any whom were crossing the equator for the first time, or any who had made themselves unpopular on the voyage were to be subjected to pranks that could easily get out of hand. He had told her that the captain and officers took no part in conducting the pranks, but did keep a watchful eye in case anything became too dangerous. There were tales, told with relish to those who were about to be initiated, of men being keelhauled almost to the point of death. The officers would only step in and put an end to it if the pranks became too vicious or too dangerous.

However, to Alice's relief, the ceremony on the *Lady Juliana* remained lighthearted and cheerful throughout. The captain had held a tight and happy ship, so none of his crew had made themselves unpopular enough to need severe punishment.

As dusk fell, all women were barred from the forecastle, where the preparations were being made, and sent below. From there they could only guess at the variety of strange sounds they heard, which went on for several hours. They could hear the officers shouting, but most times could not make out what they were saying. The ship made a sudden turn into the wind, throwing all the women around the orlop and setting many of them to swearing. Soon afterwards the women were told to come up and falteringly made their way on deck, where they stood in nervous huddles until a gong started and a clutch of noisy men scrambled over the bow and onto the foredeck. These, the women learned later, were King Neptune and his Nereids.

King Neptune was wearing the skin of a porpoise that had been caught earlier, its snout towering well above his head. His Nereids had painted their faces with red dye and wore long strands of seaweed for hair. They strutted towards the quarterdeck with *the King* waving his trident and his minions making lunges at the convicts. Pandemonium followed amongst the convicts, who squealed and jumped quickly to escape, bumping and knocking down anyone they collided with.

Alice was jostled and received a few solid thumps but was lucky enough to keep her balance.

Once on the foredeck King Neptune produced a huge ledger and began showily thumbing through it. From his list, he checked to find any officer or crew member who had not crossed the equator before. These were to forfeit a double liquor ration and had to undergo the initiation rites that had been worrying Danny.

A sudden scream from amongst a group near Alice drew her attention away from the activities on the quarterdeck. Quite a few of the women had been knocked down in the scuffling and had yelled but this was something different. This poor woman sounded to be terrified and in pain.

Many of the convicts rushed to crowd around the fallen woman and after several minutes she was picked up and carried below to the poop deck.

Attention then returned to the ceremony on the quarterdeck, but Alice could still hear the screams of the woman.

Alice watched in fear as Danny's hands were tied behind his back and he was made to sit on a plank over a barrel of foul looking water.

The Nereids, whose faces were plastered in a disgusting looking mixture of tar and dripping and heaven alone knew what other dreadful-looking ingredients, pranced around the deck looking as evil as possible.

King Neptune's demon barber approached the men on the barrels, brandishing a huge mock razor.

Alice gasped and clasped her hand to her mouth as she saw Danny struggling with the barber. Like all the men before him, he finally lost his balance and fell off the plank into the messy, slimy-looking water.

The men all splashed around desperately. Unable to get a grip on the slippery sides of the barrels they could only draw in a quick gasping breath each time they managed to push themselves high enough to get their heads clear of the water.

Surgeon Richard Alley kept a wary eye on proceedings to ensure none of the men drowned. When he felt they had struggled for long enough the order was given for them to be hauled out of the muck filled tubs. As soon as they had recovered enough breath, ropes were tired around them and they were thrown into the sea to be cleansed.

Alice heaved a great sigh of relief and scuffed a tear from her cheek as Danny was hauled back up over the rail.

At that moment one of the convicts pushed her way onto the quarterdeck and tugged at Surgeon Alley's sleeve.

'You gotta come quick, Surgeon,' she said frantically. 'Milly got knocked down an' she fell real hard. I think her baby is coming an' it is far too early.'

Looking concerned, Richard Alley hastily followed the woman to the poop.

Alice became aware suddenly that the poor woman who had been carried away was still screaming. In her worry and fear for Danny, she had stopped hearing, but now the other woman's screams tore at her heart. Instinctively, she put her hands to her belly to check her unborn child.

Nonetheless, the party on the quarterdeck continued noisily. Sailors all had to make the confessions to King Neptune, many of whom confessed to having been unfaithful to the woman they had taken us a *wife*. A generous portion of rum was handed out to men and women alike, who quickly became very drunk. Seamen's rude stories were told and for those who were still able to stand there was music and dancing on the forecastle.

Bodies littered the deck; some passed out with an excess of rum; others wildly copulating on the open deck.

Wide-eyed, Alice watched this strange, but rather exciting activity going on around her. Women kneeling, their skirts pulled up to their waists and sailors with their trousers down to their knees doing things Alice had never imagined that people might do.

'We've never done that,' she whispered to Danny.

Danny dragged his eyes away for a moment. 'I never thought of it. Maybe we could try it.' When Alice gave him a startled look he added hesitantly, 'after the baby has come out.'

When the officers decided it's had gone on long enough, they moved around the deck nudging the bodies with the toes of their boots.

'C'mon. Let's be having you out of here. I reckon you've had enough And if you haven't you must go back to your quarters.'

Alice saw Surgeon Alley approaching and clutched at his arm.

'Can you tell me how the lady is who fell and was carried away?' she asked.

The man looked at her quizzically. 'Friend of yours was she?'

Alice shook her head. 'No, but she looked as if she was going to have a baby and I was worried.'

Richard Alley shook his head and pursed his lips. 'She will probably be alright in time, but the baby was too early and I think it had been damaged when she fell. It was dead when it was born. I have given Millie some opium to stop her pain and some laudanum to help her sleep. There was really no more that *I* could do for her. I have left her in the charge of women who have borne several children and probably know more about childbirth than I.'

Alice burst into tears and gently taking her arm, Danny led her away to their sleeping quarters.

'I don't think I could bear it if anything like that happened to our baby,' she told Danny when she had recovered from her weeping. 'I love it so much already and I don't think I would want to go on living.'

Danny tightened his arms around her, wiped away her tears and kissed her forehead. 'Nothing bad is going to happen to him,' he promised. 'I will look after you and keep you both safe.'

'But what if you have to sail with the ship when it leaves this place we are going to?' Until now she had not realised that this thought had been worrying her — but it had. She was frightened. How would she; how *could* she survive without him? There was no way of knowing what sort of a place this Port Jackson was and she would not even begin to know how to start a life there without Danny. He had become a part of her — the part that gave her the strength to face up to life.

Danny shook his head and hugged her even tighter. 'That won't happen,' he said quietly. 'Captain will know you need me more than he does and I'm sure he will let me stay with you.'

Alice clung to him and tried a watery smile. 'I do pray you're right,' she said quietly. 'I couldn't bear to be without you.'

Alice awakened suddenly with an uneasy feeling. Something was wrong. The ship didn't feel right. There was an eerie stillness about it. Was it sinking?

She fearfully disentangled herself from the sheet and bent to waken Danny, who had taken to sleeping on the deck as her pregnancy advanced. His mattress was empty. Where was he? Why wasn't he there?

Stifling a sob and with her heart racing in fear Alice shuffled towards the door.

The sun, not yet risen painted, the sky a brilliant orange. Puffy white clouds appeared as bright lights and fires in the sky, dazzling Alice's eyes. For a moment she forgot her fear as she drank in the beauty of the scene.

Suddenly she realised what it was that had woken her and seemed so strange. The ship was not moving. Not at all. The *Lady Juliana* stood still and silent in the water. The sails hung motionless and there was no sound of the sea slapping and slurping against the hull.

Alice lingered in the doorway for several minutes trying to figure it out. In all her weeks at sea even on the calmest of days, the ship had been restless. Alice felt as if she was standing on solid ground. So what was wrong?

Timidly she edged her way across the deck to look over the rail. The sea was absolutely flat, so much so that it had an almost oily look. The horizon was still and the whole scene seemed unreal. It appeared to Alice more like a painting than real life.

'What's wrong? What's happened to the ship? To the sea?' she asked a nearby sailor.

The man puzzled over the strange question. 'The ship? The sea? Nothing has happened. Why do you ask?'

Alice drew a deep breath. 'Well, it's so still. The sea isn't moving. There is no wind and the sails just hang. No movement anywhere. I have never seen a sea that does not move and it frightens me.'

The man gave a great shout of laughter. 'Bless you, child. Nothing to be frightened about. We are in an area we seamen call *the doldrums*. When we crossed the equator we passed from northern to the southern hemisphere. And very often in this area, the wind dies completely and so the sea is unmoving too.

You will find that the ship does not stay as still as this for long. There are a lot of cross-currents here that'll make the ship move very strangely. That might make you feel a little bit sick until you get used to it.'

Alice nodded. He might have been speaking a foreign language for all she had understood of it, but she wasn't going to let him know that. As long as the *Lady Juliana* was not going to sink was all that mattered to her.

Thanking the man, she turned to return to her bed.

'We could well be becalmed here for days, or maybe even weeks. You can never tell, but without wind, we will go nowhere!' the man added with relish.

Alice felt her heart sink but kept on walking. Wasn't this damnable journey long enough without being stuck in one spot for weeks waiting for some wind? Not long after she returned to her bunk the *Lady Juliana* started to shudder and with the strange, frightening motion Alice's stomach started to heave.

The sailor's prediction proved correct and the *Lady Juliana* lay wallowing in a mostly empty ocean for many days. The effluent from the heads floated on the still waters and clung to the hull, bathing the convicts and crew in a sour odour once again.

The only movements to be seen were dolphins, porpoises, and shoals of fish breaking the surface. The fishing continued, much of it done by the convicts as the sailors were too busy, and the passengers and crew continued to eat well — but only after the fish had been thoroughly cleaned.

Alice was surprised that, considering the ship was hardly moving, the crew seemed busier than when there were the good trade winds to hurry the *Lady Juliana* along. There was more noise, with the officers constantly watching the sails and shouting instructions through there speaking trumpets.

Men scrambled high in the rigging, like an army of busy ants, making small adjustments. They scrambled and swung around the rigging like a tribe of monkeys, whilst Alice watched with her heart in her mouth. All this activity, so Danny told her, was because the small amount of wind in the doldrums constantly changed directions, so the sails had to be trimmed every few minutes to catch even the very slightest bit of a breeze. If this was not vigilantly attended to The *Lady Juliana* might possibly go back the way she had come.

With over two hundred and fifty people using the heads the smell of human waste clinging to and floating around the ship quickly grew. Long green ribbon-like strands of slime grew on the side of the ship and clung to all the human waste and galley refuse. With no wind to carry it away, the stench became more unbearable with each day that passed.

Captain Aitken sent men down in the boats to try to clear the mess. They spent hours every day scraping the hull as best they could, but they were fighting a losing battle. The mess and the smell increased daily.

Surgeon Alley soon grew concerned about the possibility of disease on board the *Lady Juliana*. In particular, he worried about the pregnant women.

'Is there no way we can make some headway and get away from all this muck?' he asked Captain Aitken.

The captain shook his head and chewed thoughtfully on his lower lip. 'All sorts have been tried,' he said, 'From wetting the sails to wedges to make the masts tighter in their shoes, but I don't think any of them work. The only possible way, to my mind, is manpower.'

'Manpower?' Richard Alley frowned.

'Aye.' Captain Aitken nodded. 'I could send the men down in the boats to tow the ship. 'It's not a thing I like to do though if it can be avoided because it is exhausting work.'

'I'd appreciate it if you would give that some thought, George,' Richard said quietly. 'Even if they can only move it far enough to get away from this effluent. I fear that if we have to live in these conditions much longer we might well have an outbreak of scurvy or gaol fever. In particular, I fear for the women in the orlop. They are crowded so tightly down there at water level and the smell is absolutely sickening. There is no air movement and in this hot damp climate, it must be unbearable. Would it be possible for them to sleep on the deck for the time being?'

The captain shook his head. He was a caring man but that would be just a step too far. 'No.' He said decisively. 'You know as well as I do, the trouble we have with many of them during the day even when we are able to keep an eye on them. We could not have them running loose at night. Heaven knows, they would more than likely toss overboard anyone they did not like.'

Richard Alley heaved a mighty sigh. 'Yes, I can see that. but we really must do something to improve things.

'Right.' Captain Aitken nodded and took a deep breath. 'I don't really like to do this, but I feel I have no choice. I'll order the men to stop scraping the hull and set them to tow the ship.'

With the decision made he immediately ordered that lines be attached to the bow and the men must row instead of scraping.

Day after day they spent many hours heaving on the oars, and with frequent changes of crew, the oarsmen put all their strength into their task. There was a bit of grumbling from some, but others were just happy to no longer be working amongst the effluent.

The *Lady Juliana* made slow headway but little by little she was dragged out of the worst of the mess.

His face set grimly, Richard Alley faced his captain. 'It grieves me to have to report, George, but we now have some cases of scurvy.'

George Aitken slumped into his chair and heaved a mighty

sigh. 'How has that happened? Lieutenant Edgar has been very particular about keeping a clean ship. I know he makes close inspections of the orlop, in particular, to ensure it is always scrubbed clear of any vomit or other mess.'

'My feeling is that scurvy has little to do with cleanliness. I'm certain it is more to do with a shortage of green vegetables and fruit. We have little left of the stocks we purchased in Cape Verde and what there is has spoiled badly in this heat.'

Aitken nodded and bit his lip. 'Well, I'm afraid there's not much we can do about that until we reach Cape Town. Is there no other way you can find to combat this disease?'

'We do have some cases of cabbage preserved in salt that the Admiralty gave us. I have ordered it to be soaked in vinegar, which itself is a healthy additive. this makes a reasonably palatable meal and, in addition, I have ordered that the cakes of portable soup should be prepared and given to all on board. I have also given instructions that copious amounts of barley be soaked for several hours then boiled up to make sweet-wort, with each sick person to be given several pints of this each day.'

'Will this cure them, do you think?'

Richard Alley shrugged and made a helpless gesture with his hands. 'I really can't say. All we can do is hope. It certainly won't do them any harm.'

In the days that followed, it became so hot that sleeping became almost impossible. In the orlop, the women suffered even more at night than before, with tar melting between the boards above and dripping down on them. Many received painful burns.

During the day the boiling tar bubbled up from between the decking boards, burning the feet of the convicts, most of whom were shoeless. At Thomas Edward's suggestion, the women were given permission to cut up some tarpaulins to tie around their feet.

When she wasn't safely amongst her friends, Alice huddled quietly in her corner trying hard to keep out of the way of any trouble. On several occasions, she, along with several of the other convicts, succumbed to the heat and fainted. Most of them were simply laid out on tarpaulins in the shade but any of the pregnant women were taken to the sickbay until they had recovered.

It frightened Alice to be there, for the worst cases of the scurvy victims were also there. All around her, people moaned or screamed, complaining about terrible pains in their arms and legs. many had weeping rashes on their faces and hands with bleeding blisters around their mouths. What of her baby, she wondered, if she were to catch this dreadful disease. Though Surgeon Alley assured her that scurvy was caused by a lack of essential elements in the diet, still she trembled in fear until he allowed her to leave the sickbay.

After many days of the ghostly stillness in *the doldrums*, finally, a wind picked up. Light at first, it raised a cheer from both convicts and crew as they felt the air movement; the sails filled, and the ship resumed a normal motion.

To Alice's relief, they were making headway again. They left behind the effluent smell that had been in their noses and had clung to body and clothing for all the days they had been becalmed.

A tropical sun, that appeared much larger than the one they had left in England, beat down relentlessly. Alice puzzled over the size of it but could think of no reason why it should be bigger. All she knew was that she needed to stay in the shade and avoid its rays as much as possible. That was not hard to do, as the surgeon had ordered that she must be given only light duties, to be undertaken where there was shade.

CHAPTER 17

A s the days and weeks passed they started to see more shipping. Danny told Alice it was because they were on a shipping lane, en-route to Cape Town in South Africa.

On two or three occasions Captain Aitken sent signals to a nearby ship then gave the order to heave to and his lighter to be launched.

Alice, now in her seventh month of pregnancy watched with interest as the captain climbed down into his boat and was rowed across to the other ship. To the amusement of all on board the *Lady Juliana*, he would return a few hours later in a merry mood and none too steady on his feet.

On other occasions, captains from other ships would be rowed to the *Lady Juliana* to drink captain Aitken's rum and fill their bellies at his table. If they wished, which most of them did, they were also able to satisfy other pressing needs while aboard.

Alice and her friends tried to stifle giggles later as the visitors wended their way across the deck, clearly well in their cups, to scramble down into their lighters in a most ungainly fashion.

By this time the *Lady Juliana* was suffering badly from all her months at sea, in particular, the time they had spent becalmed amongst the sludge. Damage was done by the animals lurking in the depths, nibbling at the timbers and the plant life that had rooted there. The poor old girl was springing leaks. Those above the waterline could be repaired while they were under sail, But the ones below were not so easily fixed.

To the consternation of the women, huge cauldrons were dragged onto the deck, filled with pitch, and fires were lit under them.

Alice had watched in puzzlement, but when flames appeared she struggled to her feet, her eyes wide. 'They'll set the ship on fire,' she cried in horror.

Maggie laughed and caught hold of her arm. 'Don't be panicking girl,' she told her. 'They know what they're doing. An' they had fires to boil the water when we had all them clothes to wash. The captain wouldn't allow it if it wasn't safe.'

Alice gave the nearest fire a sideways look before allowing herself to be settled again. They could say what they wanted, but she still couldn't see how it could be safe to light a fire on the deck of a ship.

The livestock, instinctively afraid of fire, were restless and skittery. Eyes rolling, they jostled around in their pens; feet stamped; sheep bleated; bullocks bellowed; poultry squawked and flapped and Alice sat on the deck, ready to jump up and run at the first sign of trouble.

When she had calmed and thought about it she smiled to herself. What would be the point in running? There was nowhere to run to, was there? If the ship caught on fire it would simply sink and she would go with it no matter where she was standing.

Later in the day, when the sun was not burning too hotly, Alice moved to the rail and stood watching curiously as pitchers of boiling tar were passed down to men sitting precariously on planks caulking the leaking areas.

While they worked, the ship's boats moved backward and forwards alongside, scraping away the barnacles and other rubbish that clung to the hull of the *Lady Juliana*. More and yet more bad areas were found and the carpenters were forced to work long hours in the relentless, blazing sun.

Even with these repairs being done George Aitken's concern about the state of his ship increased daily. There were many areas below the waterline where the wood had rotted and in more than one place the *Lady Juliana* was taking water badly.

In the bowels of the ship, teams of sailors valiantly manned the pumps. In stinking scorching humidity, they tried desperately to stay ahead of the water but seemed to be fighting a losing battle. When a man passed out through heat exhaustion he was carried to the sickbay and quickly replaced.

It was to be expected of course. Captain Aitken had been well aware, but because of all the delays — over six months laid up in Galleons Reach and more time lost in Plymouth it had certainly put an added strain on the ship.

On a visit below decks, the captain stood grimly watching the men at the pumps. They were more or less holding their own, but he knew they could not keep working at that pace indefinitely. The last thing he wanted was to work any of his men to death. Returning to the deck, he gave the order to fother the ship.

From her seat on the deck amidst her pieces of cloth, Alice frowned at the strange activity all around her.

The men were filling a large basket with ashes and cinders from the fires on the deck, along with oakum, which was chopped up pieces of old rope. Once the basket was full they wrapped it loosely in a piece of old sail. After attaching a long stout pole to the basket, they heaved it up over the rail and pushed it down into the sea.

In her curiosity, Alice got a bit too near to the action and one of the men stumbled into her.

The sailor turned, looking cross, but when he saw it was Alice his frown changed to a smile. 'Best stay back a bit lass, else you might get knocked over,' he suggested.

Alice took a couple of quick backward steps before asking, 'What are you doing?'

'We're trying to stop a leak in the bottom of a ship. This is the only way we can do it while the ship is under canvas, or indeed when she is afloat.'

'How does it work? Do you have do push that basket into the hole?'

The man gave a great shout of laughter. 'Bless you, no, child. What happens is that we use the pole to plunge the basket up and down as near to the leak as we can manage. bit by bit the ashes and oakham are shaken out and if we are lucky they get sucked in with the water and gradually choke up and seal the hole. Then the piece of sail completes the seal.'

Alice understood most of that but asked, 'Does it all stay in place then?'

The sailor pursed his lips and nodded. 'Usually, it does, but if it comes loose we will just have to do it again. if we have God on our side, it should keep us afloat until we reach a port where we can make proper repairs.'

Alice looked at him a bit doubtfully. But it didn't sound too good to her. Perhaps it might be a good idea if she started praying to this God everyone talked about.

Captain Aitken returned to the bridge and called his officers together.

'Well gentlemen,' he began. 'I have just checked below and the fothering repair appears to have been successful.'

The men around him voiced their relief and appreciation.

'However, we must now consider our options,' he continued. 'I have heard of fothered ships sailing great distances, but we are still two thousand miles short of Cape Town. Even if good winds continue it will take three weeks to get there. I certainly have no great wish to attempt such a distance if it can be avoided. Every mile we are under sail before we can safely beach the *Lady Juliana* is putting at risk the passengers, the crew and indeed the ship herself.'

The room was quiet, with all attention riveted on their captain. When he lapsed into a thoughtful silence Thomas Edgar spoke up. 'What are your plans then?' he asked.

Captain Aitken drew a deep breath. 'Well, I suggest we get the charts out, put our heads together, and find a safe harbour nearer than Cape Town's.

'The sooner we reach a port, the better,' Surgeon Alley agreed, 'And for more reasons than an unseaworthy ship.'

George Aitken threw him a questioning look.

'I have more than sixty women on my sick list. A few of them are malingerers but the majority are genuinely ill. Some of them might not survive to reach Cape Town. I am particularly concerned about the women and girls who are with child. Three of the seven are particularly unwell.'

'Aye,' Thomas Edgar agreed. 'And even if we reached Cape Town without sinking, the Dutch would never allow us into the harbour if there is disease on board.'

'No,' George Aitken nodded his agreement. 'I think our best chance will be to head to Rio de Janeiro. It is not a city I would choose to go to normally, but I can't see that we have any other choice. They probably have enough disease of their own so won't be too concerned about any we might bring.'

'Right, we'll head west, then follow the coast down to Rio de

Janeiro. It will take quite a while to do the necessary repairs. By the time we are ready to sail again, we will have had a chance to eat plenty of fresh fruit and vegetables. If luck is with us most of our invalids will have recovered their health.'

The *Lady Juliana* took a new tack and with an ever freshening wind filling her sails, she skipped along swiftly over the waves.

The news that they would be making land much earlier than expected was greeted with relief and joy by both convicts and sailors alike. The women, who were relieved that they would soon see land again; the crew who would now be able to rest and recover their strength, and the officers because they alone knew the jeopardy their ship was in.

On the last day of October, a shout from the masthead drew the attention of all on board. First, the eyes went to the figure high above them, then moved to follow the direction of his pointing arm. As one, with a hand raised to shade their eyes from the burning rays of the sun, everyone peered searchingly over the bows. It was quite some time however before anyone on deck finally spotted the darkening proof of land on the horizon.

'I see it!' a woman's voice squealed. 'Over there! Land! Look — over there!'

One after another, shouts of joy rang out. Women hugged each other. Hugged any sailor who got near enough. They danced and jumped around, some with tears streaming down their faces.

As they drew near they could see it was not a large area of land, but islands. Lots and lots of islands.

'What is this place,' Alice asked Danny. 'I thought we were going to a harbour but all that here is islands.'

Danny laughed. 'We are going to a harbour, you silly goose. James told me there at least a hundred islands in the approach to Rio de Janeiro. It will take us quite a while to sail between them all, but if you're patient we'll reach the harbour eventually.'

It was late the following evening before Alice spotted a strange-looking mountain that appeared to rise up straight out of the ocean. She had seen cliffs aplenty on the Isle of Man, but nothing to match this huge monster.

James, who had been to Rio do Janeiro on several previous occasions was happy to explain that the Portuguese had named this strange rock Sugar Loaf Mountain because it resembled the shape of a loaf of concentrated sugar.

Night was fast approaching, so Captain Aitken decided it would be prudent to anchor well offshore until the morning. Early the following day the *Lady Juliana* edged carefully across the bar.

The women excitedly crowded along the rail. There was just so much to be seen, the likes of which they had never encountered before.

In the sea, crowding all around the ship, were the strangest looking creatures Alice had ever set eyes on.

'What are those?' she asked, leaning us far over the rail as her belly would allow.

Maggie looked down to where she was pointing and twitched a shoulder. 'Buggered if I know! They don't have nothing like *them* in the Isle of man I don't think.' Grabbing a passing sailor by the arm she asked, 'What's them things?'

The man glanced down at the water. 'Them's turtles. Don't you women know nothin'?'

'Well we've never been here before, and there aren't none of them where we come from.'

The man shook his head, twitched his arm free and, mumbling something unintelligible, went off to get on with his work.

Almost as soon as the *Lady Juliana* crossed the bar and entered the harbour a whole flotilla of small, rickety-looking boats bobbed across the water towards them. Some of them looked to be not much more than bathtubs. Certainly most of them did not look seaworthy.

The convicts watched in awe as a flock of small children swarmed up the sides and onto the deck. Children with all shades of colouring, ranging from white to black. Their features ran from the finer boned European to the much broader African, the likes of which the women had never seen before. They were not to know that almost from the start of Portugal's occupation of this country, there had been extensive cohabitation between the Portuguese, the indigenous peoples, and later the Africans.

Dressed in nothing more than a small piece of cloth to cover their loins, the smallest of the boys swarmed up the sides of the ship in only seconds. Slightly larger boys clung halfway up, while the biggest ones stayed in the boat. Up this chain of humanity was passed a variety of fruit such as the women had never before seen.

Alice watched with tears in her eyes and her mouth-watering as the women who had money gleefully bought the exotic fruits from the urchins. All the convicts who had sold their bodies in the previous ports of call greedily collected fruit.

With not a penny to her name, she could not buy even a single apple. Suddenly the exciting scene she had been watching lost all its magic. Closing her eyes to shut it out, Alice bowed her head and sadly turned away. It was more than she could bear to watch.

An arm went around her shoulders and she felt something being thrust into her hands. Looking down she found herself clutching and apple, an orange and a couple of bent yellow things she had never seen before.

'Eat these up, love,' Maggie whispered in her ear, do you both good.

Alice gazed up at her with tears in her eyes. 'But I haven't any money.'

Maggie gave her a hug. 'You don't need any, my love. I've paid for your fruit.'

'But it's yours. Your money. You worked for it and you will need it when we get to wherever we're going.'

Maggie laughed. 'An' most of the time I enjoyed the work. I told you I would always look after you and that's what I am doing. I have enough money for both of us.'

The tears started to flow in earnest then. Alice threw her arms around her friend and kissed her cheek. Clinging to her like a baby monkey she said 'What would I ever have done without you? I could not have survived this ordeal without you. It is my vow that one day I will repay you.'

Maggie returned the hug, wiped Alice's greasy hair back from her face, and looked fiercely into her eyes. 'Just look here, my girl, you have nothing to repay me for. Just to see you happy and you and your baby healthy is all the payment I need. So just eat that fruit and enjoy it.'

Looking past Maggie, Alice saw boats approaching, rowed by men with jet black skin.

Nudging her friend she pointed to the boats and asked, 'Have you ever seen people that colour before?'

Maggie looked around, Studied the oarsmen and shook her head.

'Are they real people,' Alice asked, frowning.

'Must be. They are probably the African slaves we have heard talk about.'

Within minutes the boats, tied up alongside the *Lady Juliana*.

The women jostled for position at the rail, all eager not to miss any part of whatever was going on.

Recognising them as official government launches, Captain

Aitken hurried to greet his guests, brushing small urchins aside as if they were pesky flies. As his visitors climbed the rail he extended a hand to help and to welcome them aboard.

'Good morning, gentlemen,' he greeted them, hoping they would understand enough English, for he knew no Portuguese.

'We are the representatives of His Excellency the Viceroy of the Brazils, son of the King of Portugal,' one of the fancily dressed men said pompously. 'Would you be kind enough to tell us what is your business here?'

'We sail under the orders of the English government,' Captain Aitken began, 'Transporting two hundred and twenty-nine female convicts to the English colony of New South Wales. Now would you gentlemen care to come to my quarters and partake of a glass of port.'

Four heads nodded and the visitors happily turned to follow Captain Aitken.

'We have a favour to ask of His Excellency,' the captain started when the representatives were all settled with a glass in their hands. 'Our ship is very badly in need of repair and we have quite a number of people aboard who are not at all well. In addition, we have six or seven women who are pregnant and due to give birth quite soon.'

The man who was obviously in charge of the delegation nodded thoughtfully. 'And what are your plans? What is it you require of us.'

'First and foremost we need to remain here long enough to repair all the damage to our ship. That will take quite some time. We would also like to stay until all, or a least most, of our sick are returned to health. There are also the pregnant women to consider. It would be much safer, for both mothers and babies, if they could be confined here rather than at sea.'

The man thoughtfully rubbed his chin. He knew very well

that His Excellency and indeed most Portuguese had a great liking for the British, especially those bound for Port Jackson. The Governor of that colony, so he had heard, was Commodore Arthur Phillip, who had at one time served in the Royal Portuguese Navy. Any countryman of his was regarded as a respected and welcome visitor to Rio de Janeiro.

'I can not foresee any problems,' he finally replied. 'I'm quite sure His Excellency will be happy for you to stay as long as you require. Of course, you must come and make your request to him. We shall return to shore now and I will tell His Excellency to expect you later.'

Quaffing the last of his port, he pushed himself to his feet and gave an elegant bow.

When the visiting officials returned to the deck a short time later they were not quite so steady on their feet, nor was their return to their launches as dignified as their arrival.

Not long after their departure Captain Aitken's longboat was launched. He and Lieutenant Edgar appeared on deck dressed, even in those extreme temperatures, in their frock coats and tight breeches. As he gave instructions to the mate, a river of sweat ran down his face to wet the collar of his shirt.

'There will be a lot of formalities to be sorted out, so we will be gone for probably a day or two. Keep a good eye on those women, both day and night. Make sure none of them go over the side. The last thing we need is to be searching Brazil for missing women.'

'Aye aye Sir.' the mate gave a crisp salute.

The two overdressed men wiped the sweat from their faces, climbed down into their launch, and were rowed to shore.

'Why, in God's name are they wearing all them warm clothes in this heat?' Maggie asked James.

'They have to. It's the way things are done in the navy. When the officers go ashore anywhere they have to put on their best bib and tucker. As messengers of King George, it is essential for them to look their best.'

'I seems barmy to me,' Alice joined in. 'They was in a lather of sweat before they even came on deck. What are they going to be like are in a few hours?'

James shrugged. 'It's the way it is. No naval officer would go ashore in a foreign land improperly dressed.'

It was two days before the captain and Lieutenant Edgar returned. Though looking somewhat frazzled and with their clothing now quite badly stained, they had an air of satisfaction.

'How did it go?' Richard Alley asked, as soon a the officers had had time to get themselves freshened up. 'Did His Excellency agree to any of our requests?'

Captain Aitken smiled and nodded. 'I'm happy to report he was very co-operative. It helps that he has such high regard for Governor Phillip. We are welcome to stay here for as long as it takes us to do the necessary repairs, to return our passengers to good health, and to welcome all the babies into the world.'

Surgeon Alley beamed. 'That is the best news I have had in many a long day. There is no shortage of fresh fruit and vegetables, so with luck, our sick list should soon shorten. And it will be a great relief not to have to deliver any more babies than I have to at sea.'

With the next high tide near, Captain Aitken again ordered the decks cleared of all women. The crew now scrambled around, readying the ship for entrance to the inner harbour. As they passed through, an eleven gun salute reverberated round the *Lady Juliana* making her timbers shiver and once again scaring the life out of the passengers.

When the convicts were allowed back on deck they were stunned by the sight of the harbour. There were many little green island and the whole city, which climbed steeply up the hills, was surrounded by high mountains. It was a stunning sight, foreign to anything the passengers on the *Lady Juliana* had ever before seen. The harbour was enclosed by severe-looking grey fortifications, from where the canons had been fired.

Bells rang incessantly from the many churches and convents that could be seen along the shore. In the evening there was an endless sound of incantations as worshippers prayed to their various saints. The thousands of candles they burned lit the harbour at night. and the women on the *Lady Juliana* were at first awed by the sight.

There was always something of interest for the convicts to watch. It was a very busy harbour, with ships moving in, out and around it at all times. Guard-boats rowed by black slaves hustled around all the time amongst the ships, and the women watched it all with avid interest. Some, no doubt, would be wondering if escape might be possible and trying to think of a way it might be achieved.

The captain had asked His Excellency the Viceroy if his crew and certain privileged, trustworthy convicts might go ashore. He had hoped that the officers might be able to take their 'wives' for shore breaks.

His Excellency had steepled his fingers under his chin and considered the question for several minutes. 'I can allow the officers to come ashore. I can see no problem with that. I will also permit the crew to come, but only if you can give me your word they will behave in an orderly fashion. And they must be accompanied by one of my officers at all times.'

'And the women — -?' George Aitken began.

His excellency had shaken his head decisively. 'No. Not the women. You must understand that we live in very turbulent times. We have just quelled a rebellion. The leader, Joaquim Jose da Silva Xavier, was captured and executed. He was hanged and quartered in the city square. His head was displayed on a pole in the square and his limbs sent to be displayed in the towns where most of his supporters were. We hope this will be lesson enough to make sure they will not repeat their trouble-making. I have not the troops I would need to guard your convict women.'

Knowing it was important that his men should have some shore leave, George had sighed, glumly given his word and accepted the Viceroy's terms. What else could he do?

Repairs to the *Lady Juliana* went along steadily and Captain Aitken was pleased with her progress.

There was an endless supply of fruit and vegetables from the near-naked urchins who swarmed around and over the ship all day. Their wares were cheap and good. The poor souls who had been afflicted with scurvy quite quickly showed signs of improvement.

The surgeon heaved a sigh of relief. At last, all his expectant mothers were in good health again and were close to giving birth.

The British government, in all its wisdom, had anticipated that by sending over two hundred women on a months-long voyage with a shipful of lusty men there were bound to be several babies born before the ship reached its destination. This being so, they had supplied a good number of suits of 'childbed linen'.

Concerned with the torrid November temperatures in Rio de Janeiro, Richard worried that the heat within the ship would put too much of a strain on the pregnant women while they gave birth. With this in mind, he ordered that a birthing tent should be constructed on the deck. This way, if there was any breeze at all he could have the flaps of the tent opened to catch it. He gave a nod of satisfaction as he watched the suits of childbed linen being stacked in the corner. Not the ideal conditions for childbirth he conceded to himself, but the best he could manage given the situation they were in.

CHAPTER 18

The convicts were not slow to realise there would be rich pickings in this busy harbour town.

There were so many ships with crews who had not had the pleasure of a woman for many a long day, many with a pocket full of money and very little to spend it on. There were also many of the wealthier residents of Rio de Janeiro who were keen to try a bit of this new paler flesh that had drifted onto their doorstep.

Alice watched with fascination, as a steady stream of men, who's skin came in a great variety of shades, climbed on board the *Lady Juliana*.

While the convicts scrambled to try to snare the male they fancied most, the men of the crew stood close-by ready to claim their *wife's* fee the moment she had made her choice. It was always *payment in advance*.

Maggie was as keen as any, with James collecting the fee to be shared out later. Even Sarah and Lily had succumbed to the temptation. Having lost their virginity they now felt they might as well add to their nest egg for when they arrived in Port Jackson.

Alice thought about it in bewilderment. *Could she do that?* she wondered yet again. *Lie under another man for payment? Would Danny want her to? And if he did would she be upset?* She shook her head and smiled to herself. What was the use of wondering? It wasn't going to happen. No man, she was sure, would be interested in her with a belly full of baby,

Maggie, Sarah and Lily seemed to enjoy it, so maybe she would try it one day. It would be nice to have a bit of money!

Alice huddled in a corner as far away from the birthing tent as she could get. Even with her hands clamped tightly over her ears, she could not shut out the woman's screams. She didn't need to hear this. She did not want to hear this. Her own baby would be making its way out of her belly and into the world in the next few days, she knew. Was this what she had ahead of her? This terrible agony severe enough to make a woman scream for hours.

Maggie was sitting on the deck beside her. Alice could feel her friend's arms around her and cuddled in tight against her, hoping somehow to shut out the terrible sounds. It didn't work. Nothing worked. The screams continued to tear through her nerve ends and into her heart. Sobbing she clung to Maggie. 'Make it stop,' she pleaded. 'Can't somebody make it stop. Why does it have to go on?'

Maggie bit her lips as she battled to force back tears. Wiping the hair away from Alice's damp face she kissed her forehead. 'Hush love,' she said quietly. 'It will be over soon.' She covered Alice's hand with her own, hoping it would help to shut out more of the sounds.'

A whole lifetime later, or so it seemed, the screams died away to a whimper and finally stopped.

Apart from the sounds of the rigging slapping against the masts and the sloughing of the sea against the hull, there was a complete and unnatural silence.

Every person on the deck was motionless, all eyes fixed on the birthing tent as they waited for the sound that never came.

Maggie muttered, 'Oh dear God,' then clamped a hand over her mouth.

'What is it? What's happened?' Alice straightened up and looked at her friend through large, frightened eyes. The shocked look on Maggie's face made her even more fearful.

'The baby hasn't cried!'

'Why should it cry? Why does it matter whether it cries.'

Maggie gulped down a huge tremulous breath. This child, who was about to give birth, knew so little. Knew *nothing*. *Dear God*, she thought, *however will she cope when her time comes?*

Richard Alley ducked out through the flap of the birthing tent. He looked spent and pale and somehow years older. There was blood on his hands and clothes and even a few smears on his face. All eyes followed him as he stumbled to the rail and stood looking wearily down into the water. After a few moments, he drew In a deep breath, straightened and made his way up to the bridge.

Several minutes later three of the women, who had been acting as midwives, emerged from the birthing tent in tears. They merely shook their heads and not a word needed to be said.

As the surgeon entered the bridge George Aitken raised his eyebrows questioningly. He had watched Richard from the moment he left the birthing tent and could tell from his demeanour that the worst had happened. He knew everyone on the ship had been shocked by the poor woman's screams, And almost certainly everyone in the harbour, and possibly on the nearby shoreline too.

The surgeon slumped onto a seat and put his head in his hands.

Captain Aitken laid a hand on his shoulder. 'Which one was it?' he asked quietly.

'Mary Bainbridge. The poor girl didn't have a chance. She had gaol fever when she came aboard. I managed to cure her of that, but then she took the scurvy. She was very weak. She was only eighteen years of age.'

'And the baby?'

'Gone too. Dead before it was born. it was a girl child and never took a breath.'

George sighed and nodded sadly. 'We will have to hold a service as soon as possible.' He gazed thoughtfully around the harbour for a few moments. 'Unfortunately, we won't be able to give them a burial at sea, but in these torrid temperatures we must dispose of the bodies as soon as possible.'

Richard Alley nodded his agreement. 'Yes,' he sighed, 'the last thing we need now is another outbreak of disease.

Turning to Lieutenant Edgar, George said, 'Thomas go and speak to His Excellency right away. Explain to him what has happened and request that Mary and her child may be buried in a graveyard in Rio de Janeiro.

'Sir.' Thomas saluted and immediately left the bridge. Minutes later the captain's launch was in the water and Thomas was on his way to shore. When he returned some two hours later he had the necessary permission.

'His Excellency was happy to agree. He sends his condolences. I told him we do not know what religion Mary followed, but he said he would arrange for a Catholic priest to say a prayer at the interment. It's all the same God after all isn't it?'

'Thank you, Lieutenant. I will hold a service here before the bodies are taken ashore, but will change the wording slightly as it is not going to be a burial at sea.'

Mary Bainbridge's body lay on a table on the deck the following morning. She had been wrapped In the bloodied birthing sheets

255

with her baby in her arms. Some of the sailors had then stitched her into a cocoon of sailcloth, as they would have done for a burial at sea. a large flag blanketed the table and its sorry bundle.

The whole of the ship's company, officers, crew, and convicts alike, were gathered on deck. A sailor, the *husband* of Mary and father of the dead child, stood close to the table. Tears ran unfettered down his face, to drip from his chin onto his shirt.

Captain Aitken stood solemnly, bible in hand, flanked by surgeon Alley and Lieutenant Edgar.

'We are here, as you all know, to say farewell to our friend Mary Bainbridge who lost her fight for life and that of her baby. It is a sad time for all of us and I thank you for your respectful silence. I will now read the service and say the last prayers for Mary and her unnamed child.'

He paused for a moment, perhaps listening to the murmuring of sobs from the women.

'Unto Almighty God, we commend the soul of our sisters departed. Their bodies will be committed into the care of the good people and the Saints of Rio de Janeiro,' George's strong voice was raw with emotion, 'in sure and certain hope of the resurrection unto eternal life, through our Lord Jesus Christ; at whose coming in glorious majesty to judge the world. The corruptible body of those in eternal sleep shall be changed, and made unto his glorious body; according to the mighty working whereby He is able to subdue all things unto himself. We hereby commit the body of this woman, Mary Bainbridge and her unnamed girl child to his care. God bless you, my children.'

Alice was vaguely aware that a pipe was playing as the flag was removed and folded. Her mind was a turbulent mixture of fear and sorrow.

The sailcloth bundle that was Mary and her baby was lowered

with great care into the waiting launch. The captain, surgeon, Lieutenant Edgar and the father of the baby climbed down behind it and the oarsmen moved them to shore for the burial.

They left behind them a shocked silence that blanketed the whole harbour, unbroken save for the quiet sobbing of some of the women.

Shortly after their arrival in Rio de Janeiro Richard Alley approached the captain. 'I am quite concerned about the health of the women who are soon to give birth.'

'Concerned? in what way? What worries you?'

'Mostly the temperature. It is hot enough now, but summer is fast approaching, and I fear the very pregnant women will not deal well with the extreme heat.'

Captain Aitken frowned and sighed, 'There is not much we can do about the heat, Richard. Did you have some thoughts on the matter?'

'Well, I did wonder if it would be possible to allocate space on the deck to each of these women and fashion an old piece of sail in place to shade them. I would like it if they could be allowed to sleep on the deck too. That would be much cooler for them than the orlop or even the forecastle.'

George Aitken nodded thoughtfully. 'Yes, I can see that they would be more comfortable on deck and it could certainly be quite unsafe for them to be locked in the orlop at night. There would be little risk of them going overboard and attempting to escape during the night. So, yes Richard, you have my permission and blessing to arrange quarters on the deck. But only for the women who are near to giving birth. No one else.'

Richard expressed his thanks and quickly took his leave.

At first Alice was reluctant to leave Danny's bunk. She needed him near her during this frightening time.

'Think about it.' Maggie counselled her. 'More often than not Danny isn't there because he is on watch. When he is there, he has to sleep on the floor to give you comfort in the bed. It will be cooler and more comfortable for you to have a mattress out on the deck. Better for the baby too.'

Alice gazed thoughtfully over the water to the busy bustling township but said nothing.

Maggie smiled and shook her head. 'Ask surgeon Alley to give you a space near the forecastle door, then Danny will not be far away if you need him.

So it was that Alice found herself spending most of her days and all of her nights sitting under a shade right next to the door to the forecastle. If she was honest with herself, she had to admit that she was cooler and thereby more comfortable with the night breeze blowing around her.

Alice was awakened by a strange sensation in her lower belly. It wasn't a pain, just a tightening, but not the movements of the baby that she had become accustomed to.

She wriggled on her mattress, trying without success to find a comfortable position. Finally, she scrambled to her feet and crept into the forecastle. Easing herself, awkwardly onto Danny's bunk, she pressed herself close to him.

Half waking, Danny put his arms around her and she snuggled in tightly.

'What's wrong love, can't you sleep?' he whispered.

'I was asleep, but I wakened with this strange feeling.'

'Strange? What do you mean by strange?'

'I don't really know. Most of the time there is nothing, but then

I get these niggly tightening feelings. Then they go away again. I think the baby might be starting to come.'

Danny was suddenly wide awake. He sat bolt upright and moved to slide from the bed, but Alice clutched at his arm. 'Where are you going? Don't leave me,' she pleaded as she pulled him back into her arms.

Danny kissed her forehead. 'I'm not leaving you. Well, only for a little while. I'm going to fetch Surgeon Alley.'

'Don't get him yet.' Alice whispered. 'It's the middle of the night.'

'But if the baby is coming, we must have him here.'

'We don't know if it is the baby coming yet. I haven't had any pain at all, so even if it is the baby, I think it will be a long time before it is born.'

Danny reluctantly agreed to wait, and lay wide awake, holding Alice gently for the rest of a hot restless night.

When morning came and the ship was waking, Alice sought out Maggie and told her what was going on. By this time Alice's tightening sensations had become stronger and more frequent.

Without a moment's hesitation, Maggie nodded. 'Yes, I have little doubt you are in early labour.'

Richard Alley was hunkered down before his patient, who squatted miserably on the birthing chair. 'Come on Alice,' He encouraged. 'You have to keep pushing.'

Alice shook her head. Her eyes were red from crying, her face puffed up. 'I can't,' she sobbed. 'I can't do it anymore.'

Maggie wiped her damp hair from her forehead. 'Come on love,' she encouraged. 'You have to push this baby out. No one can do it for you.'

Alice shook her head and flopped forward, exhausted. 'I've tried, but it won't come out.'

As another crippling pain gripped her she tried to scream, but it came out as little more than a gurgling whimper.'

'Lie down on the sheets lass and let me check how far the baby is down.'

With Maggie's help, Alice slid down onto the sheets and curled into a ball as another pain ripped through her.

When the pain had passed, the surgeon gently turned Alice on her back and carefully felt her tummy. With a sharp intake of breath, he rolled his eyes to heaven and whispered 'Oh dear God.'

Maggie gave him a piercing look and he shook his head. 'Baby has turned and it's coming bottom first.

'Bloody Hell,' was all Maggie could think of to say and Richard nodded in agreement.

'We will have to have a go at turning it. Alice can't deliver it breach.'

'No. What do we have to do? The child has been labouring now for a day and a half. She can't take much more.'

Jane Bridger, who had been a midwife before she had been convicted of stealing a patient's baby, moved forward and nudged Richard Alley out of the way. Sitting on the bed beside Alice, she took her hand and said quietly, 'Now my lass, your baby is trying to come out bum first. You can't have it folded in two, so we are going to have to push it back where it came from and turn it around. It will hurt. I won't lie to you about that, but we must do it.'

Alice shook her head and burst into tears. 'No. Please no. It has been hurting too much for too long. I can't bear any more pain. I don't want this baby anymore. Just tell it to go away.' She broke off, squealing, as another pain hit her.

Jane rubbed her back gently. 'I'm sorry, my lovely, but there is only one way the baby is coming out, so I'm afraid you are going to have to suffer a little bit longer.'

Turning to Maggie she said, 'find me a good lot of pillows or blankets. We need to raise her bum a good bit to help me push the babe back up so I can turn it.'

Jane had performed this type of manipulation many times during her career. Sometimes it worked — more often it did not, but it had to be tried. With an air of confidence she didn't really feel, she worked between contractions pushing upward with all her might, but no sooner would she move the baby than a contraction would come and push it back. Each time Alice would give a little tired scream and plead with them to stop.

After about half an hour Jane sat back and shook her head. 'It's not going to work,' she said quietly. 'If I keep going, I'm going to kill both of them.'

Maggie, in tears by this time, looked pleadingly at Richard Alley. 'What now?' she asked tremulously.

The doctor looked searchingly at Maggie and Jane. 'There is only one other way. 'I will have to cut it out of her!'

Maggie clamped a hand to her mouth and shook her head. 'No!'

Richard Alley caught her eye and held it. 'Yes. It is the only way left and the sooner we do it the better. Poor Alice has suffered more than enough already. If we don't do it soon it's going to kill her!'

Maggie sighed miserably and nodded. This was not at all what she had wished for little Alice, but she could see it *must* be done.

'Go and get a good measure of rum and when you come back with it bring two more of the women.' When Maggie gave him a startled look he added quietly, 'We will need four of you to hold her.'

Maggie scrambled to her feet and hurried away. While she was gone Richard explained to Alice what he was going to have to do, and persuaded her to drink large doses of laudanum and morphine.

261

Maggie returned very quickly with a large glass of rum and with Sarah and Lily in tow, both looking very nervous.

Richard held the glass to Alice's lips. 'Here drink this quickly.'

Alice gulped a large mouthful then spluttered. 'That's horrible. I can't drink that.' She quickly pushed the glass away, but Richard returned it to her lips.

'You *must* drink it, my dear. It will make the pain less severe.'

Alice obediently drank the rum and shuddered as she finished it.

After telling her to lie on her back he instructed the four women in the room to hold her shoulders and legs. When he made the first incision, Alice gave a high-pitched scream that ended in a gurgle then, mercifully, she lost consciousness.

Working quickly, Richard Alley hooked his fingers under the baby's arms, lifted it out and thrust it into Jane Bridger's waiting arms. Without wasting a moment he prepared the gut to repair Alice's wound.

Jane took the baby by its feet and dangled it upside down. When it didn't cry, she gave it a sharp slap and was rewarded with an indignant screech. She sat on the far end of the bed, cleaning the baby's face and smiled up at Maggie and the other two pale, stricken looking girls.

'It's a boy!' she announced.

Maggie gave a loud whoop. 'I told you!' she said triumphantly. 'Didn't I say all along that it was going to be a boy?' Turning to the surgeon she asked, 'And Alice? Will Alice be alright?'

Richard smiled. 'She should be. I have done several of these operations before. The important thing now is to keep her wound clean and make sure it does not become infected. Alice will need to rest, and she'll be sore for a while, but she's a tough little thing she will survive this ordeal.'

Sarah and Lily smiled and nodded. 'Can I go and tell Danny?' Sarah pleaded.

Maggie laughed. 'Yes. Off you go. he's been very anxious this past two days. But tell him he won't be able to see her for a little while.'

Alice opened her eyes and looked around in dazed puzzlement. 'What's happened?' she asked weakly.

'You've had a baby is what's happened,' Maggie replied cheerfully. 'A little boy.'

'A boy,' Alice repeated in wonder. Suddenly her face clouded. 'Is he alright?' she asked anxiously.

'More than just alright,' Jane told her. 'He's perfect. Here meet your son.' She handed Alice the swaddled bundle.

Alice winced as she took her son into her eager arms and the stitches in her belly pulled. Looking down at the wizened looking face she lifted him and kissed his little red cheek. 'Hello, Daniel Michael,' she said as a tear stung her eyes. 'I promise I will always love you more than anything else in this world,' she promised.

The tiny face turned towards her with its mouth wide open.

Maggie laughed gleefully. 'And he loves you too,' she said. 'Cupboard love!'

CHAPTER 19

Ll too soon for the convicts on the *Lady Juliana*, the time had come for them to take to the high seas again. With spring marching on towards summer, each day that had passed since their arrival in Rio de Janeiro had been hotter than the day before. The women had what was, most of the time, an idyllic seven weeks to recover their health. For most of them, they had been more comfortable and better fed than ever before. The only fly in the ointment was the almost unbearable heat.

Recovering from her surgery, Alice was happy to rest in her open-sided tent on the deck, cradling her new treasure. Little Daniel Michael, named for his father and the policeman in Douglas who had treated her so kindly, was a good baby. He slept most of the time, fed greedily whenever he wakened, then went straight back to sleep.

Alice had never known such joy could exist. She couldn't stop looking at and touching this tiny person she had created. It was like the most beautiful dream and she just prayed she would not wake up and find herself back in the nightmare she had escaped from.

Danny, too, was overjoyed with his son and spent every spare moment he had with Alice and the baby. He had been physically sick when he had been told that Alice had been cut open to get the baby out. His guilt at having caused her to go through this trauma was almost more than he could bear. When he tried to apologise to Alice she just smiled and kissed him.

'There is nothing to be sorry about, my love. I — we have Daniel now and he is worth everything. I will heal and I have already forgotten most of the pain. He was worth every moment of it.'

Even so, despite Alice's reassurances, Danny still suffered at times. He assuaged his guilt by helping her with Daniel. His experience with all the younger siblings that had arrived in his life meant he knew how to handle babies and was able to offer Alice sensible advice about caring for their son.

The ladies of the night had very frequently entertained visiting males and had useful sums of money bound to their bodies. Maggie was an experienced old hand at the game but Lily and Sarah were new to it. They had been apprehensive at first, but after lying with a few men they decided that on the whole they rather enjoyed promiscuity. Most of all they enjoyed the easy money that came with it and all three of them insisted they would not do it if they were not being paid. They had more money beneath their belts than ever they'd had before.

Alice was a bit bemused by it all but had more on her mind than other peoples' sexual activities. She had Danny and he was the only man she wanted. In her daydreams she imagined them setting up home together. Danny, she was sure, would be able to turn his hand to any kind of work that came his way, while she would set up her business making and selling children's' clothes. Life for her would be better than it had ever been before. It was already better!

Although in a considerable amount of pain from the huge gash down her belly, she bore it without complaint. Richard Alley had told her very sternly that she was not to do any work *at all* until her wound was fully healed, but by the time she had recovered from the trauma of the birth she found time to be limping slowly past and soon took up her stitching again.

One morning Alice sensed a tension in the atmosphere. There was something afoot but she could not work out what it was. During the weeks they had been in Rio de Janeiro everything had been peaceful and relaxed. The men had spent a lot of their time lounging around; playing deck games; cavorting with the women, relieving their lust and generally just enjoying themselves.

Yesterday was different. Suddenly the men were busy and there was a sense of urgency on the ship.

The ship's boats had been busy since very early in the morning. The men rowed backward and forwards between ship and shore. Every barrel that still contained water was emptied onto the deck. The empty casks were lowered into the ship's boats, rowed shore and brought back a while later full of fresh water.

Today the crew seemed alert and on edge. Again the boats had been busy.

Awake and feeding Daniel, as the sky began to welcome the new day, Alice watched with interest as the boats set off once again towards the shore.

Peering through an early morning haze, she sat in the shade of her little tent enjoying a small breeze. Warm though it was, it was better than the usual still, humid, dank air that made breathing a struggle. Besides, it helped to blow away the smell from the polluted water of the harbour that clung around the ship.

When the boats arrived back they carried bags and crates full of fresh fruit and vegetables. These were quickly heaved on board and taken below deck — away from the scorching sun.

More small boys than ever, in their leaky home-made boats, arrived beside the *Lady Juliana*.

Those boats worried Alice. All of them looked as if they might sink any minute and she wondered how often this happened. And if it did, could they swim, would any of their friends rescue them or would they be left to drown? To the new young mother, it didn't bear thinking about.

The decks came alive with the grubby, loincloth clad little creatures who swarmed around the *Lady Juliana* like an army of ants.

They leaned over the rail screeching and jabbering in their own tongue to the older boys below. Fruit and vegetables flew up and were deftly caught.

The convicts, sensing this might be their last chance to stock up on the delicious foods the boys were selling, clamoured to buy as much as they could.

A collection of livestock was heaved aboard and driven through the milling mob of women and little boys, to be secured in the waiting pens.

Alice sat in her little tent watching all the activity, with Daniel asleep on a blanket beside her. She would have loved to join in and do some buying but, having no money, she had to sadly shake her head whenever a little boy offered her his wares.

It was about noon when Lieutenant Thomas Edgar strode onto the deck with a speaking-trumpet in his hand. 'I want the deck cleared,' he bellowed.

Everyone, with the exception of the army of little boys, stopped what they were doing and turned to stare at him.

'Right now!' He roared when no one moved to obey him. 'I want all these ragamuffins over the side and clear of my ship. All the women must return to their quarters. And all these tents must be taken down and cleared from the deck. This minute! Move!'

There was a sudden flurry of activity as the crewman moved to obey.

The little boys were collected, bundled over the side, and left with no alternative but to climb down the nets into their waiting craft.

Once they were all out of the way the sailors, started shepherding the women towards the hatch to the orlop deck. Some went peacefully, with muttered apologies from the men, but others put up loud arguments and refused to be moved.

Thomas Edgar heaved an angry sigh, stamped his foot, and raised his speaking trumpet to his mouth. 'Any woman still on this deck five minutes from now will be thrown in the brig and will later receive twelve kisses from the *cat*.'

The offending women stopped their shouting and turned to glare at him.

Thomas held their stare without flinching. 'Well, that is one minute wasted so far. That leaves you four, so if you have one grain of sense in your heads you will obey me!'

The following few minutes saw an undignified scramble as the women who had thought to rebel pushed and shoved to get down the hatch within the allotted four minutes.

Alice and her three friends, watching from the forecastle, giggled as they studied the melee.

'Do you think he would have done it?' Alice asked through her laughter.

Maggie frowned questioningly. 'Who? Done what?'

'Mister Edgar. Would he really have given them the cat if they had refused to go below?'

Maggie shrugged. 'Probably not, but the threat worked didn't it? They weren't game to find out.'

'Except Mavis Crowe,' Sarah put in. 'I bet he would flog her as soon as look at her.'

Maggie laughed. 'I can't understand why he hasn't dumped her overboard months ago.'

Meantime the sailors scurried around dismantling the strange array of little tents that had sprung up around the deck during their stay in Rio de Janeiro.

There followed, for the next two hours or so, all the sounds the women had now become accustomed to as the crew prepared the *Lady Juliana* for departure.

The women in the forecastle heard the almost deafening banging of the flapping sails, as the wind began to fill them, and the cracking and snapping of the rigging.

There was the usual cacophony of men's voices as Captain Aitken bellowed instructions through his speaking horn and the men shouted to each other.

The thirty or so *wives* sat in the torrid heat of the forecastle longing to be released back to the fresh air on deck. Concerned only with their own and in several cases, their babies' discomfort, few of them spared a thought for the two hundred or more women who were locked in the stinking, airless oven that was the orlop deck.

Finally came the clanking and clattering of the chain as it dragged the heavy anchor from the sea bed. There was a sigh of relief from probably every woman on board. They knew by this time that those sounds signalled that they would very soon be released into the fresh air.

Almost immediately the convicts felt the change of attitude in the *Lady Juliana* as the sails took the wind and she started to move.

Once the activity on the deck had settled down and the

women were not going to be in the way the hatch to the orlop was unbolted. There followed several minutes of screaming and swearing as the convicts pushed and shoved to escape from their hell hole.

Alice and her three friends moved to the rail to watch as the bustling town of Rio de Janeiro gradually diminished.

The boats of little boys bobbed in their wake and were gradually left behind. The women felt a thrill of both fear and excitement as the *Lady Juliana* moved out through the mouth of the harbour.

The many islands slipped past on either side of the ship and gradually the air freshened as they moved further away from shore.

So this was it then. The next step of their journey towards this unknown *place beyond the seas*. Where to next? James had told them Cape Town. But where was Cape Town? They didn't know. Time would tell.

The *Lady Juliana* made a fairly swift passage between Rio de Janeiro and Cape Town with a brisk following wind most of the way. When the sailor at the masthead shouted 'Land ahoy!' a ripple of excitement ran the length of the ship.

All heads turned towards the bow and necks craned as crew and passengers alike watched excitedly for their first sight of land in fifty days. It had been a calm and fairly uneventful voyage but had seemed to the convicts to have taken forever.

Within about two hours the strange flat top of Table Mountain appeared out of the blue hazy distance. Not long afterward the excited people on the *Lady Juliana* could see the Lions head and Devils Peak; the green hills rolling down from the mountains. Very soon they could see buildings, houses, and churches on the lower reaches of the hills and the basin between mountains and sea.

Cape Town's bay was alive with ships of all shapes and sizes. It was the busiest of harbours, used by the Dutch, French, and English to ferry goods from such places as Madras, Mauritius, Bengal, Calcutta, and Bordeaux to Holland, France, Britain, and Portugal.

There were also some American whalers and private merchantmen, some of whom had thought about setting up trade to the new colony at Botany Bay.

Before the sun had set on the 28th of February the *Lady Juliana* lay at anchor a mile or more south west of Cape Town.

With his looking glass to his eye Captain Aitken surveyed the bobbing mass of shipping. His sweep stopped suddenly and moved back.

'By God, what is *she* doing here?'

'Who, Sir?' Lieutenant Edgar questioned.

'The *Guardian*. Here, take a look. I'll swear that's the *Guardian*.' As he handed his spyglass to Lieutenant Edgar he pointed to a ship in the harbour'

'The *Guardian* it is,' Thomas agreed.

Captain Aitken frowned. 'That's strange. with the detour we took and the amount of time we spent in Rio de Janeiro I would have expected them to have been well on their way from here by now. It looks as if it may have been run aground. Certainly, it is in very poor shape.'

Early the following morning Alice was sitting near the rail, cradling her baby when she noticed a boat with several stern, official-looking men, approaching the *Lady Juliana*.

'I wonder who this lot are. They all look a bit grim,' she said.

Maggie nodded. 'James said that Cape Town belongs to the Dutch and that some of their officials would be coming to pay their respects to Captain Aitken.'

At that moment the captain and Thomas Edgar arrived on deck and moved to welcome their guests aboard.

Once the Dutchmen were comfortably settled in George Aitken's cabin with a glass of his best port to hand, all the formalities were quickly dealt with and the conversation turned to other matters.

'Is that the *Guardian* I saw in the Harbour?' George asked.

The Dutchman, Andre Van Solkema looked grim as he nodded his head and said, 'Indeed it is, Sir,' he sighed.

George Aitken frowned. 'I'm surprised to see it still here,' he said. 'We had to make a diversion to Rio de Janeiro for urgently needed repairs to the ship. Also, we had several women in an advanced state of pregnancy, so for the safety of the mothers, we lingered there until the babies were safely delivered. We spent seven weeks at anchor there, so I had expected that the *Guardian* would have been well ahead of us by now.'

'Well,' Andre Van Solkema began, 'I'm afraid the *Guardian's* is a story of great tragedy.

George Aitken gave him a startled look. 'How so? What has occurred?'

'The start of the story was the arrival earlier this year the *Sirius*, which I believe had been the flagship of the fleet that sailed from here in November 1787 to set up a new British colony. Captain Hunter had been sent here to buy as many supplies as he could possibly take on board. He told us that the new colony was in dire straits as they had been unable to get crops to grow. At the time he had left Port Jackson the population was starving and he had already been at sea for many months before he arrived here.'

George Aitken frowned. 'They must indeed be in a dreadful situation, but I'm afraid I fail to see what that has to do with the *Guardian* being here.'

'As you no doubt know, the *Guardian* was carrying supplies

— seeds, plants, farm machinery, and livestock which was badly needed in the new colony. When Post-Captain Riou arrived here and was told of the visit of the Sirius and the plight of the colonists, he decided to waste no time. He loaded as many extra plants and livestock as he could fit into his ship and set sail as quickly as possible.'

'Then why — ?' Captain Aitken glanced to where the *Guardian* lay grounded in the distance.

'He left here around the middle of December, sailing south-easterly,' The Dutchman continued. 'This brought him very close to the Antarctic areas. With all the livestock, in addition to the over three hundred people he had on board, they were using water at an alarming rate and Post captain Riou was concerned that he would not have sufficient water to last until they reached Port Jackson.'

'I'm following you so far,' said George Aitken. 'Following, but not understanding.'

Van Solkema Pursed his lips and shook his head.

'It is my understanding that Captain Riou was trying to collect ice from an iceberg, collided with it and his ship was holed. Most of the passengers and crew left in the boats, but captain Riou stayed behind on the *Guardian* along with the passengers who could not be fitted into the boats. By some miracle, he managed to keep the ship afloat and limped back here about a month after he had left.'

'And the people?' Captain Aitken asked in horror. Did everyone survive?'

Van Solkema shook his head. 'Very few I'm afraid. Post-Captain Riou would be able to tell you a lot more about it than I can,' he suggested.

Thomas Edgar's head shot up. 'He's here, is he? In Cape Town?'

'Yes. At the moment every room in every boarding house in

Cape Town is housing a survivor from either the *Guardian* or the *Bounty*.'

'The *Bounty*? What happened to the *Bounty*?' This all grew more confusing by the minute.

The Dutchman sighed. 'Well, that's another disaster for you to learn about. Perhaps when you go ashore to complete the formalities you might be able to catch up with some of your countrymen who will be able to tell you more about it than I.'

Shortly after the Dutch delegates left, the captain's launch was lowered And Captain Aitken and Lieutenant Thomas Edgar were rowed ashore.

On landing, they were taken straight away to the home of Governor van Graff to complete all the necessary formalities. With him, they had a short conversation about the two British shipping disasters and were pleased when he was able to tell them where they could locate Post-Captain Riou.

'We served together in 76, you know,' Edgar told his captain as they approached Riou's residence. 'I was master on the Discovery when Captain Cook was charting the Pacific. He's a good man. Very dependable. He will have taken this hard.'

Captain Aitken shook his head sadly. 'I can well imagine how he must feel. It will take a lot of getting over.'

When Edward Riou answered their knock on the door, he at first looked puzzled, then recognizing Thomas Edgar his face lit up. Hand extended, he said 'come in, come in my dear friend how nice it is to see you.'

As the two men moved into the room he watched them with a puzzled expression. 'I understood you had sailed with the *Lady Juliana* months before we left London.'

'I did,' Thomas agreed. 'We did,' he corrected himself before introducing his captain.

Riou studied his visitors in silence for a moment. 'Well, where — ?'

'Rio de Janeiro. The ship was breaking up and we had several women about to give birth. We would have had great difficulty in reaching Cape Town. Too dangerous to try to make the distance, so we diverted to Rio for repairs. Once there we decided to wait until the babies were safely delivered before continuing on our way,' George Aitken answered the unfinished question.

'A sensible idea,' Edward Riou agreed before a wave of sadness passed over his face. 'I have no doubt you have heard about the *Guardian* and my disaster.' It was a statement, not a question.

'We were told you hit an iceberg.'

'Yes.' Riou sighed and shook his head. 'We had taken on board a lot of extra livestock; horses; cattle; poultry; a flock of sheep, a couple of stallions and even a pair of Mauritius deer I thought someone might like to breed from. All this because we were told that they were desperately short of everything and were starving in the new colony.'

'Yes, the Dutch have told us that much.'

'Twelve days — Christmas Eve it was — and some thirteen hundred miles after we left Cape Town the lookout spotted an iceberg in the distance. I gave it some thought and decided it would be a good chance to replenish our water stocks. I positioned the ship at a safe distance and then dispatched two boats to harvest as much ice as possible. I knew this action was fraught with danger because in those icy waters you never know what might be lurking just beneath the surface. It had to be done for we were getting desperately short of water. By the time enough ice had been collected and the boats had been recovered the day was gone and night had fallen. That was when disaster struck. A bank of thick fog moved in, surrounding the ship, and the ice mountain was lost to view. We could see for no distance at all.

Of course, I placed extra lookouts all around and we struggled for hours to try to find a safe passage. Just when we thought we had succeeded The lookout in the bows spotted a huge berg. I ordered the helm to turn hard to starboard, turning into the wind, and for a brief moment, I thought we had managed to clear it. Suddenly a gust of wind caught us. The ship reared up, swung around, and drove the stern into ice that lay just below the surface. We had no chance to avoid it.'

George Aitken found himself too emotional to speak. The best he could manage was a sympathetic shake of his head.

'I'm sorry, I forget my manners. Would you gentleman care for a taste of rum or port?'

The pair from the *Lady Juliana* opted for a port and there was a momentary lull in conversation while the drinks were poured and delivered.

'When we finally broke free from the berg,' Edgar Riou continued, 'I realised the rudder has been torn away and there was a gaping hole in the hull. We twice attempted to fother her but to little avail. The hole was too large and water still continued to stream in. With luck and a lot of hard work, we managed to pull the *Guardian* clear of the ice.'

'What a terrible situation to be in,' Thomas Edgar sympathized.

George Aitken nodded in agreement. 'Go on,' he encouraged.

'I went below to check and found we were in a really desperate situation. There were a couple of feet of water in the hold and was more rushing in every moment and to make matters worse, a gale sprang up. The men were working themselves to death on the pumps, but by midnight there were six feet of water in the hold. At dawn on Christmas morning, we attempted again to fother the hole, this time with an oakum packed studding-sail.'

'So that worked did it?'

'It helped a bit George, but nowhere near enough. We did

manage to lower the flood level to about a foot and a half, but the pressure proved too much for the studding-sail and it split. The water started flooding in again.'

'Did you fother again?'

Edgars Riou sighed and nodded sadly. 'When the sail split, several of the crewmen requested permission to take to the boats. I managed to persuade them to stay until we made another attempt to fother. Sadly this second attempt also failed because the studding-sail split immediately. By nightfall, the hold was about seven feet deep in water. The ship was rolling and pitching in the gale, allowing water to flood in over the deck.'

'It sounds like a pretty impossible situation,' Thomas Edgar commented.

'Yes. At that point, it became clear we must lighten the load and jettison as much of the cargo as possible. The first things to go were the guns. Next to go were most of the animals. Some had been swept overboard when the ship caught on the ice and reared. Many of the smaller ones had been crushed when the big ones panicked. These poor animals had already suffered terribly. They had been tossed around for hours with the pitching of the ship and most were lying on the deck, many no doubt with broken legs and backs. Against formidable odds, the crew had to manhandle them over the rails and into the sea. It was a complete nightmare and I can still hear their cries before they drowned or the coldness of the water killed them. All we managed to save was a flock of twenty-two sheep and the two stallions.'

Thomas Edgar shuddered at the mere thought of it. Watching his friend, he could see a tear in his eye.

'Once the decks were cleared we had to start dragging as much of the cargo from the hold as we had the strength to manage. By the following morning, the *Guardian* was settling by the stern and the gale had ripped away her sails. Many of the crewmen, and also the convicts, asked again to be allowed to leave the ship. In all humanity, I had no choice but to agree for it was obvious the ship was doomed. I knew there was not room in the boats for everyone, but hoped the men would come to an amicable decision about who left and who stayed with the *Guardian*. As for myself, I never for one moment considered leaving. I would have preferred to go down with my ship rather than let her sink alone.'

'Was it possible to launch the boats safely in the gale?' George Aitken asked.

'Yes, but it was a formidable task. Before the boats left I wrote a letter to the secretary of the Admiralty in which I said,

Sir,
If any part of the officers or crew of the *Guardian* should ever survive to get home, I have only to say their conduct after the fatal stroke against an island of ice was admirable and wonderful in everything that related to their duties considered either as private men or on His Majesty service.

As there seems no possibility of my remaining many hours in this world, I beg leave to recommend to the consideration of the Admiral a sister who if my conduct or service should be found deserving any memory their favour might be shown to her together with a widowed mother.

I am Sir remaining with great respect
You're ever obedient and humble servant.
E. Riou.

The three men sat in stunned silence for several minutes before Edgar Riou continued. 'I gave the letter to Mister Clements who was master of the *Guardian* and put him in command of the launch. Two hundred and fifty-nine people chose to leave. That left only sixty-two of us on board to attempt to sail the ship. In addition to myself, I had three midshipmen, including young Thomas Pitt who is the nephew of the Prime Minister. There were thirty of the crew; twenty-one convicts, the bosun; the carpenter; the surgeon's mate; three superintendents of convicts, and the daughter of one of the superintendents. It was a very mixed bunch, but every one was welcome and did not hesitate to do whatever was asked of them.'

George Aitken drew a deep breath and shook his head. 'How, in God's name did you bring a rudderless ship thirteen hundred miles with such a motley, untrained crew?'

Edgar Riou gave a wan smile. 'It was not easy,' he admitted. 'By the time the boats left, the *Guardian* was almost awash, with about sixteen feet of water in the hold. We heard strange bumping sounds coming from below deck. This we found to be caused by a number of empty water-casks that had broken loose, were floating in the hold, and were trapped under the lower gundeck. This was affording us quite a bit of buoyancy, so I ordered that the gun deck hatches be sealed and caulked. We fothered the hull again to try to contain the flooding as much as possible, raised the small amount of sail we still had, manned the pumps twenty-four hours a day — and just prayed.'

'It's a miracle,' Thomas Edgar gasped.

'Aye. It is indeed,' Edgar Riou agreed. 'It took us nine weeks to reach the Cape of Good Hope. We were spotted from the land and some whalers were sent out to help bring us to safety. I can not describe my feelings when we first saw land, and soon afterward the whalers coming to our rescue. Not one of us on that ship could really believe we had survived.'

'What happened to the people who abandoned ship? Have you heard any news of them?' Thomas asked.

Edgar Riou drew a hand across his mouth and tears sprang to his eyes. Dropping his eyes to study his boots, he said 'Aye. I have heard. Of the two hundred and fifty-nine people who chose to take to the boats, only fifteen survived. The launch watched the jolly-boat sink but was unable to help. Very soon they had lost sight of the two cutters and the longboat. They themselves were lucky enough to come in contact with a French merchant-man and were rescued. There is no news of the other two boats, but I fear they are almost certainly lost.'

George Aitken nibbled at his lower lip and shook his head. 'All those lives lost,' he said eventually. 'It hardly bears thinking of.'

'I must say though that the convicts acquitted themselves extremely well. Never once did they question an order, nor refuse to obey. It is my intention, when I return to England, to request that all twenty-one of the convicts be pardoned. If it had not been for their help the ship would surely have sunk and every life on it would have been lost. I thank our Good Lord that we had those good men with us and not the crew the *Bounty* was blighted with.'

George Aitken gave him a speculative look. 'The Dutchmen mentioned that the survivors from the *Bounty* were being accom-modated in town, But they did not have time to tell us the story. What do you know of it?'

'I've heard quite a bit about it but the person to give you the clearest story would be John Fryer, who was master on the *Bounty*. William Bligh sailed for England in January, but John has remained in Cape Town. In fact, he's dining with me tonight so if you gentleman would care to join us you will be very wel-come. John will be able to tell you first hand about the mutiny and the survivors' terrible journey to safety.'

As they walked back to the harbour, George shook his head sadly. 'What a terrible tale. All those lives lost, that could have been saved if only they had stayed with the *Guardian*.'

Thomas nodded thoughtfully. 'But all those saved, who could well have died had they not had the courage to trust Edgar Riou.'

George sighed. 'Yes, and the *Guardian* lost too. Edgar did well to save his ship and at least some of the provisions and livestock. That must be one of the greatest ever feats of seamanship.'

'To sail a ship, that was no more than a raft, all those hundreds of miles without a rudder!' Thomas Edgar shook his head in disbelief. 'From what we have been told, the colonists in Port Jackson must be in dire straits.'

George Aitken nodded. 'With no crops growing. Little or no farming equipment. Few, if any, livestock. What can they be surviving on?'

Thomas shrugged and said gloomily, 'If indeed any have survived.'

His captain was thoughtful for a while, then nodding to himself he took a deep breath. 'Well, it seems to me that it is now imperative that we help them. We must take on as many extra stores as we can find room for and leave for Port Jackson as soon as possible.'

CHAPTER 20

———•••———

George Aitken and Thomas Edgar returned to their ship in a serious thoughtful mood.

'That was a rum do they had,' Edgar commented. Shaking his head, he kicked absently at a pebble.

'Yes. We have to assume some of the colonists are still alive so it's up to us to get provisions to them. There is no knowing if the rest of the fleet is close behind us, or whether they might have suffered some mishap.'

'Or even what extra supplies they will be carrying — if any.' Thomas Edgar shook his head sadly. 'Considering the length of the lay-up we had in Rio de Janeiro, I would have expected them to be ahead of us by now.'

George nodded and sighed worriedly. 'There has been no mention of them arriving here. Which is why I fear they might have foundered.'

Thomas ran a shaking hand over his face. 'Dear God, I hope not. But it is strange they have' arrived yet. Perhaps they, too, have had to go to Rio.'

'We must hope so. In their absence, the responsibility of getting supplies to the colony falls to us. As soon as the *Lady Juliana* has been repaired we must collect as many of the surviving stores and livestock from the *Guardian* as we can find space for, then set sail as quickly as possible. They could very well be dying of starvation over there.'

'If they're not dead already!' Thomas put in.

George Aitken gave him a piercing look but did not reply. That dreadful thought had already crossed his mind.

Alice watched the two men climb out of the launch and into the ship.

'The captain and Mister Edgar look worried don't they?'

Maggie looked around and studied the men. 'They do indeed. James told me there's a supply ship here that was expected to have passed us while we were laid up in Rio de Janeiro. It was supposed to be carrying desperately needed supplies to this new colony we are being sent to, but James says it looks damaged. Captain and Mister Edgar were going to see what they could find out about it.'

'From the looks on their faces, I don't think they liked whatever it was they found.'

'No. they both look a bit grim-faced don't they?'

Alice cuddled little Daniel as he contentedly suckled and told herself that whatever had happened to the other ship was not going to be any problem of hers.

Four men sat around a table in a nearby tavern that evening. They had eaten well of roast pork, roast potatoes, and vegetables, which they were washing down with several jugs of good ale.

'Can you tell us, John, What is this story we hear about a mutiny on the *Bounty*?' George Aitken asked as his curiosity got the better of him.

'It's a long story, but I will keep it as short as possible,' John Fryer replied. 'You have sailed with James Cook have you not?' He looked questioningly at Edward Riou.

Edward Riou nodded. Thomas and I were both with him on the *Discovery* when she sailed in 1776. Thomas was the master. But what has this to do with your mutiny?'

John Fryer tutted and shook his head. 'I was coming to that if you will just be patient and listen.'

Edward Riou drew a deep breath and studied his feet.

'You will no doubt remember what a fusspot James Cook was over hygiene and the cleanliness of the ship and quality of the food.'

Two heads nodded as they waited for him to continue.

'Well, Bligh followed Cook's tradition with an almost insane zeal. He was fanatical about hygiene, good food, and cleanliness. The *Bounty* was probably the cleanest ship that ever sailed. You could have eaten your excellent food straight from the deck. To keep the crew entertained and exercised he had music played, and insisted the crew must dance.

On the whole, in the early days, it was quite a happy ship. Captain Bligh had no reason to inflict punishment as, to quote him, '*All officers and men are tractable, well disposed and cheerful.*' The only fly in the ointment was the surgeon who was, in Bligh's eyes, a slovenly drunkard and not too concerned about cleanliness. I had rather expected to be Bligh's second in charge, but he appeared to develop a very high regard for a man called Fletcher Christian. I believe they had been close friends for some years, and Bligh afforded him a position that seemed to make him second in charge. So keen, was Bligh, on this man Christian that he even lent him money and in March afforded him the position of Acting Lieutenant.'

George Aitken's eyebrows shot up, but he held his counsel.

'A week or so after this I found I was having some serious problems with a man called Matthew Quintal. I reported this to Captain Bligh and on my insistence he ordered that Quintal be given twelve lashes for insolent and mutinous behaviour.'

George Aitken nodded approval. 'I must admit I do not like having men whipped, but if there is any sign of a mutinous nature it has to be scotched and the only way is with the *cat*.'

'Yes, though Captain Bligh was disappointed about having to do it. He had hoped to complete the voyage without having to mete out any punishment.'

'That's a bit of wishful thinking, on a ship full of tough men,' Thomas Edgar put in.

'Aye, well, it was done. After that, all went fairly without incident until the second day of April, when we were nearing Cape Horn. We were hit suddenly by strong gales and high seas that just would not abate. They were the worst storms I had ever encountered, with the winds bringing squalls of icy rain and hail which quickly drove us back the way we had come. In no time we were further north than we had been a week before. Several times Captain Bligh attempted to drive the ship forward, but it was impossible. At last, to the relief of everyone on board, he ordered the ship to turn and make sail for Cape Town.'

George Aitken nodded his approval. 'It was the wrong time of year to be trying to navigate Cape Horn. However, I can understand that it must have been frustrating for Bligh to have to give up and change his course.'

'I must admit I can't fault Bligh on his seamanship. It was no easy feat to turn in those terrible storms and faultlessly find his way to Cape Town. Only the very best of sailors could have accomplished it. We dropped Anchor at False Bay, just east of the Cape of Good Hope on the 24th of May and spent five weeks there repairing and reprovisioning the ship. We left there on the 1st of July and Bligh again navigated skilfully across the Southern Ocean. On the 19th of August, we sighted Mewstone Rock, on the south-eastern corner of Tasmania, dropping anchor at Adventure Bay two days later.'

'A tremendous feat of navigation, but of course he had been trained by a master.' Thomas Edgar said admiringly. 'James Cook took him under his wing and taught him a great deal.'

'On the whole, it was a pleasant time in Tasmania. Most of it was just relaxing after a very trying and at times hazardous few months. We spent quite a bit of time fishing, refilling the water casks, and felling timber. This led to some friction between Bligh and his officers, when Bligh took the carpenter, Purcell, to task because he didn't like his methods of cutting the timber. Purcell stood up to him, challenging him so Bligh withheld his rations, forcing him to toe the line.'

After we left Tasmania there was one problem after another ad the discontent just seemed to escalate.

George Aitken heaved a great sigh and shook his head.

'I think by that time Fletcher Christian was becoming resent-ful about the loan Bligh had made to him. And I think I added fuel to Bligh's anger by refusing to sign the account books unless he gave me a certificate attesting to my complete competence throughout the voyage. I was angry and disappointed that he had appointed Christian to the position I regarded as mine and was concerned about securing my future.'

'Quite right,' Edward Riou agreed, nodding vigorously.

'Well, it didn't work. Bligh refused the certificate. He sum-moned the crew, read the *Articles of War* and I was left with no option but to back down. I was forced to sign the account books. There was also trouble with the surgeon, Huggan. He had decided on bloodletting as the cure for one of the men who was suffering from asthma. The result of this was that the man developed a blood infection and died. To make a bad affair worse Huggan tried to cover his mistake by saying the man had died of scurvy. This caused Bligh to invoke his own ideas of curative diet on the entire ship's company, which caused a great deal of discontent.'

'A bad affair. A drunkard like Huggan should never have been allowed on the ship in the first place,' George Aitken said angrily.

Riou nodded. 'By this time Huggan was so helpless with drink that William Bligh was forced to cut off his supply of alcohol. And another thing that caused ill-feeling was that Bligh had the surgeon examine every member of the ship's company to check for venereal disease, and every man proved clean of disease. To make matters worse, Bligh seemed to take against Christian and despite their previous friendship, he took pleasure in humiliating him before the crew, both on the ship and the shore. I could see the storm brewing, but such was Bligh's arrogance, he seemed oblivious. The men were often flogged for wrongs they had supposedly committed that often were only in the imagination of William Bligh. Three of the men stole a small boat, arms and ammunition, but left behind a list of names, including Christian's, which Bligh was certain were the names of men who were also planning to desert.'

'That wouldn't have pleased Bligh!' George Aitken snorted.

'It did not! He challenged Christian, who managed to convince him he had no intention of deserting and so that was the end of it. The deserters were caught some three weeks or so later and were flogged.'

'Too much slack time never did anyone any good,' George Aitken said grimly

'I have to agree, but there really was very little for them to do for quite some time. In February the workload increased when the breadfruit plants had to be potted on board. There were over one thousand of them and they filled the great cabin. A few days after that we were ready to depart. Many of the men had become too fond of the lazy, indolent lifestyle they had been living and were unwilling to leave it. Bligh failed to realise just how much of an impact taking to sea would have after five months of sloth. He became angry and intolerant of any real or imagined misdemeanour and flogging became a regular event. In particular, he seemed to single out Fletcher Christian as the target for his rages.'

Thomas Edgar pursed his lips. 'Not the right way to treat your second in charge, I would have thought.'

'Well, the real troubles started when we left Tahiti. We had spent five months there, our mission being to collect as many bread fruits as possible. The local chieftains were happy to allow this in exchange for gifts from Bligh. The men spent a great deal of their time ashore without much work to be done and spent much of their time fornicating with the native women. Bligh himself, as far as I know, never found comfort with a woman, but he turned a blind eye to the men's activities. Fletcher Christian and a few of the others formed serious relationships. Venereal disease was rife in Tahiti and eighteen of the officers and men, including Fletcher Christian, had to be treated for it. The officers became lazy and discipline suffered, which infuriated William Bligh, to the point where he wrote *such neglectful and worthless petty officers were never in a ship as such as are in this.*'

'He should have maintained more discipline. Five months is too long a time to allow the men free run, then expect them to buckle down without complaint,' George Aiken said irritably. It would have served Bligh better to have found more work for the men, rather than giving them so much freedom with the native women. It breeds discontent.'

'I don't think there was any thought of mutiny until they reached the Friendly Islands. William Bligh had been there with Cook, so knew the natives to be unpredictable and possibly dangerous. This was to be the last stop before Endeavour Straight, so he wanted to pick up supplies, water, and wood. Christian was to lead the watering party and Bligh gave him muskets and ammunition but ordered they be left in the boats, to avoid antagonising the natives. The natives, however, pestered and threatened the unarmed water party, who were forced to return to the ship with their task incomplete. Bligh berated Christian, before the rest of the crew, as *a damned cowardly rascal.*'

'That should have been done in private — and only if it was deserved,' George Aitken growled.

'Which I don't think it was. It is likely the men would have been killed if they had stayed on shore. In further troubles with the natives, they stole a small anchor and an adze, for which both Christian and I were blamed and berated. William Bligh captured the island's chieftains and held them on the ship, but eventually, he had to let them go. We never did recover the stolen items and had to sail without them.'

'A small price to pay, I should think, to ensure the safety of the ship.' Thomas Edgar said quietly.

John Fryer nodded. 'By this time Fletcher had taken almost as much abuse and ridicule as he could tolerate. He had become a very depressed and angry man. At one time he even considered getting wood, making a raft and escaping to an island somewhere. There might have been trouble with the natives, but he seemed willing to take that risk. By then, of course, most of the other officers knew of his discontent and many were feeling the same.'

'That's a bad situation on any ship,' Captain Aitken said grimly.

'As it was on the *Bounty,*' John Fryer agreed. 'Two of the men, Young and Stewart, suggested that rather than desert, he should seize the ship. They assured him almost everyone on the ship had had as much as they could tolerate of Bligh's brutality and would give him their support. They told him which of the officers and crew would undoubtedly support him, and before dawn on the 28th of April, Christian made his move. He went below, to where the chest of arms was and distributed them to his staunchest supporters, then marched to Bligh's cabin. Three of the men grabbed William Bligh and tied his hands, telling him not to make any noise or he would be killed. Fearlessly he shouted as loudly as he could. The commotion from his cabin wakened me. I leapt to my feet in time to see Bligh being frogmarched away. I could not help him, however. I was ordered by the mutineers to lay down and *'to hold my tongue or I was a dead man.'*

'A frightening experience,' Thomas Edgar sympathised.

'I could hear Bligh shouting all the while, demanding to be set free and ordering the ship's company to *'knock Christian down.'* I was briefly allowed on deck to speak to Christian and I noticed he had a *sounding plummet* hanging around his neck. Then I was quickly shoved back below deck at bayonet point.'

'A sounding plummet?' Aitken questioned. 'What on earth for?'

'I think it was in his mind that if the mutiny failed he would jump overboard and the plummet would take him to the bottom. He told me that he had been in hell for weeks and that Bligh had brought this on himself.'

'A desperate man indeed,' Edward Riou said sadly.

'There was a great deal of fighting going on while I was on deck and it was impossible to tell which were Christian's men and which Bligh's loyalists. Thinking that I and midshipmen Hallet and Hayward and John Samuel were the only men on board still loyal to the captain, Christian intended to set us adrift in the small jolly-boat, but it was in disrepair. He was surprised to find that nearly half the ship's company were still loyal to Bligh, so he instead had the twenty-three-foot launch lowered. Those loyal to the captain, myself included were given about two hours to collect their belongings and get into the launch. There was not enough room on the launch for all Bligh's allies and four were to remain on the ship. With Bligh's approval, I asked Christian to allow me to stay on the *Bounty*, with the idea that at some stage I might be able to seize the ship back, but he ordered me into the launch. The men who were kept on the ship, including the armourer and the two carpenter's mates were told to stay as he would have need of their skills. They begged Bligh not to forget they had stayed against their wills and he replied, 'never fear, lads, I'll do you justice if I ever reach England.'

'Good man. Good man,' Aitken nodded his approval.

'John Samuel, a midshipman, had managed to secure Bligh's manual and some other papers, but had been unable to get his navigational charts, which represented fifteen years of his work.'

'A sad loss,' said Edward Riou, shaking his head.

'There were nineteen of us, as well as our belongings, crammed into a boat not made to carry so many. We were given enough food and water for five days, a compass, sextant, nautical tables, and Purcell, the carpenter's tool chest. The boat was dangerously overcrowded and we had only about seven inches of freeboard. Almost as an afterthought, four cutlasses were thrown down to us.'

'A frightening situation to find yourself in,' Thomas Edgar told him.

'It was,' John Fryer agreed. 'On the horizon, we could see the smoke from the volcano on Tofua. Captain Bligh ordered the sail to be raised and told us to head for there in the hope that we would find water and food enough to get us to Tongatapu. He hoped to seek help there from the King, whom he'd become acquainted with during a visit to that island with Cook, and get enough food to get us to the Dutch East Indies, It went alright to start with, but the natives became fractious and threatening. Sensing an attack was imminent Bligh ordered his shore party back to the boat. Some of the natives grabbed the rope and tried to pull the boat back, and to give Bligh credit he kept calm and led his men safely to the boat. We were struggling against the pull of the natives but John Norton, God bless his soul, leapt into the water to try to free the rope. The price he paid was to be set upon and stoned to death. After that, we were reluctant to land on any of the small islands for fear we might get the same hot reception there. We thought about Fiji but had heard stories of cannibalism there and none of us wanted to end up as someone's dinner. After a long discussion, we all agreed we should follow Bligh's suggestion that we should try to make a run for the Dutch settlement on Kupang in Timor, which was about three thousand five hundred nautical miles. We had only the food and water we had on board, which would mean we would each have to survive on a ration of one ounce of bread and a quarter of a pint of water a day.'

'How could anyone survive on such a small quantity of food and water for that great distance?' Thomas Edgar's eyes were wide with shock and disbelief.

'Well, there was no choice was there? It was that, or risk being eaten by some savage on an island! We battled storms and mountainous seas from the start of our journey. The water relentlessly heaved into our little boat and many times we were sure it was going to be swamped. Everyone baled with all their strength and somehow we managed to stay afloat, though we were all drenched and very cold. When, at last, the sun did finally shine it brought us such great joy. In our hearts, we could hardly believe we were still alive.'

Fryer's three companions sat, stunned, as they silently studied their storyteller.

'A week or so later the sun broke through and at last, we were warm again. We started to see birds, so realised we were nearing land. Against all the odds, Bligh had managed to keep his journal up to date, and on the day which he estimated to be the 28th May, we spotted an island that Bligh named Restoration Island. He managed to navigate the boat into a quiet lagoon and, late in the afternoon, ran it ashore. The island seemed uninhabited, and we were lucky enough to find an abundance of oysters and berries. We all gorged ourselves until we could eat no more.'

'Well, that was a lucky find. A real life-saver I should say.' Thomas Edgar spoke quietly in awe.

'It was that! From then on we sailed from island to island, all part of some huge reef, managing to find food on each. We were aware of natives watching us from the shore, but they made no attempt to row out to us. Tempers started to fray, as you would expect. Bligh and Purcell, the carpenter were forever at each other's throats and during one spectacular argument, Bligh grabbed a cutlass and challenged Purcell to fight him. I thought this discord was not good for morale and ordered a man called Cole to arrest the captain. Bligh turned on me then and told me he would kill me if I tried to interfere. So I had no choice but to back down.'

'It sounds as if the man has lost his mind,' Edward Riou commented.

'Aye. It appeared like it at the time. On the 2nd June, we cleared the northernmost tip of Australia and turned south-west, but we were still over a thousand miles short of Kupang. The following seven or eight days were the most unbearable of the whole voyage. The temperature was hotter than anything I had known before and there was no way in the world we could escape it. By the 11th of June, many of the men were on the verge of collapse. The following day we saw the coast of Timor and there are just no words I can think of that aptly describe my feelings at that moment.'

The other three men sat in silence for several minutes. George Aitken, elbows on the table supported his chin with his thumbs, his fingers to his lips as he slowly shook his head. 'It is indeed difficult to believe you could all have survived such a journey. It is impossible to imagine the joy you must have felt when you sighted Timor.'

John Fryer nodded. 'You know, it is hard now to even remember it clearly. But several of us were so weakened that we did not survive for too much longer. The cruel Kupang climate soon put an end to the botanist, Nelson. On the 20th of August, we took ship to Batavia, where four more of our company died. Bligh secured passages to Europe for himself, his clerk Samuel and his servant John Smith. They left on the 16th of October, bound for London to report the mutiny. The rest of us found our way here, and here we still are awaiting a ship to finally take us home.'

'I wish you a swift and safe voyage,' George Aitken told him. 'Our task now will be to careen and repair the *Lady Juliana*. 'Then we must load her with as many food supplies as we can find room for.'

'I managed to save two dozen sheep and two stallions. there are also quite a number of the provisions that were above the waterline and were not spoiled. Perhaps you might take these with you,' Edward Riou suggested hopefully,

Thomas Edgar nodded enthusiastically. 'We could most certainly take the sheep, but I'm not so sure about the stallions. Their space might be better taken up by a couple of cows or bulls.'

George Aitken stood up and flexed his shoulders wearily. 'It's time we were returning to our ship. Perhaps we might meet tomorrow and take stock of what is salvageable from the *Guardian*; and just what, if any, extra supplies we can make space for.'

CHAPTER 21

———···———

The *Lady Juliana* was laboriously emptied of her cargo. The women were taken ashore, stumbling in confusion along the jetty, some grumbling, but most were happy to be walking on solid ground at last. The ship was then beached and careened. With their recently enforced experience at repairing holes in ships, John Riou and the carpenter from the *Guardian*, volunteered their services to make the *Juliana* seaworthy as quickly as possible.

The crews of the *Bounty* and the *Guardian* were happy to lend their weight and muscle power to heave the ship onto first one side and, later, the other, to enable the patching to be done.

The sailors slaved through most of the hours of daylight, but fast though they worked, it took three weeks to have the necessary repairs completed, then the cargo they had offloaded was returned and a precise inventory was taken. George Aitken ordered that all salvageable goods be brought over from the *Guardian*, listed and carefully packed below deck. Once this was done they would know precisely how much space they had and what provisions it would be most essential for Thomas Edgar to purchase.

While the ship was beached the women had to sleep on their

mattresses on the beach. To most of them, it was a relief to be on solid ground and many saw it as an opportunity to add to the nest eggs they had been accumulating during the voyage.

The Dutch authorities had been nervous and reluctant to permit convicts to come ashore, but George Aitken had successfully used his powers of persuasion.

With his fingers firmly crossed behind his back he said, 'the convicts on my ship have all been well cared for. They are healthy, happy and I can guarantee they will cause you no trouble, nor will they attempt to escape. And, even if they wished it, where would they escape to? The mountains? The desert? None, I'm sure would want to risk being eaten by the savages.' He lifted an eyebrow.

The Dutchman studied him speculatively and scratched his head. Finally, he sighed, shrugged, and gave a reluctant nod. 'I will allow it,' he said grimly, 'But I will place extra guards on the beach. You understand?'

'I understand,' the captain agreed. He had won his case, so cared not about extra guards.

The women from the *Lady Juliana* however, did care very much about extra guards and there was quite a bit of strenuous activity on the beaches throughout the nights. The convicts were perhaps not quite as well guarded as the authorities might have hoped!

Alice spent much of her days on the shore, finding shade wherever she could, nursing her young son, and engrossed in the endless activity around her.

The ship's carpenters and blacksmith set up shop temporarily on the beach. They slaved, with very few breaks, every daylight hour in the scorching autumn sun as they battled to mend the worst of the leaks.

When the repairs were finished and the ship refloated, she was returned to her berth in the harbour, and the women ordered to reboard. Despite a constant battle with flies the women had been pleased to be off the ship. They had all enjoyed having the freedom to wander on the beach and many were reluctant to return to go back on board. The working ladies grumbled the loudest, for they could no longer earn their pennies from the militiamen.

Maggie, Sarah, and Lily were no less vociferous than the other prostitutes, while Alice still failed to understand how they could allow their bodies to be used by strangers in this way.

Maggie prayed that the child would never be forced to find the answer.

'It's imperative that we must transport as much as we possibly can. It could make the difference between life and death for whoever might have survived in Port Jackson. If they have had no supplies since they landed there they could well be starving by now. From the tale Captain Hunter had told when he returned to London in July the new colony was struggling to survive twelve months or more ago.'

He got no argument from either Thomas Edgar or Surgeon Richard Alley. Both men were keen to get the ship loaded and underway as quickly as possible.

The women on board watched with interest as the ship's boats came and went. The sailors sweated as they rowed to and from the shore with their boats piled high. Once their own cargo had been reloaded, they made a start on whatever goods from the *Guardian* that had not been spoiled.

All survivors from both the *Guardian* and the *Bounty* who were fit to work were roped in to take stock and help with the move. They struggled around the sloping decks and holds of the wrecked *Bounty*, hauling crates and kegs out from the corners they had floated or been jammed into. Eventually, seventy-five barrels of flour and one-hundred gallons of wine were lowered, amidst a volley of foul language, into boats, rowed over from the wreck to the *Lady Juliana*, and hauled on board

Men scurried around; whistled through their fingers; waved their arms. Tempers frayed in the tropical heat and fists were raised as angry men fronted up to each other like fighting cocks.

In an attempt to defuse ugly situations, George Aitken stood on the poop, bellowing orders through his voice trumpet, promising twenty lashes of the *cat* to any men who came to blows.

Heaven help any woman who got in the way as the sailors heaved, slid, and trundled heavy items across the deck.

Firmly clutching her precious bundle, Alice huddled in a corner and ensured she and Daniel were never near any danger.

Every available space on the ship was filled. Casks and crates were squeezed into every corner. The women in the orlop deck found themselves with an ever decreasing amount room to move around in.

The sails and spare canvas had been stretched out on the beach, above the high tide mark, to check for any signs of rot or mildew. Any necessary repairs had been done and along with the topmasts they were now returned to the ship and secured back in place.

The two Cape stallions and twenty-two sheep that had survived the wreck of the *Guardian* were winched on board and fastened into their pens on the deck. Lastly, the new passengers, survivors from the *Guardian*, clambered up into the *Lady Juliana*.

Three men, each with a glass in hand, sat in silence in the captain's cabin. George Aitken rubbed his chin thoughtfully. 'You have to let her have your cabin, Thomas,' he said finally.

Startled, Thomas jerked his head up to stare at his captain. Surely the man must be joking. 'My cabin?' he questioned.

George Aitken gave a quick nod of his head. 'Yes. Your cabin.'

'But why mine? And what about Mary?'

'Mary?' George frowned.

'My — um — well — *wife.*'

George Aitken impatiently flapped his hand. 'Oh, she'll have to get out too. It wouldn't do for the child to share a cabin with — em — a convict. Anyway, I imagine her father will wish to share her accommodation. He will want to be in a position to protect her from having any contact with our women.'

'I can quite understand that,' Thomas said through gritted teeth. 'But where do you propose to accommodate Mary and myself?'

His captain drew his shoulders back and glared at Thomas across the cabin. 'I suggest you find yourself a place in the forecastle or put up a tent on the deck.' When Thomas opened his mouth to protest he added, 'and I will brook no argument!'

Thomas sank back in his chair, his lips tightly clamped and glared back wordlessly.

'Now,' George Aitken changed the subject, 'we have the young lady and her father sorted, but where are we going to put all the other extra bodies we are taking on board?'

'Exactly how many are we adding?' Richard Alley asked.

George Aitken frowned and took a deep breath. 'There's that fellow Schaffer, father of the girl. I believe she is ten years of age. The man told me he was German and is going to the new colony as a settler. He was a Hessian mercenary, has fought for our King and country, so we owe it to him to make him as welcome and comfortable as possible on this voyage. He will share the cabin with the child, that will be the best way to keep her safe. Then there are the five convict supervisors. I suggest we have the carpenters build a hut on the deck to accommodate them. Are we all agreed?'

Thomas Edgar nodded glumly, still angry at the loss of his cabin.

'I can think of nowhere else to put them,' Richard Alley agreed, rather more cheerfully. 'What of the other survivors from the Guardian?'

'They were twenty-five convicts with gardening experience and were to take care of the plants the *Guardian* was carrying. The plants had to be thrown overboard when the ship hit the iceberg, and will have to be replaced at some time, but we have no time to wait for them. These prisoners, according to Edward Riou, all stayed with the ship after the accident and all behaved and acted well. Edward says that without them the ship could not have been saved. When he returns to England he intends to petition the home office for a reprieve for all twenty-five.

'They sound the type of men you would want at your side in times of trouble,' Richard Alley said thoughtfully.

'I agree, but unfortunately, we can not accommodate them, so they will remain here and will join either *Neptune*, *Surprize* or *Scarborough* when they arrive. They should not be too far behind us by now. Thomas, order the carpenters to build a hut for the five supervisors.'

'Sir!' Lieutenant Edgar jumped to his feet, snapped a smart salute, and abruptly left the cabin.

'I think our friend is not too happy with you,' Richard Alley said smilingly.

George Aitken shrugged his shoulders. 'Aye, well, needs must when the devil drives. And he will be driving us hard until we reach Port Jackson.'

'Indeed he will.'

'This is altogether the wrong time of year to be tackling the

Southern Ocean,' he said worriedly. 'We have no choice though. The delays we have encountered in Rio de Janeiro and here have lost us so much time. We can not afford to wait for a safer time. We must sail now with these provisions.' He felt every bit as grim as he looked.

'Let's hope the devil is looking the other way when we pass through,' Richard Alley said without much confidence. 'Have you thought about the young girl?'

'In what way?' George Aitken frowned at his surgeon.

'Well, I feel it would be wrong for her to witness the goings-on between convicts and crew that you — we — have been turning a blind eye to.'

George nodded thoughtfully. 'Yes. I see what you mean. I have felt, in the past, that it is beneficial to keep both men and women in a more amenable mood, by allowing nature to take its course when and where it was needed. And I'm sure this has saved us a fair amount of trouble. But you are right. With a young girl on the ship, we can not allow it to continue. I will tell Thomas to make it known to everyone that they can carry out their activities discreetly, but anyone — man or woman — caught fornicating where the child might see them, will get twenty lashes.'

Thomas Edgar sulkily passed his captain's orders to the carpenters. Huts were erected on the waist of the ship to house the additional passengers and any supplies that could not be fitted below decks.

Alice and her three friends watched the newcomers with avid interest.

'Who do you suppose she is?' Maggie asked, eyeing a smartly dressed young child.

No one had an answer. 'Maybe she's another prisoner.' Lily suggested.

Alice studied the girl. For she *was* no more than a girl. 'I think she is too well dressed to be a convict.'

Maggie nodded but said no more. James would know. She would find out from him tonight. A ship full of prostitutes certainly did not seem like the right place for this youngster!

On the last day of March, the *Lady Juliana* weighed anchor and prepared to leave Table Bay.

Nerves were on edge for both crew and passengers. Strong south-easterly winds picked up and whipped, howling through the rigging. To the crew, it was a foresight of what lay ahead of them in the dangerous waters of the Southern Ocean.

To the women, it was the realisation that they were now heading out into the wild waters that had claimed the *Guardian* at a much gentler date on the calendar. And the knowledge that their next port of call would be the *place beyond the seas*. The end of a journey into heaven knew where! They had heard so many rumours — mostly frightening. Stories of starvation; cruelty; slavery, flesh-eating savages and they knew not if any — or all — of it was true. As they sailed before a harsh wind from the shelter of Table Bay, even the most hardened of the women, but most especially the new young mothers, tasted fear like none they had ever known.

A haze lay over Cape Town and the *table-cloth* had settled heavily on the mountain. The women watched fearfully as it slowly drifted into the distance and eventually disappeared. Now they were left with nothing to look at, but the angry grey ocean.

Within days the temperature plummeted, icy rain, driven by almost gale force winds slashed down from sullen black skies.

Shivering, those women who had been lucky enough — and wealthy enough — to bring extra clothing with them, had the crew open their trunks in the hold to allow them access to warm clothing.

The poorer women, who had nothing but the itchy serge dress the prison had issued, sat shivering in their bunks or sleeping shelves.

Alice now came to treasure more than ever the shawl Michael had given her. It was too cold and, most of the time, too wet or wild, to venture out on deck, so she either lay in her bunk or sat huddled on the floor of the forecastle with her friends around her and her shawl wrapped tightly around herself and Daniel. Even with that, she was still cold and feared for Daniel.

Maggie watched her anxiously and she too worried about both the child and her baby. She had been lucky enough to bring a few pieces of clothing and was reasonably warm with a wool jacket and wrap. Seeing Alice clench her teeth to stop them chattering, she unwound her wrap and put in around the girl's shoulders.

'Here, wrap this around yourself and the baby,' she said quietly.

Alice looked up at her with tears in her eyes and shrugged it off. 'Thank you, Maggie, but you need it yourself. You feel the cold as much as I.'

Smiling, Maggie picked it up and replaced it and fastened it cozily around the baby. 'Yes,' she agreed, 'but Daniel feels the cold more than either of us. So you must have it. I'll ask James if he has any ganseys he can spare.'

Alice nodded doubtfully but accepted the gift. *Some day*, she promised herself, *I will repay this wonderful friend who has done so much for me and expected nothing in return.* She could not have known that she had already given Maggie all she could have wished for — her love. The love she had been robbed of when she had been taken from her children.

Now deep in the Southern Ocean, the *Lady Juliana* heaved and tossed in agony as she was thrashed by the turbulent seas. Huge waves, driven by gale-force winds, swept icy water over the rails and through the hawser holes. At the worst of the storms, they sheeted up over the upper decks, engulfing the bridge and the forecastle. It forced its way past the tar to seep into every last corner of the suffering ship.

Water sloshed ankle-deep around the floor of the forecastle so that Alice and her friends could no longer sit in a group on the deck. They had to be content with clinging onto their bunks and calling to each other across the cabin, trying to make themselves heard above the sound of the water that thundered against and over the *Lady Juliana*.

The hatches were kept battened down and the poor women on their overcrowded sleeping shelves in the orlop deck feared for their lives. The towering stack of containers that had been crammed in and now took up most of the space were well secured, but the convicts lived in fear of them breaking loose and falling on them.

The pumps were having to be manned twenty-four hours a day to keep the ship free of the water that was being forced between every plank and through every possible space. Even with this effort, when the seas were at their worst, the *Lady Juliana* was shipping water faster than it could be pumped out. It was now that Captain Aitken appreciated having all the extra manpower on board, for all the passengers, like it or not, were made to do their share. None complained. All willingly set themselves to any task that was asked of them.

Everyone was soaked to the skin, with no possible chance of getting dry. The damp salt spray permeated even inside the cabins.

Terrified, Alice huddled in her bunk. She had bound Daniel to her chest with the shawl, to leave her hands free to cling to the post. There was a sound that frightened her. A terrible roaring and banging. A new sound she had not heard before. The ship must be breaking up! That's what it must be. She thanked her Gods she was not trapped in the orlop. Then asked herself what difference it would make. They could not take to the boats in such huge seas! If they tried to launch them they would surely be smashed to pieces against the ship. So what difference did it make whether she was in the forecastle or the orlop? She would drown just as surely in either if the ship sank.

Squaring her shoulders, Alice glared at a wall of water that smashed against the forecastle window. No! She was not going to drown, for if she did Daniel would also. And she could not allow that! The seas would not have them.

Later when Danny finished his watch and joined her on the damp, bunk, she asked him about the strange, frightening sounds.

Smiling tiredly he said. "Tis all the water we have shipped. They're all pumping as hard as they can, every minute there is, but there is so much water in the body of the ship. Every time she heaves or rolls tons upon tons of water roll with her and crash around the bilges.

'Will she sink?'

'Bless you, no. She'll hold. Don't you be frightened about that.' Danny crossed his fingers, tightened his grip around his two loved ones and prayed that he was right.

The orlop and 'tween decks stank, for the women could not venture outside to empty the commode buckets, which now overflowed. The waste, combined with sea-water sloshed backward and forward around their frozen feet and ankles.

Now, more than ever, Alice was thankful for Danny's offer to make her his wife. The thought of being locked in the orlop was almost unbearable to her now, as was the knowledge that without

Danny's friendship, she would not have Daniel. Indeed, with the bullies there were down there, she might not have even her life.

The child, Elisabeth, the daughter of the Hessian mercenary, rarely ventured from her cabin, for the ship tossed too much most of the time for it to be safe for her on the deck. Nor was there much risk of her seeing any immoral couplings on the deck. Shortly after departing Cape Town it was too wet and cold to for sexual activities anywhere, but indoors.

The five supervisors who had joined the ship at Cape Town quickly found *wives* to give them comfort during their voyage.

Remembering the *Guardian* disaster, George Aitken posted extra lookouts before they reached the southernmost point in their voyage. Whenever an iceberg was spotted in the distance, he made sure to keep well clear. If they ran short of water, he decided, then they would just have to manage without. Although he agreed that Edward Riou's idea to collect ice had seemed a good one, he decided he would not risk his ship.

Navigator, Lieutenant Thomas Edgar had sailed these waters before, probably the only man of the *Lady Juliana* to have done so. He had been with Captain Cook in 1777 when he had charted the waters from Cape Town to New Zealand and had briefly anchored off Tasman's head in Van Diemen's Land. He smiled as he thought about it.

Captain Cook had sent men ashore to seek vegetables and perhaps a few animals to boost their dwindling stocks. The sailors had soon returned in terror. They claimed they had found huge steps cut into the hillside and were certain the land was inhabited by giants. Thomas sighed. But that had been in summer months. Even then it had been bitterly cold and the seas, wild. He had supervisors and now shared the hut on the waist of the ship. A huge commotion of shouting and swearing heralded the efforts of the orlop convicts fighting each other to reach the deck.

Eventually, they all stood in relative silence, breathlessly watching the horizon ahead.

Danny, standing with his arms protectively around Alice and Daniel was the first to spot it. "'Tis there! Do you see?'

Alice, looking to where his finger pointed saw it and almost danced with excitement. 'I see it! It's there! It's really, really there! Look, Maggie. Look!'

Maggie *was* looking and laughed with everyone else as they cheered and shouted in joy. This, they all hoped, was the end of their journey through endless unforgiving oceans. The end to their cold and their fear. Soon, so very soon, they would be off this God-forsaken lump of leaking wood and safe in a town, on land that did not constantly move under their feet.

The women lined the rails, jostling and pushing for position as the land drew closer. Land which they now knew to be part of this *place beyond the seas.*

They expected to be sent to their quarters at any moment and the hatches battened down behind them. This time they would not mind, for this would be their final lockdown before leaving this accursed ship forever. To their consternation, the *Lady Juliana* did not slow and they watched, many of them complaining loudly, as the beautiful green land slipped quickly past.

Judging by his navigation chart, Thomas Edgar knew that, depending on the wind they still had fourteen or more days before they reached Port Jackson.

Captain Aitken gave some thought to perhaps making land at Van Diemen's Land to replenish stocks, but his concern for the possible survivors at Port Jackson put paid to the idea. He felt that every day might count and he wanted to reach them as soon as possible.

The convicts stood sadly watching as the land disappeared into the mists behind them.

Danny came behind Alice where she stood at the rail and drew her into his arms. 'Perhaps the Captain is afraid of the giants,' he said, with a smile in his voice.

Alice turned her head to look up at him and he kissed her forehead. 'What giants?'

'Didn't you hear about them? When Captain Cook landed there — about fourteen or fifteen years ago, it was — he sent men ashore and they came back shaking in fear, for the people living there were giants.'

Alice laughed. 'Giants indeed! I don't believe you.'

'Well, you ask Lieutenant Edgar. He was there. He'll tell you. Maybe he even saw the giants.'

Alice still was not sure if she believed him, but content to snuggle back against Danny, she didn't argue any further.

Thomas Edgar stood before Alice with a bundle of clothes in his arms. 'I have a few things here to help you get a better start in your new life.'

Squinting against the glare of the sun, Alice frowned questioningly.

Thomas squatted beside her and offered her the clothes. 'I thought it might be better if you started in the new colony with dresses other than your prison ones. These will probably be a bit large for you, but it shouldn't take you long to adjust them.'

Puzzled, Alice scrambled to her feet and took a dress from the bundle. It was bright and cheery and looked to her untrained eyes to be of good quality. 'I don't understand. Where have they come from?'

taken his torn flesh up the masts and torn it even more. Now he must tell Alice he could not stay with her.

Alice gazed up at Danny, blurred through the tears in her eyes. 'He couldn't mean it! You have to stay! I need you,' she pleaded.

Danny swallowed the lump in his throat. 'I tried every way I could to persuade him, but he says I *have* to go. I thought about going into hiding, but he says if I do I will forfeit all my wages for the year and more I have been on the ship. Neither I nor my parents would get as much as a penny.'

Alice shook her head frantically. 'He was only saying it to keep you here. He's a kind man. He wouldn't really do it.'

Thomas Edgar, standing nearby, had been eavesdropping on the conversation. 'I'm afraid he does mean it, Alice. He has to, for without a crew his ship cannot sail.'

'But Danny is only one man. How could it make so much difference?' Alice protested.

'Because Danny is only one of many men, and there are probably half a dozen or more who wish to remain here with their wives and babies. So Captain Aitken has no choice but to refuse them all.'

Alice bowed her head and sobbed. Thomas Edgar felt his heart shift and he put an arm around her shoulder. 'I'm sorry. I would like to make it right for you, but I can't. I can only suggest that when Danny returns to England he attempts to get a berth back to the colony. Though I warn you, it might be difficult because there are few captains who would allow a crewman licence to leave a ship mid-voyage.'

Thomas Edgar left them then Alice and Danny slumped to the deck, arms tightly around each other and the sleeping baby nestled between them. For a long time, they stayed like that, quietly sobbing.

The convicts were all lined on the deck, with their few worldly goods around them. Thomas Edgar brought out the bundles of baby clothes Alice had so lovingly stitched, and he had kindly stored safely for her. With a heavy heart, he helped Danny to see her, baby Daniel and her bundles safely into the boats. He had grown fond of this gentle, brave little girl throughout the year he had known her. He had watched her grow from a timid, frightened child to a strong young woman. But would she be strong enough to face, alone whatever was ahead of her in this harsh, hungry colony? The only thing he felt at all happy about was that both he and surgeon, Richard Alley were to remain here. With luck, he hoped, they would be able to keep an eye on her.

Invited to attend Governor Phillips at his residence, George Aitken and government agent, Thomas Edgar were advised they must bring their own food and drinks as the Governor allowed himself only the same rations as his citizens. They were also warned that when the light went from the day they would have to sit in the dark as the colony had, long since, run out of candles.

In courtesy, when they did attend the Governor, they took only a meagre amount of food and one bottle of port. They also took a ship's lantern well filled with oil.

'I must admit to you, gentlemen,' Governor Phillip began', that although it is gratifying to know that England has not forgotten us, I am more than a little disappointed by the goods you have brought us. I have to agree with Judge Advocate Collins when he described them as *a cargo so unnecessary and so unprofitable*. I had asked for skilled tradesmen to help with the building of the colony. Instead, they have sent a shipload of women, mostly prostitutes by all accounts. We could certainly have wished for a more useful cargo than this.'

George Aitken sighed and nodded. 'I quite take your point.

The three had sailed within two days of each other and after anchoring overnight just outside the harbour, were warped in, in the morning.

Watchers on the shore saw bodies being heaved from the decks of these new arrivals, into the boats below. On reaching a wading distance from shore, the oarsmen tipped them into the water and returned for more.

Some of these poor souls, still manacled, managed to drag themselves toward the water's edge. Many had not the strength and lay, drowning, where they landed.

Not, at first, believing what they were seeing, the colonists stood in stunned silence.

'They're drowning,' Alice screamed, dropping the sheets she was washing and breaking into a run. 'We have to help.'

Running into the river, she caught hold of a young girl who was struggling to hold her face above the water. Clinging to her dress, she dragged her to where the water was shallow enough to safely leave her lying on her back. Leaving her there, she plunged back into the river to where she could see a man feebly flapping his arms, his face below the water.

'I've got you. I've got you,' she cried, sobbing, as she grabbed his hair to lift his face clear. He was a heavy man and she struggled to move him, but after a few moments he seemed to recover his wits and gamely struggled to help her pull him to shallower water.

Others ran to help, hurtling into the water and grabbing at the first of the skeletal humans they came to. The women and weaker men dragged the poor souls by their shirts. The stronger men picked them up and carried them on their shoulders. As fast as the rescuers worked, more dead and near-dead were being tossed out of boats.

Men and a few women lay on the beach, hundreds of them,

nearer dead than alive, shackled and too weak from being chained in the holds, to be able to stand.

A runner was sent for Governor Arthur Phillip, who arrived in a fury.

'Get every able-bodied person here,' he shouted, as more boatloads of shackled emaciated humans were dumped in the river. 'And the blacksmiths. Anyone able to knock the chains off these poor souls. I want them here and I want it done in as short a time as possible.'

Richard Alley scurried backward and forward along the riverbank, checking who lived and who did not. The bodies of the dead were left where they lay, to be buried at a later time.

The South Bank teemed with life as the colonists slaved to rescue the living dead, free them from their shackles and carry them up to the hospital. They were not heavy. Most of them were no more than skeletons.

'Where are we to put them all,' Richard despairingly asked Governor Phillip. 'The hospital beds are almost full of folk recovering from smallpox.'

'I'll order the men to rig up some temporary shelters until we can build something more permanent. 'When I get to the bottom of this evil, I'll have the heads of the perpetrators!' he snarled.

Like magic mushrooms, shelters sprang up all along the tree line. Just rough, no more than four posts with branches and leaves for a roof, but at least it served to keep the sun and most of the rain from the patients.

Alice, with Daniel bound to her back most of the time, worked tirelessly, day and night, alongside Richard Alley. Most of the other women from the *Lady Juliana* toiled, uncomplaining, beside them, most of them realising, for the first time, how lucky they had been to have sailed with such humane men as George Aitken, Thomas Edgar, and Richard Alley. During their year at sea, only five of the convict women had lost their lives, and none of them through negligence. They had all been well cared for and in the most hygienic conditions considering the hazards they had faced.

The story one of her patients told Alice, sent her running to Richard Alley. He must hear this too.

Holding the poor man's hand, she asked him gently to repeat his story.

'Captain Traill, gave us almost no food for the entire voyage,' the man told them, his voice breaking at the memory.

Her heart wrenching, Alice wiped a tear from his cheek.

'When anyone died they were left chained to us for days. We often didn't tell the guards and that way we could get the corpse's ration of food — if any came at all, that was. Eventually, the bodies were taken away and thrown over the side like a sack of old rubbish. We were hardly ever allowed on deck and after Cape Town, we never saw the light of day. All who died, and there were many, were left shackled to us until the night before we arrived here. That night when we anchored out in the bay, they spent hours collecting the bodies and throwing them over the side. I don't know how many died before we reached here, but there must have been hundreds.'

Richard Alley sat, speechless and ashen-faced. 'Thank you, my man.' He patted the man's shoulder as he stood to leave. 'I promise you,' he said grimly, 'I will report this to Governor Phillip. He is a good man and will no doubt have it investigated.'

Once outside the hut, Richard thanked Alice for bringing it to his attention. 'I will see the governor as soon as I can. Captain Traill can not be allowed to get away with this.'

Arthur Phillip regarded the surgeon in absolute horror. 'You believed the man, did you?'

Richard Alley nodded his head. 'Without a doubt, I did. What reason does he have to lie? You saw for yourself how the poor souls were put ashore.'

'I did indeed. That man, Traill must be made to account for this evil. I will speak to Captain Hill, he's master of the guard, arrived with the fleet and seems like a good man.'

William Hill, stood before the governor his head hanging and a tear in his eye as he studied his shoes. Raising his head to look the other man in the eye, he sighed and said, 'I regret it is all true. To my mind, Captain Traill is an insane sadist. He did indeed keep the convicts starving. All the captains failed to feed the convicts. It is my feeling that they wanted the convicts to die.'

Arthur Phillip shook his head in disbelief. 'Why, man? Why would they want them dead, for Christs's sake?'

'To sell their rations; their food; to line their own pockets. The convicts were rarely permitted onto the deck, so lay wasting in shackles for most of the voyage. When I questioned him about it, and about the number of deaths on his ship Captain Traill told me that it was *his* ship and it was no business of mine how he ran it. He said the government paid his company seventeen pounds seven shillings and sixpence for each convict who boarded his ship, whether they arrived here dead or alive! Britain just wanted to be rid of them.'

Arthur Phillip drew a sharp breath. 'I noticed those shackles, he broke in. 'I have never seen any quite like them before.'

'No, sir, nor had I. They were the most barbaric I have ever seen. The makers had been in the Guinea slave trade and used the same shackles used by them in that trade. They are made with a short bolt instead of chains that drop between the legs and fasten with a bandage about the waist. These bolts are not more than nine inches in length so that the poor souls could not extend either leg from the other more than an inch or two at most; thus fettered it was impossible for them to move for fear of both their legs being broken. They were completely powerless, sir. They were left to lie in their own bodily excretions, shackled to corpses, with little or no ventilation. It is testimony to the strength of humankind that a single one of them survived.'

'I can think of nothing to say, but that this evil man must be punished. It is not within the power vested in me, I'm afraid, but I will send a report to England. He must be charged with murder at the very least.'

William Hill nodded his agreement. 'To my mind, Sir, the slave trade is merciful compared with what I have seen on this fleet. I must say that my feelings have never been so wounded as on this voyage. I had never thought to see such cruelty and suffering. So much so that I don't think I shall ever fully recover my usual spirits.'

'Governor Phillip gave his shoulder a sympathetic tap. 'I'm sure you did all you could, my lad.'

'Yes, Sir, had it been in my power it would have been the most satisfying task of my life to have prevented so many of my fellow-creatures so much misery and death. There was nothing I could do. I had no authority over the ship's captains.'

'I understand your position.'

'There is one thing you should know, Sir, I believe one of the ships is carrying some sort of prefabricated hospital. It will take a lot of manpower to erect it, but I'm sure it can be done.'

Governor Phillip gave him a sharp look, then smiled thankfully. 'Thank you, my boy. Of course, it can — and must — be done. We have nearly five hundred poor souls off those ships who can neither feed nor care for themselves. Disease, lice and fleas are rife amongst them. At the moment most of them, as you know, are in makeshift shanties. I fear a great many of them are too far gone to survive, but they will have a better chance in a hospital. We must get it erected as soon as possible.'

Orders went out and the makings of the hospital were quickly unloaded and brought to shore. Every available man was set to help sort out the jigsaw puzzled of parts. In no time at all the hospital arose like the phoenix from the ashes and the patients moved in out of the rain and the dust-laden winds.

Many of the poor souls who were pulled from the sea had little or no clothing and Governor Phillip ordered every woman from the *Lady Juliana* who knew how to put a needle to cloth, to make eight hundred sets of clothing from bales of material that were aboard the Neptune. Governor Phillip had little doubt, but that Captain Traill had intended to line his own pockets from the sale of the cloth, but his protests fell on deaf ears.

Those women who were not tending to the sick sat for hour after endless hour cutting and sewing. This, they did gladly, but with heavy hearts.

Within days of the three ships arriving, bodies began to wash up on the beaches. It was complete proof, if any was needed, that indeed many bodies had been pulled from the holds and thrown into the sea during the darkness of the night before they warped into Sydney Cove.

CHAPTER 24

George Aitken clenched his teeth and shook his head. 'I am not happy with the situation, Thomas,' he admitted.

Thomas nodded. 'No, Sir, it could get quite ugly if we don't handle it properly. Several of them have gone from requesting to stay here to demanding it.'

George Aitken drew a weary hand over his face. 'How are we to handle it? I am mindful of the fact that the main cause of the mutiny on the *Bounty* was that the men did not want to leave the women they had mated with in Tahiti.'

'There is certainly a lot of unrest.'

'Aye. I *have* to be in Canton before the thirteenth of January or I will lose a very lucrative contract. If I were to lose any more of my crew I could not possibly make that deadline.'

'No, sir. I can quite see your problem.'

'It is possibly a worse problem than you realise. The Governor has ordered me to transport most of our women to Norfolk Island. This will mean more time wasted and possibly more unrest amongst the crew.'

Thomas Edgar sighed and shook his head. His thoughts went to his *wife*, and the feeling of commitment he had toward her, and he felt some sympathy for the crew. He was only thankful that his commission only took him as far as Port Jackson.

'I think I'll have a word with the Governor. Now that there are other ships here, he might agree to send our women in one of them. That might ease the situation with our crew.'

'As long as it is not the Neptune,' Thomas Edgar said quickly.

George shook his head. 'No! Never the Neptune!'

George paced in the hall of the Governor's residence while he awaited his audience. As he walked, he rehearsed his speech in his head. After a short wait, he was ushered into the office by a footman whose uniform had seen better days.

'My problem, Sir, is that many of my men are feeling resentful because they want to stay here with the women they took as *wives* on the voyage. Several also have children by them. Much as I can sympathise with them, I cannot leave them here. I have a ship to run and cannot sail without a crew.'

'Yes, I can understand that. Then you must just tell them they *have* to go.'

'This, I have done, Sir. But there is a great deal of unrest. We see the looks of hatred they direct at us, and I fear that if we have to take the women to Norfolk Island, we might meet with the same fate as Bligh.'

Governor Phillip rubbed his chin thoughtfully. 'Yes, I heard about that debacle.' After a few moments of silent deliberation, he continued, 'I will have a word with Captain Antsis on the Surprize and tell him he has to take the women and some supplies. Perhaps the Justinian Will take extra stores. Do you think this would take care of your troubles?'

George Aitken heaved a sigh of relief. 'Thank you, sir. It may not solve it completely but it should make it somewhat easier to handle the men. I would ask you to stress to Captain Antsis that the women must not be put in chains.'

'I will most certainly do that. Leave it with me.'

The *Lady Juliana* was to sail on the twenty-fifth of July and in a perhaps misguided act of kindness, Captain Aitken had allowed some of the women to spend the last few days aboard the ship with their men.

There was little for the crew to do as there was no cargo to load, so Alice and Danny spent most of their days huddled in a shady spot on the deck, enjoying each other and their baby and dreading the moment they would have to part. Like all the other couples, their nights were a frenzy of making love, perhaps for the last time ever.

Tears were shed by the bucket-load, as couples plotted ways to hide the women on board until the ship was too far north to return.

On the night of the twenty-fourth of July trouble brewed. Captain Aitken ordered the women off the ship as it was to depart early the next morning. Most of them refused to go, backed by their *husbands*. After a short, but ugly standoff the marines were sent in.

Alice, clinging desperately to Danny was picked up bodily by a marine and she was passed down to men waiting in the lighter. Other women were bundled down behind her, followed by their menfolk who scrambled down the ladders and struggled with the marines all the way to the shore.

The fighting continued, amidst the screams of women and babies, while all the residents of the shanty-town turned out to watch; to shout encouragement to the crewmen and abuse at the marines.

Outnumbered, the crew were finally forced aboard the lighters and returned to the ship.

Sobbing, Alice and several of the other women started wading out, but had to give up when the water became too deep. Forced back to shore, they sat on the beach weeping.

'Come on lass, this will do you no good.'

Alice felt a gentle hand on her shoulder and, looking up through red-rimmed eyes, found Richard Alley beside her.

'Come back to the hospital with me. Sitting here crying will do you no good. There are people in the hospital who need you.'

Nodding sadly, she clambered to her feet and trailed miserably behind him to the hospital.

Very early the following morning she stood, watching in misery as the *Lady Juliana* weighed anchor and started out of the harbour. She saw Danny at the rail and waved sadly, hoping that he would see her amongst the crowd on the shore, but she doubted that he could.

The new hospital was finished and Alice gladly helped to move all the poor souls from their makeshift huts. Many of them had died, there had been funerals every day, and very many more were in such a sad state that they were not expected to live.

Depressing though it was, Alice was glad of the work. It pleased her to give comfort to the suffering and hold the hands of the dying. Though she wept often while she toiled, it helped to take her mind off her own loss. At least she had Daniel and her three staunch friends, she told herself, which was more than poor Danny had.

Maggie, Lily and Sarah caught up with Alice as she headed for the river with an armful of soiled sheets.

'Hello,' she smiled. 'Would you walk with me to the river? I must get this linen washed as quickly as possible.'

Maggie caught her arm and pulled her to a halt. 'We haven't just come for a friendly chat, I'm afraid. We have some upsetting news for you.'

Alice stopped and studied her friends. They all looked upset; tearful and it frightened her. 'What news is that then?' she whispered. 'What's happened?'

'Captain Aitken told us this morning that we are not to stay in Port Jackson. Most of us from the *Lady Juliana* are to be sent on to a place called Norfolk Island.'

'Another island? Another sea journey? Oh, I thought we were finished with all that. I don't want to go. I want to stay here and work in the hospital,' Alice said weepily. Her throat was dry with fear.

This hospital, Surgeon Alley, and all the patients had become so important to her. The last thing she wanted was to leave them. Choking back a sob, shaking her head she gazed pleadingly at Maggie.

Her friend bit her lip and swiped a tear from her cheek. 'Well, that's good,' she said quietly, 'because you won't have to.'

Alarmed, Alice looked sharply at her friends and saw that all had moist eyes. 'Won't have to what? What won't I have to do?' she asked fearfully.

'You won't have to leave here,' Sarah answered quietly, 'for you are to stay and continue your work, but we are all to go.'

Alice shook her head frantically. 'Stay here with you all gone? No, I won't! I'll tell them I have to go.'

Dropping her bundle of sheets, she fled back into the hospital, leaving her friends in tears.

'Surgeon Alley,' she cried as she ran down the corridor.

Richard Alley appeared from a ward with a finger to his lips.

'Hush now Alice,' he said quietly, 'we have sick people here.' He had been expecting this -and dreading it all morning.

Alice stopped and threw herself, sobbing, into his arms. 'Maggie says they are to sail on to some other place and I am to be left behind.'

Richard gently disentangled her arms from around him. 'Sit down here, my dear, and listen carefully to what I have to say.'

Alice nodded mutely and collapsed miserably onto the chair he led her to.

'I have discussed this with the Governor and Captain Aitken. It was their decision that one hundred and fifty of the women from the *Lady Juliana* must be moved on to Norfolk Island.'

'But why?' Alice asked in despair. 'Why can they not stay here?'

'It is Governor Phillip's opinion that this colony can not cope with them at the moment.'

'Then I must go with them!' Alice raised her chin and glared at the man before her.

Richard shook his head. 'I particularly asked that you be permitted to stay here.' As Alice opened her mouth to speak, he held up a hand. 'Hear me out. There are several reasons that I think you should remain here. First and foremost is your safety — yours and Daniel's.'

Alice looked questioningly at him and he continued. 'We know little of how this colony on Norfolk Island are coping — or even if there is still anyone left alive there.'

'And you are sending my friends there?' Alice asked in dismay.

Richard took her hand. 'Look at me Alice,' he said sadly, '*I* am not sending anyone anywhere. It is the Governor's order. They must go and for Daniel's and your safety, you must stay. A supply ship, a contingent of marines and some male convicts will accompany your friends and, if need be, they will form a new colony.'

'Oh, but Maggie loves me. She always said she'd never leave me and would always be here for me. What am I to do without her?'

'Just what you have been doing for the past few weeks. Taking care of the sick and learning to be a nurse.'

'Oh, but — ,'

Surgeon Alley put a finger over her lips. 'No buts, Alice, they are leaving and you are staying.'

'Mavis Crowe! Who will protect me from her? Maggie has always kept me safe.'

'Mavis Crowe is going to Norfolk Island,' Richard Alley said through clenched teeth. 'And she may well be the only one of *Lady Juliana's* women to go in irons.'

'And I have no choice?'

Richard shook his head sorrowfully.

Alice stood, straightened her shoulders and held her head erect. 'Then I had better go and wash the sheets.'

She walked proudly from the hospital and into the arms of her friends.

A week after watching Danny sail out of her life, Alice stood on the river bank once again, her face wet with tears.

The *Surprize* moved slowly away from her and she stood motionless, watching her friends at the stern rail until the ship disappeared around the headland.

Alice would never see them again. Not any of them. She knew that with a certainty that tore a huge rent in her heart. Was that always the way it would be for her. Everyone who loved her would be torn from her. First, her mother, what was it, five years ago now? Yes, it must be all of that. Then Danny. Now the only really genuine friends she'd had in her life. Gone! All gone! And she knew in her heart she would never see any of them again. All she had left was Daniel. She looked down and he smiled up at her.

Unconsciously she tightened her arms around him as though she felt that any moment there would be a snap of the devil's fingers and he would disappear too.

When she looked up again the last tip of the mainsail was just disappearing behind the headland.

Richard Alley stood beside her, an empty feeling in his heart. These women had been his life for over a year now. He had cared for them, wiped their tears. Delivered their babies. He had nursed most of them through one kind of illness or another and many of them he'd brought back from the edge of death. He could only pray that their health and welfare would be well taken care of on Norfolk Island. His only consolation was that Captain Atstis had agreed to the Governor's directive that they *must not* be shackled.

With a sigh, he turned away. Taking Alice's arm he gave a gentle tug. 'Come on, lass. Nothing left to see here and there's people in the hospital who need us.'

Alice nodded and walked quietly beside him wondering what horrors life had in store for her next. She clung protectively to Daniel. God help anyone who tried to take him from her. Either they would die, or she would die stopping them!

In the days and weeks that followed, Alice learned how to kick, scratch, pull hair, and use her knees to good purpose, with Richard Alley coming to her aid on occasions. Bit by bit the men of the camp learned the hard way that she was a wildcat and was not to be tampered with.

When she wasn't caring for the sick, Alice spent many hours sitting on the riverbank watching the activity in the harbour as Daniel crawled around at her feet.

Often she would see natives in the distance. Black people were a new experience, and to her, they looked ferocious. Nervous of them, she would hug her baby tighter to her bosom.

I just wish — , Alice thought. But what did she wish? She didn't know. What she would wish for most was to get on a ship; go back to the Isle of Man; find her mother and show her her grandson. For all the years she had spent alone and fending for herself, stealing to stay alive all she had ever wanted was to find the mother whom she knew loved her. But that was never going to happen, was it?

Here, now, she was trapped in this miserable, uncomfortable hell hole of a town. She knew she was better off than most of the women, but still hated this place.

Quite a few of the women who had arrived on the *Lady Juliana* had married strangers within days of arriving. All of them desperate to grab at the security they thought that a marriage would give them.

Should she have done this? It would have given her someone, apart from Daniel, to spend her time and her life with, wouldn't it? Someone, perhaps, to care about. Then her thoughts would turn to Danny and she would know she could not just go and marry a stranger; lie with a stranger at night. Possibly bear a stranger's child. She shuddered at the idea.

Shaking herself out of her reverie, she stood up, slapped the dust from her skirt, and turned back toward the hospital. It was time, she decided, to go and hold a few hands, though there were not so many of those left now. A great number of her patients had died, despite her tireless ministrations and many who had survived had now left the hospital.

As she trudged wearily through clinging mud toward the hospital a pair of heavy horses cantered down the road, pulling a cart.

'Help me. Dear God, will someone help me,' the driver pleaded, pulling the horses to a halt at the door of the hospital.

Several men, who were standing nearby, rushed to him.'

Alice hurried her steps as she saw them lift a woman from the cart and carry her into the hospital.

Richard Alley was there quickly and instructed them to carry the woman into a ward.

'What has happened?' Richard asked, anxiously studying the face of the unconscious woman.

'She got bit by a snake. We was working in the field an' I think she stood on it. It got her in the ankle.'

'Her name?' Richard asked.

'Emma. Emma Costain. I'm her husband, Keith.'

With a sigh, Richard studied the woman. Her breathing was shallow and she was blue around the lips. He rubbed his chin worriedly. This was away out of his realm. What did one do for snakebite? What *could* one do for snakebite? This was a first for him. He looked around despairingly at the men who had carried her in and at the nurses who lingered in the background.

One of the men said hesitantly, 'Maybe we could ask the Indians? They might know. There's always one or two friendly ones hanging around.'

'Oh please, you must help her. We've a young child who needs her mother. And I need my wife,' the man pleaded. His eyes glistened with tears and fear.

Richard Alley turned decisively to the men around him. 'Can you get out there and find one of the natives as quicky as possible and bring him here.'

As one, the men rushed from the hospital.

Spotting Alice in the doorway, Richard beckoned to her. 'Will you sit with this lady until they return. There is not much we can do, but wipe the sweat from her brow and try to keep her cool. Wet a cloth and try to dribble water into her mouth if you can.'

Alice nodded, collected a cloth and a bowl of water, and moved nervously toward her patient. Sitting on a stool beside the bed she pushed the hair away from her patient's face and wiped it gently. Looking up at the lady's husband, she smiled reassuringly. 'Surgeon Alley is a very good physician. She is in the safest hands.'

The man gave her a watery smile and nodded wordlessly, though his eyes stayed dark with fear.

Alice returned her attention to her patient. Wiping the sweat and grime away, she studied the pale, sickly face. There was something familiar. A face she knew, but could not connect.

'Did your wife come here on the *Lady Juliana*?' she asked.

The man frowned and shook his head. 'The what?'

'*Lady Juliana*. That's the ship I arrived on a few weeks ago.'

He shook his head emphatically this time. 'The answer is *no*, then. Emma came with the first fleet.'

Alice looked up sharply as a group of men almost fell through the door. 'We found one,' one of the men shouted as he pushed a nervous looking black man forward.

Richard Alley rushed in. 'Is he able to help?'

One of the men shrugged and said, 'Well it's a bit hard to be sure, 'cos we don't speak the same lingo. We did a bit of signing an' he seemed to know what we was saying. He's brought a whole lot of herbs an' things.'

Richard patted the man's shoulder. He knew this man by sight and knew the Governor had befriended him, though no one could quite understand why. Pointing to Emma he made a few signals and was relieved when the man smiled and nodded his head.

Alice moved away from the cot to allow this strange, skinny very black man near to her patient. She had seen this man around the camp and had been a little afraid of him.

After a lot of hand flapping and drinking motions, the native was given boiling water, in which he infused a strange collection of leaves. Some of these he put on the snake bite, then he dripped the liquid into the woman's mouth.

For what felt like a lifetime, the group around the bed watched warily, praying, but not very confident that this witch doctor type treatment was going to work.

Alice left for a while to care for her other patients, but whenever she could find a moment to spare, she popped back to check on the snake-bite victim.

It was a long frightening afternoon for the poor husband, who sat hour after endless dreadful hour holding his wife's hand and wiping the sweat from her brow and dripping the Indian's liquid into her mouth. Occasionally he would lean over, kiss her cheek, and beg her to wake up.

With a tear in her eye, Alice wordlessly watched this show of fear and devotion.

Richard Alley stood looking down at his patient and thoughtfully rubbed his stubble chin. *Well,* he thought, *against all the odds she is still alive, And I do believe her condition has improved.*

'Mister Costain,' He said quietly. 'You've been sitting here for several hours now. 'I think it would probably do you good to take a break for a little while. Why don't you go and find something to eat and rest for a while.'

'Oh — no — I can't. My wife — .'

'Your wife is looking a little better now. Her breathing has improved, her colour is a little better and her lips not so blue.'

'Oh — but — .'

'No buts. When she wakens she won't want to find you close to collapse. Now didn't you say you have a young child?'

Keith Costain nodded and smiled enthusiastically.

The first smile Alice had seen from him — and it took twenty years from his age.

'We have a daughter. Just turned nine months of age.'

'And where is she at the moment?' Richard asked quietly.

'My master's wife has her.'

'Your master's wife?'

'Yes, I work on a farm a few miles to the West. A place called Rose Hill. My master, Andrew, came as a convict but had almost served his sentence by the time he arrived. We had become friends on the ship and when he was made a free man he was given land and took me an' Emma to help on the farm. Emma works in the house an' in the yard sometimes, but they don't treat us like servants. We are all friends and I know Jessica will be safe with Ann.'

'That sounds like a wonderful arrangement,' Richard enthused. 'Are there many here in that sort of situation?'

Keith shook his head. 'No, we have just been very lucky. 'Like I said, Andrew an' me was mates on the ship and so was Ann and Emma.'

'So you all live together do you?'

Another shake of his head. 'No. Andrew can't afford to pay us much so he gave us a little corner of a field an' we built a little wood house on it. We've got a little vegetable garden too.'

'It sounds as if you have been very lucky. Look, why don't you go home for a while Keith? Play with your daughter. Chat with your friends. And just relax for a bit.'

Keith sighed and shook his head. 'No, It's too far an' I don't want to leave Emma for long.'

Richard Alley nodded sympathetically. 'Well, go outside and sit down for a spell. I'll tell one of my helpers to bring you some food and a glass of rum.'

Keith looked reluctantly at Emma.

'Alice will look after Emma while you're gone.' he looked questioningly at the girl who quickly nodded.

'There you are — all settled.' Richard took his arm and gently eased him to his feet.

Keith nodded, laid down the damp cloth he had been using to wipe Emma's brow, and allowed Richard to lead him from the ward.

For long minutes Alice stood watching her patient struggle to breathe. Her face pale, thin and drawn, her lips almost blue, she looked like a very old lady. But hadn't her husband said they had a young child? So she couldn't be so very old, could she? There was something about this lady that troubled her.

With a shake of her head, she heaved a weary sigh and sat in the chair Keith had just vacated.

Taking up the damp cloth she gently wiped Emma's sweaty face. With care, she slowly dripped water between the dry, parched lips. Instinctively she gently took the thin hand in hers and almost immediately felt a response.

Looking up, she found two blue eyes studying her with a puzzled expression. Frowning, she returned the gaze. There was still something hauntingly familiar about the gaunt face. It was the eyes. Yes, the eyes.

'Am I dead?' Emma rasped quietly.

Alice smiled and squeezed her patient's hand. 'No, you are still alive, thanks be to God and the native man who brought you herbs.'

The woman shook her head and tears ran on her cheeks. 'I thought I must have come to heaven.'

Alice laughed. 'Not heaven, but for a while, we did think that was where you were going.'

Emma studied her again and her eyes lit up. 'You are Alice, aren't you? My Alice. Please say you are.'

Alice's laughter died as suddenly as it had started and she studied her patient carefully. 'Yes. I'm Alice, but — .'

'You don't recognise me do you?'

Alice shook her head and looked harder. Those eyes. So blue. Blue like she had only ever seen before on one person. With a catch in her voice, she whispered, 'Mam?'

Emma's eyes filled with tears again. Too choked to speak, she merely nodded and tugged at Alice's hand.

For a long moment, Alice sat looking into the eyes of this strange, yet familiar, woman. Could this be true? Could this woman be her mother? But how — ? Where — ? Was she going to waken any minute and find it was all a dream? Could it be true? She shook her head in bewilderment.

Emma smiled through her tears and nodded her head again.

Alice leapt to her feet, her heart somersaulting with joy such as she had never felt before. It was true! This was her mother! That smile! She could see it now. No one else ever had a smile like her Mam.

Sitting carefully on the bed, she gathered this gaunt sickly little bundle into her arms as if she was a child and hugged her firmly.

'I thought I had gone to heaven when I saw you there,' Emma said weepily.

'Oh, Mam, how did you get to be in this place?'

Emma's face fell and she turned her head away. 'I was arrested an' the Deemster said I had to come here.'

'Arrested?' Alice frowned. Her Mam — arrested. The most honest woman she had ever known. Always so hard working. 'Why? I don't understand.'

'I was caught — .' Emma stopped and heaved a huge sigh. 'Well, I suppose you have to know some time.' She paused, then turned to look straight into her daughter's eyes. 'I was caught with a man. Selling my body for money. All those nights when you thought I was out cleaning the rich peoples' houses, I was with men.'

Alice sat in stunned silence. Her mother — a prostitute — and she had never suspected. But how would she?

'Please don't think too harshly of me,' Emma pleaded, a tear spilling down her cheek.

'Oh, Mam, I don't think badly of you. Not at all. My best friends on the voyage here also sold themselves, but without them, I would not have survived the journey,' she said with feeling.

'I can't believe I have found you.' Emma bit her lip as she fought against more tears. 'I knew I would never get back to the Isle of Man to look for you and I thought you were lost to me.'

'I never stopped looking for you,' Alice sobbed. 'I was sure you would never leave me.'

'Nor would I. I pleaded with the constables to find you and make sure you were safe, an' they said they would. Then when the deemster said I was to be sent away, I begged him to let me stay with you, or to find you and send you with me, but he was impatient with me and said I must go alone and that you would be taken care of.'

'Oh, Mam. The constables never came.' Alice stopped and thought for a moment. 'Or maybe they did. The landlord quickly threw me out, for I had no money to pay the rent.'

'Where did you go? How did you survive?'

'I have lived on the streets. Slept in churches sometimes. I had to steal to get food to eat.' Alice dropped her eyes and drew a tremulous breath, ashamed to have to admit to her mother that she was a thief.

'And that's why you're here.' Emma murmured and shook her head sadly. 'It is my fault for not looking after you properly.'

Alice could see her mother was becoming very distressed and took her hand. 'It was not your fault. You're here because you were working to put food in my mouth and a roof over my head. I thank you for that. You were a wonderful, loving mother. I could not have asked for better.'

Shaking her head, Emma said, 'You deserved better'.

Alice smiled. 'I had a very happy life with you. But it looks as if you are in a happier way now. You have a husband. I have met him and he seems like a good man. He was very worried about you.'

Emma's face softened and for a moment she looked younger. 'Aye. I have a husband. Keith, his name is and you're right, he is a good man. Irish. With an Irish sense of humour. I think that is what carried him through a terrible time in his life.'

Alice nodded. She had met quite a few Irishmen. A lot of them had come to the Island to work and she had always found them funny. Rogues — a lot of them — but mostly nice ones. Now and again one would give her a penny — which was probably stolen, but no matter.

'That was what first attracted me to Keith. If he saw I was upset he would tell me these jokes. Silly Irish jokes — about the Irish, it's funny how they can poke fun at themselves, isn't it? But he would cheer me up and make me giggle. I don't think I would have survived it all without him. It was so dreadful to be torn away from you.'

Alice could see her mother was becoming despondent again, so bent to kiss her cheek.

'Now I think you should rest' she said quietly. 'You have been very ill today.'

Emma clutched at her hand. 'I want to talk'. Even as she said it her eyes were drooping.

Alice bent to kiss the ravaged cheek. 'We'll talk later. Rest now.'

CHAPTER 25

———••———

Richard Alley stood in the doorway for a moment watching Alice as she gazed at the woman, whose hand she clung to. He saw there was a tear in her cheek and a strange look in her eye. Concerned, he hurried forward.

'Is she worse?' he asked quickly.

Alice shook her head, too choked for a moment to be able to speak. Finally, she managed to tell him the patient was much better and had been awake for a while.

Richard frowned. 'Then why the tears?'

Alice sucked in a shaky breath and, unable to speak for a moment, she lowered her eyes and shook her head. Finally, she sobbed 'She's my Mam!'.

Richard's eyes widened. 'Your mother? This lady? Really? Are you sure?'

Alice nodded. 'Yes. We've talked, but I didn't recognise her, Mr. Alley. My own Mam and I did not know her.'

Moving to put an arm around her shoulders, Richard said, 'Well, that's understandable and I'm sure she wasn't upset by it. It's a long time since you saw her and she must have been through a very bad time since then. It is bound to have changed her.'

Alice put a hand over her mouth to stifle her sobs. 'It's just so hard to believe. I keep thinking I'll wake up and she'll be gone again.'

Richard smiled and squeezed her shoulder. 'Well, I can assure you, you *are* wide awake and it *is* true.

Alice nodded and gave a weepy giggle. 'It is as though God has finally answered my prayers. And I have been thinking — did not her husband say she has a child?'

Richard nodded. 'Aye — a daughter.'

Tears leapt to Alice's eyes again, but his time she smiled. 'So I have a little sister! I always wanted a sister."

The surgeon smiled. 'And your mother has a grandson,' he said quietly. 'they must be close to the same age.'

Alice jerked her head back to look at Richard through startled eyes. 'Oh, dear God. How do I tell my Mam? What will she think of me?'

Richard laughed. 'You just say, "Mam, I have a son — your grandson." She will be shaken for a moment, then she'll be thrilled, not only to have her daughter back but to have the added bonus of a grandson.'

Alice looked doubtful. 'Do you really think so?'

Richard nodded. 'If she's the mother you told me so much about — I know so.'

With a sigh, Alice gently trailed the backs of her fingers down her mother's tired, pale face. Nodding, she said quietly, 'she was the best mother I could have asked for. We never had any money, but she always had plenty of love to give. There was never any shortage of that.'

Richard smiled. 'Well then, I do not doubt that she will be thrilled to have a grandson to love — as well as having her daughter returned to her.'

'But what of her husband?' Alice started worrying again. 'He doesn't know me. What will he think of me? He'll know I am a criminal. Perhaps he'll forbid her to have anything to do with me.'

Richard shook his head and smiled gently. 'No, not a criminal, Alice. All you are guilty of is being a young girl trying to stay alive. Don't go looking for troubles child. Keith Costain seemed like a nice, caring man to me. Never have I seen a man so concerned about his wife. He is a good man, I'm sure, and will find room in his heart for a daughter and her child. Besides, he too is, or was, a criminal or he wouldn't be here. Would he now?'

Alice still looked doubtful, her eyes filled with fear.

Richard took her hands in his. 'Do not put stumbling blocks in your way where probably none exist. Your mother has married a good man and has given him a daughter. He so obviously cares about them both, so I have no doubt there will be room in his heart for you and Daniel.'

Keith Costain hurried nervously into the hospital.

He had been gone longer than he had intended but had felt the need to check on little Jessica. For speed, he had borrowed a horse, rather than take the wagon, but even so, it had taken more time than he had intended. However, he knew there was nothing more he could do for Emma. It was in the lap of the Gods now and he had felt fairly confident leaving her in the care of that nice young nurse. She had seemed such a gentle lass, and it had seemed to Keith that she genuinely cared.

Fearing what he might find, he hesitated just before the door to the ward. Biting his lip, he took a deep breath, stepped forward, then stopped short.

The nurse was still there. Alice, he thought the doctor had called her, sat exactly where he had left her, still holding Emma's hand. The girl watched her patient with an expression on her face that he couldn't quite put a name to. If asked, he would probably

have described it as devotion. There was a glow about the girl —
not much more than a child, but he found himself drawn to her.

As he stepped into the ward the spell was broken. The nurse
looked up at him, smiled, and made to stand. Keith stopped
her with a gentle hand on her shoulder and a nod to tell her she
should stay. Returning her smile, he sat on the far side of the bed
and took Emma's other hand.

To his unpractised eyes, Emma looked better. Lips not so blue.
'How is she?' he asked nervously.

Alice smiled reassuringly. 'She is much better. I am sure the
danger is past, but she's still very weak.'

Keith nodded, heaved a sigh of relief and tears sprang to his
eyes. He bent to lay a kiss on Emma's forehead. 'Thank God'.
Looking at Alice, he swiped a tear from his cheek and said, 'She
is my world, you know. Her an' little Jessica. Thank you so much
for your kindness. I could not have left my Emma in better hands.'

'Jessica? Is that your daughter's name?'

'Aye.' Keith smiled fondly.

'It's a pretty name.' Alice hesitated for a moment, then said
quietly, 'Emma has another daughter you know.' There was a
tremor in her voice she could not control.

Keith nodded, his smile gone and only sadness showing. 'I
know of her. She told you about her did she? It broke Emma's
heart to be taken from her. There's not a day goes by that she
doesn't speak of her. She swears she'll get back to her island to
find her one day, but I don't know where we could find the money.
You know, she loves Jessica, but there is still a huge empty hole
in her heart for the daughter she has lost.'

Alice saw the tears on his cheeks again and said quietly, 'she
has found that daughter.'

Keith frowned at her, not comprehending. 'Found her?
Where? I don't understand.'

'Do you remember her daughter's name?' For some reason she did not understand, it mattered to Alice that this kind man should know her name.

'Yes, it was Alice ...' He stopped suddenly, startled and looked questioningly at the young nurse. Realisation dawned. 'Alice? You are Alice? Emma's daughter?'

Unable to make a sound past the emotion that threatened to choke her, Alice could merely nod.

'Emma's daughter! Praise be to God! Prayer does work after all! You'll never know how we have prayed and prayed for her to find you. We never thought it would be possible. The last thing we expected was that you would find her.'

Keith leapt to his feet. Rushing around the bed, he lifted Alice from her chair and enveloped her in a huge bear hug.

'Emma feared you might be dead. Just wait until she awakens and sees you. She'll be overjoyed.'

'She already has. Just for a few minutes, she wakened and she knew me.' Looking down at her hand on Emma's she said quietly, 'I didn't recognise her. I feel so dreadful because I did not know my own mother. For years I have held her face in my memory. But I didn't recognise her.' Alice sobbed and a tear flowed unnoticed.

Keith gave her another hug and gently wiped away the tear. 'Well, bless you girl. You were nobbut a child when you last saw her. And she must have changed — and probably aged. She spent two years or more in a rotting hulk of a ship on the Thames — an' so did I. I'm sure we both look older than we are.'

Alice frowned and shuddered. 'I saw those ships when they were taking me to Newgate gaol — and heard and smelled them. It was awful. There were more of them at Portsmouth too. The stories I heard about them were heartbreaking.'

Keith nodded, then bowed his head to hide emotions that threatened, for a moment, to overwhelm him. 'No man could imagine the torture we went through, but at least we were allowed outside most days to work on the docks We were given very little food, but still had to do heavy labouring. If we fell, or collapsed, we were beaten until we either died or got up and carried on working.'

Alice gasped in horror and put a hand to her mouth. Tears sprang to her eyes. 'How could any man do that to his fellow?' she whispered.

It was brutal all right, but not as bad as what the women had to bear. They was kept chained in the holds an' rarely saw the light of day. When they needed to relieve themselves they had to do it where they sat or laid. Sometimes they were left like that for days. An' if the woman next to you died you could be left chained to her for days. It's a wonder to me how any of the women survived.' He shrugged, sighed, and added bitterly, 'Of course, a lot did not.'

Alice swiped a tear from her cheek. 'And my Mam lived through two years of that?'

Keith nodded. 'Aye, she was one of the strong ones. An' her friend Ann, the wife of my boss. They was chained together in the hulk throughout those years, an' on the voyage out here. An' I think it was just their friendship and the strength they gave each other what kept them both alive.'

'You met my Mam on the ship coming here, did you?'

'No. We was on different ships, but me an' Andrew — he's my boss now — got to be friends on the voyage an' met Emma an' Ann soon after we got here. We got married about a week later. Andrew's sentence finished soon after an' he was given some land. He got permission for me an' your Mam to go an' work for him, to start up a farm. He's got a nice house there, what I helped him to build an' we've got a shack in the corner o' his field.'

Alice reached across the bed and took his hand in both of hers.

'Oh, I'm so glad my Mam met you. It's good to know she's happy and well cared for. And so loved. Thank you for that.'

Keith looked fondly at his wife. 'Your Mam's a lass in a million, alright,' he said with a loving smile. 'She's my whole world.'

Alice's eyes glittered with tears of happiness — with joy that her mother had found such a wonderful man and was so beloved. Then her mind turned to Danny and her face fell.

Keith sensed her sadness and he took her hand. 'What is it, girlie? What's upsettin' you?'

'I loved a man. A boy really, but he was a man to me. He wanted to stay here with me, but Captain Aitken would not release him. When the *Lady Juliana* sailed Danny was forced to go with her.

Keith squeezed her hand. 'And you were left here alone. I feel your pain, Alice. Where are you living? Were you able to find decent accommodation? I know it's hard to get.'

Alice nodded. 'The ship's surgeon was staying to run the hospital here and he found a room for us — me an' five other young girls he wanted to protect.'

'So you live — fairly safe — in the hospital?'

Alice nodded.

'Not like home though, is it girlie.'

Alice smiled sadly and sighed. 'I'm not sure what a home is any more.'

Keith studied her for a moment, then had a sudden thought that lit up his rugged, almost ugly face with beauty. 'Well then, now we've found you, you must come and live with us.'

Startled, Alice looked up at him. 'Live with you? Would you want me there? Would you have room for me?'

Keith laughed. 'Of course, we would want you. Emma won't ever want you out of her sight again. An' we'll make room. Easy enough to put another room on our shack.'

Alice dropped her gaze and pulled her hand away. 'There is something I must tell you and I don't know whether you or my Mam will want me when I do.'

Keith smiled. 'I'm sure there is nothin' you could have done that could be *that* bad. So tell me. You ain't killed no one have you?'

Alice drew a deep, tremulous breath. 'I have a child! A baby! A son!'

Keith's eyes widened and he shook his head. 'A son?'

Alice gave an almost imperceptible nod. 'Yes,' she whispered tremulously and clamped her teeth on her lips.

Keith took her hand again and lifted her face with a finger under her chin. 'Nothin' bad about havin' a son. He'll be as welcome in our home as you are.'

'But Mam ...! How will Mam feel? Will she be angry that I have a child out of wedlock? Will she feel shamed?'

'Believe me, your Mam'll not judge you badly. Getting you back is all she has ever wanted and I know without a doubt she will love your child as much as she does you.' He glanced around briefly. 'Where is he?'

'In my room. One of the other girls cares for him while I work.'

'Go, fetch him. Let him be here when Emma wakes. I want to see her face when she first sets eyes on him.'

With new hope in her heart, Alice joyfully rushed off to collect her son.

Emma opened her eyes, disorientated for a moment. Keith was beside the bed holding a child and just for a moment, she thought it was Jessica. But it wasn't, was it? It was a stranger.

Holding a hand towards him she whispered, 'who ...?'

Keith smiled. 'I've met your long lost daughter. Now meet your grandson. This is Daniel.'

'Grandson? Alice? Oh, Keith, was it a beautiful dream, or is Alice really here?'

'I'm here, Mam. It wasn't a dream,' Alice said quietly. 'I am here.'

Turning her head, Emma saw her daughter sitting nervously on the other side of the bed. Confused and puzzled, she took a close look at Daniel.

'And this is your son?'

Alice nodded. 'Daniel,' she whispered.

'His father?' Emma asked quietly.

'Danny was a deckhand on the ship. He wanted to stay here with me, but the captain would not allow it.' Alice sighed and dropped her head to hide her tears. Fighting to control her trembling lips, she added, 'he thought of going into hiding until the ship had sailed, but he would have forfeit over a year's wages and he needed those to help his parents, so he *had* to leave.'

Emma shook her head angrily. 'Oh, how sad. I'm so sorry to hear that. It's not right that he wasn't allowed to stay with his family.'

'He loves me an' Daniel, an' he's going to get back to us as soon as he can. I fear it will be a long time though.'

'I've told Alice they must come an' live with us until then,' Keith said decisively.

Emma nodded enthusiastically. 'Of course, they must. The farm will be a much healthier and safer place for them. An' he'll be a little friend for Jessica.' She was almost bouncing for joy in the bed. 'My little girl. Alive and well. I thought I would never see you again.'

Seeing tears threatening again, Keith decided it was time for a change of subject.

'I'm going to put another room on our shack for them,' he said, nodding to himself. 'In fact, now I know you are alright, I will leave and make a start. It'll do for now — until I get my freedom.'

'Yes. You go. An' tell Andrew and Ann I've found my little girl,' Emma called after him as he hurried from the ward.

Keith stood, nervously twisting his cap in his hand, while Alice gazed happily around the little room.

Turning slowly, she took it all in. A small table with two chairs. One well worn, threadbare, ancient-looking armchair. A bed with a straw mattress and a faded old quilt. A cot, obviously hand-made in a hurry.

That was it. This was her new home.

Alice could still smell the newness of the wood that Keith and his friend Andrew had cut to build her little home and she was too choked to put a voice to her feelings. She became aware that Keith was talking to her.

'I know it's not much, but I'll make it better for you. I just didn't have much time, but I'll make you some good new furniture, an' your Mam'll make you some nice bed covers an' maybe a cloth for your table,' Keith was saying nervously.

'Oh, Keith.' Feeling choked, it was all she could find to say for a moment. Handing Daniel to her mother, Alice turned to Keith with love in her eyes. Hugging him, she said, 'this is the loveliest home I have ever had. It is just perfect as it is.'

Will's face glowed. An' it'll get better. When I finish my sentence, in a few months, the government will give me some land. With Andrew's help I'll build us a proper house. By the time your Danny arrives we'll have a farm of our own and a palace fit for a king.

Lightning Source UK Ltd.
Milton Keynes UK
UKHW011119051220
374629UK00001B/209

9 780645 002003